**Two brand-new stories in every volume...
twice a month!**

Duets Vol. #41

Bestselling Harlequin author Kate Hoffmann kicks off
with a special Christmas Double Duets this month.
This writer never fails to "thrill us with light-hearted
humor, endearing characters and piquant situations,"
says *Romantic Times Magazine*.

Duets Vol. #42

Talented Jill Shalvis also presents her own fun-filled
Double Duets this holiday season. "Get ready for
laughs, passion and toe-curling romance, because
Jill...delivers the goods," says reviewer Kathee Card.

Be sure to pick up both Duets volumes today!

Unexpected Angel

"I had to get my angel back."

As the conductor blew his whistle, Eric's dad crouched down beside him. "Holly has to go home, son. Her train is leaving."

"No," Holly murmured. "I can stay until Christmas."

Holly and his dad stared at each other a long time. Eric frowned. There was something funny going on here. Holly was staring at his dad the same way that pest, Eleanor Winchell, stared at Raymond, the new kid in school. And his dad was staring at Holly the same way Eric's best friend, Kenny, stared at Eric's Michael Jordan rookie card.

Kenny wriggled his eyebrows. "Kissy, kissy." He laughed, puckering his lips.

Eric looked from his friend to the two adults. Could his Christmas angel be falling in love with his dad? "You really think so?" he asked Kenny.

"Hey, I was the one who broke the news to Raymond about Eleanor Winchell. I know all about guys and chicks. And your dad definitely has the hots for your angel."

Eric thought about that for a moment, then grinned. "Cool!"

For more, turn to page 9

"So, do you buy your own underwear, or do you let your wife buy it for you?"

Tom blinked. "I—I'm not married."

"Boxers or briefs?" Claudia continued wickedly, secretly pleased that he didn't have a spouse. She found single men so much easier to intimidate—and manipulate.

"Boxers," he murmured. Slowly he skimmed over her features, his eyes resting for a long moment on her mouth. "Silk boxers."

Oh-oh. Claudia swallowed hard. "Personally, I like a man in boxers. Tighty-whiteys just don't say sexy to me."

Tom choked, struggling to regain control of the situation. "Look, I'm afraid we got off on a tangent. Could we start this interview over again?" He stood and held out his hand. "Miss Webster, it's a pleasure to meet you. I'm Thomas Dalton, general manager of Dalton's Department Store. And I'm very anxious to hear your ideas about running our intimate apparel department."

"And...I'm not Miss Webster," Claudia said with a saucy grin. "I'm Claudia Moore. And I'm applying for the position of Santa's elf."

For more, turn to page 197

HARLEQUIN DUETS

ISBN 0-373-44107-X

UNEXPECTED ANGEL
Copyright © 2000 by Peggy A. Hoffmann

UNDERCOVER ELF
Copyright © 2000 by Peggy A. Hoffmann

Visit us at www.eHarlequin.com

Printed in U.S.A.

KATE HOFFMANN

Unexpected Angel

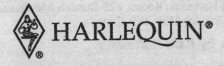

HARLEQUIN®

TORONTO • NEW YORK • LONDON
AMSTERDAM • PARIS • SYDNEY • HAMBURG
STOCKHOLM • ATHENS • TOKYO • MILAN • MADRID
PRAGUE • WARSAW • BUDAPEST • AUCKLAND

Dear Reader,

Another holiday season is here, and since I finished all my shopping last summer (I wish!), I decided to add my devoted readers to this year's Christmas list. But what do I get for the reader who has everything? Nothing I found seemed right, especially with so many tastes to take into account.

In the end, I found a present I hope everyone will like—not one, but two new stories filled with romance, humor and a lot of Christmas cheer. *Unexpected Angel* and *Undercover Elf* feature all my favorite Christmas fantasies—a small town blanketed by sparkling snow, sleigh rides at sunset, an endless supply of home-baked treats (in fiction, they're calorie free!) and not one, but two handsome men to share it all with.

So consider Alex Marrin and Tom Dalton my gift to you. Curl up in front of the fire with some hot apple cider and a plate of those calorie-free Christmas cookies you've been trying to avoid, and enjoy!

Happy holidays,

Kate Hoffmann

P.S. I love to hear from my readers. You can write to me c/o Harlequin Books, 225 Duncan Mill Road, Don Mills, Ontario, M3B 3K9, Canada.

Books by Kate Hoffmann

HARLEQUIN TEMPTATION
731—NOT IN MY BED!
758—ONCE A HERO
762—ALWAYS A HERO
795—ALL THROUGH THE NIGHT

With special thanks to Faye and Charles McDaniels,
who shared their love of horses with me
and gave me a peek inside the stable doors.

1

IT WAS ALL EXACTLY as he'd remembered it. The little candy cane fence, the gingerbread cottage with the gum-drop roof, the elves dressed in red shoes with jingle bells around the ankles, and the tinsel-trimmed Christmas tree. Eric Marrin's heart skipped a beat and he clutched his mittened hands to still the tremble of excitement.

He peered around the chubby kid standing in front of him and caught a glimpse of the man he'd come to see, the man half the kids in Schuyler Falls, New York, had come to see this night. "Santa Claus," he murmured, his voice filled with awe.

As he stood in line waiting to take his turn on Santa's lap, he wondered whether his name was on the "nice" list. Eric made a quick mental review of the past twelve months.

Overall, it had been a pretty good year. Sure, there'd been the time he brought the garter snake into the house and then lost it. And the time he'd put his muddy shoes in the washing machine with his dad's best dress shirts. And the time he'd gotten caught down at the railroad tracks squashing pennies on the tracks with his best friends, Raymond and Kenny.

But in the whole seven and a half, almost eight, years of his life, he'd never done anything naughty on purpose—except maybe for today. Today, instead of going straight home from school, he'd hopped a city bus with

Raymond and jumped off right in front of Dalton's Department Store. Riding the city bus alone was strictly against his dad's rules and could result in punishment harsher than anything he'd seen in his life. But, technically, he hadn't been alone. Raymond had been with him. And the trip had been for a very good reason. Even his dad would have to see that.

Dalton's Department Store was considered by everyone in the second grade at Patrick Henry Elementary School as a shrine to Santa Claus. From the day after Thanksgiving until the hours leading up to Christmas Eve, children flocked though the shiny brass revolving doors and up the ancient escalator to the magical spot on the second floor where Santa and his minions reigned supreme.

Raymond claimed that a meeting with Dalton's Santa was much better than a visit to any other Santa in New York. Those others were all just "helpers," pretenders dressed up like the real Santa to help out during the Christmas rush. But this Santa was special. He had the power to make dreams come true. Kenny even knew a kid who'd gotten a trip to Florida just because his dad had lost his job right before Christmas.

Eric reached into his jacket pocket and pulled out the letter. He'd used his very best penmanship and sealed the note in a colorful green envelope. He'd even added some of his favorite smelly stickers to decorate the outside, just to make sure the letter stood out from all the others. For this was the most important letter he'd ever written and he'd stop at nothing to make sure it got into Santa's hands.

He watched as a little girl in a blue wool coat slipped her own letter into the ornate mailbox outside the Candy Cane Gate. She'd sealed it in a plain white envelope, addressed in sloppy crayon. Eric smiled. Surely her letter would be passed over for his. He closed his eyes and rubbed the lucky penny he always kept in his pocket. "Don't mess up," he murmured to himself. "Just don't mess up."

The line moved forward and Eric shoved the letter deeper into his pocket. First, he'd plead his case with Santa, and if the opportunity presented itself, he'd slip the letter into Santa's pocket. He could imagine the jolly old man sitting down at dinner that night and tucking his glasses into his pocket. He'd discover the letter and read it immediately.

Eric frowned. If he really wanted to do the job right, he'd come down every night after school with a new letter each time. Santa would have to see how important this was to him and grant his wish. Maybe they'd even become best friends and he'd invite Eric over to play at the North Pole. And he could bring Santa to school for show and tell! That old sourpuss, Eleanor Winchell, would be so jealous she'd have a cow.

Of course, Eleanor had read her letter to Santa out loud in front of Miss Green's class, a long recitation of all the toys she'd need to have a satisfying Christmas, the pretty dresses she'd require. She'd also informed the class that she planned to be the very first in line to give her letter to Santa once the Gingerbread Cottage opened for business at Dalton's.

Secretly, Eric hoped that Eleanor's letter would get lost in the shuffle, and that she'd fall through the ice on the Hudson River and she'd be swept downstream to torment some other kids at a grade school in faraway New York City. She was greedy and nasty and mean and if Santa couldn't see that from her letter, then he didn't deserve to drive a magic sleigh! Eric's wish for Christmas didn't include a single request for toys. And his Christmas wish was anything but selfish; it was as much for his dad as it was for himself.

Two years had passed since Eric's mom had walked out. He'd been five, almost six, years old and Christmas had been right around the corner. The stockings were hung and the tree decorated and then she'd left. And everything had turned sad after that.

The first Christmas without her had been hard, mostly because he thought she'd be coming back. But last Christmas had been even worse. His dad hadn't bothered to get a tree or hang the wreath on the door. Instead they'd left Thurston, their black lab, in a kennel, and flown to Colorado for skiing. The Christmas presents hadn't even been wrapped and Eric suspected Santa had passed them right by because their condo had a fake fireplace with a really skinny chimney.

"Hey, kid. You're next."

Eric snapped his head up and blinked. A pretty elf, dressed in a puffy red polka-dot jacket and baggy green tights, stood at the gate and motioned him closer with an impatient expression. Her name tag said Twinkie and he hurried up to her, his heart pounding. He was so nervous he could barely remember what he wanted to say.

"So," Twinkie said, "what are you going to ask for?"

Eric gave the elf a suspicious glance. "I think that's between me and Santa," he replied.

The elf chuckled. "Ah, the old Santa-kid confidentiality agreement."

Eric scowled. "Huh?"

Twinkie sighed and rolled her eyes. "Never mind."

He shifted back and forth between his feet, then forced a smile at the elf. "Do you know him pretty well?"

Twinkie shrugged. "As well as any elf," she said.

"Maybe you could give me some tips." He opened his pocket and showed her the envelope, making sure that she saw his name scrawled in the upper left corner. If Santa didn't remember who he was, he'd be sure Twinkie did. "I really need him to read my letter. It's very, very, *very* important." He pulled a bright blue Gobstopper out of his other pocket. "Do you think if I gave him—"

She studied the envelope. "Well, Eric Marrin, I can tell you this. The big guy doesn't accept bribes."

"But, I—"

"You're up, kid," Twinkie said, pushing him forward, then quickly turning to the next person in line. Eric approached slowly, reviewing all he planned to say. Then he crawled up on Santa's lap and drew a steadying breath.

The smell of peppermint and pipe tobacco clung to his big red coat and tickled Eric's nose. His lap was broad and his belly soft as a feather pillow and Eric leaned closer and looked up into the jolly old man's eyes. Unlike the elf, Eric could see that Santa was patient and kind. "Are you really him?" he asked. Some of the kids at school claimed that Santa wasn't real, but this guy sure looked real.

Santa chuckled, his beard quivering in merriment. "That I am, young man. Now, what's your name and what can I do for you? What toys can I bring for you this Christmas?"

"My name is Eric Marrin and I don't want any toys," he said soberly, staring at a coal-black button on the front of Santa's suit.

Santa gasped in surprise. "No toys? But every child wants toys for Christmas."

"Not me. I want something else. Something much more important."

Santa hooked his thumb under Eric's chin and tipped his head up. "And what is that?"

"I—I want a huge Christmas tree with twinkling lights. And I want our house all decorated with plastic reindeer on the roof and a big wreath on the door. I want Christmas cookies and hot cider. And Christmas carols on the stereo. And on Christmas Eve, I want to fall asleep in front of the fireplace and have my dad carry me up to bed. And on Christmas Day, I want a huge turkey dinner and cherry pie for dessert." The words had just tumbled out of his mouth and he'd been unable to stop them. Eric swallowed hard, knowing he was probably asking for the impossible. "I want it to be like when my mother lived with us. She always made Christmas special."

For a long moment, Santa didn't speak. Eric worried that he might toss him out of the Gingerbread Cottage for demanding too much. Toys were simple for a guy who owned his own toy factory, but Eric's request was so complicated. Still, if Raymond was right, this Santa was his best shot at granting his Christmas wish.

"My—my mom left us right before Christmas two years ago. And my dad doesn't know how to do Christmas right. Last year, we didn't even have a tree. And—and he wants to go skiing again, but if we're not home, we can't have a real Christmas! You can help me, can't you?"

"So you want your mother to come home for Christmas?"

"No," Eric said, shaking his head. "I know she can't come back. She's an actress and she travels a lot. She's in London now, doing a play. I see her in the summer for two weeks and she sends me postcards from all over. And—and I know you can't bring me a new mother because there's no way you can make a human in your toy factory. Not that I wouldn't like a new mother, but hey, I know she won't fit in the sleigh with all those toys and you'd never be able to get down the chimney carrying her in your sack and what if my dad didn't like the kind you brought and—''

"What exactly do you want?'' Santa asked, jumping in the moment Eric took a breath.

"The best Christmas ever!'' he cried. "A Christmas like it used to be when my mom was here.''

"That's a pretty big wish,'' Santa said.

Eric cast his gaze to the toes of his rubber boots. "I know. But you're Santa. If you can't make it happen, who can?''

He risked a glance up to find Santa smiling warmly. "Do you have a letter for me, young man?''

Eric nodded. "I was going to put it in the mailbox.''

"Why don't you give it to me personally and I'll make sure I read it right after Mrs. Claus and I finish our dinner.''

Reaching in his jacket pocket, Eric withdrew the precious letter. Did this mean that Santa would grant his wish? Surely it must mean that he'd consider it. "Eric Marrin,'' he murmured pointing to the return address, just to make sure. "731 Hawthorne Road, Schuyler Falls, New York. It's the last driveway before you get to the bridge. The sign says Stony Creek Farm, Alex Marrin, owner. That's my dad.''

"I'm sure it's on my map,'' Santa said. "I know I've been to your house before, Eric Marrin.'' He patted Eric on the back. "You're a good boy.''

Eric smiled. "I try,'' he said as he slid off Santa's lap. "Oh, and if you hear I broke the rules coming to see you tonight, maybe you could understand? I know I'm supposed to go home directly after school, but I really

couldn't ask my dad to bring me here. He's very busy
and I didn't want him to think that I—''

"I understand. Now, do you know how to get home?"

Eric nodded. The city bus would take him back in the
direction of his school and he'd have to run the mile
down Hawthorne Road to make it home before dinner.
He'd already told Gramps he'd planned to play at Raymond's house after school and Raymond's mother would
drive him home. He'd have to sneak into the house unnoticed, but his father usually worked in the stables until
supper time. And Gramps was usually busy with dinner
preparations, his attention fixed on his favorite cooking
show while the pots bubbled over on the stove.

Eric waved goodbye to Santa and, to his delight, Santa
tucked his letter safe inside his big red jacket. "Some of
the kids at school say you aren't real, but I'll always
believe in you."

With that, he hurried through the crowd and down the
escalator to the first floor. When he'd finally reached the
street, he took a deep breath of the crisp evening air.
Fluffy snowflakes had begun to fall and the sidewalk was
slippery. Eric picked up his pace, weaving in between
holiday shoppers and after-work pedestrians.

The bus stop was on the other side of the town square.
He paused only a moment to listen to the carolers and
stare up at the huge Christmas tree, now dusted with
snow. When he reached the bus stop, a long line had
formed, but Eric was too excited to worry. So what if he
got home a little late? So what if his father found out
where he'd been? That didn't matter anymore.

All that mattered was that Eric Marrin was going to
have the most perfect Christmas in the whole wide world.
Santa was going to make it happen.

"I DON'T LIKE THIS. This whole thing smells like month-old halibut."

Holly Bennett glanced over at her assistant, Meghan O'Malley, then sighed. "And last week you thought the doorman at our office building was working as an undercover DEA agent and our seventy-year-old janitor was an international terrorist. Meg, you have got to get over this obsession with the news. Reading ten newspapers a day is starting to make you paranoid!"

As she spoke, Holly's breath clouded in front of her face and a shiver skittered down her spine. She pulled her coat more tightly around her body, then let her gaze scan the picturesque town square. There was no denying that the situation was a little odd, but danger lurking in Schuyler Falls, New York? If she took a good look around, she would probably see the Waltons walking down the street.

"I like to be informed. Men find that sexy," Meghan countered, her Long Island accent thick and colorful, her bright red hair a beacon even in the evening light. "And you're entirely too trusting. You've lived in the big city for five years; it's time to wise up." She sighed and shook her head. "Maybe it's the mob. I knew it! We're going to be working for wise guys."

"We're two hundred miles north of New York City," Holly cried. "I don't think this is a hotbed of mob activity. Look around. We're in the middle of a Norman Rockwell painting." Holly turned slowly on the sidewalk to take in the gentle snowfall, the quaint streetlights, the huge Christmas tree sparkling with lights in the center of the square. She'd never seen anything quite so pretty. It was like a scene from *It's A Wonderful Life.*

One side of the square was dominated by a majestic old courthouse and the opposite by a department store right out of the 1920s called Dalton's, its elegant stone facade and wide plate-glass windows ablaze with holiday cheer. Small shops and restaurants made up the rest of the square, each and every one decked out for the Christmas season with fresh evergreen boughs and lush, red ribbon.

Meg surveyed the scene suspiciously, her eyes narrowing. "That's what they'd like us to think. They're luring us in, making us feel comfortable. It's like one of those stories where the town appears perfect on the surface but it's got a seamy underbelly that would—"

"Who is luring us in?" Holly demanded.

"Exactly my point," Meg said. "This morning, we get a mysterious letter with a huge check signed by some phantom client with very poor penmanship. We're given just a few hours to go home and pack, then take a train halfway across the state of New York and you don't even know who we're working for. Maybe it's the CIA. They celebrate Christmas, don't they?"

Holly glanced at Meg, then looked down at the letter clutched in her hand. The overnight missive had arrived in the Manhattan office of All The Trimmings just that morning at the very moment she'd learned her struggling business was about to finish yet another year in the red.

She'd started All The Trimmings five years ago and this Christmas had become a turning point. She was nearly twenty-seven years old and had all of $300 in her savings account. If her company didn't show at least a few dollars profit, Holly would be forced to close down the tiny office and try another line of work. Maybe go back to the profession she'd trained for and failed at first—interior design.

Though she had plenty of competitors, no one in the Christmas business worked harder than Holly Bennett.

She was a Christmas consultant, holiday decorator, personal corporate Christmas shopper and anything else her clients required. When called upon, she'd even dressed a client's dog for a canine holiday party and baked doggy biscuits in the shape of candy canes.

She'd started off small, with residential installations, decorating New York town houses both inside and out. Her designs became known for unique themes and interesting materials. There'd been the butterfly tree she'd done for Mrs. Wellington, a huge Douglas fir covered with colorful paper butterflies. Or the decorations she'd done for Big Lou, King of the Used Cars, combining gold-sprayed auto parts ornaments and nuts and bolts garland. Over the next few years, she'd taken on corporate clients—a string of shopping malls on Long Island, a few boutiques in Manhattan—and the demand for her services had required a full-time assistant.

Holly had always loved Christmas. From the time she was a little girl, she'd anticipated the start of the season, officially beginning the moment Thanksgiving was over and ending on Christmas Day—her birthday. No sooner had her mother put away the Indian corn and Horn of Plenty centerpiece than she'd retrieve all the beautiful Christmas ornaments from the dusty old attic of their house in Syracuse. Next, Holly and her dad would cut down a tree and the whirl of decorating and shopping and cookie-baking wouldn't stop until midnight on the twenty-fifth, when she and her mother and father would tumble into their beds, exhausted but already planning for her next birthday and the Christmas that came with it.

It was the one time of year she felt special, like a princess, instead of the shy, unpopular girl she'd been. She'd done everything to make the holiday perfect, obsessed with the tiniest details, striving for perfection. Holly's mother had been the one to suggest that she turn her degree in interior design toward something more seasonal.

At first, Holly had been thrilled with the strange path her career had taken and she'd doted over the designs for her earlier clients. But lately, Christmas had become synonymous with business and income, profits and pressure, not happy memories of her childhood. After her parents had moved to Florida, Holly usually spent the holidays working, joining them once all her clients were in bed on Christmas night.

Without a family Christmas, she'd gradually lost touch with the spirit of the season. But it was impossible to make the trip to Florida and still keep watch over her business. So Christmas had turned into something she barely tolerated and had grown to dread, filled with last-minute details and loneliness. She sighed inwardly. What she wouldn't give for a real family Christmas this year.

"I've got it!" Meg cried. "This guy we're working for is in the witness protection program and he's left his family behind because he doesn't want to burden them with—"

"Enough," Holly interrupted. "I'll admit, his request for an immediate consultation is a bit unusual. But look at the bright side, Meg. Now that all our other holiday installations are complete, we really don't have that much to do." She could certainly find time to make Christmas perfect for a client who chose to pay her a $15,000 retainer for a two-week project, even if he *was* in the witness protection program.

"Nothing to do?" Meg asked. "We've got six new commercial installations with mechanized reindeers and sleighs to maintain and you know how temperamental those singing reindeer are. And that tree we did for Farley's courtyard on Park Avenue is going to take a lot of maintenance. If we get a stiff wind, all the decorations will end up in the East River. Plus we've got a list of corporate Christmas gifts we still need to shop for.''

''We can't afford to turn this job down,'' Holly murmured. ''I've already spent my inheritance keeping this business afloat and my parents aren't even dead yet!''

''So how are we supposed to know who we're meeting?'' Meg asked.

''The check was from the TD One Foundation. And the letter says he'll be wearing a sprig of holly in his lapel.''

That very moment, Holly saw a tall gentleman approaching with the requisite holly. She jabbed Meg in the side and they both smiled graciously. ''No more cracks about the mob,'' she muttered.

''Miss Bennett? Miss O'Malley?''

''He knows our names!'' Meg whispered. ''He probably knows where we live. If we make a run for it now, we might be able to get to the train before he sets his goons on us.''

He held out his hand and Holly took it, noticing the fine cashmere coat he wore and the expensive gloves. Her gaze rose to his face and she felt her breath drain from her body. If this man was a mobster, then he was the handsomest mobster she'd ever seen. His dark hair ruffled in the wind and his patrician profile looked like carved marble in the dim light from the street lamps.

''It's a pleasure to meet you,'' he said. ''And thank you for coming on such short notice.''

''Mr.—I'm sorry,'' Meg said, holding out her own hand. ''I didn't catch your name.''

His cool expression didn't change as he brushed off

her indirect question. "My name isn't important or necessary."

"How did you know it was us?" Meg asked, her eyes narrowed in suspicion.

"I just have a few minutes to talk, so why don't we get down to business." He reached for a manila envelope tucked beneath his arm. "All the information is here," he said. "The contract is for $25,000. Fifteen for your time, ten for expenses. Personally, I think $25,000 is entirely too much, but then, it's not my decision. Of course, you'll be required to stay here in Schuyler Falls until the day after Christmas. That won't be a problem, will it?"

Startled by the odd demand, Holly wasn't sure how to respond. Whose decision was it and what decision was he talking about? "Usually we suggest a budget after we've done a design, and once that's approved, we work out a timetable for installation. I—I don't know what you want or where you want it and we're up against a tight deadline."

"Your brochure says 'We make Christmas perfect.' That's all he wants, a perfect Christmas."

"Who?" Holly asked.

"The boy. Ah, I believe his name is Eric Marrin. It's all in the file, Miss Bennett. Now, if you'll excuse me, I really must go. I have a car waiting for you just over there. If you have any problems with the contract, you can call the number listed on the front of the folder and I'll hire someone else to do the job. Miss Bennett, Miss O'Malley, have a merry Christmas."

With a curt nod, he turned on his heel and disappeared into the crowd of shoppers strolling through the square, leaving both Holly and Meg with their mouths agape. "Gorgeous," Meg murmured.

"He's a client," Holly said, still stinging from his

abrupt manner. "And rude! Besides, you know I'm engaged."

Meg rolled her eyes. "You broke up with Stephan nearly a year ago and you haven't seen him since. He hasn't even called you. He's not much of a fiancé if you ask me."

"We didn't break up," Holly replied, starting off toward the car parked on the other side of the square. "He told me to take all the time I needed to decide on his proposal. And he has contacted me. I had a message on my machine a few weeks ago. He said he'd call me after the holidays and that he had something very important to tell me."

Meg grabbed her arm and pulled her to a stop. "You don't love him, Holly. He's snooty and self-absorbed and he has absolutely no passion."

"I *could* love him," Holly said, a defensive edge to her voice. "And now that my business will be in the black, I'll have some independence. I won't be marrying him for his money, for a secure future. We'll be equals."

Meg paused for a long moment, then groaned. "Oh, I didn't want to tell you this," she muttered, "especially right before the holidays. But I read something in the papers last month and—"

"If this is another story about underworld crime, I—"

"Stephan's engaged," Meg blurted out. "That's probably what he wants to tell you. He's marrying the daughter of some really rich guy. They're getting married in June in the Hamptons." Meg slipped her arm around Holly's shoulders. "I shouldn't have told you like this, but you have to put Stephan out of your life. It's over, Holly."

"But—but *we* were engaged," Holly murmured,

stunned at the news. "I finally made my decision and—and—"

"And it wasn't right. Holly, why do you think it took you a whole year to decide? It's because you didn't love him. Someday you'll meet a man who'll sweep you off your feet, but that man wasn't supposed to be Stephan." She patted her back sympathetically. "So, let's just focus on work, all right? We've got a new job that pays $15,000. Open that envelope and let's hear what we have to do."

Numbly Holly tore open the envelope. In her heart, she knew Meghan was right. She didn't love Stephan, she never had. She'd only decided to accept his proposal because no one else had bothered asking. But the news still stung. Being rejected by a man—even a man you didn't love—was still humiliating.

She drew a shaky breath. So she'd pass this Christmas as a free woman—no family, no fiancé, nothing but work to occupy her time. Holly pulled out a sheaf of papers from the envelope. Clipped on top was a letter, written on wide-lined paper, in a childish scrawl with smeared lead pencil. She skimmed through it, then moaned softly, her troubles with Stephan suddenly pushed aside. "Oh, my. Look at this."

Meg snatched the letter from Holly's fingers and read it aloud. "Dear Santa, my name is Eric Marrin and I am almost eight and I have only one Christmas wish." She glanced at Holly and grinned. "W-U-S-H. I would like you to bring me a Christmas like me and my dad used—Y-O-U-S-T—to have when my mom lived at our house. She made Christmas…" Meg frowned at the spelling. "Seashell?"

Holly sighed. "Special." She flipped through the rest of the papers, long lists of items suggested for Christmas gifts and decorations and special dinners and activities, all to be paid for by an unnamed benefactor.

Meg waved the letter under Holly's nose, her apprehension suddenly gone. "You have to take this job, Holly. You can't let this little boy down. This is what Christmas is all about." She glanced around the square, then fixed her gaze on the department store. "Dalton's," she murmured. "You know, I've read about Dalton's, last year in some upstate newspaper. The article said their Santa grants special wishes to children, but no one knows where the money comes from. Do you think that guy was—"

Holly shoved the papers back into the envelope. "I don't care where the money comes from. We have a job to do and I'm going to do it."

"What about our clients in the city?"

"You'll take the train back to the city tonight and take care of them, while I do the job here."

Meg smiled. "This will be good for you, Holly. No time to be lonely for your family, no time to think about that jerk, Stephan. An almost unlimited budget to make a perfect Christmas. It's like you've won the lottery or died and gone to Christmas heaven."

Maybe this was exactly what she needed to rediscover the spirit of the season! All the way up from the city, she'd stared out the train window and watched the picturesque Hudson Valley scenery pass by. And when they'd stepped off the train, she'd been transported to another world, where the commercialism of Christmas hadn't quite taken hold.

Here, people smiled as they passed on the street and children laughed. From every shop doorway, the sound of Christmas music drifted out on the chill night air, mixing with the jingle bells from a horse-drawn carriage that circled the square. "It is perfect," she murmured, the lyrics from "Silver Bells" drifting through her head. And spending Christmas in Schuyler Falls was a far sight better than passing the holiday buried in year-end tax reports for her accountant.

She drew a deep breath and smiled. "Maybe I'll have a merry Christmas after all."

THE ANCIENT ROLLS ROYCE turned off the main road into the winding driveway of Stony Creek Farm just as Holly finished rereading her contract. The ride from downtown Schuyler Falls was even more picturesque than the train ride upstate, if that was possible. The old downtown gave way to lovely neighborhoods with stately brick and clapboard homes, built as summer homes for wealthy New Yorkers in the early part of the century, those who enjoyed the waters of nearby Saratoga Springs. Then, the streetlights disappeared and the houses became fewer, set back from the winding road and nearly hidden by thickets of leafless trees.

Somewhere in the darkness, the Hudson River streamed by, the same river she saw from her high-rise apartment on the west side of Manhattan. But here it was different, more pristine, adding to the magical atmosphere. The chauffeur, George, kept up a steady stream of informative chatter, giving her the history of the town and its people, yet steadfastly refusing to reveal who had hired him. She did learn that Stony Creek Farm was one of the few active horse breeding farms left in the area, owned by the Marrin family, longtime residents of Schuyler Falls.

As they slowly approached the main house, Holly peered through the frosty car window. On either side of the driveway were long white barns flanked by well-maintained plank fences. The house wasn't nearly as grand as some she'd seen, but it was large and inviting with its white clapboard siding, deep porches and green shutters.

"Here you are, miss," George said as he pulled to a stop. "Stony Creek Farm. I'll wait out here to take you back to town if you'd like."

She nodded. They'd dropped Meg at the train station to catch the late train back and Holly had picked up her overnight bag from a locker there. But as the hour was late, she'd decided to find a hotel after she'd introduced herself to Eric Marrin.

In truth, now that she was here, Holly wasn't quite sure how to broach the subject of her assignment. Her contract expressly forbid any mention of who'd hired her or who was paying the bill, not that she knew herself. But for all the Marrins knew, she was a complete stranger intruding on their lives. "Why don't you wait at the end of the driveway," she said. With no visible transportation back to town, Eric Marrin and his father would be compelled to invite her inside.

George hopped out of the car and ran around to open her door. As she stepped out, she didn't see any sign of Christmas, no wreath on the door, no lighted tree shining through a front window. Holly slowly climbed the front steps, then reached out for the brass door knocker. She snatched her hand back. What was she supposed to say?

"Hi, I'm here to grant your Christmas wish." She swallowed hard. "My name is Holly Bennett and I've been sent by Santa Claus." She was allowed to say she worked for the fat guy in the red suit, that much her contract did state.

"This is crazy," she muttered, turning around. A cold wind whipped around her feet and she tugged the lapels of her coat up around her face. "They're not going to let a perfect stranger in the house."

But the prospect of finally turning a profit was too much to resist. Perhaps she could even give Meg a well-deserved bonus this year. Gathering her resolve, Holly reached out and pushed the doorbell instead. A dog barked inside, and a few seconds later, the door swung open. The light from the foyer framed a small figure, a pale-haired boy with wide brown eyes and a curious expression. His large black dog stood next to him, eyeing Holly suspiciously. This had to be Eric Marrin.

"Hi," he said, his hand resting on the dog's head.

"Hi," Holly replied nervously.

"My dad's still in the barn. He'll be in soon."

"I'm not here to see your dad. Are you Eric?"

The boy nodded.

Holly held out her hand and smiled. "I—I'm…I'm your Christmas angel. Santa sent me to make all your Christmas dreams come true." She was sure the words would sound ridiculous once they left her mouth, but from the look on Eric's face, she couldn't fault her choice. An expression of pure joy suffused his features and the dog wagged his tail and barked.

"Wait here," he cried. The boy raced off into the house and returned a few moments later. He shrugged into his jacket, tugged on his mittens and grabbed her hand. "I knew you'd come," he said, his voice breathless with excitement.

"Where are we going?" she asked as he dragged her down the front steps, the dog trailing after them.

"To see my dad. You have to tell him we can't go to Colorado for Christmas. He'll listen to you. You're an angel."

They followed a snow-covered path toward the nearest

barn, the cold and damp seeping through Holly's designer pumps. A real angel wouldn't mind the wet shoes, but they were her favorite pair and she'd spent a week's salary on them. She made a note to herself to use part of her budget for some cold weather essentials, like waterproof boots and socks, a necessity while working for a client who didn't bother shoveling the snow.

"Did you talk to Santa?" Eric asked. "He must have read my letter right away. I only gave it to him a few days ago."

Holly hesitated for a moment, then decided to maintain the illusion. "Yes, I did speak to Santa. And he told me personally to give you a perfect Christmas."

When they reached the barn, Eric grabbed the latch on the double door, heaved the doors open and showed her inside. A wide aisle ran the length of the barn, covered in a thin layer of straw and lit from above. "Dad!" Eric yelled. "Dad, she's here. My Christmas angel is here."

He hurried along the stalls, peering inside, and Holly followed him, steeling herself for his father's reaction. What she wasn't prepared for was her own reaction. A tall, slender man suddenly stepped out of a stall in front of her and she jumped back, pressing her palm to her chest to stop a scream. She'd expected someone older, maybe even middle-aged. But this man wasn't even thirty!

Holly looked up into the bluest eyes she'd ever seen in her life, bright and intense, the kind of blue that could make a girl melt, or cut her to the quick. He was tall, well over six feet, his shoulders broad and his arms finely muscled from physical labor. He wore scuffed work boots, jeans that hugged his long legs and a faded corduroy shirt with the sleeves turned up. Her eyes fixed on a piece of straw, caught in his sun-streaked hair.

He took a long look at her, then glanced over his shoulder at his son who continued to search each stall. "Eric?"

The little boy turned and ran back to them both. "She's here, Dad. Santa sent me an angel." He pointed to his father. "Angel, this is my dad, Alex Marrin. Dad, this is my Christmas angel."

She fought the urge to reach out and rake her hands through his hair, brushing away the straw and restoring perfection to an already perfect picture of masculine beauty. Holly coughed softly, realizing that she'd forgotten to breathe. She struggled to speak beneath his piercing gaze. "I—I've been sent by Santa," she said in an overly bright tone. "I'm here to make all your dreams come true." She sucked in a sharp breath. "I—I mean, all *Eric's* dreams. All Eric's *Christmas* dreams."

She watched as his gaze raked along her body, boldly, suspiciously. A shiver skittered down her spine and she wanted to turn and run. For all Eric's excitement at her arrival, she saw nothing but mistrust in this man's expression. But she held her ground, unwilling to let him intimidate her.

Suddenly Alex Marrin's expression softened and he laughed out loud, a sound she found unexpectedly alluring. "This is some kind of joke, right? What are you going to do? Start up the music and peel off your clothes?" He reached out and flicked his finger at the front of her coat. "What do you have on under there?"

Holly gasped. "I beg your pardon!"

"Who sent you? The boys down at the feed store?" He turned and glanced over his shoulder. "Pa, get out here! Did you order me an angel?"

A man's head popped out of a nearby stall, his weathered face covered with a rough gray beard. He moved to stand in the middle of the aisle, leaning on a pitchfork and shaking his head.

"She's my angel," Eric insisted. "Not some lady from the feed store."

The old man chuckled to himself. "Naw, I didn't send you anything. But if I were you, I wouldn't be refusing that delivery." He winked at Eric. "We could use an angel 'round this place."

"That's my gramps," Eric explained.

"Who sent you?" Alex Marrin demanded.

"Santa sent her," Eric replied. "I went to see him down at Dalton's and I—"

Alex's attention jumped to his son. "You went to see Santa? When was this?"

Eric kicked at a clump of straw, his expression glum. "The other day. After school. I just had to go, Dad. I had to give him my letter." He took Holly's hand. "She's here to give us a Christmas like we used to have. You know, when Mom was..."

Alex Marrin's jaw tightened and his expression grew hard. "Go back to the house, Eric. And take Thurston with you. I'll be in to talk to you in a few minutes."

"Don't send her away, Dad," Eric pleaded. His father gave him a warning glare and the little boy ran out of the barn, the exchange observed by his glowering grandfather. The old man cursed softly and stepped back into the stall. When the door slammed behind Eric, Alex Marrin turned his attention back to Holly.

"All right," he said. "Who are you? And who sent you?"

"My name is Holly Bennett," she replied, reaching into her purse for a business card. "See? All The Trimmings. We do professional decorating and event planning for the Christmas holidays. I was hired to give your son his Christmas wish. I'm to work for you through Christmas day.''

''Hired by whom?''

''I—I'm afraid I can't say. My contract forbids it.''

''What is this? Charity? Or maybe some busybody's idea of generosity?''

''No!'' Holly said. ''Not at all.'' She reached in her coat pocket and took out Eric's letter, then carefully unfolded it. ''Maybe you should read this.''

Marrin quickly scanned the letter, then raked his hands through his hair and leaned back against a stall door. All his anger seemed to dissolve, his energy sapped and his shoulders slumped. ''You must think I'm a terrible father,'' he said, his voice cold.

''I—I don't know you,'' Holly replied, reaching out to touch his arm. The instant she grazed his skin, a frisson of electricity shot through her fingers. She snatched them away and shoved her hand into her pocket. ''I've already been paid. If you send me away without completing my duties, I'll have to return the money.''

He cursed softly, then grabbed her hand and pulled her along toward the door. Holly wasn't sure whether to resist or go along with him. Was he going to toss her out on her ear? Or did she still have time to argue her case?

''Pa, I'll be back in a few minutes,'' he muttered. ''I've got some business to take care of with this angel.''

2

"I WANT HER TO STAY!"

Alex ground his teeth as he stared at his son standing on the other side of his bed. Eric, dressed in his cowboy pajamas, had folded his arms over his chest, set his chin intractably and refused to meet Alex's eyes. He used to see Renee in his son, in the dark eyes and wide smile. But more and more, he was starting to see himself, especially in Eric's stubborn nature. "I know I've made some mistakes since your mother left and, I promise, I'll try to make things better. We don't need this lady to give us a nice Christmas."

"She's not a lady," Eric said with a pout. "She's an angel. *My* angel."

Alex sat down on the edge of the bed and drew back the covers. "Her name is Holly Bennett. She gave me her business card. When was the last time you heard of an angel who had a business card?"

"It could happen," Eric said defensively. "Besides, her name doesn't make a difference. It's what she can do that counts."

"What can she do that I can't?" Alex asked. "I can put up a Christmas tree and tack up some garland." He patted the mattress and Eric reluctantly crawled beneath the covers.

"But you can't bake cookies and make ornaments and—and—the last time Gramps made turkey it tasted like old shoes!'' He slouched down and pulled the covers up to his chin. ''If you haven't noticed, Dad, she's really, *really* pretty. Like supermodel pretty. And she smells good, too. She's mine and I want to keep her!''

Alex didn't need to be reminded of the obvious. If she hadn't introduced herself as a mortal being, he might have believed Holly Bennett truly was heaven sent. She had the face of an angel, a wide, sensual mouth and bright green eyes ringed with thick lashes. Her wavy blond hair had shimmered in the soft light of the barn, creating a luminous halo around her head and accentuating her high cheekbones and perfectly straight nose.

No, that fact didn't get past him. Nor did his reaction to her beauty—sudden and stirring, almost overwhelming his senses. Over the past two years he'd managed to ignore almost every woman he'd come in contact with, not that there had been many. Running a horse breeding operation didn't put him in the path of the opposite sex very often.

He'd ignored social invitations and community events, secluding himself on the farm day and night and losing himself in his work. The last woman he'd touched was Eric's teacher, Miss Green, and that was a benign handshake at the parent-teacher conferences. Never mind that Miss Green was fifty-seven years old and smelled of chalk dust and rose water.

But Holly Bennett wasn't a spinster schoolteacher and she was hard to ignore. His fingers tingled as he remembered touching her, wrapping her delicate hand in his as he dragged her out of the barn. She was waiting downstairs at this very moment, waiting for him to decide her fate, and his mind was already starting to conjure excuses to touch her again.

''She could stay in the guest room,'' Eric suggested.

Alex leveled a perturbed look at his son. "I'm not allowing a perfect stranger to—"

"Angel," Eric corrected.

"All right, a perfect angel, to stay in our house."

"Then she can stay in the tack house. No one's stayed there since Gramps moved back into the house. *He* thinks she's pretty and nice."

"How do you know?" Alex said, raising an eyebrow.

"I can just tell." His son set his mouth in a stubborn straight line.

Alex covered his eyes with his hands and moaned. If he sent Holly Bennett packing, Eric would never forgive him. And he wouldn't hear the end of it from his father. Aw, hell, maybe it wasn't such a bad idea having her around. He hated stringing lights on the tree. The smell of evergreen made him sneeze. And he was more comfortable with curry combs than cookie cutters.

Besides, Christmas had always reminded him of Renee. Every ornament, every decoration brought back memories of their time together, time when they'd been a happy family with a bright future. The week after she'd left, he'd thrown out every reminder of Christmas she'd brought into the house, vowing to discard anything that brought thoughts of her betrayal.

But here was a chance to begin anew, to create Christmas traditions only he and Eric shared. Sure, Holly the Angel would be around, but she was nothing more than an employee, a helping hand during a busy season. And he was curious to learn who was paying her salary, a secret he might learn given time. "All right," Alex said. "She has three days to prove herself and if everything's going all right, she can stay."

"Then we're not going skiing in Colorado?"

He sent his son a grudging smile. "No, we're not going to Colorado. But you're going to have to deal with her. I'm not going take care of her the same way I have to take care of Thurston and the horses. She's your angel.''

Eric hit him full force against the chest, throwing himself at Alex and wrapping his arms around his father's neck. The boy gave him an excruciating hug and beamed up at him. "Thanks, Dad. Can I go tell her?"

Alex ruffled Eric's pale hair, a flood of parental love warming his blood, then kissed his son on the cheek. It took so little to make Eric happy. How could he think of refusing him even a bit of joy? "Crawl back under the covers and I'll tuck you in. Then I'll go down and tell your angel."

Eric gave him another quick hug, then scrambled back between the sheets. As he did every night, Alex tucked the blankets around his son, then tickled his stomach. "Who loves you the most?"

"You do!" Eric cried.

Alex brushed the hair out of Eric's eyes, then stood. But as he walked to the door, his son's voice stopped him. "Dad? Do you ever miss Mom?"

His hand froze on the doorknob and Alex turned around. He wasn't sure what to say. Did he miss the fighting, the constant anger that bubbled between them? Did he miss the sick feeling he got every time she went into the city, knowing she was meeting another man? No, he didn't. But he did miss the contentment he saw in his son's eyes whenever Renee was near. "Your mom is very talented. She had to leave so that she could be the very best actress she could. But that doesn't mean that she doesn't love you just as much as I do."

Though his question hadn't been answered, Eric

smiled, then sank back against the pillows. "Night, Dad."

Alex released a tightly held breath as he slowly descended the stairs, wondering at how he'd managed to dodge yet another bullet. Sooner or later, Eric would demand explanations and Alex wasn't sure what to tell him. So far, he'd always managed to evade the truth. But could he tell an outright lie to his son?

He turned into the library and stopped short. Holly sat primly on a leather wing chair staring at the dying embers of a fire in the fireplace across the room. She was like a vision from paradise and Alex found himself tongue-tied. She'd removed her coat and tossed it over the back of the chair, revealing a pretty red jacket, cinched in at her tiny waist and a slim black skirt that revealed impossibly long legs. He'd never met a woman quite as cool and sophisticated as her. But though she appeared to be all business, there was an underlying allure that was hard to ignore. "I'm sorry to keep you waiting," he muttered. "If you'll just tell me where your things are, I'll get you settled."

She straightened at the sound of his voice then neatly crossed her legs. Alex stood beside his desk and let his gaze drift along the sweet curve of her calf. When she cleared her throat, he snapped back to reality and silently scolded himself. If Holly Bennett would be hanging around this holiday season, he'd have to prevent all future fantasizing!

"Thank you," she said in a quiet voice, "for allowing me to stay."

"I suppose I should be thanking you," Alex replied. "Eric requested you be offered a guest room, but—"

"Oh, no!" Holly cried. "I have a budget. I can afford

to stay at a hotel. And I'll rent a car to get back and forth.''

"If you'll let me finish," Alex said. "I agreed that you can stay for the next three days. I can't imagine you'll need any more time than that. And you can stay in the tack house. It's quite nice. There're a couple of guest rooms with private baths and small kitchenettes. And you can use the pickup to get around. I can use my dad's old truck.''

"But I've been hired to stay through Christmas day," she replied. She stared down at her lap, then glanced back up at him. "I know this is a little strange, me barging into your lives. Believe me, this is not the typical job for me. But I do intend to do it right and that will take more than three days."

"How long can it take to put up a Christmas tree and a few strings of lights?" he demanded.

She looked at him disdainfully, as if he'd just asked her to build the Queen Mary III overnight. "Actually, Mr. Marrin, the job will take quite a bit of time and attention. You have no decorations up and, from what your father tells me, you don't have any in storage. Between the exteriors and the interiors, there are at least three days of *planning* to be done. And with the budget, I can do some very special things. And I've got baking to do and menus to plan and if you'd like to throw a party or two I'm perfectly capable of—"

He held out his hand to stop her. "Slow down, Betty Crocker."

"Martha Stewart," she muttered.

"What?"

"Betty Crocker is a face on a cake box. I'm really much more like Martha Stewart." She sighed impatiently and stared at her hands.

"All right. Why don't we just see if everything goes all right, then we'll talk about extending your...earthly incarnation. But first, maybe you'd like to tell me who's financing your visit."

She shrugged her delicate shoulders. "I told you, I don't know."

"Don't know, or can't say?"

"Both," Holly murmured.

A long silence spun out between them as Alex watched her intently. She shifted in her chair, and for a moment, he thought she might bolt. "She left two years ago," he said, meeting her shocked gaze coolly. "Four days before Christmas. That's what you've wanted to ask, isn't it?"

"It—it's none of my business," Holly replied as if questioning her curiosity was nothing more than an insult. "I don't think it's necessary for me to become personally involved in your lives to do my job. I'm here to give your son, and you, a perfect Christmas. I'm very good at my job, Mr. Marrin, and I don't think you'll be disappointed."

"This is for my son," Alex replied. "Not me. Eric misses his mother around the holidays. Things have been difficult for him. He doesn't see much of her."

The meaning of his words couldn't have been clearer. He wasn't looking for another wife and he didn't want Holly Bennett to pretend to be Eric's mother. He watched as she rose to her feet, her demeanor growing more distant with each passing moment. "If that's all, then I'll be saying good night. I've got a busy day in front of me tomorrow. If you'll just point me in the direction of the tract house—"

Alex chuckled. "*Tack* house. It's where we keep the saddles and bridles. We call that tack."

"I'm going to be sleeping in a storage shed?" she asked.

"I assure you, Miss Bennett, it's quite nice. Now, where are your things?" Alex asked.

"My things?"

"Your halo and harp? You know, all your angel accoutrements?"

"My luggage is in the car. The driver is parked at the end of the driveway."

Alex nodded. "I'll go get your bags and then I'll show you to your room."

"Mr. Marrin, I—"

"Alex," he said, pulling the library door open for her. He placed his hand on her back as she passed, then helped her into her coat. His palms lingered on her shoulders for a few seconds, her silken hair brushing his skin. Reason told him he'd have to draw his hands away, but it had been so long since he'd touched a woman, smelled the fresh scent of a woman's hair, fought the overwhelming longing to make love to—

Alex opened the front door and showed her out, drawing a deep breath of the crisp night air. The cold revived him, clearing his mind. Granted, she was beautiful—and thoughtful—and unquestionably single-minded. But the last thing he needed in his life was a woman and all the trouble that came along with a romantic relationship.

No, he'd keep his distance from this angel. And if he knew what was good for him, he'd put any devilish fantasies right out of his head.

"SHE'S AN ANGEL. I SWEAR!"

For a moment, Holly wasn't sure where she was. Were the voices part of a dream? Slowly everything came back to her. She'd spent the night in Alex Marrin's tack house.

Though she'd anticipated a storage shed, her room looked more like a quaint B & B than a barn. A beautiful field-stone fireplace dominated one wall of her bedroom, while the others were paneled with warm knotty pine. Across from the iron bed was a tiny galley kitchen and a white-washed table and just outside the door was a pretty sitting area, decorated with old harnesses and riding prints and yellowed photos of very large horses.

"She doesn't have wings," said an unfamiliar voice.

Holly slowly opened her eyes. When her vision focused, she found two little faces staring at her from close range. One she recognized as Eric Marrin. The other, a gap-toothed, freckle-faced boy, observed her as if she were an interesting lab specimen, pickled in formaldehyde and floating in a jar.

"Can she fly?" he said, lisping slightly through his missing front teeth.

"Jeez, Kenny, she's not that kind of angel!" Eric said. "She's a Christmas angel. They're different."

"What's wrong with her hair?" Kenny asked.

Holding back a smile, Holly sleepily pushed up on one elbow. She looked at Eric then Kenny. "Good morning." Kenny jumped back from the bed, a blush staining his cheeks, but Eric happily plopped down on the patchwork coverlet.

"This is my friend, Kenny. He lives down the road. We go to school together."

Holly ran her fingers through her tangled hair and yawned. Judging by the feeble light coming through the window, it was still well before eight. The boys were dressed in jackets, both carrying backpacks. She groaned softly. Though her bed had been wonderfully cozy, her night had been plagued with strange and disjointed dreams. Unbidden images of Alex Marrin had been punctuated with a recurring nightmare that had her endlessly untangling tinsel and searching for the single bad bulb in a mile-long string of lights.

Why did Alex Marrin fascinate her so? Until yesterday evening, she'd been ready to spend her life with Stephan! Yes, Alex was incredibly handsome. Perhaps it was the rugged, salt-of-the-earth image. Or maybe it was the wounded look she saw, deep in his eyes, the wariness that seemed to pervade his lean body whenever he looked at her. He seemed to exude excitement and a little bit of danger.

"Does she have a magic wand?" Kenny asked, regarding her from beneath a scruffy wool cap.

Eric rolled his eyes. "Angels don't have magic wands. Fairy godmothers do. And wizards."

Holly should have explained to the boys that "Christmas angel" had been a metaphorical reference, a way to explain her place in this whole scheme as granter of wishes. She could have just as easily called herself a Christmas genie. "Why don't you just call me Holly," she suggested, too sleepy to make sense of her new job.

"We brought you breakfast, Holly," Eric said, retrieving a battered cookie sheet from a nearby table and setting it on the bed. "Dad says I'm in charge of feeding you. Cap'n Crunch, Tang and toast with grape jelly. After you're finished we'll show you around the farm. I've got my own pony and a pinball machine in my bedroom."

"Here you are!"

Holly glanced up to find Alex Marrin looming in the doorway of her room. He was dressed much as he had been the previous night, in rugged work clothes and a faded canvas jacket. But his hair was still damp from a shower and he was freshly shaven. She scrambled to pull the covers up over the gaping neck of her camisole, then felt a flush of embarrassment warm her cheeks.

"You're late for school," Alex said to the boys. "Come on, I'll drive you."

"But Holly needs a tour," Eric said. "We always give company a tour."

A crooked smile touched Alex's lips and he glanced at Holly. "She's still half asleep." Eric gave his father a pleading look. "I'll show her around," he finally replied, "when I get back. Now let's move!"

The boys called out a quick goodbye, then rushed out. Alex's gaze met hers for a long moment and she tried to read the thoughts behind the enigmatic blue eyes. "I'll just be a few minutes. Enjoy your breakfast." With that, he turned and followed the kids. With a soft moan, Holly stumbled out of bed, wrapped the quilt around her shoulders and crossed to the window, watching as they walked past the house to the driveway beyond.

Of course she was fascinated with him. He was the first man to wander into the general vicinity of her boudoir in nearly a year! And though Stephan had always taken his manly duties quite seriously, he'd never set her pulse racing the way Alex Marrin did. Perhaps it had been fate that had kept her from accepting Stephan's proposal. Perhaps, deep down inside, she knew there was a man out there who could make her feel...Holly groped for the right word. Passion?

She leaned against the windowsill and pressed her nose to the cold glass. She had never considered herself a passionate woman, the kind of woman who could toss aside all her inhibitions and give herself over to a man's touch. But then, maybe she hadn't been touched in just the right way.

"And you think Alex Marrin is the man to do it?"

Holly shook her head, then wandered back to the bed. Sure, there was a certain irresistible charm about him. The easy masculine grace of his walk, the casual way he wore his clothes and combed his hair with his fingers. Any woman would find that attractive.

But there was more, Holly mused. When she looked at Alex Marrin, unbidden and unfamiliar desire surged up inside of her, disturbing thoughts of soft moans and tangled limbs and overwhelming need. Her stomach fluttered, but Holly knew the sensation would never be satisfied with Tang and Cap'n Crunch.

"He's a client," she murmured to herself. Though that wasn't entirely true, since the mysterious benefactor was the one paying her salary. Still, she'd be better off if she kept her distance. This was strictly professional! With a soft oath, she crossed back to the bed, picked up her cereal bowl and took a big bite.

"*Ugggghhh!*" The sweetness of the cereal made her gag and she spit it out, wiped her tongue with the paper napkin, then guzzled down the tart and barely dissolved Tang. The toast was just as bad, cold and overloaded with jelly. Holly dropped it back on the plate and wiped her hands. "At least I won't have to worry about those fifteen holiday pounds."

By the time a soft knock sounded on her door, nearly twenty minutes had passed. She'd dressed, restored some order to her hair and applied a quick bit of mascara and lipstick. Holly took one last look in the mirror then called out. Slowly Alex opened the door, but he ventured only a few steps inside. "You're not ready," he said, taking in her choice of wardrobe, the cashmere sweater set, the wool skirt and her water-stained leather pumps.

Holly glanced down at her clothes, then back up. "I'm

sorry. This is all I brought. I thought I'd go out today and get some more casual clothes.''

"Those shoes won't do." Alex stalked out of the room and returned a few moments later with a pair of tall rubber boots. He dropped them at her feet. "Put those on."

Holly glanced down at the high rubber boots, encrusted with who knows what and at least six or seven sizes too big. There were probably spiders lurking inside their dark depths. She crinkled her nose and shook her head. "Thank you, but I think I'd be more comfortable in my own shoes."

He shrugged. "Suit yourself. We'll start with the barns." Alex stepped aside and motioned her out the door.

"Actually, I don't need to see the barns," Holly said, grabbing her coat, "unless you'd like them to be decorated, too. I really need to start in the house. I've got to measure the rooms and decide on an approach. I think we should stay with more primitive, country themes. Besides, I'm really not very good with animals—dogs, cats, goats, horses."

He gave her a puzzled look. "I think the standard decorations would be fine," he said, striding out of the tack house. "You know, shiny balls and tinsel garland."

She closed the door behind her and shrugged into her coat. "No! I meant real animals. They don't like me. As a child I had a rather unfortunate encounter with a Guernsey cow."

"This is a horse farm," he said. "If you plan on staying until Christmas, it'll be hard to avoid the animals."

Resigned to her fate, Holly hurried after him, her heels sinking into the soggy snow along the path. They began with a tour of the barns, Alex showing her the indoor arena first. She stood on the bottom rung of the gate and watched as Alex's father ran a horse in circles around the perimeter of the arena.

"Why does he have the horse on a leash?"

Again, she caught him smiling. "That's called a lunge line," he said. "It gives him more control. Some of our horses don't need it."

Their tour didn't stop for long. He turned away from the arena and led her back to the main aisle of the barn.

"How many horses do you have?" she asked.

"We have about seventy horses on the farm," Alex replied. "Just over forty thoroughbred broodmares, twenty-seven yearlings that we'll sell at auction in January, a few retired stallions, a few draft horses and some saddlebreds. In the summer we can have another twenty horses that board and train here while they're racing at Saratoga. They use the outer barns and the track."

"That seems like a lot of horses." Holly sighed. "Actually, one horse is one too many for me. I once had this horrible experience with a horse, the kind that pulls the carriages around Central Park. It was frightening."

He forced a smile. "We're really a small operation compared to some. In my grandfather's day, we were a lot bigger. But we've got a good reputation and great bloodlines. Our yearlings fetch a high price at auction."

He reached in his shirt pocket and handed Holly a few sugar cubes, then pointed to the horse in the next stall. "That's Scirocco, grandson of Secretariat. He's one of the old men we keep here and he's retired from fatherhood. He's got a sweet tooth and he likes the ladies."

"If you don't use him how do you get...horsey babies?"

"Foals. And that's all done scientifically now," Alex

said. "These days, you don't need the actual stallion, just what he has to offer."

Holly frowned. "You mean he doesn't get to—"

Alex shook his head. "Nope."

With a frown, Holly held the sugar between her fingers, just out of the horse's reach. "That seems so cruel. What about his needs?" Though she'd never liked animals and considered them smelly and unpredictable and frightening, she couldn't help but feel sorry for the old horse—even though he did have very big teeth.

"Believe me," he muttered. "A male doesn't always have to follow his...instincts." Though the discussion was clearly about a horse, Holly couldn't help but wonder if there might be another meaning to Alex's words.

Alex put the cube in her palm and pushed her hand nearer. The moment the horse nibbled the sugar, she snatched her fingers away. "Animals hate me," she said nervously, her attention diverted by the gentle touch of his hand. "Dogs bark at me and cats shed. I—I won't even tell you about my run-ins with chickens and ducks."

"Funny, he seems to be quite taken with you," Alex replied, capturing her gaze with his. For what seemed like an eternity, neither one of them moved. Holly wasn't even sure her heart was still beating.

Somehow, she didn't think Alex was talking about the horse this time, either. Uneasy with the silence, she braced her hand on the edge of the stall door and tried to appear casual and composed, as if handsome men stared at her every day of the week and she barely noticed. "If we're through here, I think we should—ouch!"

Holly jumped back, a sharp pain shooting through her finger. But she moved so quickly that she didn't notice the danger lurking right behind her. Her foot sank into a warm pile of horse manure. She tried to gracefully extract herself but when her heel struck the smooth floor beneath, her foot skidded out from under her. With a soft cry, she landed on her backside, right in the middle of the pile of poop.

The smell that wafted up around her made her eyes water and Holly moaned softly, not sure how to cover her embarrassment. She glanced down at her finger and found it bleeding. "He bit me!" she cried, holding out her hand.

She heard a low whinny come from the stall and saw the vicious horse watching her with a mocking eye and a smug smile, his lip curling over his huge fangs. Alex held out his hand and helped her struggle to her feet. "I'm sorry," he muttered through clenched teeth. "Scirocco can be a little aggressive when it comes to treats. And that should have been cleaned up."

Holly winced as she tried to shake the filthy shoe off her foot. But the horse poop had seeped inside and it stubbornly clung to her toes. "Just because you haven't had sex for a few years, doesn't mean you have to take it out on me!" She glanced up to find Alex looking at her with an astonished expression. Holly felt her face flame. "I—I meant the horse, not you."

"I'm sure you did." With an impatient curse, Alex scooped her up in his arms and carried her across the barn to a low bench.

She might have protested, if she hadn't enjoyed the feeling of his arms cradling her body. He lifted her as if she weighed nothing more than a feather. But before she could start to like the feeling too much, Alex dropped her to her feet, causing her knees to buckle slightly.

"Sit," he ordered.

Holly twisted to see the damage done to her favorite coat, hoping to hide the flush that had warmed her cheeks. But standing on one foot, she almost lost her balance again. Alex grabbed the collar of her coat to steady her, then slipped it off her shoulders and tossed it over a nearby stall door. He shrugged out of his own jacket and held it out to her.

When Holly pushed her arms into the sleeves she could still feel the heat from his body in the folds of fabric. His scent drifted up around her, a mix of soap and fresh air and horses, a welcome relief from her previous *parfum* and a reminder of the time spent in his arms. "Thank you," she murmured.

"Now, sit," Alex said. He knelt down in front of her and gently removed her ruined shoe. The mess had seeped through her panty hose and stuck in between her toes. He circled her calf with his hands, then slowly ran his palms toward her ankle. But the imagined caress ended abruptly when he tore through the nylon at her calf. She sucked in a sharp breath as he skimmed her stocking down along her leg and bared her foot. "You should have worn those boots."

"I told you animals hate me," she reminded him, a bit breathlessly.

"I'm sure Scirocco had this all planned. He's grown to be quite a curmudgeon in his retirement and, in truth, has a real talent for torturing our female guests." With that, he pushed to his feet and disappeared into a small alcove nearby. She heard water running, then leaned back against the barn wall.

"They say horse poop is the best beauty treatment for the skin."

She glanced to her right and saw Alex's father peeking out from a nearby stall. Though he'd introduced himself the previous night, they hadn't shared but a few words. But Holly already knew she'd found a friend in Jed Marrin. The man had a devilish sense of humor and an easy-going manner that his son seemed to lack.

"You know, Miss Bennett, you're the first woman we've had at this farm in two years. And I don't mind saying, you're a far sight nicer to look at than these old nags."

"Thank you, Mr. Marrin."

He winked. "You can call me Jed if I can call you Holly."

"All right, Jed."

He nodded to her foot. "Around here we call that a Stony Creek pedicure."

A small giggle slipped from her throat and Holly stretched her leg out in front of her, turning it from side to side. "Once I tell all my friends in the city, I'm sure you'll be able to package some of this stuff and make a million."

"Well, we got plenty of inventory," he said. "And I account for all of it, it seems."

Alex returned with a bucket of soapy water, a first-aid kit, and the pair of boots she'd refused just minutes before. "Except for that little item you missed in front of Scirocco's stall," he said. He gave his father an irritated look and the old man winked at Holly again, then went back to his work in the stall. Holly watched him until she felt Alex's hands cup her foot. Slowly he placed it in the bucket of warm water and began to rub.

Holly gulped nervously, wonderful sensations surging up her leg. She'd never considered the foot an erogenous zone, but with her pounding heart and her swimming head, Holly knew she'd be forced to revise her opinion. What Alex Marrin was doing to her toes was simply sinful! Biting back a moan of pleasure, she scrambled for a topic of conversation.

"How long have you lived here—on the farm?" she murmured, her voice cracking slightly.

"My whole life," Alex said, moving his hands up to her ankle. "My great-grandfather owned this place before he turned it over to my grandfather, who turned it over to my father, who turned it over to me. It's been in the family since the early 1900s. There used to be lots of breeders and boarders in the area, but now, we're one of the last. Most of the thoroughbreds are raised south of the Mason-Dixon line."

He took her foot from the bucket and dried it with a rough towel, then slipped her foot into the rubber boot. She kicked off her other shoe and the second boot followed the first.

"Now that we've tended to your bruised pride, let's see about that finger." Alex took her left hand and gently examined her finger. He pulled a bandanna from his jeans and wrapped her wound. "It's not so bad. I've got antiseptic and bandages here."

"Shouldn't I get a shot?" she asked.

He sent a withering glare Scirocco's way. "Don't worry, he's not rabid."

He bent over her finger, his clumsy attempts to render first aid undeniably charming. Holly smiled inwardly. It felt good to have a man worry over her, even a man as indifferent and aloof as Alex Marrin. Maybe getting bitten by a horse and sitting in horse manure wasn't such a bad trade-off for his attentions.

He carefully washed her finger with a soapy rag, then doused it with antiseptic. A bandage followed. "There," he said. "All better." Alex pressed his lips to her fingertip.

Holly blinked in surprise and when he glanced up, she could see he was similarly startled by his own action.

"I—I'm sorry," Alex stammered, suddenly flustered. "I'm so used to fixing Eric's cuts and scrapes, it's force of habit."

She smiled and withdrew her hand. "It does feel better." Holly drew a shaky breath.

He nodded, his jaw suddenly tight, his eyes distant. Alex cleared his throat, clearly uneasy in her presence. "Well, I should really get back to work," he murmured. "The house is empty. You can look around, get your bearings. Make yourself a decent breakfast."

With that, he turned and walked out, leaving Holly still wrapped in his coat, her finger still throbbing and her leg still tingling from his touch. She clomped toward the door in the oversized boots, wondering if there'd ever come a time when she'd understand Alex Marrin. In the end, she decided it didn't matter. She was here to do a job and nothing Alex did or said—including kissing her fingers or massaging her feet—would change her life in the least.

3

"SHE'S A PRETTY LITTLE thing. And don't tell me you haven't noticed. Every time I turn around, you're touchin' her or starin' at her. Last night at supper you almost tripped all over yourself helping to clear the table. You never do that when I cook."

"Maybe if you cooked as good as she does, I would," Alex murmured, not loud enough to reach his father two stalls away. He turned his focus back to the dandy brush he was smoothing over the coat of his favorite mare, Opal. Never mind that he'd been brushing the same spot for nearly ten minutes, caught up in an idle contemplation of the beautiful woman who'd suddenly barged into his home and his life.

How many times that day had he been tempted to wander back to the house, to casually search for a hot cup of coffee or quick snack with the real purpose of seeing her again? According to Jed, she'd spent the entire day yesterday with a tape measure and notepad in hand, scribbling down ideas. And when Jed had begun dinner preparations, she'd swooped down and changed his menu plan, whipping up a deliciously rich Beef Stroganoff to replace the pan-fried steaks his father usually managed to blacken.

That morning at breakfast, she'd blithely prepared another stunning culinary event of scrambled eggs, bacon and homemade biscuits. He'd given her the keys to the truck, expecting her to go right out and buy herself a decent pair of boots—and the ingredients for a gourmet supper that evening. But careful observation of the garage proved that she hadn't left the house at all.

"You don't have to act like you're not listening," Jed muttered, now leaning up against the stall gate. "I've seen the way you look at her."

"And how's that?" Alex asked, unable to ignore the bait.

"Like maybe not every woman in the world is trouble?" his father replied. "Like maybe it's about time to put your problems with Renee in the past?"

Alex bit back a harsh laugh. He'd never put his problems with Renee in the past. Every day he was reminded that he'd failed at marriage and that his son was suffering for that failure. "I made a stupid decision marrying Renee. Hell, we only knew each other for a few months before I asked her to marry me."

"That's the way it always has been for Marrin men," his father said. "We meet the woman of our dreams and it's love at first sight."

"She wasn't the woman of my dreams," Alex muttered. "And neither is Holly Bennett. I won't be making the same mistake twice."

"I don't know. This one's different," Jed said. "She didn't screech and holler when she ended up backside down in a pile of steaming horse apples. Takes a special kind of woman to maintain her composure in the presence of manure."

"She's a city girl. All manners and sophistication. My guess is she can handle herself no matter what might come along."

"Your guess?" Jed scoffed. "It wouldn't hurt you to get to know her. That little girl is working her tail off for your son. She's up at the house right now scurrying around like a squirrel in a nut factory. I've never seen a body get so worked up over Christmas cookies. She's sent me to the store twice today to fetch her ingredients. Says we're havin' cocoa van for dinner. I figure that's some kind of fancy chocolate dessert shaped like a truck.''

"*Coq au vin,*" Alex corrected. "Chicken in wine sauce.'' His stomach growled in response and he realized that he hadn't bothered with lunch that day.

"Oh, yeah? Well, that's even better.''

"It would do you well to remember that you've got work in the barn," Alex said, tossing the dandy brush into the bucket as he grabbed the handle. "Your job doesn't include fetching for her. She can drive herself to the store.''

She could do a whole lot more than drive, Alex mused. His thoughts drifted back to that first morning, when he'd carried her in his arms and kissed her bandaged finger. Though the gesture had been instinctive, his reaction hadn't been. In truth, he'd wanted to draw her into his embrace and cover her mouth with his, to see if the taste of a woman was still as powerful as he remembered.

Alex cursed softly. So he'd been a long time without feminine companionship. Hell, it went deeper than that. In his whole life he'd only had a handful of women. He'd met Renee nine years ago, when they were twenty. He'd asked her to marry him three months later. Not much time for sowing wild oats, Alex mused. Maybe that's why he found himself so attracted to Holly. She was a confident and sophisticated woman, she was beautiful, and she was in close proximity. He dropped the bucket on the concrete floor with a clatter. And that's exactly how it had all started with the fickle Renee.

He stepped out of the stall to find his father leaning against a post, a piece of timothy clenched in his teeth, his gaze fixed on Alex. "Don't ruin this for Eric," Jed warned. "Be nice to her or stay away. There's no middle ground here."

Alex shook his head, then stalked to the door, the faint sound of Jed's chuckle echoing through the silent barn. Of course, he'd be nice! He wasn't some rube from upstate New York, some farm boy lacking in manners. He could certainly maintain a cordial relationship with Holly Bennett—and without lapsing into sexual longing every few minutes!

He wasn't prepared for the assault on his senses when he walked in the door. Christmas carols piped cheerily from the stereo in the family room, filling the house with music. The scent of baking was thick in the air and he followed his nose into the kitchen. She'd started a fire in the family room fireplace and the wood snapped and popped. But it was the kitchen that stopped him short.

Every surface, from countertop to table to the top of the refrigerator, was covered with neat rows of cookies, arranged in military precision, each regiment a different variety. Holly, humming along with "Silver Bells," popped up from in front of the oven, a cookie pan in her hand. She froze at the sight of him, their gazes locking for a brief moment, before she smiled and set the pan down. "Hi," she murmured.

"What's all this?" Alex asked.

"I've just been doing a little baking. I had your father run to the store for some staples—flour, butter, eggs, chocolate."

Alex's brow quirked up, amused by her penchant for understatement. "A little baking? We could keep a small third world country in cookies for a year."

Holly glanced around the room, as if she'd just realized how many cookies she'd baked. "Right. I—I guess I did get a little carried away. But you have to have variety. One or two different cookies on a plate doesn't look nearly as festive as ten or twelve. Here, let me show you."

She snatched a plate from the cupboard and artfully arranged a selection of cookies. Then she ladled a fragrant liquid from the battered crockpot into a mug and dropped in a cinnamon stick. "Mulled cider," she said. She placed the plate of cookies and the mug in front of him, then crossed her arms. "Go ahead. Try it. The cider is a perfect accompaniment for the butter cookies."

She watched him intently and he slowly reached for a cookie.

"No!" she cried.

Alex pulled his fingers away. "No?"

"Try that one first," Holly said. "And then that one. The pecan shortbread is an acquired taste. More of a tea cookie. Not as sweet as the others."

He took a butter cookie filled with jam and coated with toasted coconut, then popped it into his mouth. He was prepared to offer lavish compliments, knowing that Holly would be shattered if he just swallowed it and nodded in approval. But Alex stifled a soft moan as the impossibly fresh cookie simply melted on his tongue. He had to admit that he'd never tasted anything quite so good. Cheap store-bought cookies had been the norm in the Marrin household for years and since no one bothered to close the bag, they were usually stale after the first day.

"I'm going to make some gift boxes for them," she said, turning back to the pan of cookies on the stove. "Eric and I can use some Christmas ink stamps to decorate them and then we'll line them with cellophane and gold foil and tie them with a pretty ribbon and—"

"Why?" Alex asked, surreptitiously snatching a handful of cookies and dropping them into his jacket pocket. "You could have bought cookies. It wouldn't have made any difference to us."

"That's not the point," Holly said, clearly stunned by his obtuse views on the matter. "You can't give friends and relatives store-bought cookies! It's—it's just not done."

"Wait a second. We're giving all these cookies away?" He grabbed two more handfuls and managed to hide them in his pockets before she turned around.

"With all the friends and relatives that stop by over the—"

Alex cleared his throat, after downing another cookie. "Ah, there won't be any friends," he said, his mouth full. "No relatives, either."

"You don't have any company? But it's Christmas!" Holly cried. "Everyone has company at Christmas!"

He shrugged. "We live a pretty quiet life here."

"But—but—what are we going to do with all these cookies?" She studied the countertop, then smiled. "What about the feed store? And Eric's teachers? And his bus driver?"

He grinned, then snatched up another handful of the pretty little butter cookies with jam in the center. "And we can have cookies for supper. And they're great for breakfast. And lunch. For a guy who usually eats toast two out of three meals, cookies are like gourmet fare."

"Speaking of dinner," Holly said. "I was hoping to take Eric out shopping tonight after we eat. We need to buy decorations for the house. I thought we'd start at

Dalton's and look for Christmas tree ornaments. Would that be all right?''

Alex circled the counter, examining another variety of cookie. Holly watched him, her wavy hair tumbled around her face, streaks of flour caught in the strands and smudged on her cheeks. He stood next to her and looked down into her eyes. Lord, she was pretty. "As long as he finishes his homework, he can go," Alex murmured, his gaze skimming over her features.

"I—I used to make these cookies with my mother," Holly explained, turning back to her work. "Every Christmas. I know all these recipes by heart." She picked up a frosted Christmas tree and took a delicate bite. "The taste brings back so many memories." A wistful look crossed her face. "It's funny the things you remember from childhood. "

Alex sighed. "Maybe that's why Eric wrote the letter. He's looking for a few memories." He drew a deep breath. "I should thank you," he said.

She glanced up, her eyes questioning. "For what?"

"For all this. For taking the time." He reached out and gently wiped the smudge of flour from her face, letting his thumb brush across her silken skin. But he couldn't bring himself to break the contact, an undeniable attraction drawing them ever closer. Alex bent near, wanting, needing to kiss her.

"Holy cow! Look at this!"

Alex jumped back, startled by the sound of his son's voice. Nervously he raked his hand through his hair, then forced a smile. He expected Eric to be staring at them both, wondering why his father had been contemplating kissing the Christmas angel. But his son's attention had been captured by the cookies. Kenny stood at his side, his own eyes wide with anticipation.

Alex glanced back at Holly and found the color high in her cheeks. Had his son not come in at that very moment, he knew he would have swept her into his arms. How would he have explained such a sight to Eric? Good grief, the last thing he wanted to do was confuse Eric with adult matters. Holly Bennett was here for only two weeks. He had no intention of making her a permanent fixture at Stony Creek Farm.

"I need to get back to the barn," he murmured, grabbing his mug of cider. He circled around the counter, then ruffled Eric's hair. "Holly is going to take you shopping tonight, Scout. You can go as soon as you get your homework done."

"Wait!" Holly cried. "You can't leave yet. We need to discuss all my plans."

"Dad!" Eric groaned. "You have to discuss her plans!"

"With just two weeks, we'll have to adhere to a strict schedule," Holly began. "And I'll need you to approve my ideas for the interior and exteriors. And as I said before, I've decided to use a rustic theme, which is something I've—"

"I'm sure anything you suggest will be fine," Alex said. "If Eric likes it, I will, too."

He hurried out, anxious to put some space between them. The door clicked shut behind him and he started back toward the barn, ready for a few more hours of hard work. But halfway there, he found himself craving another cookie. He reached in his pocket and found a pretty checkerboard cookie, then popped it into his mouth. But it didn't satisfy him. Alex raked his fingers through his hair. Maybe it was the baker and not the baked goods he was really craving. Unfortunately that was a craving he'd have to learn to ignore.

HOLLY STARED OUT the frosty window of the pickup truck as it bumped along the road leading to downtown Schuyler Falls. Snowflakes, caught in the headlights, danced on the road in front of them. On her right, Eric sat, his eyes wide with excitement, his little body squirming against the seat belt. She'd never met a child quite so sweet and kind as Eric Marrin. His enthusiasm for the season seemed to spill over on to her, making her look forward to every minute leading up to Christmas Eve.

She risked a glance to her left, at Alex, who sat behind the wheel of the truck, silent, stoic, his strong, capable hands wrapped around the wheel, keeping the truck safe on the slick road. Holly hadn't planned to invite Alex along. After their encounter in the kitchen that afternoon, any contact with him was fraught with peril. Instead of thinking about cookie recipes and menu plans, she always seemed to lapse into a contemplation of Alex's broad shoulders or his stunning features or his long, muscular legs. Or his lips, those hard, chiseled, tempting lips. Even now, she couldn't help but sneak a few long looks at him under cover of the dim interior of the truck.

She shouldn't have invited him, but once she learned the truck didn't have an automatic transmission, she'd had no choice. He'd agreed grudgingly, grumbling that he'd never finish all his work in the barn after an evening wasted with shopping. But she knew enough to require only a ride to and from Dalton's. Taking a man—especially a man as stubborn and moody as Alex—through the front doors of a department store could be a disaster of biblical proportions. Men just didn't appreciate the sheer joy of a good retail experience.

"How about some music?" Holly suggested, reaching over to flip on the radio. A blare of Aerosmith split the air behind her head and she jumped, pressing her hand

to her chest. A tiny smile quirked the corners of his
mouth at her reaction. She quickly found some Christmas
music and, before long, she was humming softly along
with Miss Piggy and the Muppets in a rousing rendition
of "The Twelve Days of Christmas." Both Eric and Alex
stared at her as if she'd suddenly gone mad.

"You know, in times past, Christmas was celebrated
over a twelve-day period," Holly said. "This Christmas
carol is nearly three hundred years old and it's steeped
in tradition. Back then, people gave gifts on each of the
twelve days."

"You don't say," Alex muttered.

"Twelve days of gifts?" Eric gasped.

"I've been thinking of decorating the living room with
a Twelve Days' theme." She stole a glance at Alex, hoping that he'd offer at least one opinion on her decorating
ideas. Was he completely bereft of Christmas spirit? And
good taste?

"Can we get reindeer?" Eric asked. "Big plastic reindeer with lights inside like Kenny has at his house? Dad,
you could put them up on the roof."

Holly winced inwardly. Reindeer were fine for shopping malls but a bit too tacky for such a pretty setting as
Stony Creek Farm. "Perhaps we could find something a
little less—"

"Now there's an idea I like," Alex said, barely able
to suppress a teasing grin. "The more stuff on the roof,
the better. And we've got all that space on the lawn, too.
And along the driveway and around the barns. We could
make it look just like…Vegas in the Adirondacks!"

"Yeah!" Eric cried. "Just like Vegas!" He leaned
over to look at his father. "What's Vegas?"

"It's a place where bad Christmas decorators go to
die," Holly said, shooting Alex an impatient glare. She

turned to Eric. "I don't think we're going to find plastic reindeer at Dalton's."

"Dalton's has everything," Eric said. "Raymond has lights on his tree that look like bugs! You get lots of 'em and it looks like the tree is crawlin' with bugs. His mom got them at Dalton's. Can we get some of those lights?"

Holly swallowed hard. "Bugs?"

"Oh, I think a bug tree would be perfect," Alex said. "How does the song go? Twelve crickets chirping, eleven spiders crawling, ten worms a-wiggling."

Holly glanced over at him and caught him staring at her, his eyes bright, his jaw twitching with humor. "I thought you didn't want anything to do with my plans." Their gazes locked for a moment and Holly felt her breath catch in her throat. Though at first his expression seemed benign, when she looked into his eyes she saw something there, intense, magnetic, almost predatory. She quickly looked away, hoping that he couldn't see the flush heating her cheeks.

"Eric wants the bugs," he said with a grin.

He really was a handsome man when he smiled. Strong and vital, and oh-so sexy. At times so serious and then downright silly. What woman in her right mind would choose to leave a man like Alex Marrin?

"I can work with bugs," she murmured, outvoted two to one. "I'm flexible." Though Holly preferred to do things her own way to insure that everything fit in with an overall theme, she'd done a few bizarre themes in the past. A trout fishing tree for a dyed-in-the-wool sportsman and a tree decorated with little plastic internal organs for a doctor's home. She gnawed on her lower lip. Horses probably had bugs of some sort, horse cooties. She could work it in.

As she mulled over her plans, her gaze dropped to her

leg, to the spot where it pressed against Alex's thigh in the cramped confines of the truck. Even through her coat, she could feel his warmth, warmth that slowly seeped through her bloodstream until the chill had been banished from her fingers and toes. How easy it would be to reach over and run her palm along the faded fabric of his jeans, to feel the hard muscle and warm flesh beneath. To let it slide higher and higher until—

She gulped convulsively. "We'll have to have two trees," Holly said. "A very nice formal tree in the living room and a…a bug tree in the family room. And the library could use a tree, too."

"Cool," Eric said. "We never had three trees before! Santa's gonna love our house."

Holly turned to Alex but his gaze was fixed on the street ahead. The pretty homes had given way to businesses as they approached the town square. A few minutes later, the truck pulled up in front of Dalton's Department Store. "I'll pick you up in three hours," Alex said. He reached behind Holly and gave Eric's head a tousle. "Be good for Miss Bennett, Scout. Stay right with her and don't wander off."

He turned his attention to Holly and she wondered when he'd remove his arm from around her shoulders. He was so close she could feel the warmth of his breath on her cold cheek. She let her head tip back slightly, amazed at how perfectly her nape felt in the crook of his arm. "Maybe you could buy some new clothes," he suggested. "And a sturdy pair of boots while you're at it."

He pulled his arm out from around her shoulders. Holly forced a smile, then slid across the seat and hopped out of the truck right after Eric. Before she could say another word to Alex, Eric grabbed her hand and dragged her to the wide glass windows, pushing through the crowds that had gathered there.

"Look at the trains!" he cried, pressing his face against the glass like the rest of the kids lining the windows. He drew her to the next window. "And these bears play in a band! See how they move?"

As Eric pulled her to the next window, she glanced over her shoulder and found Alex watching them. He'd stepped out of the truck and now stood with his arms braced on the hood, his gaze following them both. From this distance, she couldn't read his expression, only that he wasn't smiling. For such a seemingly unaffected man, he was endlessly complicated, his mood shifting in the blink of an eye.

When she looked for him again a moment later, the truck was gone and Holly felt strangely disappointed. It had been so long since a man had looked at her with anything more than mild interest. And so long since she'd even bothered to care. With a soft laugh, she pulled Eric away from the windows. "Come on, we have shopping to do!"

They hurried through the revolving door, then stopped inside the grand entryway of Dalton's. Holly felt as if she'd been instantly transported back in time. This was the way shopping used to be, with smiling salesclerks who called you by name and uniformed doormen who welcomed you with a nod. The terrazzo floors shone and the smell of lemon oil drifted off the rich mahogany paneling.

As they strolled past the perfume counter, she noticed the huge Christmas tree set in the center of the store. Slowly her eyes rose, higher and higher, up through a soaring atrium three stories high. Above her, shoppers rested along the railings, staring out at the twinkling lights and shiny ornaments. A tiny thrill raced through her and, for a moment, she felt like a young girl again, full of the excitement of the season.

"It's magical," Holly murmured. "And a real tree. I wonder how they got it in here?"

"They always have a big tree." Eric pulled her along toward the escalator. "First, we have to go see Santa. Then we can look at the tree."

"I thought you already talked to Santa," Holly said, hurrying to match his pace.

"I have to thank him," Eric said.

"For what?"

"For you!"

Holly's heart warmed at his innocent compliment. She'd only been a Christmas angel for a few days, but she already knew it was the best job she'd ever had. Devoting herself to the happiness of a sweet boy like Eric Marrin could hardly be called work.

They stepped onto the old escalator and ascended to the second floor, then joined the long line of children waiting at the gate to a cute little gingerbread village. The place was lined with aisles of toys, but Eric didn't even notice, his gaze fixed squarely on the entrance to Santa's kingdom.

As they waited, Holly was reminded of her childhood, how resolute she'd been in her own belief in Santa, and how she had challenged anyone who told her differently. Here, with Eric's hand clutching hers, she could almost believe again in the pure magic of Christmas, and the warmth and security of a family to share it with.

"Hey, kid! What are you doing back here?"

They both turned to see one of Santa's elves approaching—Twinkie, by her name tag. Holly felt Eric's hand squeeze hers a little tighter. "Hi, Twinkie! Look what I brought. It's my Christmas angel."

The elf stared down at Eric, her hands braced on her hips. "Your what?"

"My angel. Her name is Holly and Santa sent her to me. She's going to make my Christmas perfect. I came back here to thank him."

The elf's gaze rose to Holly's face and she stared at her shrewdly, her pretty features pensive, curious. A bit too curious for Holly's liking. "Santa sent you?" she asked. "That's not true, is it?"

Holly glanced over her shoulder, uneasy with the elf's sudden interest in private matters. "I—I'm really not at liberty to say," she replied. "Come on, Eric, we'll come back a little later and thank Santa. We've got a lot of shopping to do." She tugged on his hand and led him away.

"Wait," the elf cried, weaving through the waiting crowd. "I just have a few questions to ask."

They lost the elf somewhere in bed linens, crouching behind a pile of down comforters to conceal themselves and holding their breaths as Twinkie's jingling elf boots passed by. When Holly was sure they were safe, she pulled Eric to his feet. "Maybe it would be best if we didn't tell anyone else about your Christmas angel," she suggested.

"Why?"

Holly scrambled to come up with a logical reason. "Because we wouldn't want all the other kids to ask for their own angels. There are just so many angels to go around and we wouldn't want anyone to be disappointed."

Eric nodded solemnly. "Yes. Maybe that would be best."

As they searched out the tree trimming department, Holly glanced down at Eric and smoothed his mussed hair. He looked up at her and smiled, his whole face radiating joy. How different he was from his father, Holly mused. While Eric Marrin wore his emotions on his sleeve, his father hid them behind a stony face. While Eric was friendly and outgoing, Alex Marrin was aloof and indifferent.

She sighed softly. She'd stepped into the lives of these two males intending to do her job and make her $15,000. But this was more than a job. It was a chance to make a real difference in Eric's life, to give him something that he'd been missing. If the contract were canceled tomorrow, Holly knew she'd never be able to abandon the job. She was already falling under the spell of the little boy's charm.

She drew a steadying breath. Now, if she could only avoid doing the same with his father.

A FRESH DUSTING OF SNOW had fallen that morning and, in the waning light of day, it sparkled like tiny diamonds. Alex drew a deep breath of the cold afternoon air. As he looked out over the rolling land, the thick trees and wide meadows, he smiled. This was his land, his future—and the future of his son. Nothing could tear him away from this place. Not even a woman.

Renee had tried to draw him away, to force him into her life in New York City. But when he'd insisted they come back to Stony Creek when she got pregnant, she'd had no choice but to agree. From the day she set foot on the farm, he knew she didn't belong. It shouldn't have come as a surprise when she left six years later, but it did.

He glanced back at Holly, who trudged through the

snow in his footsteps, Eric at her side. The two of them, bundled against the cold, held hands, Eric staring up at Holly as if she really were an angel sent from above. But to Alex, she'd become a siren sent by the devil himself, sent to torment and tempt him with her beauty and her allure. She didn't belong here, either. Even dressed in insulated boots and a thick wool field jacket, she still looked like a city girl.

He vowed to maintain his distance from her again and again, but at every turn, she was there, asking him questions, seeking out his help. He'd had his resolve sorely tested trying not to touch her while he drove them back from their shopping spree at Dalton's last night. And when she thanked him for carrying her parcels into the house, he'd fought an overwhelming urge to bend a little nearer and kiss her. Even this morning at breakfast, he couldn't seem to keep his eyes off of her, preoccupied with a covert inventory of her pretty features.

And now, even with the cold air and the bright sunshine, he wanted to pull her into his arms and tumble into the snow. Instead he was forced to focus on the task at hand—finding three suitable Christmas trees for the house. He stopped to stare up at a twelve-foot balsam pine, then waited for Holly and Eric to catch up.

"How about this one?" he asked.

Holly's gaze skimmed over the height and width of the tree, then she slowly circled it, taking in its every detail. She'd already rejected the past forty-seven trees he'd shown her and if she rejected another, he'd be hard-pressed not to toss her in the nearest snowbank and continue the search without her.

"I don't know," Holly said. "It seems a little bare on the other side. And it's really not very thick." She sighed. "It would be much more efficient if we just went to a tree lot and bought three trees. We just don't have the time to search.''

Alex ground his teeth as he attempted to bite back a sarcastic retort. This is precisely why he didn't shop with women. Whether they were looking for something as complex as panty hose or something as simple as a damn Christmas tree, they always had to turn it into a major production. "We'll put the bare spot against the wall," he said. "No one will know it's there."

"*I'll* know," Holly said. "And it won't be perfect."

"Nothing I show you is going to be perfect," Alex replied. "It's not supposed to be perfect. The reason we're cutting our own tree is that we always cut our own tree. It's family tradition."

"You don't have to get mad," Holly shouted. "I'll find a tree. It will just take time. Sometimes my father and I would search for days for just the perfect tree."

Alex stopped and slowly turned to Holly. "Days? We've been out here four hours and that's three hours longer than you deserve. It's getting dark, you've seen hundreds of trees. Balsam, white pine, Scotch pine. Ten-feet tall, twelve-feet tall, thick and thin, short needles, long needles. Just tell me what you want!"

"I want something special," Holly said. She crossed her arms over her breasts and stared at him, her nose rosy, her eyes bright. "Perfect."

"Perfect. The only perfect thing you're going to find in this woods is a perfect lunatic with a perfectly honed ax and a perfectly sharpened saw, and a perfectly reasonable reason to murder you if you don't pick out a tree right now!"

She gave him a haughty look, refusing to back down. "If you're going to be so belligerent, why don't you just go back to the house?"

"Belligerent?" Alex asked. "You think this is belligerent?" He reached down and picked up a handful of snow, packing it with his gloved hands.

Holly held out her hand to warn him off. "Don't even think of throwing that at me."

Alex ignored the warning, taking her words as a challenge. When he refused to put the snowball down, Holly scrambled to make her own ammunition, enlisting Eric's help. Alex released a tightly held breath. Though he'd derive great pleasure in giving her a faceful of snow, it wasn't going to get them out of the woods any faster. "All right," he said, tossing his snowball aside. "Truce. But you've got thirty minutes to find a decent trio of trees or I'm going to leave you out here to freeze."

"Hey, Dad, you're a poet and you don't even know it!"

Alex turned on his heel and started down the trail once again. But the shock of cold snow on his bare neck stopped him short. With a low growl, he slowly faced them. They both looked guilty as sin, satisfied smiles pasted on their rosy-cheeked faces. He raised his brow at Eric and his son tipped his head toward Holly.

In one smooth motion, he scooped up a handful of snow, packed it tight and took a step toward her. He was about to show her exactly who wore the pants around Stony Creek Farm. Holly let out a tiny shriek, then spun around and headed for the safety of a small tree.

Eric grabbed up a snowball and threw it at Alex, hitting him on the thigh. Alex scowled at his son. "So that's the way it is. You're going to side with the girl?"

"She's my angel and I have to protect her." He thumped his chest with his fist. "And this is war!" Eric let out a piercing battle cry, then scampered over to Holly's hiding place.

A full-scale battle erupted with Alex taking the brunt of the assault. He tore through the trees, looking for Holly only to get ambushed by another snowball from Eric. And when he took off after Eric, Holly would come to the boy's rescue with a barrage of snowballs meant to lay him low.

Breathless and wet with water running down his neck and settling near the small of his back, Alex decided to employ a new strategy—stealth. He gathered up a handful of snow and tiptoed through the trees, stopping to listen every few seconds. His efforts paid off, for a few moments later, he came up behind Holly.

Slowly he crept toward her as she peered out from behind a squat little fir tree. At the last minute, she heard him and, with a loud yell, Alex grabbed her from behind and playfully wrestled her down into the snow. He caught her wrists in one hand and pinned them above her head. She didn't have time to scream before he washed her face with the snowball. Coughing and sputtering, she looked up at him, her lashes covered with ice crystals.

But the battle between them quickly faded as Alex stared down at her. She lay perfectly still, her slender body stretched beneath his, their hips pressed together. Her breath came in quick, deep gasps, visible in the cold air. And though he refused to let her go, she didn't attempt to shout for Eric's help.

He gently wiped the snow from her eyes. "Do you surrender?" Alex asked, keenly aware of the deeper meaning to his question.

She nodded, her gaze fixed on his, her lips parted. He brushed a strand of hair from her cheek and, to his surprise, she turned her face into his palm, tempting him with a subtle sign of her desire, closing her eyes to await his kiss. Groaning softly, Alex bent nearer, already anticipating the warm sweetness of her mouth, the flood of need that promised to rush through his bloodstream.

But a moment before their lips met, Alex heard a rustling in the nearby trees. He released her wrists and pushed up, bracing his arms on either side of her head. When Eric's scream split the cold, silent air, Holly stiffened beneath him, then began to wriggle.

Alex groaned. "The kid has impeccable timing."

"Let me up!" she cried.

The electricity between them died instantly, doused by a healthy dose of reality. When Alex saw Eric's boots beneath the trees, he rolled to the side. Holly scrambled to her feet and frantically began to brush the snow from her clothes. "You shouldn't have done that," she murmured, refusing to meet his gaze. "I—I'm here to do a job and nothing more. I trust you'll remember that from now on?"

Alex smiled as he struggled to his feet, evidence of his desire pressing against the snow-dampened fabric of his jeans. "Hey, all's fair in love and war," he replied. "Isn't that what they say?"

She opened her mouth to snap out a reply, but just then Eric appeared from behind the tree. He took in his father's appearance, then grinned. "Holly got you good!" he cried. "We win, we win!"

Alex cleared his throat, then nodded. "Yeah, Scout, Holly got me good."

The "victor" pasted a bright smile on her face and held out her hand to Eric. "We better get going," she said. "We still have three trees to find." Without looking at Alex, she brushed by him and trudged off on her quest for perfection.

When Alex caught up to them, a full five minutes later, he'd managed to quell his physical reaction to their encounter, but couldn't banish the sense of regret he felt. What might have happened if they'd been alone in the woods, without interruption? Would they have given in to their attraction, finally and fully? She'd wanted him to kiss her. He'd seen it in her eyes, in the way her mouth quivered slightly, in the soft clouds of frozen breath that betrayed her excitement. But how much longer could they both deny what was so blatantly obvious? They wanted each other, in the simplest, most primal way.

"Come on, Dad!" Eric called. "Holly found a tree she likes."

She stood beside a balsam that resembled every other balsam she'd rejected, her hands clutched in front of her, her attention firmly on the tree. "This is the one," she murmured, again refusing to look at him.

Alex circled the tree, knowing full well that she'd chosen the first thing she'd come upon. It was clear she'd do anything to escape his presence, including settling for a substandard tree. "What about this bare spot?" he asked.

"We can put it against the wall," she said, her earlier enthusiasm diminished, her expression uneasy. "And that little one, over there, will be fine for the library. And the one over there for the family room. If you'll just cut them down, we can be on our way."

She was upset, but Alex wasn't sure why. Could he have misread her reactions? Had he been so long without a woman that he couldn't tell the difference between desire and distaste? He cursed inwardly, cursed his runaway urges and his unbidden reaction to them. "Eric, why don't you take Miss Bennett back to the house. She looks a little...cold."

That brought a response, narrowed eyes and cheeks

stained red from more than just the frigid air. "I can find my way back on my own," she said defensively.

"I'm sure you can. But I'd feel better if Eric showed you the way. He knows this land as well as I do."

Alex watched them go, standing in the same spot until they disappeared behind a low rise in the landscape. Then with a soft groan, he sat down in the snow. Though he'd tried his best to resist her, there was no denying the truth. He wasn't going to be satisfied until he kissed Holly Bennett, long and hard and deep. Maybe then, he'd be able to put this strange fascination behind him. That was the answer, then. At the next available opportunity, he'd pull her into his arms and kiss her. And finally, that would be the end of it.

Or maybe, it would just be a beginning.

4

THE FLAMES IN THE fireplace had ebbed to glowing embers by the time Holly finished decorating Eric's tree in the family room. He'd grown bored with hanging ornaments and was now fast asleep on the sofa, his head nestled against Thurston's stomach. Though Alex appeared to be absorbed in the newspaper, Holly felt his gaze on her every time she turned her back, making the hairs on her arms prickle and tingle.

How had things moved so quickly between them? Just three nights ago, she was standing on his front porch, a complete stranger, and now they were lusting after each other like love-starved teenagers. Though she'd tried to control her impulses in his presence, she always seemed to forget herself, to ignore the woman she was supposed to be.

Holly had never put much stock in passion. She and Stephan had shared a satisfying relationship in bed, but it had never been fireworks and angel choirs. But then, she'd never expected that, so how could she have known what she was missing?

Now she did. That little flutter that leaped in her stomach every time she looked at Alex. The ache she felt deep in her core every time he brushed against her. The look she saw in his eyes when he meant to kiss her. She'd come to crave them all.

Her head warned her to keep her relationship with

Alex strictly business. But her heart said there was more than just business between them. After their tumble in the snow, she could think of nothing more than finishing what they'd started, giving in to the kiss that hadn't happened. But where would a simple kiss lead? The only path Holly could see was the path to a broken heart and she was determined to avoid that route.

She placed the last ornament on the tree, then stepped back. Though she hadn't been completely sold on the idea of a "bug" tree, she had to admit the nature theme worked well. They'd added bird ornaments to the ladybugs and butterflies and bees, along with Eric's dragonfly lights. Holly had found natural garland made of tiny pinecones and dried wildflowers to emphasize the backyard garden theme. Though it wasn't her most sophisticated tree, it had its charms. "What do you think?" she murmured, staring up at the birdhouse that topped the tree.

"Pardon?"

Holly tweaked one of Eric's dragonfly lights, then turned around. "What do you think?"

Alex glanced down at Eric. "I think I'd better put this guy to bed." He set his newspaper down, then reached out to slip his arm beneath his son. The little boy opened his eyes and yawned.

When he caught sight of the tree, ablaze with the twinkling dragonflies, he smiled sleepily. "Cool," he murmured. He pushed up from the sofa and crossed the room. Wrapping his arms around Holly's waist, he gave her a hug, warming Holly's heart. "See you in the morning, Holly."

She patted his head, then watched as he returned to his father's side. They both walked out of the room, leaving her with a tiny smile on her lips. The love between father and son was so apparent, so assured that she felt the power of it just being near them. She'd shared the same security with her own father, the unfaltering bond between parent and child. Someday, she'd have that for herself, a child to love her unconditionally.

But when she conjured herself a family, the picture was no longer vague and unfocused. Eric was the child she pictured as her own. And Alex Marrin had taken over the role as fantasy father and perfect mate. Not that she wanted to marry *him* and have *his* children. But she wanted a father for her children who could love as deeply as he did.

Holly sighed softly, then began to gather the boxes and bags scattered around the floor. When she'd tidied the room, she walked over to the light switch and flipped the lights off. This was always her favorite moment, when the tree came to life in front of her eyes. She wasn't sure how long she stared at the tree, enjoying the pungent odor of fresh pine and the soft light thrown across the ceiling.

"Beautiful."

She turned to find Alex standing a few feet behind her. "You like it?"

"I wasn't talking about the tree."

Holly felt a blush warm her cheeks. How a simple compliment could disarm her! Especially when it came from Alex Marrin. "I think the bugs work."

"Would you like a glass of wine?" Alex asked.

Holly nearly caught herself accepting his offer. "Now that I've finished here, I should get to work hanging the garland in the library. And I've got to plan for the—"

He took her arms and slowly turned her around. Without hesitation, he cupped her face between his hands and brought his lips softly down on hers. The kiss was so gentle, so unexpected, that Holly wasn't sure what to do.

No surge of indignation washed over her, no embarrassment or guilt. Just warm and wonderful pleasure.

His mouth lingered over hers for a long time, testing, tasting. Holly slid her palms up his chest and wrapped her arms around his neck, sinking against him. When he tried to pull back, she urged him not to stop, her fingers splayed across his nape. A soft moan rumbled low in his throat as the passion grew between them by degrees.

"I've been wanting to do this since that very first night," he murmured, his breath soft against her cheek. He traced a line of kisses from her jaw to the notch at the base of her neck. "Tell me you wanted this, too."

"I—I'm not sure," Holly murmured, tipping her head back to fully enjoy the feel of his mouth on her skin. She thought she knew exactly what she wanted, to maintain a safe distance from Alex. But now, she found herself wanting his kisses much more.

Alex furrowed his hand through her hair, then forced her to meet his gaze. "Why do you deny this? We're attracted to each other, Holly. It's really quite simple."

"But it's not," she said. "I'm here to do a job. And I have a life back in New York City, a career and business to run."

He arched his brow. "I'm not asking you to stay," Alex murmured. "This isn't a proposal of marriage."

Holly drew in a sharp breath, the warmth his kiss had brought leaving her body. She placed her palms on his chest and pushed him away. "Which is exactly why we can't do this," she said.

"You want an engagement ring before you'll let me kiss you again?"

"No!" Holly cried. "Don't be ridiculous."

"Then what is it?"

She scrambled for a sane reason why she couldn't allow herself to be seduced by Alex Marrin's charm. But nothing she came up with made the least bit of sense. Why not kiss him, as long as it felt good? Why not let passion take its course? It's not as if she were engaged to Stephan! She was a single woman, free to explore her passions with whatever man she chose. "There's another man," she blurted out, taking the first excuse she could find.

Alex nuzzled her neck playfully. "There won't be after tonight."

"It's quite serious." She felt his lips abandon the pulse point on her neck. His shoulders stiffened and he drew away.

"You're engaged?" He stared at her as if she'd suddenly sprouted horns and a pitchfork tail.

The emotion in his eyes, barely controlled anger, self-loathing, made her retreat a step. "No. I—I mean, yes. We've known each other for ages and last Christmas Stephan asked me to marry him." It wasn't really a lie, just not the entire truth.

"I don't see an engagement ring," Alex said.

"I don't need a ring to remind me of how I feel."

"And how do you feel when you're with him, Holly?" Alex asked. "Does he make you feel the way I do? All warm and breathless? Out of control? Willing to do anything for this?" He caught her around the waist and yanked her closer.

"Stop it," she warned, her gaze transfixed by the desire blazing in his eyes, her voice lacking any conviction.

He leaned closer. "Make me." With that, he lowered his mouth to hers. She expected all the anger she saw in his expression to flow into his kiss. But it wasn't there. Only need, desire so fierce that she could feel it flooding into her body from his. And when he drew away, leaving her breathless, her instinct was only to lash back at him for taking away every ounce of her self-control.

"You can't change the past by punishing me. I'm not her, Alex, and when I leave after Christmas and all the decorations are put away and all the cookies are eaten, you won't be able to blame me. I won't be abandoning you. I'll just be going back to my life."

He cursed softly, then turned away from her. The heat from his body suddenly disappeared and Holly shivered. "Well, I guess that answers all my questions," he said. He rubbed his hands together, then glanced around the room. "Do you need any help cleaning up here? If not, I've got work to do in the barn."

"That's it?" Holly asked.

He forced a smile. "Don't worry, Miss Bennett. I won't be kissing you anytime soon. Unless, of course, you beg me to." With that, he grabbed his jacket and strode to the back door.

The sharp sound of it slamming made her jump and she pressed her palm to her chest, only to find her heart beating like an overwound clock. "Good," she murmured, "I'm glad that's all cleared up." She took in a shaky breath, then turned to finish tidying up the family room. But her body trembled so uncontrollably that she finally had to sit down.

This was good, wasn't it? Alex didn't want her anymore. No more lustful looks, no more passionate longing. No more kisses? Holly groaned and put her face in her hands. Now, if she could just convince herself that this was what *she* wanted, she might be able to concentrate on the job at hand. And not on the breathless, reckless, wanton way Alex Marrin made her feel.

"GET PACKED AND TAKE the first train up here," Holly ordered, trying to keep the edge of hysteria from her voice. "There's a train at 8:20 that arrives here just before noon."

"Mom?"

"No! It's Holly."

For a long moment, there was no sound on the other end of the line. Then a groan and a dramatic yawn from Meg. "Holly? It's five in the morning!"

"I know what time it is," Holly said, pacing back and forth alongside her bed. "I want you up here today. At the latest, tomorrow morning. You're taking over this assignment."

Meg's astonished gasp was audible through the phone lines, but that didn't sway Holly. She'd spent a sleepless night scarfing down Christmas cookies and weighing the consequences of remaining at Stony Creek Farm. While waiting for the sun to rise, she'd decided that leaving was the only option she had. Even though Alex had vowed to keep his distance, Holly was convinced, sooner or later, she'd go begging. And when she did, it wouldn't be for mere kisses. No, she'd want more from Alex Marrin.

Her mind wandered back to the kiss they'd shared, the unbridled desire he'd ignited inside her. The moment his lips had touched hers, Holly knew she wanted him. But a tiny corner of her brain blared out a warning she couldn't ignore. She'd known Alex for less than a week and she was ready to toss aside her inhibitions!

How could she possibly know what she wanted? It had taken her almost a year to decide she wanted Stephan and look how badly that turned out! No, Holly Bennett never made spur-of-the-moment decisions. She always weighed all her options carefully, made a plan, considered every angle.

Though an affair with Alex could be wonderfully exciting, it was also a dangerous proposition. She already knew he wasn't the type of man to give his heart freely. His divorce had obviously left scars, deep and painful. And he'd already made his feelings quite clear. He was attracted to her, but there'd be no proposals of marriage, no happily ever after. Whatever she might imagine between them, it would only be sex to him.

"What's this all about?" Meg asked, her voice ragged with sleep.

"I just think you'd be better suited to this assignment."

"Why?"

"Well, you're much—" Holly searched for a plausible reason "—much stronger than I am."

"If there's heavy lifting to be done, why don't you hire someone?" Meg suggested. "We certainly have the budget."

"That's not what I mean," Holly said, dragging her overnight bag from beneath the bed.

Meg paused. "What *do* you mean? Has something happened? You sound upset."

"I'm fine," she said, throwing the bag open.

"You're lying," Meg countered. "I can always tell when you're lying, even over the phone. What's up?"

Holly paused, wondering if she should tell Meg the entire story or just the bare facts. "All right. There's this man. Actually, Eric Marrin's father, Alex. And we have a—a thing between us."

"A thing? Did you get all prissy with him? You know how men hate that. I'm always telling you, you have to be more flexible and more—"

"I wasn't prissy!" She sat down on the edge of the

bed. "Just the opposite. Whenever I'm around him, we end up kissing. Or almost kissing."

"You kissed a man?" Meg took a moment to digest the startling news. "You kissed a man! We are talking about on the lips, aren't we?"

"Once. He almost kissed me in the snow and in the kitchen. And then, there was the time he kissed my finger, but that doesn't count."

"It doesn't?" Meg asked.

"Well, I don't think kissing a girl's hurt finger can qualify as a sexual overture."

"Honey, just because I haven't had a date in six months, doesn't mean *you* can't enjoy yourself."

"I have a reputation to protect," Holly replied.

"Now you *are* being prissy."

"I can't allow myself to have personal feelings for a client." She held her breath, hoping that Meg wouldn't realize that Alex Marrin wasn't exactly a client. Since he wasn't footing the bill for her time and effort, then she was completely free to strip naked and dance around his kitchen in her apron and oven mitts if she felt so inclined. "Please, Meg, you have to help me. If I stay here, I'm not sure what I'll do."

"Gee, you might just go crazy and make wild, passionate love to the guy. And that might be exactly what you need!" Meg cried. "Holly, you have your life so perfectly planned right down to the underwear you're going to wear next Thursday. Maybe it's time you tried a little spontaneity."

"This is not about my character flaws, Meg! This is about sex! Sex with a man who's probably really, *really* good at it. Needless to say, I'm very bad at it. Now, if you want to be hanging tinsel with me next Christmas, you better pack your bags and take the first train north."

"I've got work to finish here," Meg protested. "The soonest I can get on a train is tomorrow morning."

Holly wasn't in the mood to argue any longer. It would require her to convince Meg that her business reputation was more precious to her than a few nights of torrid sex with Alex Marrin. And right now, even she knew that would be a lie.

She gave Meg a few more instructions, listened to a recitation of her phone messages, then hung up, placing the phone softly in the cradle. With a quiet moan, Holly buried her face in her hands and flopped back onto the bed. How could she have made such a mess of this all? Perhaps if she'd just been firm that first time he almost kissed her.

But it went back farther than that. From the moment they'd met in the horse barn, she felt it. A force drawing them together, magnetic, powerful and completely uncontrollable. As if all her carefully cultivated reserve had suddenly vanished, Holly felt like a woman driven by impulse rather than good common sense.

Rolling over on her stomach, she grabbed the phone book from the bedside table and flipped through it, looking for a cab company, desperate to do something sensible. Though the train didn't leave until that afternoon, the sooner she made her escape, the easier it would be on all of them.

The owner of Schuyler Falls' only cab company answered after seven or eight rings and sounded as if he'd just crawled out of bed. She made arrangements for him to pick her up at the end of the driveway in a half hour. That would give her enough time to finish packing and write a quick note to Eric explaining her sudden departure.

When she had finally stuffed the last bit of clothing

into her suitcase, she quickly snapped it shut then grabbed her coat. Holly took one last look around the room, then walked out of the tack house. The sun wasn't even up, but the yard lights lit the way up to the house. She hurried across the porch, eager to avoid the barns, also brightly blazing with light.

But as she turned the corner on the tack house porch, she ran face first into a lean, hard, finely muscled chest, clothed in a familiar canvas jacket. Her bag slipped out of her hand and landed squarely on the toe of her shoe. Holly yelped in pain, then hopped around on one foot. When the pain subsided, she managed to look up into Alex's face.

His eyes darted to her bag. "What's this?" he asked with a frown.

Wincing with pain, Holly snatched up her suitcase and moved around him. "I'm leaving," she said, limping as fast as she could.

"Today?"

"You can finish the other trees and put up the garland around the door and the mantels. You only wanted me to stay for three days and I did."

He fell into step beside her as she started down the porch steps. "That was then," he said. "We discussed this and I told you I—"

"It doesn't make a difference. I think it would be best if I left. I've called my assistant, Meghan O'Malley. She'll be arriving here tomorrow to tie up any loose ends."

"But Eric wants *you*," Alex said, placing his hand on her elbow. "You're his Christmas angel." He drew a long breath, then sighed. "This isn't because I kissed you, is it?"

Holly laughed dryly, ignoring the tiny tremor that

raced through her body as his fingers clutched her arm. "Don't flatter yourself," she lied. She pulled out of his grasp, but as soon as her foot hit the walk, it skidded out from under her. She bumped down onto the icy walk, rebruising her already bruised backside.

What was it with this place? When Alex wasn't sweeping her off her feet and kissing her, she managed to sweep herself off her own feet at every turn! Intent on putting some distance between them, she struggled to stand. "I don't want to be anyone's angel," she said.

Alex reached out to help her up, but she slapped his hand away, knowing precisely what his touch could do to her. She brushed the snow off the back of her coat, then hoisted up her bag again and set off at a quicker pace. This time he didn't bother to follow her. "Eric will like Meg. She's really much better with children than I am."

"You're pretty damn good with kids yourself."

Holly stopped, stunned by the unsolicited compliment. She slowly turned to find him staring at her, his gaze fierce, unwavering. "Do you really think so?" she asked.

His expression softened. "Don't go. Eric will miss you. I don't want him to pay for my mistakes."

"Then you admit kissing me was a mistake?" Holly asked, not really ready to hear his answer.

"No. That's not what I meant."

"What is it you want from me?"

Alex's jaw tightened and he shook his head, his mood darkening in the blink of an eye. "Am I supposed to know? I don't know how I feel about you, Holly. Or what I want. I don't think you do, either. But we're never going to find out if you run back to New York like some scared little rabbit."

"I came here to do a job," she said. "But I can't do my job if you're trying to kiss me at every turn."

"And you feel like you're betraying your fiancé?"

Holly frowned. "My fian—oh, yes. My fiancé. That's exactly how I feel," she murmured, nearly forgetting the lie she'd told him the night before.

"An engaged woman doesn't just go around kissing other men," he said.

Holly gasped. "I—I don't kiss at all! You're the one who kissed *me*. And you don't kiss like a gentleman!"

A sardonic grin touched his lips. "I'll take that as a compliment."

"Exactly my point. You are no gentleman." She spun on her heel and started back down the walk, this time avoiding the icy patches. But her progress was stopped when his hand grasped her arm. To fend him off, she swung her suitcase at him. But in her haste to pack, she'd neglected to secure the latches firmly and it flew open, sending her clothes flying over the snow.

Lacy black panties fell at his feet and he bent down to pick them up. He held them out, hooked on one finger and when she reached for them, he snatched them away. "You accuse me of being no gentleman. I'd say these prove you're not the lady you claim to be."

Holly glared at him, her anger bubbling inside. But beneath the anger, there was something else, something more powerful. An impulse, an urge to walk right up to him and kiss him again, to prove what he already knew. To make him feel exactly the way he made her feel. She took a step toward him, grabbed his face between her hands and gave him a punishing kiss, her tongue invading his mouth, her teeth grazing his lower lip. When she was quite positive she'd gotten the desired reaction, she stepped back and shrugged nonchalantly. "Keep the panties then. You can use them to decorate the other Christmas tree.''

With that, she turned on her heel, leaving her possessions scattered in the snow. Her heart threatened to pound right out of her chest, and for a moment, she felt a little dizzy. Though it wasn't the most dignified of exits, it would have to do. Because Holly Bennett was through feeling anything at all—including uncontrollable desire—for Alex Marrin. And that kiss proved it!

THE FIRST TRAIN BACK to New York that day was scheduled to leave Schuyler Falls at three o'clock in the afternoon. Since Kenny hung around the train station a lot, he knew all the schedules by heart, even all the stops between home and New York City. Eric had rushed from the bus stop a half block away, hoping and praying that his watch was a few minutes slow. He paused outside the doors with Kenny to catch his breath, just as the speaker above their heads crackled.

"Ladies and gentlemen, passengers with tickets for the three o'clock train to New York City's Penn Station, with stops in Saratoga Springs, Schenectady, Albany, Hudson, Poughkeepsie, and Yonkers, may begin boarding on track one.''

"We're too late!" he cried.

"Naw," Kenny replied. "They always board fifteen minutes before the train leaves."

Eric yanked the door open, clutching the special gifts he was carrying, then raced inside. But a quick search of the waiting area found no sign of his Christmas angel. He caught sight of the conductor standing at the door to the tracks. He'd come to meet his mom at the train a few times when she visited, so he knew he could get out on the platform to look for Holly. But what if she'd already boarded?

"Just be cool," Kenny said. "Act casual, like we're going to get on the train." They pulled their hoods up, like the guys in the spy movies did, then strolled outside to the platform.

"I can't see anything! The windows are all dark!" Eric cried.

Kenny shrugged. "Then you're just going to have to go on board. You won't need a ticket. Just tell 'em your mom already got on while you were in the can."

Eric's heart beat at a lickety-split speed and he felt as if he might lose the lunch he'd eaten at Kenny's house. He slowly gathered his courage. This was his angel and he'd do anything to keep her! When he got close enough to the car's steps, he nearly turned back. But the conductor spoke first, startling Eric.

"Are your folks on the train already, boys?" the conductor asked.

"No!" Eric said at the same time Kenny said, "Yes!"

"His mom is," Kenny said. "I'm just here to say goodbye."

Eric gave Kenny the elbow. Though he was a good liar, he was a real chicken when it came to the hard stuff, like getting on a train without a ticket. Eric nodded in agreement. Though he usually tried not to lie, this was important. If he didn't say yes out loud, maybe it wouldn't be such a big lie.

"Go on, then. Hop aboard."

He couldn't believe his luck! The guy was just letting him walk onto the train! Without a ticket, even. He gave Kenny one last look, then scrambled up the steps and walked into the car on his left. He found Holly just a few seats away. She sat with her head against the back of the seat, her eyes closed.

"You can't leave," he said as he plopped down in the seat next to her. When she opened her eyes, Eric shoved a fistful of plastic flowers under her nose, then followed it with a Snickers bar. He'd found the flowers in Kenny's garage and the Snickers was left over from lunch. But it was the best he could do.

"Eric! What are you doing here?" Holly asked, straightening in her seat.

"I came to bring you back," he said. "I don't know why you're mad at me, but—"

She smiled in that soft way that she always did, the way that made him feel all safe inside. "Oh, Eric, I'm not mad at you. I just have some important business in the city."

"Well, if you are mad, I brought you flowers and candy. Kenny says his dad is always bringing his mom flowers and candy when she's mad and it makes it all better."

"How did you get here?" Holly asked.

"I took the bus. Kenny knows all the schedules. He's like a genius when it comes to buses and trains."

"Then you got my letter?"

"I wanted to come and get you this morning, but Dad told me no. So I went over to Kenny's to play and then we just kind of walked to the bus stop and here I am. Kenny's outside." Eric leaned over Holly's lap and pounded on the window, then waved at Kenny. He glanced around the train car. "You know, they don't even ask for your ticket when you get on the train."

"You have to get off," Holly said. "Before the train leaves the station."

He shook his head. "Nope. I'm going to New York with you. I'm going to have Christmas at your house."

He could imagine what Christmas was like at Holly's house. She'd have a huge tree with billions of presents underneath, all wrapped up in paper and ribbons until no one could guess what was inside. She'd have a special plate and cup to leave out for Santa, one with his name on it. She'd let him get up as early as he wanted on Christmas morning. And after he opened all his presents, she'd make waffles with chocolate chips and bacon fried crispy. And fresh squeezed orange juice without the schnibbles.

"What about your dad? And Kenny's parents? They'll be worried about you."

"Kenny knows where I'm going. He'll tell Dad and Gramps. When do we leave? Can we go sit in the car with the glass top?"

Holly groaned, then grabbed Eric by the hand. "You're not going anywhere. And I guess I'm not, either. We're going to get off this train and I'm going to take you home before your dad misses *you* and blames *me*."

Eric grinned and jumped up from his seat. "I knew I could get you back. So what was it? The candy or the flowers?"

She climbed down the steps, then reached back for Eric and swung him down behind her. "It was that smile of yours," she said, tweaking his nose. "You're a very charming young man."

"He doesn't take after his father."

The sound of his father's voice sent a shiver of regret through Eric's body. He slowly looked up and found his dad standing on the platform, Kenny at his side, his face all red like a tomato. Slowly he retreated behind the protection of Holly's long coat. Now he was going to get it.

No video games, no television for a week, and no playing with Raymond or Kenny after school until probably forever.

"I stopped by Kenny's to pick you up, Scout," his dad said, his eyebrow arched. "I thought we'd go out and get those reindeer for the roof." He crossed his arms over his chest. "But you weren't there. Kenny's mom was about to call the police until I told her I knew where you both were."

Eric squirmed uneasily, clutching Holly's hand so hard he might break her fingers. He knew coming here was a risk, but he had no choice. "We were just standing near the bus stop," he explained. "And then the bus came and…we just hopped on!"

"Yeah," Kenny said. "We were only gonna see who was inside, but then the doors closed and off we went."

"Off we went," Eric repeated. He sighed, then stepped out from behind Holly. "All right, it wasn't really like that, but I—I don't care if you're mad. I had to get my angel back."

The conductor picked up the step from the platform and hopped onto the car behind Holly. He blew his whistle and called out, "All aboard."

"Holly has to go home," Alex said. "Her train is leaving."

"No," Holly murmured.

His gaze snapped from Eric to her. "What?"

They stared at each other for a long time, Eric glancing between the two, his face wrinkled into a frown. There was something funny going on here. Holly was staring at his dad the same way Eleanor Winchell stared at Raymond when she told him she loved him and wanted to marry him. And his dad was staring at Holly the same way Kenny stared at Eric's Michael Jordan rookie card.

"I don't have to go home. I'll stay until Christmas."
She drew in a deep breath, then started toward the station,
missing the stunned look on his father's face and the long
breath of air that came out of him like a stuck balloon.
Eric's dad started after her, leaving Kenny and Eric
standing on the platform.

Kenny wiggled his eyebrows and laughed raucously.
"Kissy, kissy," he murmured, puckering his lips.

Eric frowned. Could his Christmas angel be falling in
love with his dad? And could his dad feel the same way
about Holly? "You really think so?" he asked.

"Hey, I was the one who broke the news to Raymond
about Eleanor Winchell. I know all about chicks. Your
dad has the hots for your angel. And I think she feels the
same way."

Eric took a moment to digest the notion, then grinned.
"Cool," he raved. He grabbed Kenny's hand and ran
after Holly. When he caught up to her, he took her hand
and swung it between them. "When we get home, can
we make that gingerbread house from the magazine? The
one with the gumdrops on the top?"

"We can do whatever you want," Holly said.

"Good," Eric said with a secret smile. "'Cause my
dad really loves gingerbread."

5

THE HOUSE WAS FILLED with the scent of warm spices, cloves and cinnamon and ginger. An "Alvin and the Chipmunks" Christmas album chirped cheerily from the stereo while Eric sat at the end of the counter squeezing icing onto freshly baked gingerbread men. His lack of coordination made the men look as if they'd just returned from a gingerbread war, eyes and mouths displaced, pants hanging down over feet, hands mangled. But Holly was beginning to realize that perfection didn't always come from appearances. Instead it came from the joy on the frosting-stained face of a little boy she was slowly growing to love.

The pieces to a gingerbread house were cooling on the table as Holly pulled a gingerbread cake from the oven, the fragrance swirling in the air in front of her. "How's it going?" she asked Eric. "Are you almost finished?" She snatched up a cookie and took a bite. "Yummy!"

Eric put another flourish of frosting on the last man, then sat back, pensive. "We should have some gingerbread girls," he finally said. "You know, in case the boys get horny."

Holly nearly choked on the cookie, coughing and patting her chest, her eyes watering. "Wh-what?"

"It's not good to have all boys. It's like us, here at the farm—me, Dad and Gramps. When it's all boys it's not as much fun. We get kind of horny."

"Hor-horny?" She schooled her voice into casual indifference. "Where did you learn this word?"

"From Raymond. He says when his dad goes away on business, he gets horny for his mom. And when he comes home, they're all happy again."

"And what do you think horny means?"

Eric rolled his eyes, as if she were the biggest idiot he'd ever met. "It's like lonely," he said, swiping a glob of frosting off the counter and popping his finger into his mouth. "It's kind of a dumb word for lonely since it reminds me of horny toads." He studied one of his gingerbread men for a long moment. "I think my dad might be horny. So it's good you're here."

Holly braced her arms on the edge of the counter and steadied herself. Without any parental experience behind her, she wasn't sure what to do. Should she gently explain the true meaning of the word to Eric? Or should she try to preserve at least a small measure of his innocence? Since she had no intention of fulfilling Alex Marrin's horny desires, she decided to let it go.

"Do you ever get horny?" Eric asked.

"No!" Holly cried, the answer coming out much louder than she intended. "No. Never."

"Hmm. I guess it must only be boys then." He twisted until he was kneeling on the kitchen stool, his elbows braced on the counter. "You should take some of that cake down to the barn for my dad," he suggested. "Since he didn't come up for dinner, he must be really hungry."

Holly considered his suggestion for a moment. Alex probably was hungry and the gingerbread could serve as a peace offering of sorts. Besides, she hated living in limbo like she was, not knowing what he was thinking or how he felt. If she were going to spend another two weeks in this house, they'd have to develop some kind of truce or Eric would begin to notice the tension between them. "You're right," she murmured. "Why don't you get back to the library and finish your homework? And when you're finished, make sure you take a bath and wash all that frosting from your hair. Your grandfather can help you. Tell him I've gone down to the barn. He's in the library watching television."

A wide grin split Eric's serious expression. "Great! And don't forget the coffee. Cream and two sugars. That's the way my dad likes it." With that, he raced off to find his grandfather, his footsteps echoing through the empty house. But a few moments later, he ran back into the kitchen, breathless, his eyes bright. "Can you take the ribbon out of your hair?"

Holly frowned, then reached back and pulled the ribbon and the elastic from her haphazard ponytail. Her hair tumbled around her face and Eric smiled and nodded. "There," he said, "that's better." A second later, he was gone again.

Holly quickly tidied up the kitchen, stacking the gingerbread men at one end of the counter. Then she sliced a generous chunk of the warm gingerbread cake, wrapped it in a clean dish towel and filled a battered thermos with coffee. She checked her reflection in the kitchen window before she tugged on her wool jacket, slipped on her boots and made her way down to the barns.

Both barns were brightly illuminated, light spilling out of the high windows to sparkle in the snow. Holly chose the north barn, yanking open the heavy door and slipping inside. She wandered down the aisle, peeking into each stall, but Alex was nowhere to be found. She turned around and—

"Hi," he murmured. He stood in the center of the aisle, his hair damp with perspiration, his shirt unbuttoned to the waist. His forearms, so well muscled, gleamed. He didn't move and seemed unable to take his eyes off of her.

She held out the thermos and the gingerbread. "I—I brought you some coffee, and a slice of gingerbread cake. Eric helped me make it."

Alex quickly removed his leather gloves, then took the proffered snack. "Thanks," he murmured, moving to take a seat on a nearby bale of straw.

Holly rubbed her hands together, glancing around nervously. "Well, I should get going, I've got—"

"Stay," he said. "You can share my snack." He slid over to make a place for her on the bale, then poured coffee into the top of the thermos and handed it to her. "I almost didn't recognize you in those clothes," he said, splitting off a piece of gingerbread cake for her. "You look like you belong here."

He should recognize the clothes, she mused, since he'd picked them all up from the snow that afternoon and returned them to her room in the tack house. Her mind wandered to an image of him folding her underwear, but she brushed it from her mind. Holly clasped her hands over her knees. "You didn't come up to the house for supper."

"I thought maybe you'd rather I stayed away."

Holly sighed. "This is your house, Alex. I'm just a guest here."

He drew a deep breath. "Then tell me," he said. "What are we supposed to do?"

She twisted her fingers together, staring at them. Better that than staring at his naked chest, contemplating the soft line of hair that started at his collarbone and ended somewhere below the button on his jeans. "I don't think it would be wrong for us to be friends," she suggested.

"I'm going to be here until Christmas. If you plan to avoid me, you're going to be spending a lot of time in this barn."

"It's not so bad out here," he said. "I've got a lot to do. And though I love my horses, I'm not tempted to kiss them." Already, she'd grown familiar with his dry wit and his self-deprecating humor. Grinning, he took the cup of coffee from her hand and took a sip, then another bite of the gingerbread. He moaned softly, then shook his head. "You're really good at this. This cake is wonderful. There is more, isn't there?"

"Up in the kitchen." Holly hid her pleasure at his compliment, searching for a change of subject so he'd stop staring at her the way he was. And so she'd resist the urge to brush her fingertips over his chest. "What do you do out here with all your time?" she asked.

"You really want to know? I didn't think you were much of a farm girl, after your first experience in the barn—your Stony Creek pedicure."

Holly felt her cheeks warm. "It's not so bad once you get used to the smell. And have a proper pair of boots. Though this place could use some potpourri and a few barrels of lemon oil, I think—"

"Potpourri?"

"It's a mix of different dried flowers, sometimes spices or herbs. You put it in sachets and you can heat it in water. It gives the room a wonderful ambience. Or you can tuck it in a lingerie drawer."

He put on a serious expression. "I've always thought my lingerie drawer needed a…what was it?"

"Sachet," Holly said, giggling. "I have a recipe for a Christmas blend with dried apples and cinnamon sticks. And another with pine needles. Although you'd probably need a truckful of the stuff to make this place smell like a lady's boudoir.''

"Yeah," Alex said. "And the effort would be lost on the horses. If it smells like apples, they'd probably eat it.''

The teasing give-and-take of their conversation surprised her. She'd anticipated nothing but tension between them, but the easy set of his shoulders, his crooked smile, told her differently. Maybe they could be just friends.

"Would you like me to show you around?" Alex offered after he finished the last bite of gingerbread cake. "You didn't get much of a tour that first day."

Holly nodded. He stood and held out his hand to her, then pulled it back when he realized they probably shouldn't touch each other again. He covered his blunder by shoving his hand into his jeans pocket and taking another sip of his coffee. In truth, Holly would have liked to hold his hand, but maybe this was for the best.

Side by side, they strolled down the long aisle that ran the length of the barn. Holly peered into a stall, bracing her arms on the edge of the high gate. A pretty brown mare kept one eye on her and the other on the food she was munching. Unlike the vicious beast, Scirocco, this horse looked sweet and docile. "Who's this?"

"This is Jade. Her official name is Greenmeadow Girl. But we always give our mares nicknames. Usually precious gems or flowers.''

"Eric was complaining that there were no girls on the farm. I guess he forgot about all the horses," Holly said.

A frown wrinkled Alex's perfect brow. "He was complaining?"

"Yeah." She laughed softly, then sent him a sideways glance. "And make a note to talk to him about the meaning of the word 'horny.' He has it confused with lonely.''

Alex's eyes widened and he gasped. "What do you two talk about when you're baking?"

"That's strictly between us," Holly said with a sly smile. She climbed up on the first rung of the gate. "So is Jade going to have a baby?"

"A foal. And yes, she is."

"Who delivers the baby?"

"They kind of take care of that on their own. Sometimes they need my help or the vet's. Hopefully it'll happen after the first of the year."

"Why is that?" Holly asked. "For tax purposes?"

Alex chuckled. "If they're born before January 1, they're considered a two-year-old at next January's auction, instead of a yearling. So if Jade foals early, we usually don't bother discovering that foal until after the first of the year."

"This seems like a lot of work for just you and your father."

"We've got a couple of high school kids that come in every evening and on weekends to clean stalls and groom the horses. It's not hard work when you love your job."

Holly nodded. "I guess not." She moved to hop off the gate, but her heel caught and she stumbled. In an instant, Alex's hands circled her waist, steadying her as he lowered her to the ground. But this time he didn't draw away. Instead he idly smoothed his hands from her waist to her hips.

It was Holly who broke the spell, Holly who took a step back. She forced a smile. "I'd better finish cleaning up the kitchen. I'll leave the gingerbread cake out for you."

He nodded, the barest hint of gratitude curling his lips. "I suppose I'll see you tomorrow?"

"Tomorrow," Holly murmured. Her pulse pounding,

she spun on her heel and hurried out of the barn. But she didn't slow her pace until she reached the house. She stopped, her hand on the door, her quickened breath clouding in the cold air.

She could still feel the warm imprint of his hands on her waist and she groaned softly. "If this is what gingerbread and coffee does to the man, I better not try my lemon meringue pie on him."

ALEX STOMPED THE SNOW OFF his boots, then pushed open the back door to the house. He'd been working in the barn all day, taking a short break only for the sandwiches Jed brought down at noon. But he'd finished all his work in anticipation of a Christmas tradition that hadn't been observed since before Renee left.

It was one of his favorite holiday activities, a tradition that he remembered from his own childhood. He and Jed had tossed the tarp off the old cutter and wiped down the cracked leather seats. He'd gathered up a stack of clean blankets, oiled the jingle-bell traces and given Daisy a grooming until her winter coat shone.

As he stepped inside, he drew a deep breath, new and tempting odors assailing him every time he returned to the house. He'd become continually amazed at the transformation Holly had wrought. Room by room, his house was becoming a Christmas showcase, filled with beautiful decorations, fragrant garlands, twinkling lights and candles. And still, the florist trucks arrived with more, the deliveryman from Dalton's hauling yet another bag of decorations up the front steps, and Jed, as besotted by Holly as Eric, squired her around town to every shop that carried Christmas merchandise.

He found Holly in her usual spot, in front of the stove, peering into a steaming pot of water. "What are you cooking up now?'' he asked, stepping to the sink to wash his hands. He grabbed a towel from the rack, then noticed it had pretty little embroidered Christmas trees along the hem. He carefully replaced it, then wiped his damp hands on the thighs of his jeans.

''It's wonderful! Perfect!'' Holly murmured. ''Look, I found a mold in the back of the cupboard.''

''There's mold in the—''

''No, a mold. It must be at least a hundred years old. Collectors pay exorbitant amounts for these things. I probably shouldn't even be using it but—''

''There's stuff in this house that my great-grandmother cooked with,'' Alex said. ''You should see the attic. So what's so special about this?''

''I think it's an English mold, made especially for plum pudding. That's what I'm making. It's steaming in the pot right now. We'll have it with Christmas dinner.''

''Hmm,'' Alex said. ''I like pudding. But where did you get the plums?''

Holly glanced over at him with an odd expression, as if she'd just realized he was there. Sometimes she got so wrapped up in her Christmas preparations she lost all contact with reality. ''There are no plums in plum pudding. It's a traditional Christmas dessert made with raisins and figs and suet and bread.''

Alex wrinkled his nose. ''Suet?''

''Yes. It steams for six hours and then you wrap it in a brandy-soaked cloth until Christmas. And then you re-warm it and drizzle hard sauce over it.''

Wasn't suet what Jed fed the chickadees? So far, he'd loved everything Holly had offered him, but suet? ''Hard sauce. And that's made with…let me guess…nuts and bolts? Or maybe gravel?''

Holly rolled her eyes. ''I guarantee you're going to

love it. I haven't made a plum pudding since I was very young. We always used to have it at my house for Christmas dinner.''

He nodded, then moved to the cookie jar to see what new treat awaited him today. "Then you're going to stay for Christmas dinner?'' he asked, trying to sound nonchalant.

Holly shifted uneasily. "My contract requires that I stay, unless you don't want me to stay. It's entirely up to you.''

"No, no,'' Alex said. "I wouldn't want you to be in breach of your contract.'' They stood in uncomfortable silence for a long moment. "So, are you almost ready to go?'' he asked. "Make sure you dress warm. Once the sun goes down, it gets chilly.''

"Where are we going?''

"Didn't Eric tell you? I'm taking you both out for a sleigh ride as soon as he gets home from school. I've got Daisy all hitched up. It's a full moon tonight, so we'll be able to see.''

"Oh, that sounds like fun!'' Holly cried. The color rose in her cheeks with barely suppressed excitement. Alex felt a flood of warmth race through his body at her natural beauty. She was dressed much like she had been last night in the barn, in casual clothes, her wavy flaxen hair pinned up in a careless knot with tendrils brushing her face.

Right on cue, Alex heard the front door slam and Eric came stomping through the house, dragging his backpack behind him. "Hey, Scout!''

"Hey, Dad. Hey, Holly.''

"Why don't you change real quick and put on a warmer jacket. Remember, we're going to take Holly out in the sleigh.''

Eric glanced between Holly and Alex, then hesitantly shook his head. "I—I can't, Dad. I know I promised this morning, but Kenny has this science project he has to do and he needs my help. His mom is coming right over to pick me up and I'm supposed to have supper with them. It's really important."

Alex studied his son shrewdly. Somehow, he didn't think Eric was being entirely truthful. He had that same tight smile he used when he was faking sick before school or covering up a bad report from his teacher. "But I have this all planned. Are you sure you don't want to go?"

"It's not that I don't want to go. I can't." Eric swallowed and pasted an even tighter grin on his face. "It's ignorant rocks. Kenny doesn't know anything about them and I have to help him."

"Ignorant rocks? Don't you mean igneous?"

"Yeah, that's it. So why don't you and Holly go anyway? I wouldn't want her to miss it." He turned to Holly. "It's the most fun."

Alex nodded, suddenly aware of his son's motivations. His heart twisted in his chest and he cursed silently. He should have been prepared for this. There was no way Eric could avoid seeing Holly as a potential mate for his dad. She was pretty and smart and exactly the kind of woman a boy like Eric might wish for his new mother. But building up his hopes, only to have them dashed when Holly left, was something that Alex could not allow. It had taken Eric almost a year to get over his mother's desertion. How long would he mourn after Holly left?

"All right," Alex said. "We'll just cancel for today. We can go another day."

"No!" Eric cried. "I—I mean, today is the best day.

And—and what if the snow melts? Then Holly wouldn't get a sleigh ride at all."

A car horn beeped outside the front door and Eric snatched up his backpack and ran out of the room. "I gotta go!"

"Have Kenny's mom bring you home by eight," Alex called.

"Bye, Dad. Bye, Holly. Have fun!"

The door slammed behind him and Alex leaned back against the counter, crossing his arms over his chest. "I guess it's just the two of us. Unless you don't want to go," he murmured.

"No, I'd like to go. As long as you have Daisy all hitched up. And the moon is full. Besides, I already finished my report on ignorant rocks."

Alex laughed. "Then grab your mittens and hat and let's go."

"Wait," Holly said. "I'll make some hot chocolate and wrap up some cookies."

"You do that and meet me at the barn," he said. He pulled his gloves from his pockets, then strode to the back door. "Don't be too long." But she didn't hear him. She was already dumping milk into a pan and dropping in a chunk of chocolate, lost again in plans, this time for a perfect sleigh ride.

Alex ambled down to the barn, whistling a cheery version of "Jingle Bells" as he walked. He found Daisy waiting in front of the north barn, Jed adjusting her harnesses.

"Where're Holly and the boy?" he asked.

"Eric has a school project he's doing with Kenny. Holly is whipping up some hot chocolate. She'll be along in a few minutes."

Jed raised his eyebrow. "Eric's not going along?"

"Naw," Alex replied. He noticed the leery look on his father's face. "Do you want to come and be our chaperone?"

Jed laughed, then rubbed his stubbled chin. "You want me to come along? If you're scared to be alone with the little lady, I can always—"

"I'm not afraid to be with her," he protested. "We're getting along just fine now that we've come to an agreement."

"What's that? An agreement to pretend that you don't care about her? Well, that's the dumbest thing I ever did hear."

"That's the way she wants it," Alex said.

"What a woman says she wants and what she really wants are sometimes very different. Haven't you figured that out yet?"

"All I know is that I'm not going to be kissing her again, that's for sure—unless she asks. And I don't expect that anytime soon."

His father chuckled and shook his head. "Holing yourself up at this farm for the past two years hasn't done you any good, son. If you really want that little lady, then let her know. Sooner or later, she'll come over to your way of thinking."

"And what is my way of thinking?" Alex asked.

"Why, I suspect, you're in love with her. You just haven't realized it yet." He gave Daisy a pat on the neck, then wandered back toward the barn, mumbling to himself.

"I barely know her!" Alex called.

Jed turned around. "That's right. We Marrin men don't need much time. It was that way with your grandpa and your great-grandpa and me. When we see the gal we want, we get matters settled right off."

"But I only knew Renee for three months before I decided to marry her. And that didn't work out."

Jed nodded. "Yep. I coulda predicted that. You took too long in deciding. Three months. That one was doomed from the start."

Alex muttered a soft oath as his father walked into the barn, then efficiently began to rearrange the blankets beneath the seats. Jed had refilled the kerosene lamps that decorated the front corners of the cutter and even tossed in an old moth-eaten lap robe that he remembered from his childhood rides.

Though he tried to occupy himself with preparations for their ride, he couldn't ignore his father's words. Was he really falling in love with Holly Bennett? How could that be? He'd known her less than a week. He couldn't possibly fall in love in a week!

Alex stepped back from the cutter and raked his hands through his hair. Alone with Holly, snuggled beneath cozy blankets, in the midst of a moonlit night. This was an evening planned for lovers.

"Maybe this wasn't such a good idea after all," he muttered.

HOLLY'S SPIRITS SOARED as they skimmed over the snow. The jingle bells on the horse's reins rang sharp and clear in the silence of the outdoors. The only other sounds, the creak of old leather and the dull thud of the horse's hooves in the snow, played a strangely soothing counterpoint in the waning light of day.

Here in the crisp evening air, she felt the spirit of the season surround her, engulf her, until she had no choice but to laugh out loud. They glided through rolling snow-covered meadows, pastures for the horses in the summer, down lanes flanked by old stone fences that divided forest from field, and through lightly wooded glades, where the bare trees shivered in the wind.

Her cheeks and nose, ruddy with the cold, were nearly numb, but the rest of her body was toasty warm beneath the heavy lap robe. Alex urged Daisy into a quick trot and they flew through a drift of snow, the sleigh rising up in the air. Holly screamed before she hit the seat with a bump, then giggled.

"Whoa! Slow down there, Daisy," Alex called. They rounded a short bend in the lane and then he drew the horse to a stop. Holly looked out on the vista, a wide expanse of land that dropped gently to a winding creek below. The shallow water, not yet frozen, bubbled over rocks and glinted in the low angle of the setting sun. "That's Stony Creek," he said.

The sun hung low over the horizon, streaking the sky with pink and gold. "I don't think I've ever seen a more beautiful spot," Holly murmured. "Your farm seems to be blessed with so many pretty spots."

Alex smiled. "I think so, too. And every season brings something new. There's a grove of wild plum trees just down there that burst into bloom in the spring. As a kid, I used to ride out here in the fall and pick the plums from the back of my horse. My mom would turn them into jam."

"Does Eric do that now?"

Alex shook his head. "Naw. No one to turn the plums into jam."

Holly sighed. "Maybe I'll come back in the fall and do that for him. I've never made wild plum jam. I'll bet it's good."

"You'd do that?" Alex asked, his gaze intense, skimming the features of her face as if he were trying to read her mind, discern her true intentions.

"Of course. Why not?" she said, covering her offer with an air of indifference.

"I just figured you'd go back to the city and forget all about us," Alex said.

Holly felt the heat rise in her cheeks, driving away the cold. She tore her gaze from his and stared out at the landscape. "I don't think I could ever forget this place. It's given me back Christmas." She distracted herself by tucking the robe around her legs. "These past few years, I've almost dreaded the holidays. It's all been about business. I work and work to make everyone else's Christmas perfect and when Christmas Eve finally comes, I'm left wondering why I feel so sad."

"We're two of a kind, then," Alex said. "I always tried to work up some enthusiasm for Eric's sake, but the holidays just brought back bad memories."

"But this Christmas is different for me," Holly continued. "I'm happy. Joyous might be a better word." She turned to face him, only to find his eyes already fixed on her.

Slowly he reached over and brushed a strand of wind-whipped hair from her cheek, then hesitantly drew his hand away. "I'm happy, too," he murmured. The deeper meaning of his words hung between them in the cold air and Holly didn't need to question the cause of Alex's happiness. It was there in his expression, the smile that barely touched his lips, the warm light in his eyes. She swallowed hard, willing him to lean closer and kiss her, for this time, she wouldn't fight him. This time she wanted him.

But when he refused to make a move, Holly nearly screamed in frustration. What was stopping him? She certainly acted like she wanted him to kiss her, didn't she? Short of closing her eyes, throwing herself at his chest and puckering up, how much more obvious could she be? But as moments passed, excruciatingly long moments, she remembered his words after the last time they kissed.

She groaned inwardly. Did he really expect her to beg? Oh, this was just like him, to taunt her with her own reservations, to make her feel all warm and mushy inside, then coldly refuse to respond. Well, she could be just as hard-hearted as he was. She didn't need his kisses and she'd prove it!

Holly sat back in the seat. "Let's go," she said.

He arched his eyebrow, his smile turning sardonic. "Do you want to drive?"

Holly took the reins from his hands. If he wanted her in control, then she'd take control! "All right. This doesn't look too hard. There's no clutch, no gearbox. What do I do?"

He wrapped an arm around her shoulder and took her hands in his. "Weave the reins through your fingers like this. Give it a firm touch, but not too firm. She needs to know you're in control." He raised Holly's hands and let the reins drop gently against Daisy's rump. "Hup, Daisy girl. Get along."

The horse lurched into action, quickly breaking into a brisk trot. Holly clutched the reins and fixed her eyes on the horse's bobbing head. But her mind was focused on the feel of Alex's arm around her shoulders, the warmth that seeped through his jacket, the faint scent of his aftershave. She'd never known a man to smell as...manly as Alex Marrin. No fancy designer cologne nor expensive shampoo, just all man—rugged, windblown, suntanned man.

The further they went, the more her mind wandered, to thoughts of his smooth, muscled chest, his flat belly, the sinewy strength of his arms. Shoulders so broad and a waist so narrow it made her ache with the need to look at him. Piece by piece, she mentally removed his clothes until—

Holly coughed softly. "How do I stop?" she demanded, her voice cracking slightly.

Alex looked down at her, his chin grazing her temple. "Stop?"

"Yes!" she cried. "How do I stop the horse? I want to stop now."

"Pull back," he said. "Whoa, Daisy. Whoa, girl."

When the cutter slid to a stop, she shoved the reins back into his hands. He swung his arm over her head, a perplexed expression on his face. "Do you want to go back to the house?" he asked.

Holly shook her head. "No."

"What do you want?"

"I—I want you to kiss me," she said. She drew in a deep breath, then let it out very slowly, clouding the air in front of her face. Until now, she'd listened to her head instead of her heart. But suddenly her head was starting to agree with her heart.

Why shouldn't she have exactly what she wanted? She'd spent her whole career planning for the future, waiting for Christmas to come. It was about time she lived for now, lived for this very moment when desire danced between them. "I'm not going to ask again," Holly murmured. "I'm not going to beg. So, if you want to kiss me, you'd better do it now or lose your chance."

He chuckled softly. "You think I want to kiss you?"

Her head snapped around and she narrowed her eyes. "Don't you?"

Alex shrugged lazily. "I'm not sure. I hadn't really thought about it."

An aggravated moan slipped from her throat and she pushed aside the lap robe and slid to the far edge of the seat. All she wanted was a simple kiss. Why did he have to make it so difficult? "Then don't. I don't care. I—I just thought you might want to. You looked like you did."

"Maybe I do," Alex finally said, a wicked grin twitching at his lips. "But with you over there and me over here. Well..." He lifted the lap robe, inviting her back beneath its warmth. When she relented and slid over the cracked leather seat, he slipped his arm back around her shoulders and she grudgingly settled against him. But he still didn't make a move.

"You can do it anytime now," she muttered.

He caught her chin with his finger and turned her face up until she was forced to look at him. "The truth is, I want to kiss you," he said, bending nearer, "wherever and whenever I want. I want to be able to pull you into my arms and taste your mouth. And I want you to kiss me back, to go soft against me, to wrap your arms around my neck and run your fingers through my hair."

"I—I can do that," Holly stammered, staring into his eyes, aware of the passion burning there. All her resolve vanished and Holly was certain of what she wanted. "Really, I can."

"Then maybe we should give it a try?"

Dazed, she blinked and waited, waited for that exquisite moment when his lips would touch hers, that instant when his tongue would take possession of her mouth. And then it happened, a kiss she'd been waiting for her entire adult life, from a man she'd been searching for since she'd first become aware of the opposite sex. And it all happened as he said it would, lips touching, tongues tasting, and her heart threatening to burst from her chest.

She slipped her arms around his neck and furrowed her fingers through his hair. A soft moan rumbled deep in his throat and the kiss gradually intensified, growing more frantic with every passing breath. He took her face between his hands and molded her mouth to his, stealing her breath and making her pulse race even faster.

Holly felt giddy, light-headed, so much so that she forgot to think and merely felt. All her doubts and insecurities vanished as desire surged between them and a simple kiss became so much more. She brushed aside his canvas jacket and pressed her palms against his warm chest, the flannel of his shirt soft beneath her fingertips.

But that wasn't enough for Holly. She wanted to touch him, really touch him, to feel his skin beneath her hands. With shaking fingers, she unbuttoned his shirt, craving his warmth. He did the same, unzipping her jacket and slipping his hands beneath her sweater to circle her waist. On and on, the kiss went, never breaking contact, growing more desperate until they nearly tore at each other's clothes.

Holly had almost dispensed with the buttons of his shirt when she was thwarted by yet another layer, his thermal undershirt. His lips still clinging to hers, Alex yanked both shirts out of the waistband of his jeans. He grabbed her hands and slid them beneath, her fingers skimming over the rippled muscles of his stomach until she felt his heart beating beneath her palms.

Alex slowly leaned her back onto the cool leather of the seat, drawing the lap robe around them and shutting out the cold night air. As he nuzzled Holly's neck, she opened her eyes to see a single star gleaming in the deep blue sky. She smiled and tried to think of a wish, then closed her eyes again when she realized she wanted nothing more than what she had at this very moment.

As he trailed kisses along her neck, Holly arched beneath him. Perhaps she did want more. Naked limbs twined beneath twisted sheets. The sweet weight of Alex Marrin stretched over her body. Desire so intense that nothing could satisfy it but the ultimate act of passion. Though that wouldn't happen tonight, Holly knew it would happen soon.

Now that they'd taken the first step, there would be nothing to do but rush headlong toward the inevitable, a runaway horse headed straight for the edge of a cliff. But Holly wasn't afraid. Even if they parted ways on Christmas Day, she'd always have her one perfect Christmas with Alex Marrin, a Christmas filled with passion and excitement. And those memories would be enough to last all the Christmases of her life.

She tugged his head back, then gently kissed him, running her tongue along the crease of his mouth before drawing away. "I packed some hot chocolate and cookies. Maybe we should take a break."

He smiled languidly then braced his hands on either side of her head. He wouldn't push her. Holly saw it in the way he looked at her. Alex was willing to wait until she was ready and that made her want him even more. He gave her a quick kiss, rubbed his nose against hers and sat up. "I've learned one thing from you, Holly Bennett."

She sat up beside him, straightening her clothes. "And what's that?"

"When you offer me food, I'd be a fool to refuse."

Holly tipped her head back and laughed. Alex wrapped his arms around her and hugged her tight, then nuzzled the top of her head. "And when I offer you kisses?" she asked.

"Well, given the choice, I think I'd give up the cookies, and the cake, and anything else you'd offer. The way to a man's heart is not always through his stomach."

6

"A LITTLE TO THE LEFT... No, now a little bit back toward the right. Okay, up, up, up. Oh, there. Stop. Don't move."

Alex balanced on the ladder, his arm outstretched, his hand clutching the fresh pine garland that Holly had purchased for the front porch. He'd already affixed a lush swag of fruits and nuts and greenery just above the front door and hung tiny wreaths in all the windows on the facade of the house, but the garland seemed to be taking an inordinate amount of effort. He'd already sneezed five times and he could feel another tickle growing in his nose from the scent of evergreen.

He rubbed his nose, which threw off his balance, which set the ladder to wobbling. Alex had no choice but to drop the garland and grab hold with both hands, or take a nasty tumble into the bushes.

"Oh, no!" Holly cried. "That won't do."

Alex stared down at the garland, now draped over the yews that fronted the porch. "I think it looks nice right where it is," he said. "Besides, my arms are getting sore. Can't we just tack it up and be done with it?"

Holly shook her head and grabbed the garland, handing it back up to him. "It has to hang evenly or you'll notice it every time you drive in the driveway. It has to be—"

"Perfect," Alex completed. "Yeah, I kind of figured that."

She hitched her hands on her waist and giggled. "I'll make you a deal. If you help me finish this, I'll be very, very grateful after you crawl down from that ladder."

"And will that gratitude be expressed in the form of a kiss?" he asked, holding the garland back up on the eave of the porch.

"You'll just have to wait and see."

The past three days had been near perfect. Holly had busied herself with decorating the house and baking Christmas treats. She'd crafted delicate snowflakes from frosting and made a wreath out of tiny shiny ornaments. She'd filled the house with candles and, in the evening, lit them all, suffusing the house with wonderful scents. And after the day's work was finished and Eric had been tucked into bed, he and Holly would curl up on the sofa, the fire crackling and the tree twinkling, and talk as if they'd known each other for years.

Though he wasn't really sure what had brought about the change in her, he wasn't about to question it. He felt like a teenager again, stealing kisses while the late movie played, wondering just how far he could go before she said no. It had been so hard to hold back, for he wanted nothing more than to possess Holly, both body and soul. But after their shaky start, he wasn't willing to risk another retreat. If she ran again, he wouldn't have the courage to bring her back. A desertion now would likely tear him apart.

"That's it!" Holly cried. "Hold it right there." She scurried to collect the hammer and nails they were using to fix the garland to the porch, then handed them up to him.

When the garland was finally perfect, Alex stepped down from the ladder. He tossed the hammer into the snow, snaked his arm around Holly's waist and yanked her against him. "Now, for that kiss."

He dipped her back and kissed her thoroughly, making her sigh with need. And when he'd had enough, he didn't stop, but delved into her mouth just once more in case he didn't have another chance to sneak a kiss until that evening.

A low rumble sounded from the end of the driveway and Alex groaned as the school bus rolled to a stop on the road. He set Holly upright, straightened her jacket, then grinned. "Eric's home."

She gave his hand a squeeze, holding it behind her back until they saw Eric through the trees. They hadn't really discussed their relationship. Though Alex was certain it was a relationship, talking about it might make it seem too real, too fragile and too temporary. But one thing was understood—they'd keep their attraction a secret from Eric. It was for the best because Alex knew his son harbored some hope that Holly would become a permanent part of their lives.

But Alex also knew Holly had a life back in New York City, full of parties and theater and sophisticated friends—and a fiancé she'd neglected to mention in days. He'd love to believe she'd stay, but giving up a career and her plans for the future for life on an upstate horse farm, becoming an instant mother to a seven-year-old boy, wasn't something most women would choose to take on. He had to be satisfied with the time they had together. When her job was finished, he'd let her go.

"Dad!" Eric called, waving as he ran up the driveway. "I have to talk to you." He raced up to the porch and threw his backpack on the steps. "In private."

"Am I going to be making a call to Miss Green?"

"No! It's something else." He glanced at Holly. "Man talk."

Holly grabbed up the tools they'd used. "I've got some decorating to finish inside. We'll have supper around five if that's all right."

"Six," Eric said. "Me and my dad have stuff to do."

Alex smiled at Holly and she returned the favor, sending a flood of warmth through his bloodstream. Every day, she was more beautiful. He wondered what stroke of luck had sent this angel knocking at his door. Who was responsible? If he ever found out, he'd have to make a point to thank the person.

When Holly had closed the door behind her, Alex sat down on the porch step and patted the spot beside him. But Eric refused the invitation. "We have to go right now."

"Where?" Alex asked.

"Shopping. We have to get Christmas presents for Holly. She's going to be here on Christmas morning and she has to have something to open." He grabbed Alex's hand and pulled him to his feet. "If we go now, we can be back before dinnertime. And she won't even know."

Alex hadn't thought about a gift for Holly. Knowing her, she'd pick out the perfect present for the two of them, a thoughtful gift filled with obvious meaning. But what was he supposed to choose for a woman who wasn't his girlfriend or his lover, a woman who had wandered into his life and would soon wander out? It would take time to find the perfect gift for Holly, one that would say just enough about his feelings but not too much.

"Then we better get going," Alex said, jogging toward the pickup parked in the driveway.

"We only have eight shopping days until Christmas," Eric reminded him.

Alex pulled open the truck door and jumped inside, then reached over to open Eric's door. When his son had his seat belt fastened, he started the truck and steered it down the driveway and onto the road into town.

Eric wriggled in his seat, zipping and unzipping his jacket. "I have to get just the most perfect present."

"I'm sure anything you get Holly will be fine," Alex murmured, his mind on his own choices. Perfume? Candy? A pretty sweater?

"No, it has to be special. If I get her the right present, then maybe she'll stay."

Alex was tempted to stop the truck in the middle of the road and set his son straight. But he couldn't deny that he harbored some of the same hopes. Was there a chance she'd stay? If he said the right thing, did the right thing, would she consider giving up her life in New York? "Scout, I don't think that's the right reason to get Holly a gift. You should get her something because she's been nice to us and because she made your Christmas wish come true. But you can't expect her to give up her life and her job to stay with us."

Eric shrugged. "It could happen."

They drove for a long time in silence, Alex's eyes fixed on the road, but his thoughts elsewhere. He'd always anticipated problems with Eric when it came to a new woman in their lives. Eric still held Renee up as the ultimate mom, even though she only saw him a few times each year. They had a special connection that couldn't be diminished by time apart.

"Would you like to have a new mom?" Alex asked.

"I know my mom isn't coming back to live with us. And I think you need a wife."

"Don't worry about me," Alex said. "I'm doing all right."

A light snow started to fall as they reached the downtown area. Alex found a parking space just off the square and he and Eric joined the holiday shoppers as they hurried toward Dalton's. Eric didn't even bother to linger over the windows, so intent was he on his mission.

They passed through the revolving doors and stopped once inside. "So what were you thinking about?" Alex asked, hoping his son might be able to give him a few pointers. He'd never been much good at figuring out what women liked. And Holly would be very particular about the perfume she wore or the scarves she chose.

Eric grabbed his hand and dragged him over to the far side of the main floor, past perfume, past accessories and directly to jewelry. He pressed his nose up against the glass case and carefully scrutinized a selection of precious gemstones fashioned into earrings, rings and necklaces. "These are pretty," he said.

"And a little out of your price range," Alex said.

"How much?" Eric asked the salesperson.

The man perused the case. "The least expensive item would be the birthstone earrings. They're ninety-nine."

Eric glanced up at his father. "I have ninety-nine cents," he said.

Alex smiled and placed his hand on Eric's head. "I think he means dollars."

A crestfallen expression suffused Eric's face. But then he suddenly brightened. "You could buy her the earrings. Or a bracelet. Or a diamond ring." He looked up at the salesman. "Do you have any diamond rings?"

The salesman gave Alex a questioning look, then proceeded to the next case. "We have some lovely rings here. Do you know what style she likes? We have brilliant cut, marquis, emerald cut, and a variety of settings in gold and platinum."

"Let's look at them all," Eric said.

Alex wasn't about to argue. In truth, he was curious. When he married Renee, he only had enough money to buy her a cheap ring with a barely visible diamond. He wasn't even sure what an engagement ring cost. It couldn't hurt to look.

The salesman set the velvet case in front of them. Eric peered at the selections. "I think she'd like that one," he said, reaching up and pointing to the largest diamond in the front row.

"How much is that one?" Alex asked.

"This is a one-carat emerald-cut diamond of impeccable color and clarity in a platinum setting. It's just under nine thousand."

Alex blinked. "Nine thousand. That's a lot of molasses and oats."

"Excuse me?"

"Nothing." He bent down until he was eye-level with Eric. "Scout, I think we can find something else for Holly besides a diamond ring. Maybe a pretty bracelet or a sweater."

Eric gave one last look to the diamond rings then nodded. "We could sniffle some perfume," he said. "Holly always smells really good. I bet she uses a lot of that stuff."

The salesman put the diamond rings back in the case, locked it, then leaned over the counter. He motioned to Eric and the little boy pushed up on his tiptoes. "Try bath salts or scented lotion. That's what I usually get my wife for a Christmas gift and she loves it."

"I bet they have some nice gift boxes at the perfume counter," Alex suggested to his son.

Eric took one last look at the rings, then nodded. "That

would probably be better. Those rings are real little. She could lose it.''

Alex breathed a small sigh of relief as they strolled back to the perfume counter. But his mind was still on the diamond rings. Which one would she like? Holly had very sophisticated taste and, though she dressed in a simple, elegant manner, she seemed to be drawn more toward traditional things. There was a pretty ring in the top row Alex was certain she'd—

He cursed to himself. What the hell was he thinking? They'd barely shared their first kiss a few days ago and he was already thinking engagement rings?

Alex sighed. If he knew what was good for him he'd head right to the scarf department.

HOLLY GLANCED AT THE CLOCK over the kitchen sink then wiped her hands on a dish towel. She'd just finished a duo of tiny pinecone wreaths that she planned to hang on either side of the library fireplace. Eric was stretched out on the sofa watching a favorite *Star Wars* video. And Alex had ventured out to the barn nearly three hours before, promising to be back in a few minutes.

She wandered over to the sofa and ruffled Eric's hair. "Come on, buddy. It's half past nine. Time for bed."

Except for the obligatory groan, Eric didn't protest. Pleased with another successful foray into parenting, Holly slipped him a cookie as they walked through the kitchen, then accepted his quick peck on the cheek before he crawled up the stairs. She'd never spent much time around kids and had always doubted her ability to parent. But with Eric, she'd seemed to fall into it naturally.

They were friends, but she'd also managed to cultivate a level of respect between them. Eric listened to her and did his best to please. And the rare times that he misbehaved in her presence, she'd merely have to look at him sternly and he'd shape up. But there was something more she'd found with Eric. Holly had no doubt that he cared about her, maybe even loved her. And her feelings had grown just as strong.

Now, when she thought about the day she'd leave Stony Creek Farm, she didn't only think about leaving Alex. She thought about saying goodbye to Eric. She couldn't imagine walking away from him without tears in her eyes.

Holly brushed the thoughts aside, determined not to dwell on the future. She glanced around the room. Jed had gone to bed an hour before, and with nothing else to do in the house, Holly decided to return to the tack house—after she made a quick stop in the barn. She tucked a few cookies in a cheerful linen Christmas napkin, then poured some spiced cider into Alex's thermos, before heading out.

She expected to find him hard at work or deeply involved in some project. But when she slipped through the door of the north barn, she found Alex halfway down the main aisle, his arms braced across the top rung of a stall door, his attention focused on the horse inside.

She slowly approached. "Alex, is everything all right? I thought you were coming back to the house." In truth, she'd looked forward to their time alone together all day, although she couldn't admit that aloud. Holly still wasn't sure what they were doing since neither one had broached the subject of their relationship. But without a few moments alone with him, Holly knew she'd pass a restless night, wondering if she'd done something wrong.

At the sound of her voice, Alex glanced her way, then turned back to the stall. "I don't know. She's acting restless."

Holly followed his gaze. It was Jade, the sweet-tempered mare she'd come to trust. The one she'd been sneaking sugar cubes to the past three days. "Is that bad?"

"It could mean she's going to foal early."

Holly groaned inwardly. "Or could it mean she's had too much sugar?" He frowned at her. "I'm sorry. I know I should have asked, but I've been giving her sugar every time I come down to the barn. She's the only horse who's been nice to me and I figured since we were becoming friends, I would—"

Alex pressed a finger to Holly's lips. "A few sugar cubes a day won't hurt her."

"How about six?" Holly asked, wincing.

He shook his head, then turned away. "I don't think that's the problem."

Holly sighed in relief. Good Lord, the last thing she wanted to do was kill one of Alex's horses. "Then what is?"

"She's due to foal in mid-January but last year she foaled in late November and lost the foal." He shook his head. "She's got a great pedigree. If she'd go full-term, the foal could grow to be a great horse."

"Isn't there something you can do?" Holly asked. "Couldn't you call the vet? Give her some drugs? Get her off her feet?"

"With horses, it's sometimes best to let nature take its course. Just watch and wait."

Holly sighed. He seemed so distant, so preoccupied. He'd always been attentive to her, but then they'd only been romantically involved for a few days. There were so many things she didn't know about him. Did he need her here for support or would he rather be alone? Holly wasn't sure what she was expected to do.

"I—I'll leave you to it then," she finally said. "Eric went to bed. There's some pecan pie on the stove if you're hungry and I brought you some cookies and cider." She set the thermos and the cookies on a nearby barrel. "I'm going to bed."

"Thanks," he murmured distractedly.

"All right, then. Good night."

She turned to leave, but at the last moment he caught her around the waist and pulled her close. "I'm sorry," he said, nuzzling his face in her hair. "Stay. I don't want you to leave just yet."

"But you're busy. I don't want to—"

"Looking at you always takes my mind off my problems." He turned her to face him and wrapped his arms around her waist, pressing his hips to hers.

"So, would you like to roll around in the hay?" he teased.

"Why don't we start with a kiss in the barn," she murmured, "and see where that leads."

He tipped her chin up and grazed her lips with his. Holly's knees grew weak and she wondered whether she would ever refuse him anything. With every day that passed, she needed him more—and not just in the physical sense. In the course of a single day, she'd think of so many things she wanted to tell him, little thoughts that came to her mind, bits of information she knew he'd enjoy.

A few days ago, after he'd first kissed her on their sleigh ride, she'd convinced herself that she could still walk away, that on the evening of Christmas Day, she'd pack her bags and take the train home with no regrets. All she needed to do was maintain her distance, protect her heart.

But now, she knew that was impossible. And that

knowledge wouldn't change the reality of their situation. After she left, they'd never see each other again.

Holly wrapped her arms around his neck and kissed him hard, trying to commit the kiss to memory, to burn the wonderful sensations into her brain. Someday, she'd want to remember, wouldn't she? Or would she pray to banish the memory from her mind? It really didn't matter because nothing would make her forget Alex Marrin—not time, not distance and never another man.

He responded to her passion immediately, his hands skimming over her body as his tongue plundered her mouth. Frantic with need, he scooped her up into his arms and carried her to the end of the aisle, to a huge pile of straw.

"It doesn't look very comfortable," she said.

"It's scratchy and dusty and it will get in your hair," he said.

"But every girl has to have at least one roll in the hay with a man, doesn't she?"

With a playful growl, he tossed her into the straw and she pulled him down on top of her. Dust clouded up around them and Holly sat up, sneezed once, then twice. "It always seems so romantic in the movies."

"It can be very romantic," Alex said, nibbling on her neck. "Let me show you." His hands slid beneath her jacket and he pushed it off her shoulders and tossed it aside. His fingers found the hem of her sweater, bunching it in his fist then tugging it over her head. In short order, he yanked his own flannel shirt over his head, adding it to the growing pile of clothing beside him.

Holly closed her eyes and reveled in his touch, the deft workings of his fingers as he unbuttoned her shirt. They'd never gone this far before, never ventured into such intimate territory. His lips trailed over her collarbone, then drifted lower still.

Holly's mind raced. Was this what she really wanted? Would she be able to live with herself in the morning? And why hadn't she made these decisions earlier, before she became entangled in the heat of the moment? Her breath caught in her throat as he placed a kiss on the warm swell of her breast. And then, all the questions didn't matter. He captured her nipple, his lips damp through the sheer fabric of her bra.

She arched beneath him, moaning softly with his brazen caress, then skimmed her hands over his shoulders, his chest, his belly, conscious of every muscle, every inch of warm, hard flesh. Vague dreams that had disturbed her sleep now became reality, an intense, stirring reality that was hard to deny. She needed Alex, his touch, his taste. And his heart.

"I guess this *can* be romantic," she murmured in his ear.

Alex drew back and looked down into her eyes. "This is where I kissed my first girl."

"On this very hay?" she asked skeptically.

"No, that hay became compost a long time ago. But in this barn. In one of those stalls near the end. Her name was..." He frowned. "I can't remember her name."

"And will you remember my name?" Holly asked, reaching up to stroke his cheek.

The smile slowly faded from his face and she felt him stiffen. He opened his mouth to say something, then snapped it shut.

"Did I say something wrong?" she asked, trying to read his emotions in his eyes.

Alex shook his head and rolled off her. As an afterthought, he plucked at the front of her blouse, carefully covering exposed skin. Then he sat up, leaving her a view of the tensed muscles in his neck and back. "About that..." he said.

"What?"

"You know. When you leave. We haven't talked about it. In truth, I think we've been avoiding it."

Holly reached out to touch him and he jumped slightly. "I don't need any promises," she said. "Promises you can't keep."

"I'm just not very good at happily ever after," he said. "I don't know how to make it happen. And if we had...a future, I know that sooner or later, I'd mess up and you'd leave." He furrowed his fingers through his hair. "Maybe this was a mistake. We shouldn't form any attachments. It will only make things more difficult."

Holly quickly buttoned her blouse and reached behind him to grab her sweater. Suddenly a simple roll in the hay had turned complicated. "I—I really should go to bed. I'll see you in the morning."

She scrambled up from the pile of straw, frantically brushing the remnants from her clothes as if that might brush away the embarrassment. Why couldn't she have left well enough alone? She knew better than to bring up the future.

When she finally reached her room in the tack house, she locked herself in her bedroom and prayed that he wouldn't follow her. Right now, she needed to put Alex Marrin and all the feelings he stirred inside of her firmly aside. She had a week to go until Christmas, a week to repair the mistakes she'd made.

But try as she might, Holly couldn't regret the question she'd asked. Would he remember her after she was gone? Or would she fade into the past, a brief interlude during a magical holiday season, a fantasy that, with time, became less real?

"I'll just focus on the job," she murmured. Holly pressed her palms to her eyes and flopped back on the bed. But how could she possibly do that with Alex so near? In her heart, she knew they belonged together. But would she ever be able to banish his memories of the woman who'd hurt him so badly?

She sighed deeply. Holly knew she could try. But she wasn't sure yet whether she had the courage to accept what might become of her heart if she failed.

ALEX STOOD IN THE SHADOWS of the hallway, the last light of day throwing the house into a cozy glow. He'd come in from the barn to find the kitchen empty, no cookies baking, no pudding steaming. Then the sound of a piano playing "Jingle Bells" drifted through the house and he had decided to follow it.

He found Eric and Holly in the living room, sitting at the piano that hadn't been played since he'd bought it. Renee had decided she'd get more roles if she knew how to sing and dance, so he'd bought the piano the very same Christmas she'd walked out.

"All right," Holly said. "Now, you play the melody and I'll play the harmony." She counted off the time and they started, then stopped, then started again. Over and over again, she and Eric tried to make it through the song, but at the first mistake, they'd dissolve into peals of laughter.

She never lost her patience with Eric's fumbling attempts, teasing him and tickling him when he'd almost made it through without a mistake and encouraging him when he'd get frustrated. She'd make a wonderful mother, Alex mused. Not just to any man's child, but to *his* child—and the children they could have together.

When they'd finally made it through "Jingle Bells," Holly clapped and cheered for Eric and he stood and took a bow. Then she played a pretty version of "White Christmas," surprising Alex with her skill at the piano. Had she taken lessons as a child? He shook his head. He knew so little about her, about her childhood, about the men in her past, her dreams and goals.

He did know a few important things, though. Holly Bennett was kind and thoughtful, vulnerable yet strong, a woman with an incredible capacity for passion and yet a comforting streak of practicality. He'd grown so accustomed to her little quirks, her need for perfection, that they'd become endearing. All these qualities made up the woman he'd fallen in love with.

"Should we try another?" Holly asked.

"I want you to stay here forever," Eric cried. "You could teach me all kinds of songs."

"That would be nice," Holly said with an indulgent smile. "You'd be a very good pianist in no time at all."

"Will you stay?"

Holly hesitated. "Eric, I have to go back to New York. My job is there. And—and the man I'm going to marry is there."

Eric chewed on his bottom lip. "But couldn't you marry my dad?"

"I don't think your dad is ready to get married again. But someday, I'm sure he will. He'll find the perfect woman and she'll love you and take care of you and you'll be a happy family."

"But you're the perfect woman. You're an angel."

Alex stepped out of the shadows and moved into the room. Eric noticed him first and jumped up from the piano bench. "Dad, Holly taught me to play 'Jingle Bells'! Listen."

He counted off the rhythm and they played the duet flawlessly, Holly embellishing her part until the song sounded like a concerto. When they finished, Alex smiled and clapped and his son beamed.

"We can play it again," Eric said.

Alex chuckled. No doubt he'd be hearing it several times every day until Christmas and long after. "Why don't you wait until your grandfather comes in from the barn," he suggested. "I'm sure he'd like to hear it. In fact, why don't you go down and get him. It's nearly dinnertime. And I need to talk to Holly alone for a minute."

Eric nodded, then ran out of the room. A few moments later, they heard the back door slam and Alex leaned up against the doorjamb, his arms crossed over his chest. "I don't think you should do that," he murmured.

Holly frowned. "I don't understand. You don't want him to play the piano?" She sighed. "I know it's not very macho, but boys take piano lessons, too. In fact, they've found that musical knowledge helps a child in math and—"

"That's not it," Alex said. "I don't think you should let Eric grow so attached to you. He'll only be hurt when you have to leave."

"I haven't done that!" Holly cried. "Just the opposite. But I can't control his feelings. He feels what he wants to feel."

He wasn't the only one, Alex mused. "Well, then find a way to unattach him."

Holly shook her head. "No."

"No?"

"I won't do that. I won't keep him from caring about

me. And you can't stop me from loving him. The only way you can is if you tell me to leave. Do you want me to leave?''

"I didn't ask you to come here. We were fine on our own until you showed up."

"Is this about last night?" Holly asked.

"No," he said.

"I thought we understood each other. I came here to do a job and when that's finished, I have to go back to New York. Eric is going to have to learn that people will come into his life, but there's no reason to feel a loss when they leave."

"You weren't here when his mother left. You don't know what he went through."

"I'm not his mother," she said.

"But you could be," Alex countered angrily, "and he knows that."

"Then you have to talk to him. You have to explain."

"You're the one he wants. You're the one I—" He drew a sharp breath. "He won't understand. You're his angel. He thinks you belong to him. To both of us."

"Don't be silly. He knows I have to go back. I told him that."

"He does? Then why was he helping me pick out an engagement ring for you?"

Holly gasped. "What?"

"Last night. We went to Dalton's and he was looking over engagement rings. He got quite an education on cut and clarity."

"I have never asked for an engagement ring!" Holly cried. "And I certainly wouldn't marry you if you offered me one."

"And I don't want to marry you, either!" Alex replied.

"Well, I wouldn't marry you if you paid me a million dollars."

"And if I had a million dollars, I certainly wouldn't pay you to marry me!"

"Why are we screaming at each other?" Holly cried.

"I don't know." He turned away from her, unable to look at her angry eyes and her beautiful face any longer. He wanted to yank her into his arms and kiss her senseless, to forget the indecision and anxiety that had suddenly invaded their relationship. Why did this have to be so difficult?

"Do you want me to leave?" Holly asked softly.

"No," he said. "That's exactly the point. I don't want you to leave but I don't see how you can stay without hurting Eric." His statement seemed to take her by complete surprise but Alex didn't regret speaking the truth. Couldn't she see how he felt? Wasn't it obvious? Or had he hidden his feelings for such a long time he'd built an invisible wall around his emotions? "Just be careful, all right?"

"All right," she said, her voice cool. "After all, you're the boss." She stood up and started for the kitchen. "Now, if you don't have anything else to discuss, I've got fruitcake to make."

He grabbed her arm as she passed. "I don't like to argue with you," he murmured.

"Then don't," she snapped. "We only have a week until I have to leave. It's silly to spend it shouting at each other."

"And silly to spend it making fruitcake," Alex countered.

"Well, I can't have Christmas without fruitcake. It's perfect for Christmas morning. Toasted. With a cup of good coffee." She walked out of the room toward the kitchen. It was only then that Alex realized they'd solved nothing. They'd begun with a problem and finished with fruitcake and they were both still angry!

He followed her to the kitchen and watched as she pulled ingredients from a grocery bag and tossed them on the counter. She seemed determined to ignore him, refusing to say another word. When she opened a container of nuts, they sprayed all over the counter, but she didn't flinch. Instead she gathered them up and began to neatly chop them into little bits.

"You know, many people have the wrong impression about fruitcake. They think fruitcake is a brick of oversweet candied fruit that would be better used as a doorstop than a Christmas treat. Well, let me tell you. *Real* fruitcake has nothing to do with that stuff that's filled with preservatives and pressed by machines into molecular density so high you could use it for ballast on the Titanic. My fruitcake is light and airy and it tastes— perfect!"

"Do we really have to talk about fruitcake?" Alex asked. "I get the feeling you still have a few things to say to me."

"What would you like to talk about? Pfefferneuse? Springerle? Lebkuchen? Baked goods seem to be the only safe subject for us."

"That's not true," Alex said.

"But it should be, because that's what I'm here for. To bake cookies and trim the tree. To spend money on Christmas tea towels for the guest bathroom and cinnamon-scented candles for the kitchen. This is what my life has become and the first time that I step outside it and share my feelings with a real family, I get my fingers slapped. So I'll just cream my butter and sift my flour and we'll all be much happier." She wiped her hands on a kitchen towel. "Now, if you'll excuse me, I have a fruitcake to bake."

Alex stood in the kitchen for a long moment, desperate to repair the damage he'd done. He'd never seen Holly quite so hurt. It wasn't that he didn't want her to care about Eric, but he had to protect his son. In the end, he decided to make a quiet retreat. And until he knew precisely what to say to make her feel better, he wasn't going to attempt an apology.

For Alex sensed that he and Holly were teetering on the threshold of something neither one of them were ready for. And he wasn't sure he wanted to be the one to take the first step.

7

THEY'D GONE NEARLY twenty-four hours without speaking, Holly stubbornly refusing to give in and Alex avoiding her at all costs. The tension between them was so thick, she could cut it with a knife, even one of Alex's famously dull kitchen knives! She'd considered an apology, but then decided she'd done nothing wrong. He was angry at her because she was being kind to his son. What did he expect her to do? Though "nice" wasn't part of her contract, she considered it an important quality for a Christmas angel.

Besides, how could she keep from falling in love with Eric Marrin? As for Eric's father, she'd come to regret her earlier good opinion of him. His moods could turn on a dime, from unrestrained desire to cool indifference. She should never have kissed him that day in the sleigh! She should have kept things simple between them.

A thump sounded above her head and Holly jumped. She usually wrote unusual noises off to Eric, but he'd gone outside long ago. She looked up, but nothing was amiss with the ceiling. A series of bumps followed, like footsteps on the roof. Curious, Holly wandered through the house and stepped out onto the front porch. She found a ladder leaning up against the porch roof.

By the time she found a vantage point on the snow-covered front walk, she knew what was up. Alex stood on the porch roof, hefting a huge plastic reindeer up a shorter ladder that lead to the ridgepole of the house. He slipped once and Holly held her breath, pressing her palm to her fluttering heart.

"Be careful," she cried.

He glanced over his shoulder, surprised to see her standing below. "I don't need your advice. I think I can line eight tiny reindeer up without supervision."

"Actually there should be nine. Dasher and Dancer and Prancer and Vixen. Comet and Cupid and Donder and Blitzen. There is some controversy about Donder. Some people call him Donner, but I prefer the traditional Donder. And then there's Rudolph. That's nine." She glanced at the remaining reindeer laying in the snow on their sides. "Nine tacky reindeer," she murmured.

"I'm not putting them up for you, I'm doing it for Eric. So he'll see I can decorate as well as you."

Holly glanced around. "Where is Eric?"

"He went to get an extension cord from the barn."

"That reindeer is too low in the front," she said.

"It's fine," he shouted.

"He looks like he's in a rut," Holly shouted back.

He muttered beneath his breath, just softly enough so Holly couldn't make out the words. No doubt they disparaged her keen sense of perfection. But he did adjust the reindeer so it stood straight. After he fastened the plastic reindeer to the roof, he crawled back down for the next one.

But when he picked it up Holly noticed that it had a red nose. "That's Rudolph," she said. "He's supposed to be first."

"Well, he's going to be second," Alex said.

"Eric will notice. His nose lights up all red like a big old beacon. Everyone will notice Rudolph isn't in the front."

Alex tucked Rudolph under his arm. "Are you here to make my job more miserable, or did you have something to say to me?"

"Actually, I do have something to discuss. I haven't seen any Christmas presents for Eric around the house. Either they're very well hidden or you haven't gotten around to shopping yet." She withdrew a folded sheet of paper from her jeans pocket and held it out to him. "I've made a list of things Eric has mentioned along with a few suggestions for Jed. If you'd like me to shop for you, I can as part of my duties. Of course, there will have to be gifts for Eric from Santa and from you and Jed. And they all have to be wrapped in different paper to maintain the illusion. I've purchased some nice French gift wrap and velvet ribbons and I—"

"I'm sure I can handle it," he said, snatching the list from her fingers. With that, he turned back to the ladder and began to climb up to the porch roof. When he finally settled himself on the peak of the roof, he wrestled Rudolph into the second spot. But the reindeer apparently didn't agree with the choice, because it promptly tipped over on its side and skidded down the roof. When it hit the porch roof it became airborne for a moment before crashing down along the slope and falling off the gutter edge.

Holly had never seen a reindeer truly fly until this moment and she couldn't help but giggle. She stepped back and the reindeer landed a few feet away, headfirst in a snowbank. "Rudolph doesn't take kindly to running behind another reindeer," she shouted.

"Are you personal friends with plastic reindeer?"

She stepped over to the fallen decoration and picked it up. The red nose was cracked and an antler had broken off, but he still seemed to be electrically sound. Holly patted the plastic animal on the head, then sat down on the front steps, Rudolph beside her. As expected, Alex joined her a few moments later.

"So, when do you plan to shop?" Holly asked. "Some of the toys on the list might be sold out if you don't go soon."

Alex hooked his thumbs in the back pockets of his jeans and stared down at her. "I think I can handle Christmas shopping for my son. I know what he likes."

"I was just trying to help," she said. "That's what I'm here for."

"And how much longer will you be here?" Alex asked. "I know you're supposed to stay until Christmas Day, but I'm sure you're anxious to get back. Your fiancé must want you home for the holidays, doesn't he?"

Holly frowned. "My fiancé?"

"Yeah, the guy you're supposed to marry?" He paused. "I heard you mention him again when you were talking to Eric."

"You were listening?"

"He's my son. I have to protect him. I've been thinking if you stay for the holidays, it might send the wrong message. And it might be harder for him when you leave."

"I would never deliberately hurt him," Holly murmured.

"Every day you're here he becomes more attached. You know that."

Holly's anger rose anew. Why was she being punished for feelings she had no control over? "Then I'll leave," she said. "I'll finish my work this week. I can prepare your Christmas dinner early and you can simply reheat it. I'll be out of here by Friday or Saturday afternoon at the latest."

To her surprise, he didn't try to convince her to stay. Instead he nodded curtly, then made to go back to work on the rooftop. But before he climbed the ladder, he turned back to her. "Do you love him?" Alex asked.

"Eric? Of course, I love him. Who wouldn't? He's a wonderful boy and you should be very proud."

His stony expression cracked for a moment. "No," he murmured. "I meant your fiancé."

Holly shrugged as she considered her answer. She knew the truth, but she found in the lie a way to protect her heart, to exact a little revenge for his boorish behavior. "I suppose I do." She smiled smugly. "He asked me to marry him and he's the only offer I've had."

He kicked a clod of snow with the toe of his boot, avoiding her eyes. "Well, then I guess you should marry him."

"Yes, I guess I should," she murmured. Holly slowly stood, then forced a smile. He'd made his feelings perfectly clear. There was no future here for her. The wonderful days they'd spent falling in love were in the past. Her time at Stony Creek Farm was as she always knew it to be—a job and nothing more. "Well, I suppose I'd better finish the rest of the decorating in the next couple of days. I've got shopping and cooking to do. Do you have any requests for dinner on Christmas Eve and Christmas Day?"

He shook his head. "Whatever you suggest will be fine."

His voice was cool, indifferent, and she wondered how he could simply forget what they'd shared. She shoved the reindeer at him then hurried inside the house.

When she reached the solitude of the kitchen, she braced her hands on the edge of the counter and drew a calming breath. "Just do the job," she said. "Just do the job and everything will be all right."

With a silent oath, she yanked open cabinet doors and began to pull out ingredients. She'd make the best Christmas meals she'd ever made—Beef Wellington for Christmas Eve, and a plump roast turkey for Christmas Day, with all the trimmings, so tasty that he'd moan with pleasure and regret ever sending her away.

She grabbed a bag of cornmeal and tore it open. First she'd make corn bread for the turkey stuffing. And then she'd prepare the brioche pastry for the Beef Wellington. And after that, she'd put the final touches on her decorations, making the house shine like something out of the December issue of *House Beautiful*.

"I'll make him sorry he sent me packing," Holly muttered. "One taste of my sausage and cornmeal dressing and he'll never forget me."

"BUT YOU HAVE TO COME!" Eric cried. "It's my holiday pageant. I'm going to play the bells along with "Santa Claus is Comin' to Town." It's the most important part. Miss Green said so. And—and Eleanor Winchell is playing Mrs. Santa Claus and she looks just like a big red tomato with legs in her costume."

Alex stood behind his son, his hands on Eric's shoulders. He'd tried to convince him that Holly had too much work to do, but Eric could not be swayed. "Holly's been working really hard, Scout. Maybe she'd like a little time to herself."

"I do have a lot of work to do," Holly murmured, though Alex couldn't imagine what was left to be done. The house looked like a page out of some glossy magazine, every detail perfect. She'd been cooking up a storm in the kitchen, and though he'd generally been absent from the house, he could smell the results of her efforts every evening when he came in from the stables.

She glanced across the room at him and her gaze lingered for a long moment. He'd changed from his usual dress of jeans and flannel work shirt into a wool jacket and finely pressed khakis. He'd even taken care with his hair, using a comb instead of his fingers, and had exchanged his comfortable work boots for fashionable loafers. Though he might not be as sophisticated as her "fiancé", some women found him attractive.

Alex met her gaze, trying to read her expression. At first he'd thought nothing of pushing her away. After all, she didn't really care. But lately, whenever they glanced at each other, he saw a tiny flicker of hurt in her expression, as if she were trying to maintain her composure but fighting her emotions.

"We really would like you to come," Alex said. Though the invitation was genuine, his voice sounded forced.

They'd shared only polite conversation over the past four days, a word here, a comment there. In truth, they behaved precisely as he might have expected when she arrived, maintaining a cordial business relationship and a careful distance. She had stopped eating dinners at the house, fixing her own in the little kitchenette in her room.

Every evening, she and Eric would tackle another craft project for the holidays and he'd excuse himself to go to the barn, only returning to the house after he saw the lights in the tack house go on. And when Eric had asked her to take him shopping for Christmas presents, she'd passed the job off to his grandfather.

Alex should have been happy. After all, he was the one who suggested she put some distance between herself and Eric. But in truth, the atmosphere around the house was anything but festive. A depressing gloom now seemed to hang over them, Holly on one side of a dark cloud of confusion and he and Eric on the other. And all of them anticipating the day she'd leave with varying emotions.

Holly placed her hand on the top of Eric's head and looked down at him. "I really would like to come, but I just can't take the time away. I've got pies to bake and peanut brittle to make. You want a perfect Christmas, don't you?"

Alex cleared his throat. "Eric, go get your jacket. And put your boots on over your good shoes. We have to leave in a few minutes."

When he left the room, Alex turned back to Holly. "I do want you to come. It would make Eric so happy."

"Are you asking me to come along for Eric? Or because you want me to?"

"Both," he said. "I'd like you to be there."

Holly considered the invitation for a long moment, then nodded. "All right. I'll go. Should I change?"

"You look nice the way you are," he said. She was dressed in a pretty celery-green sweater set and a black corduroy skirt that showed off her long legs. Her pale hair was pulled back in a pretty patterned scarf and she wore just enough makeup to highlight her incredible beauty. In his eyes, she was perfect.

He held out his hand. "Come on. We don't want to be late for Eric's big debut."

Holly grabbed her jacket from the back of a kitchen stool and began to tug it on. But Alex took it from her hands and held it out behind her. "I appreciate this."

She didn't say another word, all the way to school, sitting on the far side of the truck, when he helped her back out of her coat in the lobby, even when he slipped her hand into the crook of his arm as they walked toward the gymnasium. She simply smiled woodenly and stared straight ahead. So much was left unsaid between them, neither one of them wanting to venture into territory better left undisturbed.

How many times had he fought the urge to pull her into his arms, to say all the things he'd been thinking about the two of them, to put things back the way they were, so full of warmth and excitement? But when he opened his mouth, doubts rushed up to drown his resolve. He didn't want to make another mistake. Divorcing Renee had been bad enough, but to love then lose Holly would tear his heart in two. And it might destroy what was left of Eric's trust as well.

As they walked into the dimly lit gym, Alex watched every head turn to stare at them. The status of his social life had been a matter of some curiosity around town. Behind the suave and wealthy Thomas Dalton, president of Dalton's Department Store, Alex Marrin was considered quite the catch for Schuyler Falls' single women. And now, without warning, he suddenly appeared with a beautiful woman on his arm, and to a school function at that!

"Why are they staring?" Holly murmured.

Alex gave her hand a squeeze. "They're staring at you."

"Why?"

"This is the first time I've been out in public with a woman since Eric's mother walked out."

"You haven't had a date in two years?" she asked. "Why not?"

"I guess I hadn't really found anyone I wanted to date—until you."

"This is not a date," she snapped.

Alex grinned ruefully. "Can we pretend it is? It'll put all the matchmaking mothers off my scent for a while. You wouldn't have to kiss me. Just look at me adoringly every now and then and act like every word I say is the most fascinating thing you ever heard."

This brought a tiny giggle and Alex felt the tension between them crumble a bit. "And what happens when you go out in public the next time?" she asked.

He shrugged. "Rent a date? 1-800-HOT-BABE? Or maybe I just won't go out again for a year or two."

Alex wove his fingers through hers as they made their way to their seats, finding a spot in the middle of a row not far from the front. When they settled, he handed her a program. "I know you probably haven't ever been to a school pageant, but I think I should give you a few tips."

"What kind of tips?"

"No matter how bad it is, don't laugh. You can smile, but you can't laugh. I find that biting the inside of my bottom lip can be helpful. Believe me, it's going to be really bad. Children this age are incapable of standing in front of a crowd of people and acting normal. And Miss Green's second-grade class won't be driving the Vienna Boys Choir out of business anytime soon. Their singing closely resembles shouting."

"I'm sure I'll enjoy every minute," Holly said.

When the gymnasium was nearly full, the lights dimmed even further and the murmur from the crowd quieted. The pageant began with the first-grade students. Almost on cue, as the music teacher raised her arms to conduct, video cameras began to whir and flashes popped. The children barely paid attention to their song, preferring instead to search the audience for their parents, bother the student standing next to them, or find an original way to play with their clothes. Thankfully the first-graders only did one song before scurrying off the stage.

Eric's class came on next. Holly reached out and took Alex's hand, giving it an encouraging squeeze. He glanced at her and found her gnawing at her bottom lip. "Are you all right?"

"I'm really nervous for him," she said. "He's been talking about this solo all week and I think he's really worried he'll mess up."

"Eric doesn't get nervous," Alex said.

"Yes, he does. He doesn't say anything, but I know how much he wants to do well."

Alex sat back in his chair, pondering Holly's keen insight into his son as he stared down at her delicate fingers. He'd always thought of Eric as such a confident kid, jumping into every situation with careless abandon, then shrugging off any failures as if they didn't matter in the least. He'd never considered that Eric might be hiding his fears and insecurities, living up to an ideal of masculinity that he saw in his father. A mother would notice these things—if Eric had a mother to raise him.

He stole another glance at Holly. She'd make a wonderful mother. Even now, she sat on the edge of her seat, awaiting Eric's big moment in the spotlight, her smile tight, her shoulders tense. She loved his son and admitted that freely. With a woman like Holly, maybe Eric might experience the softer side of life, the side filled with hugs when he felt scared and kisses when he cried.

"There he is," Holly murmured, pointing to the far end of the group. She waved as Eric scanned the crowd and when he saw them both, he beamed with a wide grin. "We should have brought a camera. He looks so sweet, doesn't he?"

Eric and the rest of the little orchestra wore jaunty

Santa hats and stood at a table, their bells spread in front of them. As the song began, they raised their mallets and the harmonies chimed out along with the vocals. Eric's face was set in fierce concentration as he played.

Suddenly he lost his place and looked up at the teacher hopelessly, chewing on the rubber mallet nervously. Alex heard Holly draw a sharp breath and she nearly broke his fingers clenching his hand. But then the music teacher nodded at Eric and he joined back in. Holly relaxed, releasing her tightly held breath. And when it was all over, she jumped to her feet and clapped.

"Bravo!" she cried, beaming at Eric and waving.

Alex glanced around to find the rest of the parents staring at her and he grabbed Holly by the arm and tugged her back down in her chair. "This isn't Lincoln Center," he whispered over the polite applause. "There won't be any encores."

Her smile was exuberant and her eyes were bright with pride. "Didn't he do well? I think he lost his place for a moment, but then he joined right back in. He had such composure. I think he had the most notes to play, don't you?"

Alex couldn't resist. He slipped his arm around her shoulders and pulled her closer. "I haven't seen you this excited since you found that moldy thing for the pudding."

A pretty blush stained her cheeks and she averted her gaze. "I'm sorry, I shouldn't have—"

"No," Alex interrupted. "It's nice that you care so much."

The rest of the program passed slowly, each grade level playing two songs for the audience before filing off the choir risers. The evening ended with the entire school and audience joining in a rousing chorus of "We Wish

You A Merry Christmas,'' complete with a figgy pudding verse.

They met Eric in the hallway outside his classroom. He bounded up to them, anxious to gather compliments for his performance. Alex gave him a gruff hug and ruffled his hair. "You were great," he said.

Then Holly bent down and took Eric's hands. "It was so wonderful," she said. "You played so well and I could hear your bell all the way to where we were sitting. You were definitely the best."

"I messed up a little," he admitted.

"I hardly noticed. And I don't think anyone in the audience could tell. I think they were all so caught up in the beautiful music and the singing. It was very professional."

"Really?" Eric asked. "Like something you would see in New York?"

"Absolutely," Holly replied. "Better than what I've seen in New York."

She took his hand and they started toward the front door of the school. Alex stood in the hallway watching the two of them together, his son and the woman he was fast falling in love with. He raked his hands through his hair, then slowly shook his head.

"Well, Marrin. If you really love her, then I guess you're going to have to find some way to convince her to stay." He took a deep breath, then started after them. "Either that, or risk the wrath of an angry seven-year-old."

HOLLY LAY ON HER BED in the tack house, staring up at the ceiling, her hands folded over her chest. To say she was confused was an understatement. Alex Marrin had become the master of mixed signals. First, he wanted her to stay. Then he wanted her to go. And now, she wasn't sure what he wanted.

After they'd returned home from Eric's pageant, she'd excused herself to go back to the tack house. But he'd grabbed her hand and asked if she'd like to join him and Eric for hot cocoa and cookies before the night ended. They'd popped in *How The Grinch Stole Christmas* and sat around a fire in the family room, reliving the highlights of the evening and laughing along to Dr. Seuss.

And when Eric finally wandered off to bed, Alex had joined her on the sofa. But instead of letting the evening spin out in front of them, she panicked and jumped up, mumbling some feeble excuse about calling Meg before it was too late. Then she made a hasty exit and closed herself safely in her room where she found some solitude to think.

What had she been so afraid of? That Alex might just kiss her and start everything all over again between them? In her present state of mind, she could just about walk away without shattering into a million pieces. She still had a chance of going back to her life in New York and putting her time at Stony Creek Farm in the past.

But how would he feel? Was she giving up on them too soon? Her contemplation of Alex Marrin's sudden turnabout was interrupted by a knock on her bedroom door. She glanced over at the clock at her bedside. It was past eleven. There was only one person who would come knocking at such a late hour and Holly wasn't sure she wanted to answer.

He knocked again and Holly covered her eyes, willing him to go back to the house and make her life simple again. But when he knocked for the third time, she sighed and rolled off the bed. She pulled the door open to find

Alex standing on the other side, bags and boxes piled so high in his arms that she could barely see him.

"I saw your light on," he said from the other side of a huge Lego set. "I—I thought I'd bring these down."

Holly grabbed the top of the stack, uncovering his head and shoulders. Their gazes met and she felt a shiver skitter down her spine. Why was he doing this to her? Weren't things already settled between them?

"You said you'd wrap them and I wanted to get them done before Eric finds them and knows what I'm getting him. I'm going to hide them in the loft above the other bedroom. I don't think he'll find them there." He set the rest of the presents on the bed, then stepped back, rubbing his hands together. "I went a little nuts."

Holly stared at the pile of toys and sighed. "I guess I could work on these tomorrow morning before I leave."

"You're leaving tomorrow?" Alex asked. Then he nodded, drawing a sharp breath. "That's right. Tomorrow."

"I thought I would. Saturday is Christmas Eve and the train will be packed with travellers. I wanted to get an early start."

Alex nodded silently. "I guess that would be best."

"Yes," she said.

The conversation between them faded and they stood watching each other uneasily. Holly waited for him to leave, to make some silly excuse and walk away. But in the end, he muttered a soft curse, crossed the space between them in two long steps and pulled her into his arms.

A tiny cry slipped from her lips as he brought his mouth down on hers, more a surprise than a protest. She'd tried so hard to commit the taste of him to memory, but nothing prepared her for the sheer intensity of his kiss. His tongue teased hers, first gently, then demanding her unfettered response.

Holly moaned softly as her knees went weak. His hands spanning her waist, Alex slowly pushed her back toward the bed. When the edge hit her knees, he stopped and reached around her, sending toys and boxes and bags flying across the room. Then, he gently pushed her down and lowered himself to lie beside her.

His hand skimmed along the front of her cashmere cardigan then splayed on her belly, softly massaging her waist as he kissed her again. "I'm sorry," he murmured, his breath warm against her mouth. "I've made such a mess of things."

"No," she said, pressing her finger to his lips. "No apologies. This is all that matters. Just this night. I don't need any more than this."

"Holly, I need to tell you—"

She cut off his words with a kiss, furrowing her fingers into his hair at his nape and pulling his mouth down on hers. He grabbed her hips and rolled her over on top of him, settling her against his body, his broad chest and lean, long legs.

Every shred of common sense she still possessed told her to stop before they went too far. But her common sense was silenced by her need—for his taste, his touch, his smell. His fingers wove through her hair, pulling it down around them like a curtain of flax, shutting out the world and the past.

With every breath, Holly sank further into the magic of the moment, the pure sensation of his touch, the warmth of his body. A hunger to possess him surged up inside of her, but she didn't feel the urgency she felt that night in the stable. Tonight, they had all the time in the world.

Slowly his hands explored her body, toying with the buttons of her sweater before moving on. But when his hands skimmed beneath the cashmere to cup her breasts, Holly moaned, arching her back and bracing her hands on either side of his head. She pushed away from him and stood beside the bed. Alex watched her through passion-glazed eyes, his elbows cocked behind him.

A tiny smile curled the corners of Holly's mouth as she reached for the top button of her sweater. She flipped it open and Alex sent her a devilish grin. Another button followed and he growled playfully. When she finally finished, he made a move to join her, but Holly held up her hand, warning him to stay where he was.

She toyed with him, letting the sweater fall off her shoulders and feeling for the first time the power of her femininity. With just a casual smile or a suggestive movement, she could pique his desire, make him feel a need so powerful he ached to touch her. No man had ever wanted her more than Alex did. She could see it in the way his gaze caressed her body, taking in every detail with a lazy appreciation.

When she reached for the clasp at the front of her bra, Alex shook his head. "No," he murmured. Slowly he rose from the bed to stand in front of her, his head bent. "Let me."

His fingers dipped between the soft swells of her breasts and with a careless flick, her bra fell open. She wasn't embarrassed by her nakedness, but emboldened. She reached for his jacket and tugged it off, then set to work on his shirt. Piece by piece, the fabric barriers dropped until he stood before her, bare-chested. He gently drew her into his arms and skin met skin, the heat from his body seeping into hers in a delicious rush.

As if they existed in another world, a world of endless

nights, they slowly peeled the rest of their clothing off of each other. Every movement gave time to tease, to explore, to tantalize until Holly couldn't deny the passion that swelled inside of her. When they were both naked, she took a step back and looked at him, so strong and yet strangely vulnerable. At that moment, Holly knew he was all the man she'd ever want.

They tumbled back onto the bed together, limbs tangling, skin tingling. Soft moans mixed with urgent whispers and Holly's senses whirled with the heady scent of him, the damp of his tongue on her nipple and the harsh sound of his breathing. No words were needed between them and when he retrieved a foil packet from his wallet, Holly took it from him and quickly sheathed him.

They seemed to respond to each other instinctively, as if they'd always been meant to reach this moment in time, this instant when his body became one with hers. And as he entered her, his hips sinking against hers, Holly looked up at him. All the emotion was there in his eyes, the unspoken love, the undeniable need, and every nerve in her body sang.

She didn't need to hear that he loved her, for she knew it in her heart. And if he never uttered the words aloud, never acknowledged his feelings, she still knew that, for a single night, she was the woman of his dreams. Holly reached out and cupped his cheek in her palm. He pressed a kiss there, then closed his eyes.

He moved slowly at first, but then uncontrollable desire took hold of them both. Deep in her core, Holly felt the tension grow with each thrust, a strange compelling need that begged to be satisfied. And when he slipped his hand between their bodies to touch her, she cried out with the intensity of the sensation, falling headlong into her release. Alex followed her, calling out her name again and again as he came inside of her.

And later, after they'd made love once again and he lay beside her, Holly reached out to touch his face. As a young girl, she'd had dreams of meeting a man she could truly and deeply love, with fierce passion and utter stillness. But as she grew older, she'd given up those dreams for a more pragmatic approach to love, never realizing the woman she really was inside. With Alex, she'd become more than she'd ever been, a woman filled with light and life and a love that overcame all her doubts and inhibitions.

"I love you," she murmured, so softly that, if he did hear, he'd think it was only a dream. "And if this is the only night we have between us, I'll still love you." She placed a kiss on her fingertips, then touched his parted lips. Holly watched him for a long time, her eyes growing heavy with sleep. And when she finally drifted off, his head nestled against her shoulder, her sleep was deep and dreamless.

8

THE SUN WAS STILL FAR below the horizon when Alex opened his eyes. He drew a deep breath, taking in the sweet scent of Holly's hair. Sometime during the night, he'd tucked her against his body, her backside nestled in his lap, his arms wrapped around her waist. She fit so perfectly against his body, as if they were meant to begin and end the day together just like this.

When he'd brought the pile of presents to her room, he never thought they'd end up in bed. He just wanted to see her face one more time before he went to sleep, needed to assure himself that she was there. But, somehow, the tension between them dissolved completely and the inevitable came to pass. Hell, it had been so long, he'd wondered whether he still knew how to please a woman.

His thoughts wandered back to the moment when he'd moved inside of her, to the single shattering second when she arched beneath him and found her release. Perfection, he mused. He'd never made love so completely, so intensely. The very act seemed to seal a trust between them that couldn't be broken.

Alex glanced over at the clock on the nightstand: 5:00 a.m. Jed would be up and around soon, ready to get to work in the barn. If he slipped out now, he'd be able to change into his work clothes and make it to the barn without any unanswerable questions from his father. But the bed was warm and Holly's body soft, and he'd be crazy to leave.

What a change. He'd been a fool up until the moment he'd kissed her last night, determined to develop some immunity to her charms, convinced that she'd hurt him like Renee had. But he was older now and much wiser. And he didn't look at Holly through a veil of boyish exuberance and innocence. He saw her as she really was—as a woman he could spend a lifetime loving.

He picked up a strand of her hair and brushed it against his chin, wondering what the morning would bring. Would she regret what had happened or would she realize her future was with him? Alex pressed a kiss against the curve of her shoulder. She stirred slightly, then sighed and fell back into a deep sleep.

He had no right to expect anything from her. What had she said? No promises? He'd vowed never to make promises to a woman again. But the prospect of promising to love and honor—hell, even to obey—didn't seem so unnerving, not when the woman standing with him at the altar was Holly.

He slowly sat up, pulling his arm from beneath her and shaking it to restore circulation. The chill air of the bedroom sent a shiver over his naked chest and he reached over to tug the quilt up over her bare skin, allowing his fingers to linger just a little longer. He fought the temptation to wake her and make love to her again. They'd only fallen asleep a few hours before. He and Holly had a lot to talk about when she woke up and he needed her to be well-rested.

He crawled out of bed and began to search the room for his clothes, tugging them on as he found them. Embers from a fire he'd built for them both, glowed among the ashes, providing just enough light to see. When Alex was finally dressed, he crossed back to the bed and squatted down beside Holly.

He smoothed a strand of hair from her eyes and his gaze skimmed her peaceful features. She'd never been more beautiful to him than at that moment, not because they'd just made love, but because he realized that she was the woman he loved.

"Hey," he murmured. "Wake up, sweetheart."

Her eyes fluttered, then opened, and she smiled at him sleepily. "Why are you leaving? Is everything all right? Is it Eric?"

"No," he said, brushing a kiss along her lips. "I need to get back to the house. Jed will be up soon and then Eric. I'm always there when Eric gets up."

"Mmm," she said, snuggling further under the covers. "Will you come back after he goes to school?"

"I promise," Alex replied. "If you promise you won't move until I get back."

"I promise."

This time he kissed her long and deep, before dragging himself away. "I'll be back," he murmured. Reluctantly, Alex closed the door behind him, then hurried back to the house, the cold air clearing his head with the swiftness of a sledgehammer. The kitchen was dark when he walked through, heading straight for the coffeemaker.

"You're up early."

The sound of Jed's voice startled him. He glanced over his shoulder and watched as his father strolled into the kitchen. Jed was already dressed, but hadn't bothered to shave that morning. He pushed Alex aside and started to make coffee, filling the pot with water and dumping coffee into the filter.

"Or maybe you haven't been to bed yet," Jed said.

He gave Alex the once-over, then chuckled. "Aren't those the same clothes you were wearing last night?"

"What are you? Chief of the fashion police? You've never noticed before when I've worn the same clothes two days in a row."

"Those aren't your work clothes." He stuck his coffee mug under the stream of fresh coffee, filled it half full, then exchanged it with the pot. "And, there was never a beautiful woman staying in the tack house before." Jed took a slow sip of his coffee as he stared shrewdly at Alex over the rim of his mug. When he set the mug down, he sighed. "You want her to stay, don't you?"

Alex ran his hand through his hair. "Yeah, I guess I do." He cursed softly. "But I'm afraid to ask her."

"Why?"

"Because I'm afraid she'll refuse. Or even worse, I'm afraid she'll accept. And then I'll screw it up all over again, the same way I did with Renee."

"Son, you didn't mess up with Renee. You did everything you could to hold that marriage together. How many other men would let their wives live in New York half the days of the year? She was the wrong woman for you. Maybe now, you've found the right one."

"I thought Renee was the right one."

"No, you thought Renee was glamorous and exciting and sophisticated. You were starstruck. And Renee thought you were rich enough to finance her acting career. She was selfish. If she hadn't gotten pregnant two months after the wedding, you probably wouldn't have lasted a year."

"So that only proves I've got rotten judgment when it comes to women. Up until this moment, I actually believed Renee married me because she loved me. Thanks for the insight, Dad."

His sarcasm wasn't lost on Jed. The old man chuckled. "That's what I'm here for."

Alex raked his fingers through his hair again and pressed the heels of his hands against his temples. "How the hell am I supposed to know how I feel? I've known Holly for two weeks, give or take a few days. I don't know anything about her family, I don't know what perfume she likes, what her favorite color is."

"There are a lot of things you *do* know."

"I don't know whether she'd want to live here, on a horse farm in upstate New York. She's a city girl. Her friends are there, her career. What is she going to do on this farm?"

"You know what's in your heart, Alex. That's all you really need to know."

"What about what's in *her* heart?"

"Well, that you won't know until you ask her. But I can tell you this, if you let her leave without telling her how you feel, you'll always wonder." Jed rubbed his chin. "Wait here. I have something that might help you decide."

He hurried off into the dark of the house while Alex poured himself a mug of coffee. If only he had more time with Holly. A month or two. Maybe a little more. Then he could rid himself of the last traces of doubt. Hell, everything seemed so simple, lying in bed with Holly in his arms. But in the growing light of day, it wasn't easy at all. After just two weeks, planning a future with Holly was a big gamble. He'd lost the gamble once and he was loathe to take the risk again.

But if he didn't take the risk, what kind of future was he making for himself? A long life of solitude, a cold bed and an empty heart. Raising a son without a mother.

Never filling the house with all the children he once wanted to have.

Alex smiled. Holly would give him beautiful children. Perhaps a little girl with pretty green eyes and golden hair. And a little brother for Eric. If only Holly would stay, his life might mean something again.

"I've wanted to give this to you for a while," Jed said as he came back into the kitchen. "But I thought it might not be the right time. Here," he said, handing Alex a tiny velvet bag.

Alex loosened the drawstring and tipped the bag upside down over his palm. A ring fell out, a large diamond in an antique platinum setting. "Mother wore this," Alex said. "I remember."

Jed nodded. "And your grandmother. And your great-grandmother. Your wife should wear it, don't you think?"

"Renee was my—"

"I didn't think she deserved it," Jed said. "As it turns out, I was right. But I think that ring would look mighty pretty on Holly's finger."

Alex shook his head. "Marriage. That's a big step. I'm not ready to jump into that mess again. And I'm certainly not going to ask Holly after just two weeks together." He held the ring between his fingers. It would look beautiful on Holly, slipped over her slender finger. Holly loved tradition and old things.

"You're a Marrin. It's not supposed to take time. If she's the one, then you need to ask her."

"I think that family tradition ought to stop with my generation. I have to think of Eric, too." He glanced up at Jed. "What if things don't work out? He was so hurt when Renee left. I don't want him hurt again. Not like that."

Jed rested his hand on Alex's shoulder. "Don't waste too much time chewing on this, son. If you let her leave, you might never get her back."

His father grabbed his mug of coffee and his jacket from the back of a chair and slipped out of the house, leaving Alex to contemplate his choices. But no matter how he looked at his situation, he couldn't come up with a logical plan.

Maybe love wasn't supposed to be logical, Alex mused. Maybe it was supposed to be crazy and irrational, driving a man to distraction. It was all so much easier when he was younger, the choices so clear, the consequences still unknown.

He placed the ring back in the velvet bag, then wandered upstairs to his bedroom. He caught a glimpse of himself in the mirror above his dresser. His eyes were bleary and his hair still tousled by her fingers. But there was something there that hadn't been before—a peace, a calm, as if he'd finally found a center to his life.

Now, if he could only make it last.

"HOLLY! HOLLY, ARE YOU HERE?"

Holly slowly opened her eyes. She rolled over to find the bed empty, the spot where Alex had spent the night no longer occupied. He'd gone sometime before sunrise, leaving her to catch up on all the sleep she'd missed. Holly smiled, then pulled the covers up to her chin. She felt relaxed, completely sated—she took a peek under the covers—and completely naughty. She couldn't remember ever sleeping naked.

"Holly, it's me. Eric." A soft rap sounded at the door. "Can I come in?"

She sat up in bed, knowing that Alex hadn't locked the door behind him. It could only be locked from the inside. "Wait a minute!" she called. "Just let me get dressed." Leaping from the warm bed, Holly searched the room for anything to wear. She tugged on the sweater she'd worn the night before, then yanked on the bottoms of her new flannel pajamas. Christmas presents were still scattered all over the room. With the expertise of a professional soccer player, she kicked them under the bed.

The doorknob turned. "Are you awake? Can I come in?"

She raced back to the bed and grabbed a Widgie Midget miniature toy robot and shoved it under her sweater. Then she casually sat down on the edge of the bed. An instant later, Eric threw the door open and raced inside, a long florist's box in his arms. He stumbled as he neared the bed and the box went flying, falling open on the patchwork quilt. "Holly, look! You got flowers! They just brought them. And they're not even plastic!"

Eric crawled up on the bed and carefully scrutinized the flowers from close range. "I think they're roses."

"Alex," Holly murmured. She wrapped her arms around herself and sighed. What a wonderful way to start the day, she mused. A bleep and blurp sounded from beneath her sweater and she remembered the little robot she had hidden there.

"What was that?" Eric asked.

"Just my tummy," Holly replied. "I guess I'm a little hungry."

Eric frowned in confusion. "My tummy never makes sounds like that, even when I'm starving."

"Good morning."

They both looked up and saw Alex standing in the doorway. He was dressed in his work clothes, his hair windblown and flecked with chaff, his arms spread across the width of the doorjamb. Eric bounced up and down on the bed and pointed to the roses. "Dad, look at what Holly got. Flowers."

For a long moment, their gazes locked and memories of the night before came flooding back, the frantic need, the ache to touch him, and the final surrender. Holly felt her face warm with a blush and she wondered how long it would be before they shared a bed again. Would he come to her tonight? Or would they steal some time together during the daylight hours? "Thank you," she said, sending him a silent smile of gratitude.

Alex shrugged. "You're very welcome. But if you're thanking me for the flowers, I didn't send them."

She blinked, then glanced down at the roses scattered across the bed. "Then who did?" Holly asked. "Who would send me two dozen roses?" She gently tickled Eric's knee. "Did you send me flowers?"

"Maybe there's a card," Alex suggested, stepping into the room, now curious himself.

Eric rummaged through the box and came up with a small envelope. "Here it is. Should I read it?"

"If you can," Holly said.

He pulled the card from the envelope and scrunched his face as he looked at it. "Merry Christmas. Call me. Love—Step—Step—Hand. Who is Step-Hand?"

Holly snatched the card from Eric's fingers, gasping when she re-read the inscription. "Stephan?" she breathed. The robot squeaked from beneath her sweater again, causing a giggle from Eric. "But—I don't understand. Why would he—" She snapped her mouth shut. Could he have changed his mind about marrying that other woman?

"Who's Stephan?" Eric asked.

Alex took another step toward the bed. "Eric, go help

your grandfather in the barn. He's working in Emmy's stall.''

"But Holly is—"

"Eric, do as I say. Now." His voice had suddenly chilled and his expression grew hard. The boy saw the change on his father's face and knew not to argue any further. He sighed dramatically, then clomped out of the room, shooting Alex a perturbed look as he passed.

An uneasy silence began the moment the door clicked shut. Holly flicked the card with her finger and tried to avoid Alex's penetrating gaze. And Alex stood silently near the bed, waiting for some explanation.

In truth, Holly had none. She couldn't imagine why Stephan would send her flowers—especially now. Unless...she swallowed hard. Unless he wanted her back. "This doesn't make any sense," she murmured, forcing a smile.

"I agree. Flowers from a fiancé. What are the odds?"

Holly cursed beneath her breath. "I don't have a fiancé! I mean, I could have had a fiancé, but when he asked, I told him I needed time to think. And—and I just never got back to him with an answer. And then he got engaged to someone else and I just assumed it was over between us."

"So when you told me you were engaged, that was a—"

"A slight exaggeration," Holly admitted. She groaned. "All right, it was a lie. But I had my reasons."

"Well, he's obviously changed his mind."

"No! He couldn't have. He's getting married in the Hamptons in June. I haven't spoken to him in nearly a year. He didn't even know I was here!" Holly cried.

"Do you love him?"

"No!" Holly cried, stunned that he'd ask her such a

question. "Do you think I would have made love to you if I still loved him?"

"I don't know you well enough to know what you'd do," Alex muttered.

"He can't possibly believe I'd still want to marry him. I—I said no!" She winced. "Or at least I should have. Since I didn't give him an answer, wouldn't you think he'd interpret that as a no?"

"I wouldn't," Alex said. He shook his head. "When you told me you were engaged, I didn't really believe you. I just thought you were saying that because you wanted to protect your virtue."

She stared at the card, baffled. "Well, we both know how safe my virtue was with you."

Though Holly hadn't meant to be hurtful, Alex caught the hint of regret in her voice. "Holly, there were two of us in this room last night. Neither of us wanted to stop." He crossed the room to the bed, gathered up the flowers and tossed them on the floor. Then he sat down beside her and took her face between his hands. "Forget him. He's been out of your life for a year. What we have is real and it's happening now." He wove his fingers through hers. "Holly, I want you to stay. Not just for Christmas, but forever."

His words didn't register at first, unable to penetrate her preoccupation with the roses. Something wasn't right here. Stephan was engaged, to a woman with money. He'd never give that up for Holly. And he certainly wasn't the type to send flowers. "I—I should call him," she said.

"No," Alex replied. "You don't have to call him. Holly, listen." He tipped her chin up until she met his gaze. "I need you. Eric needs you. And I want you to stay."

Her eyes went wide and she blinked, finally hearing his haphazard proposal. "You want me to stay? But— but I thought you weren't ready to—"

He reached out and cupped her cheek in his hand, stopping her words. "I know I haven't made my feelings very clear, but I know this much—I'm in love with you, Holly, and I want you to be a part of our lives."

Holly wasn't sure what to say. Though she'd dreamed about a future with Alex and Eric, she never thought it would come to be. In truth, she'd convinced herself it was an impossibility! But this wasn't a real future he offered. In truth, he hadn't made any more promises than he had earlier.

What could she expect? They barely knew each other. A marriage proposal would be foolish at such an early stage, especially considering Alex's track record. But could she give up her life and her career in New York for the mere possibility of a life with Eric and Alex? Could she become a lover to Alex and a mother to Eric without knowing the future? And though she'd come to recognize her potential as a parent, taking on that responsibility full-time was another matter. What if she wasn't a good mother? What if she made mistakes and messed up Eric's life? Alex would never forgive her.

And then there was Alex. Though she'd fallen in love with him, she still barely knew him. What if his feelings faded? What if he realized later he'd made a mistake in asking her to stay? Could her heart take the pain of leaving both Alex and Eric after becoming a part of their family for real?

"Aren't you going to give me an answer?" he asked.

"This isn't a marriage proposal, is it," she said.

Alex's jaw grew tight, his eyes hard. "You know my track record with that."

Holly frowned. "I—I'm not sure. I'll have to think about it. We'll have to talk about it."

Alex cursed. "Like you thought about the other guy's proposal? Ignoring it for a year while you hoped it would go away? I'm not going away so easily. I want an answer now."

Holly drew a deep breath, regret filling her expression. "My answer is I can't give you an answer now. There are just so many things I have to consider."

"Then last night meant nothing to you?"

"Alex, last night was wonderful. I've never felt such...passion. But it's just a beginning. I can't change my whole life based on one wonderful night in bed. Even if it *was* really good. I'm a practical person. If you really knew me, then you'd understand." She picked up a rose from the floor and stared at it, frowning. "And as much as I'd love to accept, I'm obviously not free to do that right now. I have to go back and give Stephan an answer. Until I do that, I can't give *you* an answer."

Alex stood, anger evident in his expression. "I should have known. I should have trusted my instincts," he muttered. He stalked to the door and yanked it open. "Well, when you do come up with an answer, be sure to let me know. I wouldn't want to be kept hanging for a year."

Holly jumped as the door slammed behind him. She stared down at the roses scattered on the floor. How could Stephan do this to her? She'd finally put him in the past and had fallen in love with another man, a man who'd asked her to become a part of his life. And now, she had no choice but to go back to New York and give him an answer she should have given him a year ago. No, she wouldn't marry him! If she were going to marry anyone, it would be Alex Marrin. The only problem was, he hadn't asked.

So why was she determined to return to New York? She didn't have to answer Stephan at all. It had been a year and he'd already found another woman. Her answer should have been obvious. And all she had waiting back in the city was a job she'd grown to hate and a business that barely stayed afloat from year to year.

Holly sighed. Maybe she just needed an excuse, a chance to give herself some time to figure out an answer for Alex. He was the man she really loved, the man she should want to spend her life with. Closing her eyes, she tried to calm the confusion in her mind. She had only dreamed about a future with Alex. And now that her future was close enough to grab, she couldn't reach out and take it, couldn't believe that it might be real.

She flopped back onto the pillows and let images of the previous night drift through her mind. A shiver of desire skittered up her spine as all the feelings they'd shared came rushing back. Intense feelings. Feelings that Holly knew might last a lifetime if she'd only give them a chance. But could she base her whole future on overwhelming passion and desperate love? Or did there have to be more?

HOLLY TOOK A LAST LOOK around the kitchen, a place that had become as familiar as the back of her hand. She'd arranged everything exactly the way she wanted over the past few weeks, utensils in handy spots, staples where she could get at them quickly. This was her kitchen now and she wondered whether it might revert to the mess she'd found it in, like a testosterone jungle swallowing up civilization.

She'd spent her time finishing preparations for the Marrins' Christmas Eve celebration and Christmas dinner, occupying her mind with recipes rather than regrets.

"The Beef Wellington is kind of tricky," she said as Jed listened intently. "I've rolled out the pastry and all you have to do is enclose the filet inside. Work very quickly so that you can get it right into the oven. Otherwise the pastry will get doughy. Then bake thirty to forty minutes. The meat thermometer should read precisely 125 degrees. Watch it carefully."

She handed Jed the two pages of directions for the Beef Wellington. She wasn't about to tell him that the recipe was straight out of Julia Child—*Filet de Boeuf en Croûte*. He already looked intimidated enough. Holly forced a smile. "Don't worry. This is the most difficult thing. The turkey for tomorrow will be a breeze. You just have to stuff it right before you put it into the oven. The stuffing is in the green bowl." She handed him another two pages.

Jed nodded solemnly. "I—I think I can do that."

She handed him another sheet of paper. "Here are all the directions for all the side dishes. And diagrams of the table settings. Don't forget to change the candles. Red for tonight, white for tomorrow."

"That's important?" Jed asked.

"Very," Holly said. "I've ironed all the table linens and carefully folded them. The poinsettia print is for tonight, the white cutwork tablecloth is for tomorrow. Come to think of it, I should probably just set the table for tonight and save you the time." She turned to hurry to the dining room, but Jed's voice stopped her.

"Couldn't you stay?" he reminded her. "I've never stuffed a bird before and this Beef Burlington kind of has me flummoxed. I'm not sure I've ever used a meat thermometer before."

"Wellington. And I—I can't stay. I've got...business

back in New York. Something I have to take care of right away."

"He asked you to stay, didn't he," Jed said.

"I'd really rather not talk about it," Holly said. "I'm a little confused right now and the more I think about it, the more confused I get. My brain is starting to hurt. I—I just need some time. This is a very big decision for me. I don't want to make a mistake."

"Well, he's not doing much better. That boy's cleaned out stalls so good you could eat off the floor. If you had a mind to, that is. There'll be no more Stony Creek pedicures."

Holly had wondered what Alex had been doing for the past twenty-four hours. She hadn't caught a single glimpse of him, not that she'd been looking. He was obviously still angry over her refusal to give him an answer. But no amount of convincing would change her mind. Holly had always taken her time making decisions and planning her future. She wasn't about to uproot herself and move to Schuyler Falls after one night of incredible passion, no matter how wonderful he made her feel or how strongly he professed his love.

She had to consider her options, to carefully contemplate every detail until she knew things would turn out perfect. But was that ever possible? Every couple went into a relationship expecting it to turn out perfect and that didn't always happen. Alex had tried once before and failed. Would they also be a casualty of the odds? Were the odds already stacked against them? Or had fate purposely brought them together?

She sighed. "Well, I think we've covered everything. My bags are by the front door and my train leaves in thirty minutes. We should probably get going." Holly gave Jed an encouraging smile. "Don't worry, you'll do fine. And the Beef Wellington will taste great even if it is a little overcooked and the pastry is doughy.'' She grabbed her coat from the back of a chair and shrugged into it. ''I better say goodbye to Eric. Do you know where he is?''

''He's waiting on the front porch. You make your farewells and I'll get your bags and warm up the truck,'' Jed said.

Holly nodded, then slowly walked to the front door. She found Eric sitting on the steps, staring out at the snow-covered driveway, Thurston lying next to him in a spot of sunshine. She quietly closed the door behind her then sat down beside him. He didn't look at her and she could see he was close to crying.

Slipping her arm around his shoulders, she pulled him closer and kissed the top of his head. ''We've had a good time, haven't we? You got your perfect Christmas, didn't you?''

He nodded. ''It would be more perfect if you'd stay,'' Eric suggested. ''I was thinking you could be my mom...if you wanted to.'' He glanced up at her, his gaze full of hope.

''I don't know what the future holds,'' Holly said. ''Maybe someday, I will be your mom. Or maybe someone wonderful will come along and make you and your dad very happy. But that doesn't mean I'll ever stop loving you.''

''Yeah,'' Eric said. ''That's what my mom said when she left.''

Holly felt his words stab into her heart, robbing her of her breath. She pushed back her own tears. Why did this sweet child have to suffer for their indecision? Why couldn't they all be a happy family? ''Well, just pretend that I'm a real angel. And believe that I'll be watching over you from a long way away.''

Eric reached into his pocket and withdrew a crudely wrapped box. ''It's a Christmas gift. I bought you bubble bath, but then I decided to give you this instead. You can open it.''

Holly tore the wrapping and picked through the little box lined with cotton. She withdrew a chain. Hanging from it was a penny, shiny and nearly flattened paper-thin. ''It's beautiful,'' she said.

''It's my lucky penny. Me and Kenny and Raymond put pennies on the train tracks and when we came back the next day they were squished. I had this penny when I went to see Santa, when I asked him for you. Now, you can have it. For luck.''

Holly slipped the chain around her neck, a tear slipping from the corner of her eye, her heart nearly breaking. ''Thank you, Eric. It's the best present ever.''

He grinned, then stood up and wrapped his arms around her neck. ''It's for the best angel ever.'' He finally let go of her neck, then turned and raced back inside the house, Thurston trotting after him.

Holly drew a deep breath and rose, the penny still clutched between her thumb and index finger. Then she started down the steps. Jed waited for her in the truck, her bags already tucked in the back. She walked slowly, hoping that Alex would magically appear and sweep her into his arms so she couldn't possibly leave. That's what she wanted, wasn't it? She wasn't ready to make a decision, not yet, but she didn't want to leave. With a few hundred miles between them, she was afraid her attraction to Alex would fade a little, the hazy world of passion they'd shared would disappear and she'd never see this place again.

When she reached the truck, she grabbed hold of the door handle, then turned around for one last look. To her surprise, she saw Alex standing by the corner of the porch, his hands hitched on his waist, his hair blown by the crisp wind. Holly felt her breath catch in her throat, exactly the way it had the very first time she'd set eyes on him.

Alex took a single step nearer. "I guess this is goodbye then," he called.

She moved away from the truck. "I suppose it is, at least for the time being."

He stared down at his feet. "Are you going back to him?"

Holly shook her head. "I don't love him. And I'm going to tell him that."

"And after that? Will you come back and give me an answer?" Alex asked.

Holly nodded. "I promise. I will."

Jed beeped the truck horn and Holly jumped. She glanced over her shoulder and he pointed to his watch. Then she turned back to Alex. He was staring at her across the distance between them. Without thinking, she ran to him, then pushed up on her toes and brushed a kiss across his cheek. "Merry Christmas, Alex."

He stared down into her eyes and, for a moment, she considered staying, his gaze a connection that couldn't be broken, a connection she didn't want to break for fear they'd never be able to find it again. But then she slowly backed away and got into the truck.

Holly watched him through the back window of the pickup as they bumped down the long driveway to the road. Just before the house disappeared from view, he raised his hand and waved. Her heart ached and her mind whirled with regret, but she forced herself to turn around and look at the road ahead.

"I will come back," she murmured softly. "I promise." But though she said the words, Holly wasn't sure she meant them. After all, this was just supposed to be a job, a two-week project to put her company back in the black. She was never supposed to fall in love.

9

THE TRAIN RIDE BACK to the city seemed to drag on endlessly for Holly. She tried to be excited about going home, tried to muster enthusiasm about getting back to the hustle and bustle of a normal life. But with every mile that passed, Holly's thoughts roiled with regret and indecision. For two weeks, she'd lived a different life, quiet and important, filled with people who cared about one another. What did she have waiting in the city except twinkle lights and pinecone garland and hand-blown Polish ornaments? A girl certainly couldn't snuggle up with those late at night.

As the scenery flew by, she slowly savored the memories of her night with Alex, trying to recall in perfect detail every moment of every minute, choosing to focus on the passions rather than the problems afterward. Interspersed with the passion was the laughter, images of Eric baking cookies and Jed standing behind her, taking notes, as she cooked. Alex's gentle teasing and stolen kisses.

After living at Stony Creek Farm, her life in the city appeared banal and bleak. Did she really care whether she put the finest holly or the freshest mistletoe in her Christmas arrangements? Did she really care whether her ornaments were real mercury glass or just a cheap knock-off? And if she had to convince one more rich matron that white twinkle lights weren't the only choice for a

Christmas tree, she surely would scream. Holly tipped her head back and sighed.

"The holidays are difficult for everyone, dear."

Holly glanced at the elderly lady sitting next to her. The plump little woman had boarded in Schenectady, and though Holly made it quite clear by her expression that she'd rather sit alone, the lady plopped down beside her. She smelled of lemon verbena and she carried a battered carpetbag that Holly estimated was at least a hundred years old. Her perfume gave Holly a strange sense of déjà vu and then she remembered that her grandmother always used to wear a dab of lemon verbena beneath each ear.

"I'm fine," Holly murmured, turning away to stare out the window. "I'm just tired."

"Are you going to visit relatives? I'm going to see my daughter. She lives in Brooklyn. Perhaps you know her? Selma Goodwin?"

Holly shook her head. "No, I don't know her."

"She leads such an exciting life in the city. Always so busy, working hard, taking care of her family. Sometimes I think she forgets to stop and smell the roses. Do you?"

"Have a family?"

"Smell the roses."

"No," Holly said. "I don't smell the roses." She laughed dryly. "In fact, roses are precisely what got me here in the first place. If it weren't for those damn roses, I'd probably be spending Christmas with Alex and Eric, not sipping low-fat eggnog alone in my apartment. And if Christmas Eve alone isn't pathetic enough, tomorrow I get hit with the double-whammy. Christmas Day *and* my birthday."

"Add a little brandy to that eggnog and you won't feel so bad, dear. Back in my day we didn't use antidepressants when we were blue. We just dipped into the brandy snifter.'' The woman giggled as if she were revealing her darkest secrets, then patted Holly's hand. ''Why don't you tell me all about it? Perhaps I can help.''

All of a sudden, Holly felt the undeniable need to unburden herself. After all, she hadn't been able to make any sense out of the past few weeks. Maybe, looking at the whole situation from an objective point of view, this stranger could. She took a deep breath and went back to the beginning. ''It all started when I got a job as an angel—not a real angel, but a Christmas angel.''

The story poured out of her as the train rumbled through Albany and Hudson, the scenery flying by as she told of her growing feelings for Alex Marrin and his son. The woman didn't say much, but when she did comment, her words were frank and to the point and her questions direct.

''At first we didn't get along,'' Holly admitted, ''but then everything changed between us. Do you believe in love at first sight?''

The woman shrugged. ''I suppose love is love, whether it happens immediately or whether it takes a long time. What I do know about love is that you have to listen to your heart, dear. When I met my Harold, I thought he was the cat's pajamas. But he was all full of himself and didn't even notice me. When he finally did bother to look, he fell hard. I found out later that he ignored me because he was scared of me. Do you believe that? Afraid of me. Deep down inside, I knew he loved me, though.''

''What was he afraid of?''

''I suppose he was afraid that he might not have what it takes to keep me happy. But being with him was all the happiness I needed.'' She sighed. ''Do you love this man?''

''I do,'' Holly said. ''And I know he loves me. But is

that enough? And how do I know that love will last?" She sighed. "I just have so many questions and no answers." She looked at the older lady bleakly. "Do you have any answers for me?"

The train slowly came to a stop, and for the first time, Holly noticed that they'd pulled into Penn Station, their ride through the city going completely unnoticed. The woman stood up and straightened her tidy little suit. "Only you know how to make your dreams come true, dear. If you listen to your heart, you'll never go wrong." She tucked her carpetbag under her arm. "Well, dear, it was a pleasure talking with you. Do have a Merry Christmas, won't you?"

"Wait," Holly said. After such intimate conversation, the woman couldn't just walk away. There was so much more to discuss! "I didn't even introduce myself. My name is Holly. Holly Bennett. What's your name? Maybe we could catch a cup of coffee." Suddenly she didn't want to go home to her cold, empty apartment. She didn't even have a Christmas tree of her own.

The woman glanced around and then a smile curved her lips and she gave Holly a wink. "Most people call me Louise. But you can call me…your Christmas angel."

Then Louise stepped out into the aisle, and before Holly could even stumble out of her seat, she'd been swallowed up by the crowd of holiday passengers anxious to get off the train. Holly dragged her luggage from the overhead shelf and forced her way into the aisle. "Wait! Louise! I wanted to thank you. And tell you that—"

By the time she got off the train, her Christmas angel had disappeared. Holly lugged her bags down the platform, wishing that she'd had just a few more minutes with Louise, received a few more bits of sage advice.

"'Only you know how to make your dreams come true,'" Holly murmured. "I could make my dreams come true right now if I wasn't such a dope. I could listen to my heart and change the course of my life."

Her spirits suddenly lifted and her surroundings brightened. In an instant she was filled with holiday cheer and Holly hurried toward the terminal, weaving through the crush of the crowd. This could be the very best Christmas ever and all she had to do was ignore all the questions in her head and listen to her heart. As she walked through the doors, she glanced around frantically, trying to figure the most direct way to the ticket counter. With all the holiday travellers, she would be lucky to get a ticket. If she couldn't, there was always the bus. Or a rented car. Heck, she'd walk if she had to, but she was going to get back to Schuyler Falls if it was the last thing she did.

"Holly!"

She heard her name above the din of the crowd and she stopped and glanced around. "Louise?"

"Holly, over here. It's me! Meg."

Holly stood on her tiptoes and scanned the crowd, catching sight of Meg's curly red hair about fifteen feet away. She worked against the traffic and it took her nearly a minute to make it to the spot where her friend stood. "Meg, what are you doing here?" she asked breathlessly. "Is everything all right?"

"Not exactly. I called the farm. Alex Marrin told me you'd left on the first train." She shoved her hands into the pockets of her coat and stared at the floor, two spots of color reddening each cheek. Meg wasn't easily rattled and Holly had never seen her look so uneasy.

"What is it?" Holly asked. "Is it Eric?"

Meg shook her head. "I've done something I don't think you're going to like. But I want you to know, I had

the very best intentions. I just really didn't expect you to
come back. I thought you'd realize you were in love with
him and you'd stay. And that would put an end to all
your doubts. But my plan kind of backfired.''

Holly frowned. "Meg, what did you do?"

Meg winced, then shook her head. "I sent the roses
and signed Stephan's name.'' She cover her face with her
hands. "I'm a bad, bad friend. And a terrible business
associate. And I wouldn't blame you if you hated me
forever and fired me on the spot. I just thought if you
were forced to make a choice you'd realize—''

Holly laughed and threw her arms around Meg's neck,
stopping her explanation. "*You* sent the flowers." She
pressed her palm to her chest. "Thank God. Do you
know what this means?"

"That I'm out of a job?"

Holly hugged her again. "No! It means I don't have
to face Stephan and tell him that I never wanted to marry
him. God, I wasn't looking forward to that."

"Then I still have a job?"

"I could never fire you. Besides, after today, you're
the president and sole owner of All The Trimmings. And
I'm moving to Schuyler Falls to live with the man I
love."

"What? You're going to marry Alex Marrin?"

"Well, he hasn't asked me yet. But I'm going to do
my best to convince him that I'll make a wonderful
wife," Holly said, grabbing her bags from the floor. "I
should have stayed in the first place, but the train ride
gave me a chance to realize how I feel. The farther I
traveled from Alex and Eric, the more I ached to see them
again. I'm in love with Alex Marrin and I want to have
a life with him. He loves me, Meg. And I'm going to

buy a ticket back to Schuyler Falls and be a part of his family."

"HOW LONG UNTIL THE TRAIN leaves? I hope it leaves soon. Do you think Holly will be happy when we show up at her house? Can I sit by the window?"

Alex watched through the lightly falling snow as his son paced back and forth across the station platform. He'd tried to convince Eric to wait inside, where it was warmer, but he needed space to move and a chance to burn off a little of his excess energy. They had a long train ride ahead of them and Alex hoped Eric would spend it sleeping, giving him plenty of time to plan a strategy.

It had taken all of two minutes for him to regret letting Holly go that morning. He fingered the ring in his pocket. The truck had barely been out of sight and he was already wondering how he'd be able to get her back. He'd cursed his pride and his cowardice at not asking her to marry him, then tried to come up with a plan to convince her they belonged together for the rest of their lives. Luckily, Eric had forced his hand, taking another jaunt to the train station without his father's permission. So they'd both ended up here at the Schuyler Falls train station, awaiting the next train to New York City.

"How could you let her leave?" Eric asked, sitting down next to him, then immediately standing.

"I was momentarily insane," he said, then leveled his gaze at his son. "Like you were momentarily insane when you hopped the bus and came down here to the station all on your own."

"You found me," Eric said. "Even though I didn't tell you where I was going, you knew where to find me."

"Your little adventures to the train station and Dalton's Department Store are going to stop. Or you'll be grounded until you're eighteen and I'll take away every Game Boy you own and hope to own.''

"It's worth it," Eric said. "We're going to get my Christmas angel back. You can have all my toys. And you can even have the car that Gramps was going to give me when I learn to drive."

"You want Holly back that bad?"

Eric nodded. "I want her to come and live with us forever. And bake me gingerbread and teach me how to play the piano and tell me how to act around girls."

Alex arched his eyebrow. "Holly talked to you about girls?"

"We talked about everything," Eric said. "She really knows a lot about girls, probably because she is one."

"Yeah, that helps. It's hard to navigate the female mind without a map."

"Yeah," Eric agreed. "And you're not good at it at all, Dad." He sent him a pointed glance, as if he'd suddenly become the parent and Alex was now the child. "You better hope this works. I don't want you to blow it again."

"And what if it doesn't work?" Alex asked. "Eric, you understand that I can't make Holly come back if she doesn't want to. You can't force someone to love you."

"She does love us," Eric said, his tone guileless, yet supremely confident.

"How do you know that? Did she tell you?"

"She didn't have to say it, I just know it. You can tell by the way she looks at you. You know, when you're not looking. She looks all mushy and romantic, like Eleanor Winchell looked when she had a huge crush on Raymond." He raised his voice to imitate his nemesis. "Oh, Raymond, you're so strong. And you're so good at soccer. Can you carry my books? Will you buy me a candy bar?'' He scoffed. ''Like she needs another candy bar.''

Alex jumped in at the first break in Eric's diatribe. ''So what did Holly tell you about women? I mean, girls.''

''She said that if you treat 'em nice, the good girls, the ones worth liking, will be nice back. And if they're not, then they're not worth knowing.''

''Well, I guess that pretty much sums it up.''

Eric sat down next to him and patted Alex's knee. ''So, when does the train leave? Is it time yet? Can we get a soda in the dining car?''

Alex sat back on the bench and crossed his legs in front of him. Truth be told, he hadn't been very nice to Holly. He should have told her flat out that he wanted to marry her, that she meant the world to him and he couldn't live without her. He should have pushed aside all his doubts and taken a chance.

''There it is!'' Eric shouted, jumping to his feet and pointing down the tracks.

''That's not it, Scout. That train's going the wrong way. That one's coming from New York. Our train doesn't leave for another forty-five minutes.''

''How long will it take us to get there?''

''A little over three hours. It'll be very late when we get to Holly's. She might be asleep.''

''Will it still be Christmas Eve?'' Eric asked.

''Nope, it'll be Christmas Day.''

Eric sighed as he sat back down beside Alex. He swung his feet in front of him and hummed a chorus of ''Frosty.'' Alex watched him for a long moment, then fixed his gaze on the approaching train. He'd never done anything like this in his life, taken such a risk with his heart, and he was doing it fully aware of the consequences. But he'd never know unless he tried and the rewards were certainly worth the gamble. He just hoped Eric wouldn't take it too badly if it all fell apart.

The train slowed as it approached the station, the brakes grinding and the engine rumbling. Eric covered his ears and laughed, then jumped up to watch the conductor as he hopped off the train and placed the step at the door to the third car.

Through the lighted windows of the train, Alex could see the holiday travelers crowded into the seats and pushing down the aisle. For a moment, he saw a woman who looked remarkably like Holly. And then she was gone. Alex shook his head. She'd been on his mind all day long, images of her swirling in his head until he knew the only way to stop them would be to see her again.

What would he say? He'd have to start with an apology—first, for waking her, second, for showing up unannounced, and then, probably for everything he'd done wrong in the past two and a half weeks. After that was finished, he'd have to explain how he felt. He'd plead his case, hoping to convince Holly to give up her life in New York for a life as a wife and a mother at Stony Creek Farm. If she insisted on living in the city, he'd have to find a way to keep the farm running until Eric was ready to take over. It wouldn't be easy, but it wouldn't be impossible. And then, there was—

Eric tugged on his jacket sleeve. "Dad! Dad, look!"

"It's not time yet, Scout."

"No, look!" Alex turned and followed Eric's pointed finger, but all he saw were hurrying passengers.

"At what?"

"It's our Christmas angel!" Eric cried.

She materialized out of the crowd as if by magic, the passengers suddenly parting to leave her standing on the platform alone. The light above her head bathed her in luminescent beams, reflecting off the softly falling snow until it looked as if she were showered with tiny diamonds.

Alex slowly rose and took a step toward her, not sure whether she was real or just a dream. Either way, she was the most beautiful thing he'd ever seen. And if he knew only one thing, he knew he was looking at his future.

THE PLATFORM WAS CROWDED as Holly descended from the train, luggage and shopping bags jostling her as passengers passed. Now that she was here, she wasn't certain what she was supposed to do. Everything had been so clear, standing in the middle of Penn Station, her return ticket clutched in her hand. But now that she was back in Schuyler Falls, her doubts had crept back.

It was just after seven and she imagined that Alex and Eric and Jed were probably just sitting down to her carefully prepared Beef Wellington. Or maybe they'd gone to church. "I'll call first," Holly murmured, turning to search out a pay phone. "Maybe I shouldn't call. What if he tells me to go back home? What will I do then?"

There had to be cabs waiting in front of the station. She'd buy a ride to Stony Creek Farm and stand on Alex's porch once again, praying that he'd let her into his life as he'd done that first night. He'd said he loved her. If that was really true then he'd have to be happy to see her again.

She started toward the doors to the station, but her attention was caught by a tall figure standing at the end of the platform. Her heart fluttered and her breath caught. Though she couldn't see his face clearly in the feeble light, she knew who it was.

He took a step closer and Holly's knees went weak. She dropped her bags beside her, and though she wanted to run to him, to throw her arms around him and kiss him, she suddenly couldn't move.

Alex slowly approached and everything around her, the train, the passengers, the brightly lit station, faded into the background. All she could hear was her heart beating in her chest and all she could see was the man she loved, walking toward her.

When he finally stood in front of her, Eric hovering behind, she reached out to touch him, just to make sure he was real. His jacket was soft, his muscled chest warm beneath the fabric. "You're here. How did you know I was coming back?"

"I didn't." He reached in his pocket and held up a train ticket. "Eric and I were coming to New York to get you."

Tears sprang to the corners of Holly's eyes and ran down her cheeks. She brushed them away with shaking fingers. "You were?"

Alex nodded. "I know I've made a real mess of things, Holly, but I swear, I'm going to make it all up to you. Starting now." From his pocket he withdrew a small velvet bag. "I should have given this to you when I first asked you to stay, but I'm glad I saved it for now, when I can do things right." He took a diamond ring from the little bag and held it up to her. "Holly, I love you. And I'll never stop loving you. Will you marry me?"

"Marry you?"

He nodded. "I never want to let you go again. I want you in my life—and Eric's—forever. Marry me, Holly. Make my life perfect."

Holly watched as he slipped the ring on her finger. The diamond glinted in the glare from the light above her head. "This ring has been worn by three generations of women—my mother, my grandmother and my great-grandmother. All women loved by Marrin men. And I want you to have it."

Tears welled up in her eyes, blurring her vision until the entire scene seemed more like a dream than reality. But it was wonderfully real. And if she'd had any doubts at all, they were gone now, banished to the past, never to be heard from again. The scene was perfect, the three of them standing on a deserted train platform, holiday music crackling from a speaker overhead, and snow falling all around them as the train pulled from the station.

Eric moved to her side and took her hand. "Please say yes," he murmured. "Please say yes."

Holly glanced down at Eric and gave his hand a squeeze. "Yes," she murmured. Then she looked into Alex's gaze and nodded. "Yes, Alex. I will marry you."

Eric shouted for joy and jumped up and down as Alex pulled her into his arms. He took her face between his hands and kissed her, softly and gently, a kiss filled with love. Then he picked up Eric and gathered them both in his arms. Holly laughed and tipped her face up to the falling snow.

She'd always worked so hard to give other people a perfect Christmas. But now, standing here with Alex and Eric, she realized that a perfect Christmas didn't have anything to do with fancy trees and pretty gifts. A perfect Christmas was about love and happiness, about family and home. And for Holly, this was finally *her* perfect Christmas.

Epilogue

ERIC LAY ON HIS STOMACH in front of the blazing fire in the library. Wads of paper were strewn all around him and his new toys were temporarily forgotten for a much more important matter. They'd just finished a huge turkey dinner, the conversation centering on wedding plans and a honeymoon for three at Disney World.

Eric glanced over his shoulder. Gramps was snoozing in a chair, his third piece of cherry pie half-eaten on the table beside him. Thurston was curled up near the window. And his dad and Holly were snuggled up on the couch, talking in quiet tones and laughing.

They'd spent the night in the barn, watching Jade give birth to a pretty little filly. And this morning at breakfast, after they sang "Happy Birthday," his dad had presented Holly with a special birthday present—Jade's foal. Eric smiled. Now he knew Holly could never leave. She had her own horse at Stony Creek Farm. She'd even given it a name already. Since she'd known the Marrin horses were named after gemstones or flowers, she hadn't pondered it for more than a moment. She'd simply held up her left hand, smiling, and stated, "Diamond."

Eric turned back to the letter. When he'd asked for a Christmas angel, he'd never expected to get a brand-new mom. But he couldn't think of a better Christmas gift than Holly, except for...He clutched his pencil in his hand and carefully considered the text of his letter. This letter had to be perfect—as perfect as the last letter he wrote to Santa. For this time he was asking for something really big! He had almost a year to get the letter just right before he'd deliver it directly to Santa at Dalton's Department Store, a year to work on his penmanship and choose the right envelope.

He stared down at the letter, stumped by the next word. Eric softly sounded it out. "B-R-U—" No, that wasn't right. "How do you spell 'brother?'" he called out.

"Why do you need to know how to spell that?" his dad asked.

He sat up and faced the sofa, deciding whether he should tell Dad and Holly about his newest letter to Santa. Heck, it couldn't hurt. To make this Christmas wish come true he'd need all the help he could get. "I'm writing to Santa and asking him to bring me a baby brother," he replied.

His father gasped and Holly's eyes went wide. "A brother?"

"Yeah. After you and Holly get married, it would be all right, wouldn't it? I'd ask for a real good baby, one that didn't cry and barf all the time."

"We haven't really talked about that," his father said. He turned to Holly. "Have we?"

Holly shrugged. "What about a sister?" she asked.

He watched as they kissed for about the billionth time that day. Eric figured he'd have to get used to all the smooching if Holly was going to marry his dad.

"A girl?" Eric crinkled his nose. "If there are no boys left, I guess a girl would be all right...as long as she doesn't turn out like Eleanor Winchell."

Eric's dad wrapped his arm around Holly's shoulders and drew her near. "I think she'd turn out just like Holly. Pale hair and pretty features and as sweet as sugar."

"Then I'd like her," Eric said.

His father motioned to Eric. "Bring that letter here, Scout," he said. Eric crawled across the room, the paper clutched in his hand. He gave it to his father, then sat back on his heels and watched as he folded it up and handed it to Holly.

"What am I supposed to do with this?" Holly asked.

"File it," Dad said. "For future use."

"Future?" Holly asked.

Eric's father chuckled. "Yeah. We'll work on it later tonight."

Eric grinned, then crawled back to his spot in front of the fireplace. He tore a fresh sheet of paper from his pad and snatched up his pencil. Now that he had the brother taken care of, he could ask Santa for something else. Maybe if he wrote a really good letter, he could get them two babies.

"Yeah," he murmured. "Two babies. Twins—a boy *and* a girl." Now *that* would be a *perfect* Christmas!

The Harlequin Reader Service® — Here's how it works:

Accepting your 2 free books and gift places you under no obligation to buy anything. You may keep the books and gift and return the shipping statement marked "cancel." If you do not cancel, about a month later we'll send you 2 additional novels and bill you just $5.14 each in the U.S., or $6.14 each in Canada, plus 50¢ shipping & handling per book and applicable taxes if any.* That's the complete price and — compared to cover prices of $5.99 each in the U.S. and $6.99 each in Canada — it's quite a bargain! You may cancel at any time, but if you choose to continue, every month we'll send you 2 more books, which you may either purchase at the discount price or return to us and cancel your subscription.

*Terms and prices subject to change without notice. Sales tax applicable in N.Y. Canadian residents will be charged applicable provincial taxes and GST.

If offer card is missing write to: Harlequin Reader Service, 3010 Walden Ave., P.O. Box 1867, Buffalo NY 14240-1867

NO POSTAGE
NECESSARY
IF MAILED
IN THE
UNITED STATES

BUSINESS REPLY MAIL

FIRST-CLASS MAIL   PERMIT NO. 717   BUFFALO, NY

POSTAGE WILL BE PAID BY ADDRESSEE

HARLEQUIN READER SERVICE
3010 WALDEN AVE
PO BOX 1867
BUFFALO NY 14240-9952

Play The
Lucky Hearts Game

and get...

FREE BOOKS & a FREE GIFT...
YOURS to KEEP!

Yes! I have scratched off the silver card. Please send me my **2 FREE BOOKS** and **FREE MYSTERY GIFT**. I understand that I am under no obligation to purchase any books as explained on the back of this card.

Scratch Here!
then look below to see what your cards get you...

311 HDL C6J6   **111 HDL C6JW**

NAME   (PLEASE PRINT CLEARLY)

ADDRESS

APT.#   CITY

STATE/PROV.   ZIP/POSTAL CODE

Twenty-one gets you
2 FREE BOOKS and a
FREE MYSTERY GIFT!

Twenty gets you
2 FREE BOOKS!

Nineteen gets you
1 FREE BOOK!

TRY AGAIN!

Offer limited to one per household and not valid to current Harlequin Duets™ subscribers. All orders subject to approval.

Visit us online at
www.eHarlequin.com

KATE HOFFMANN

Undercover Elf

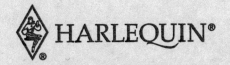

TORONTO • NEW YORK • LONDON
AMSTERDAM • PARIS • SYDNEY • HAMBURG
STOCKHOLM • ATHENS • TOKYO • MILAN • MADRID
PRAGUE • WARSAW • BUDAPEST • AUCKLAND

1

"I'M HERE TO APPLY FOR the position of elf."

Nine words Claudia Moore never in her life expected to say—at least, not in that order. Those words and "Sure, I'd love a root canal" and "Gee, I need to gain some weight" and "Yes, I know precisely what's wrong with my car."

She dropped the job application on the secretary's desk then pasted a suitably hopeful smile on her face. It had all come to this, the nadir of her career as a freelance journalist. Her talents as a reporter had been reduced to convincing some pencil-pushing personnel manager at Dalton's Department Store that she'd make the best darned Santa's elf they'd ever had. Claudia almost wished they'd turn her away as unqualified, though that would have been the worst humiliation of all.

The gray-haired secretary scanned the application with shrewd eyes, then glanced up. "Mr. Robbins will be with you in a few moments," she said in a prim voice. "If you'll take a seat, I'll tell him you're here."

Claudia did as she was told, neatly folding her hands on her lap and keeping her spine ramrod straight. She had to at least appear as if she wanted to make a good impression, that becoming an elf was her life's dream. Her thoughts wandered back to the job history she'd fabricated for the application. She'd tried to imagine what sort of background a good elf would possess, then hoped her job listings were so vague and long ago that Dalton's wouldn't bother with references. Camp counselor, day care assistant, swimming pool lifeguard. If she had bothered with summers off in high school and college she might very well have worked at all these jobs.

Though misrepresenting herself tweaked her sense of journalistic integrity, she didn't think a few little white lies would hurt this time. After all, she'd come to a crossroads in her career. Tired of living like she had in college, scraping just to get by, Claudia had decided to make her move.

From the moment she had published her first newspaper, the *Maple Street Chronicle,* at age eight, she'd been destined to be a journalist. Born an only child to an unhappy couple who struggled to make ends meet, Claudia was expected to live the dreams her mother never had—to graduate high school, find a nice young man with good prospects and have a big, happy family.

Instead, she gave up the social whirl in high school to work part-time at the *Buffalo Beacon,* forgoing football games and school dances for the smell of newsprint and the sound of the presses. She'd left home right after graduation and put herself through college, taking on odd jobs and writing articles that paid enough to cover the cost of a pizza every now and then. And since college, she'd worked freelance as a stringer for all the major New York papers. But the newspaper business had become harder and harder to crack, corporate-owned newspapers operating with a skeleton staff of seasoned veterans.

But Claudia had guts and tenacity and unwavering confidence, stopping at nothing to get what she wanted. Some might have called her single-minded, stubborn or outspoken, but she considered those qualities crucial for a good investigative reporter—if she'd ever get a decent story again.

She used to get assignments for hard-hitting pieces, chemical dumping, political corruption, corporate fraud. But lately she'd been forced to take any assignment she could find—her recent clips included "How to Divorce Your Hairdresser" and "Doggie Day Care." But Claudia was a resourceful woman, a woman who could sniff out a story where there wasn't one, a woman who could turn lemons into lemonade. A regular Woodward—or Bernstein.

"Yeah, like this story is as big as Watergate," Claudia murmured. "They'll call it Santagate."

The idea had come from the Saratoga Springs *Chronicle*, a feel-good story that mixed a little mystery with holiday cheer and altruistic giving. The article, headlined "Small-town Santa Makes Christmas Dreams Come True," told the story of a young boy who'd asked the Santa at Dalton's Department Store in Schuyler Falls for a special gift last Christmas—a new wheelchair for his sister. Along with a wheelchair, a brand-new van appeared in the family's driveway on Christmas morning. No one knew where it came from or who had paid for it and the management was stubbornly closemouthed.

In an age when every corporation and most individuals crowed about their charitable deeds, silent altruism was almost unknown. She figured a feel-good story like this would be hot news around the holidays so she pitched it to the biggest paper of all: the *New York Times*.

The editor for statewide features jumped at the chance and gave Claudia two weeks to learn the identity of the mysterious benefactor and interview recent recipients. Claudia planned to know the guy's hat size and his high school GPA inside of three days. And there was a bonus to this assignment. If the article was good, her editor promised, then Claudia's name would move to the top of the list. She'd be among the candidates to fill an upcoming vacancy at the *Times,* covering statewide features.

"Are you the one waiting for the interview?"

Claudia jumped to her feet, startled by the deep, commanding voice. But she barely had a moment to answer. The man, dressed in a beautifully tailored suit, strode right by her into a nearby office, allowing her just a brief glimpse of his back—wide shoulders, narrow waist, long legs. She wasn't sure whether to follow, but took a few tentative steps forward.

"Are you coming?" he shouted from inside his office. "I haven't got a lot of time."

"Typical," Claudia muttered. "You haven't even started the interview and already you can't follow orders." She hurried after him, then took a chair on the other side of his desk. Compared to her own desk in her tiny Brooklyn apartment, his was pathologically neat. It was only when her eyes fell on the brass nameplate that she realized there had been a mistake. She wasn't in Mr. Robbins's office at all.

"Thomas Dalton," she murmured. Her eyes went wide as she got her first look at the man, who according to her research, ran Dalton's Department Store. Claudia had expected him to be older, fiftyish, maybe a little gray around the temples with a slight paunch hidden by a nice suit. But this man had caught her by surprise.

Thomas Dalton was handsome in the way that made women swoon. Tall and lean, he wore his clothes with a casual elegance, as if he hadn't bothered with what he was putting on that morning, yet knew it would be perfect. Though the suit gave him an air of age and authority, he couldn't hide a streak of boyish appeal. His skin was tanned and his hair a little too long to be proper. And if he was thirty, she mused, then his birthday hadn't been more than a few days ago.

And there was something else, something Claudia had seen time and time again in wealthy and powerful men, something that seemed perfectly natural in Thomas Dalton. In just a few seconds, she could see he expected to control everything and everyone around him, simply by virtue of a withering glare or an impatient word. He was doing it now, staring across the desk at her, his expression both aloof and irritated at the same time as he waited for her to speak.

Why would he concern himself with interviewing a lowly elf? she wondered. Claudia wasn't about to question her luck. Nor would she ever let a man get the better of her, even a man as sexy as Thomas Dalton. Instead she'd turn this little misunderstanding to her advantage! And perhaps she wouldn't even have to spend a single day as an elf.

Claudia's mind began to form a strategy. Keep him talking but keep him off balance. And when he was most vulnerable, hit him with the tough questions. At the same time, she'd do well to convince him she was the one for the job of lowly elf, just in case it came to that.

He picked up a file folder and slowly perused it. "Lingerie," he finally murmured, a hint of boredom in his voice. "Tell me your take on the underwear business."

Claudia blinked. So she *was* in the wrong office, with the wrong man. Though if she were stranded on a desert island or trapped in a stalled elevator or locked in a very small closet, Thomas Dalton would rank right up there on her list of the *right* men. This was a stroke of luck.

"Well," she began, gathering her thoughts. "Everyone wears underwear." That one statement summed up just about everything she knew about lingerie! So much for playing along.

"Actually, marketing reports show there's a growing number of people who don't wear underwear at all," he replied, his voice now challenging, his eyebrow arched.

He was trying to rattle her. He obviously didn't know Claudia Moore! "Do you?" she asked. The moment the question shot out of her mouth she wanted to snatch it back. Impertinence would never get her this job. But her instincts as a reporter often took over without warning. The reporter runs the interview. Never give up control. Forget propriety or you'll never get to the truth.

"I beg your pardon?"

"Do *you* believe that?" she amended.

"I want to know what you think," Dalton countered, his gaze fixed on hers. "You're the one looking for a job."

Lord, he had the most intriguing eyes, vivid green and coolly perceptive. He watched her shrewdly and Claudia felt a little shiver skitter down her spine. In truth, everything about him was beyond average—shoulders just a bit broader, hair just a shade darker, profile just a tad short of perfect.

She swallowed hard and tried get her mind back on the task at hand. "In my experience with underwear, I'd have to say that…I like it. I choose my underwear very carefully. First for fit, because underwear that's too tight can be bothersome. And underwear that's too loose can cause unsightly lines. Then there's the fashion impact. I enjoy knowing if I'm in a serious accident, I'll be wearing something pretty when they cut my clothes off. Do you buy your own underwear or do you let your wife buy it for you?"

He blinked, clearly taken aback by her audacious inquiry. "I—I'm not married. And when I need underwear, I call down to the men's department and they deliver them to my office in a nice Dalton's gift box."

"Boxers or briefs?" Claudia asked, amused by his discomfort and secretly pleased that he didn't have a spouse. She found single men so much easier to intimidate—and manipulate.

"Boxers," he murmured. Slowly he skimmed over her features, his eyes stopping for a long moment at her mouth. "Silk boxers."

Claudia swallowed hard and tried to maintain her crumbling composure. Thomas Dalton had a way of looking at a woman that made her wonder just what he was thinking. Was he tempted by her lips? Or was he thinking about kissing her? Or was there spinach caught between her teeth? "Patterned or plain?" she asked, anxious to keep the conversation going and her mind on the job at hand.

"Patterned. Small patterns." He shook his head. "No pastels. Why the hell are we talking about my underwear?"

"You wanted my take. Personally, I like a man in boxers. Tighty-whiteys just don't say sexy to me."

Dalton cleared his throat. "I'm afraid we got off on a completely irrelevant tangent and we should just start this interview all over." He stood and held out his hand and Claudia leaned forward to take it.

"Miss Webster, it's a pleasure to meet you. I'm Thomas Dalton, general manager of Dalton's. And I'm very anxious to hear your ideas about running our intimate apparel department."

"And…I'm not Miss Webster," Claudia said, sending him an innocent look, distracted by the feel of her fingers caught in his hand, the gentle power they exerted. "I'm Claudia Moore. I'm here to interview for the job of elf."

Dalton frowned, his jaw growing tighter by the second and his icy facade cracking a bit. "You're what?"

"I'm hoping to become an elf. I was supposed to have an interview with Mr. Robbins. I thought you were him."

"But I was talking about lingerie," he said. "Do you think I discuss these matters with everyone who walks in to my office?"

Claudia shrugged. The naive act was working well. "I was a little surprised, but I really need this job. You could have told me about your sex life and I would have given you advice, as long as you hired me."

A smile touched the corners of his finely sculpted mouth, before he pressed his lips into a harsh line again and glared at her. Claudia's blood warmed. He realized she'd been toying with him and now he was deciding what to do about it—join the game, throw her out of his office and his store, or hire her on the spot.

"I'm very excited about becoming an elf," Claudia said.

He stared at her for a long moment. "And why is that?" His words were clipped, but she didn't hear any anger in them.

"I've heard all the stories. About the Dalton's Santa being special. I read that he grants Christmas wishes to deserving children. Wonderful wishes."

"I wouldn't know," Dalton replied.

"But why not? The Santa is your employee. And you're in charge, aren't you?"

His jaw twitched. "Right now, that might be debatable."

"Well, I want to be part of making children's dreams

come true. I want to meet this man and...and bask in the purity of his goodness.''

Footsteps sounded on the marble floor outside the office. ''Mr. Dalton, I—'' The secretary stopped short as she caught sight of Claudia. ''Here you are! I thought you'd left.''

''Miss Moore has been chatting with me,'' Dalton said, giving Claudia an odd look as he pushed to his feet. ''Mrs. Lewis, please tell Robbins that I'd highly recommend Miss Moore for the job. She's confident and clever...and possesses all the qualities we look for in a good elf.''

''Well, come along then,'' the secretary said, motioning her to the door. ''We don't want to keep Mr. Robbins waiting any longer.''

Claudia stood and nodded, then glanced up at Thomas Dalton. He circled his desk and moved to her side. ''Well, Miss Moore, it was a pleasure meeting you. And I hope Dalton's will offer you the 'basking' you desire.''

This time when he took her hand in his she couldn't help but notice the details of his fingers, well-shaped and strong, and the flood of heat that seeped up her arm. For a long time, he didn't let go and Claudia was beginning to wonder if he might want her to stay and continue their conversation. ''You can call me Claudia,'' she finally said. ''It was a pleasure meeting you, Tom. Or is it Thomas?''

He smiled again, warm, charming, so different from the aloof facade he'd maintained during their meeting. ''Business associates call me Thomas,'' he corrected. ''My friends and relatives call me Tom. But if you want to become an elf in my store, you'd better call me Mr. Dalton.'' With that, he let go of her hand. But she'd become so caught up in his touch that she let her fingers hang in midair.

Mrs. Lewis coughed softly and Claudia quickly turned and hurried out the door. She glanced back once and found him staring at her, an enigmatic smile on his face. When she reached the safety of the reception area, she drew a shaky breath. If Thomas Dalton knew anything about his Santa's charitable deeds, he wasn't going to give them up easily. But that didn't mean Claudia wasn't going to try. She'd just have to keep him off balance and chip away at that icy reserve. Sooner or later, he'd crack.

No, nothing would stand in the way of getting this story. Not even the handsome and incredibly sexy Thomas Dalton.

"I DON'T KNOW WHY WE CAN'T seem to find good elves. That last one you hired was—"

"I didn't hire him," Tom said distractedly, "Robbins did. He seemed to think since the candidate was short and had a rosy nose he was eminently qualified. He failed to notice the smell of whiskey on his breath, which caused the red nose. If you're so determined to continue with this, you really should interview your own elves, Grandfather."

Tom's grandfather, Theodore Dalton, shook his head, his thick silver hair falling down in a wave on his forehead. "I can't be bothered with personnel matters. Besides, you have plenty of time to take care of these things for me, Tommy. It's not like you have a social life."

Tom groaned inwardly. Sure, he had plenty of time. He'd been stuck in Schuyler Falls for the past seven years, learning the ins and outs of retailing and waiting for the day when his grandfather and father would transfer him to the Manhattan office of Dalton Enterprises. He could run the store in his sleep, yet he couldn't under-stand why he was still banished to the smallest holding in Dalton's vast list of assets.

"As far as I'm concerned, we should put an end to this business," Tom muttered. "If you want to give your money away, Grandfather, then do it outside the auspices of the store. You have your own foundation. This scheme has gone on far too long and it gets more complicated and time-consuming every year."

They strolled through the housewares department, both of them walking with their hands clasped behind them, aware of all they passed. Dalton's Department Store was a throwback to a time long gone, a time when every town of a certain size had a department store, run by a local family. His great-grandfather had spared no expense, the wide aisles paved with terrazzo floors, the walls of deep mahogany and smelling of lemon oil. Most of the em-ployees had been with the store for their entire adult lives, lending a deep sense of tradition and permanence to Dalton's.

Dalton's was also supposed to be the first step up the ladder of the family empire, a job that would lead to greater things. Tom's father, Tucker Dalton, had run the store in his younger days and now worked out of New York City, watching over the real estate and financial holdings of the family. Various uncles and cousins held executive positions. And Tom's grandfather, now retired, spent winters at his home in Arizona, returning north only for the holiday season and his secret passion for playing Santa. Tom was the only one still stuck out in the boon-ies.

His grandfather cleared his throat. "Tell me some-thing, Tommy. How long has it been since you've had a woman?"

Tom gasped and stopped in the middle of the aisle. "What did you say?"

"A woman. How long since you had sex? Don't worry, you can tell me. I'm very discreet."

"What does that have to do with anything?"

His grandfather shrugged. "Actually, nothing. I was just curious. At my age you get curious."

"I'm not going to talk to you about my sex life! The problem is not sex, the problem is boredom. Grandfather, I can do this job in my sleep. You know that. I've maximized profits, improved marketing and streamlined merchandising. Why not send me down?"

"There are many things still to do here and I'm not sure you're ready to move on. If you're bored, I'm sure you'll find ways to keep yourself occupied."

In truth, Tom *had* found something—or someone—to pique his interest. His mind conjured up an image of Claudia Moore, as it had so many times since they'd met, her face appearing in his mind, the sparkling eyes and mischievous smile. "Robbins hired a new elf yesterday and she starts this afternoon," he said, anxious to change the subject. "She's very pretty."

His grandfather stopped near a display of blenders and stared at Tom. "Pretty? How pretty?"

Tom hesitated. Had he said that out loud? He usually wasn't one to verbalize his thoughts but Claudia Moore had an uncanny knack for making him say and do things quite out of character. That tart tongue of hers had the ability to both charm and disarm him. "Very," he replied, keeping his tone blasé. "She has a nice figure. And dark hair that curls around her face." Her image came into sharper focus. "And she has an...enchanting smile. And lovely eyes."

"What color?"

He shrugged. "An odd mixture of brown and gold. I'd call them amber. Very...captivating."

"It seems you know this elf quite well." His grandfather clucked his tongue and waved a finger at Tom. "Don't forget the first rule of retailing at Dalton's," he teased. "Rule number one. Never—"

"I know, I know. Never get mixed up with the help," Tom finished. Not that he'd ever been tempted before. But Claudia Moore had already tested his resistance in that area. After just one meeting, he'd wanted to get to know her better, to spend a little more time trading witty remarks and clever comebacks. He enjoyed the challenge.

"No, that's not rule number one," Theodore said. "That's rule number three. Rule number one is never pass up a chance to charm a beautiful woman. That's how I met your grandmother, you know. She was standing behind the candy counter wearing a cute paper hat and a Dalton's striped apron. She smiled at me, I smiled at her, and the rest is history."

"I'm not going to socialize with an elf," Tom said, doubting his own words before he even said them. "Or an employee. I know better than that." But he could have a little fun with her while she was here, couldn't he? Just to help him pass the time.

His grandfather stopped at a table of linen napkins and carefully straightened the arrangement before moving on. Then his attention turned to a display of candles across the aisle. "Just don't dip your wick in the company ink, Tommy, that's all you have to remember."

Tom chuckled. "I'll be sure to do my wick-dipping outside the store."

"By the way," Theodore murmured. "I'm taking a trip into the city a week from Friday."

"Oh, no," Tom warned. "You can't just slip news like

that by me so I won't notice. I'm not going to do it, Grandfather. I'm not putting on that suit and sitting on that silly chair all day long listening to a bunch of babbling children with toys on the brain.''

When Theodore Dalton didn't like what he was hearing, he usually refused to listen, a trait he'd passed on to his grandson. ''Playing Santa is part of our family tradition, an eighty-year tradition I take very seriously. I did it, your father has done it and now you will. It builds character and it defines who we are. And when your grandson is running this store, you'll be glad of his help every now and then. Besides, this will give you more time with that enchanting little elf.'' His grandfather glanced at his watch, then excused himself to get ready for his duties as Santa Claus.

Tom watched him hurry off, then sighed deeply. He truly loved his grandfather, but he couldn't understand his devotion to this silly Santa tradition. He knew the story. The year the store opened, great-grandfather Thaddeus Dalton decided that financial success needed to be tempered with humility. It was always best to remember those whose lives weren't easy. So Thaddeus became the first Dalton Santa to grant secret wishes and continued until his death in 1988. And he believed it was crude to brag about charitable gifts, so the secrecy became part of the tradition.

Back in the 1920s, an envelope of cash beneath the front door was impossible to trace. But lately, the Christmas wishes were becoming far too elaborate, with so many outside people involved. Sooner or later someone would talk, interested in the media attention the revelation would bring. Tom had urged his grandfather to use the money in a more efficient way, to donate a lump sum to a worthy cause in Schuyler Falls, to buy computers for the school or a new wing for the library. His grandfather did both, but still refused to give up his work as Santa.

Tom could tolerate the whole idea of secrecy, but certainly not when he got drawn into playing Santa. After all, as general manager of the store he had a reputation to protect! What if his employees recognized him behind the voluminous beard and the padded suit? Would they still respect him? He cursed softly. If Claudia Moore was any example, he'd have cause to worry.

"That elf," he muttered. He'd never met anyone quite like her, never experienced such instant attraction or nagging irritation. She was like a very beautiful...mosquito!

Maybe his grandfather was right—he'd been too long without a woman. Since his engagement had fizzled three years ago, Tom had barely bothered with a social life. Schuyler Falls was a small town and most of the single women in it considered him a prime catch, pursuing him ruthlessly at every social event he attended.

He'd had a few brief affairs since he'd broken his engagement, the relationships based more on physical gratification than real emotion. But lately, he wanted something more. Not just sex, as his grandfather had suggested, but something much deeper. He wanted a woman who could hold his interest outside the bedroom, an independent woman who challenged him, who made every day interesting.

When he reached the reception area outside his office, he stopped at Mrs. Lewis's desk and picked up his messages, flipping through them quickly. Then he tossed them back on her desk, causing Mrs. Lewis to regard him with a concerned eye.

"Is there anything I can do for you, Mr. Dalton?"

Tom paused, then nodded. "Would you bring me the

personnel file for Claudia Moore? Robbins should probably have it on his desk.''

Her eyebrow arched. "Isn't she the elf we hired yesterday?"

"Tell him I'd like her work schedule as well."

Mrs. Lewis's concern now swung to unabashed curiosity. "Is there a problem?"

Tom shook his head. "No problem. Just bring me the file."

He'd barely settled in behind his desk when Mrs. Lewis bustled in with the requested file. She held it out to him with a disapproving expression. He'd known Estelle Lewis since he was just a kid, when she was hired as his grandfather's secretary, then worked for his father. She was more like a favorite aunt to Tom than an employee. "Don't look at me like that. We hired her. I always review the personnel files of our new hires."

"Only after I remind you seven or eight times. Remember the first rule of retailing at Dalton's?"

"It's the third rule now. Grandfather changed the order."

Mrs. Lewis gasped, appalled by the news. "I wasn't informed. Why wasn't I informed?"

Tom chuckled. "You can discuss that with Grandfather. You know where to find him."

She sniffed, then turned on her heel and stalked out the door. Tom had no doubt she'd have a few choice words for Theodore Dalton, but he wasn't going to worry about that now. Instead he flipped open the file. The first thing he found was a copy of the photo from Claudia's store ID. He picked it up and studied it intently.

Even in such a poor photo, he was reminded of her fresh-faced beauty. She didn't wear much makeup and her shoulder-length dark hair was styled in a practical yet careless manner. He'd only seen her once, but already knew her fashion sense stood quite a distance left of conservative. But the photograph didn't hint at the depth of her personality, her scathing wit, her talent for setting him off balance, her incredible disdain for his ego.

What was a smart and beautiful woman doing working as a lowly elf? From her educational background alone, she'd be qualified for any number of jobs on the sales floor or maybe even in the corporate offices. Why spend her days working at what he considered the most menial job in the store?

Tom grabbed her schedule and noticed that Claudia was due to start work at noon. Perhaps he'd wander down to the second floor and inspect the North Pole Village. He'd managed to avoid the chaos in the toy department since Santa had arrived the day after Thanksgiving. But now there was something much more interesting to see than crying children and impatient parents and frazzled sales associates, something to alleviate the tedium. There was Claudia Moore, his very intriguing elf.

"I HAVE TO WEAR *THIS*?"

Claudia stared into a full-length mirror in the employee locker room behind the toy department. She adjusted the close-fitting bodice of her jacket and tugged on the short skirt, but it still pricked at her skin. The elf costume had to be at least forty years old, hand-tailored of itchy red wool with giant green polka dots, smelling of mothballs. All this over baggy green tights.

"It's darling, isn't it?"

Claudia turned to gape at her immediate supervisor, Mrs. Eunice Perkins, the elderly woman who ran Dalton's toy department. Just the thought of working as an elf was humiliating enough, but wearing the costume would be pure torture. "There has to be something else I can wear. Something in a nice purple silk? Even polyester would be acceptable."

Mrs. Perkins withdrew a silly little tasseled hat from the garment bag and shoved it on Claudia's head, adjusting it to a rakish angle. Now she looked like she'd just stepped out of a Christmas production of Robin Hood. "Mrs. Theodore Dalton designed these costumes when we added elves in 1949," Eunice explained. "I was just a salesclerk back then, right out of high school. It was after the war and all the soldiers were coming home. It was an exciting time."

She dove back into the bag and retrieved a pair of shoes with upswept toes and jingle bells around the cuff. "Here are your booties, dear. And your name tag. Whenever you're out on the sales floor, you'll be known as Twinkie. You're part of the 'Inkie' crew. Twinkie, Winkie, Dinkie and Blinkie." Eunice dropped to one knee and helped Claudia slip into the little shoes, then stood and hurried out of the locker room.

"Twinkie?" Claudia followed hard on Eunice's heels, into the adjoining lunch room. "Like the snack cake?" she inquired.

"It helps maintain the illusion for the children. Visiting Santa should be a magical thing."

Claudia caught up to her, unused to the pace that most of the sales associates maintained, a businesslike march with arms pumping. "I won't actually have to deal with children, will I? I mean, I'm not very good around them. And the truth be told, I'd rather just tidy up around the Gingerbread Cottage, maybe patrol the North Pole Village, run errands for Santa."

Eunice stopped and turned to her. "What fun would that be? You'll mind the Candy Cane Gate, dear. Allow one child through the gate at a time and try to entertain a bit if you can. Tell a few jokes, sing a few songs. We don't want any crabby children sitting on Santa's lap.''

"Speaking of Santa," Claudia began. "What do you know about him?''

"Just the usual. He lives at the North Pole with Mrs. Claus and the elves. He has a sleigh and eight reindeer. He's a jolly old fellow with—''

"No, no, no," Claudia interrupted. "I mean, what do you know about the real man under the costume? Who is he?''

"Dalton's Santa *is* the real Santa, dear! And don't you let anyone else tell you otherwise.'' Eunice winked, her eyes glittering with amusement. "Now lace up your booties and meet me out on the sales floor. I'll introduce you to the other 'Inkies.'''

Left alone in the lunch room, Claudia could do nothing more than scratch…and whine at the pitiful state of her journalism career. Reduced to prancing around in an elf outfit, reduced to being called "Twinkie" by irritating children. Claudia yanked her elf jacket up, then scratched her stomach, moaning in relief as the itching stopped.

"Miss Moore?''

Claudia spun around at the sound of the familiar voice. But she didn't bother to cover her midriff, even when Tom Dalton's gaze drifted in the direction of her naked stomach. Why should she be embarrassed? She did her sit-ups every night. And what better way to keep him off balance than allowing him an unobstructed view of her belly button. "The name's Twinkie," she muttered, reaching around to scratch her back, the fabric of her jacket pulling tight against her breasts.

His gaze flickered for a moment as it rose to her chest,

then jumped up to her face. "You look like a very un-happy elf."

Maybe she didn't look happy on the outside, but she was certainly pleased to see him. She wondered when he'd come looking for her. After their interview, she'd sensed that he'd enjoyed their verbal sparring. Claudia had a keen insight into human nature and she could tell Tom Dalton was interested, if not highly attracted. And she could use that to her advantage.

"You know, it's no wonder you're advertising for elves," she said. "These costumes should be outlawed. In addition to my wool allergy, my boots are too tight and I think the moths have made a home in my hat." She wasn't going to add that she'd managed to find out nothing in regard to her story, not one single bit of in-formation in twenty-four hours.

"I think you look very elfin."

She scratched her shoulder, noticing the slight smile he tried to hide. "If you came here just to laugh at me, you might as well be of some use while you're doing it." She turned and presented her back to him. "Scratch."

"Miss Moore, I really don't think—"

"Oh, just do it!" she cried, impatient. "Before I go crazy."

With hesitant fingers, he reached out and raked his fingernails between her shoulder blades. Her eyes drifted shut and Claudia sighed, leaning into his touch, enjoying the feel of his hands. "These outfits are fifty years old. Couldn't you afford something more comfortable for your employees? To the right...now up a bit...there, right there."

Tom cleared his throat, then did as he was told. "The

costumes are a tradition,'' he said, his voice somber. ''And no one's ever complained.''

''They were probably afraid you'd fire them. If we elves had a union, this never would have happened.'' She arched her neck, caught up in the delicious patterns Tom's fingers drew across her back. His hands moved to her shoulders, the scratching giving way to a gentle massage. It had been so long since anyone had rubbed her back...so long since a man had touched her...so long since—

Her eyes snapped open and she stiffened slightly. This would not do! At all costs, she had to keep her objectivity. Even when faced with a scratchy old elf costume and a handsome back scratcher. She stepped away from him, then turned around and gave him a nervous smile.

His eyes met hers, his green gaze penetrating, discerning, shrewd. ''What about you, Miss Moore? Aren't you afraid I'll fire you?''

''For what reason?'' Claudia asked. ''An allergy to wool?''

''For insubordination,'' Tom replied with a sardonic smile. ''For failing to show me the proper respect. For making me scratch your back?''

Claudia rolled her eyes. ''Is stroking your ego part of my job description too?''

For the first time since she met him, Thomas Dalton laughed, a warm, rich sound that washed over her in wave after wave. ''And do you ever think before you speak, Miss Moore? Or are you as surprised as I am by what comes out of your mouth?''

Claudia straightened her outfit, adjusted her hat, then grinned at him. ''If it bothers you, Tom, you can always fire me.''

He nodded, his arms crossed over in front of him. She

noticed the way his shirt hugged his chest, wondered what his body was like beneath the business attire. Shoulder pads and a good cut on a suit could only do so much.

"Why an elf, Miss Moore? I read your personnel file. You have a college degree, some experience as a freelance writer. You're probably qualified for any number of positions here at Dalton's."

"I need the money," she lied. "I've got Christmas gifts to buy and bills to pay. I figured my chances of getting this job were pretty good. A girl doesn't need a post-graduate degree to wear this outfit."

"Why don't you let me look for a different position for you? We always need sales help. And the pay is better."

"Why? Are you ashamed to be seen scratching a lowly elf's back, Tom?"

He shook his head. "I'd prefer that you addressed me as Mr. Dalton."

Claudia shrugged. "We've discussed your choice of underwear. It's a little hard putting you on a pedestal while I'm thinking about you in silk boxer shorts, no pastels." She stepped around him and headed toward the door to the sales floor.

"Miss Moore!" His voice echoed off the high ceiling.

Startled, she glanced back over her shoulder to find him staring at her, a scowl furrowing his brow. Claudia winced inwardly, chiding herself for her plain talk. Good grief, would she ever learn to control her mouth? One of these times, she'd push him too far. "Yes, Mr. Dalton?"

"I'll have new costumes made immediately. Please let Mrs. Perkins and the rest of the elves know."

She turned back to the door and smiled smugly. It seemed she had Mr. Thomas Dalton exactly where she wanted him—wrapped around her little elfin finger. Now all she had to do was figure out a way to get him to reveal all his family secrets. Once she did that, Claudia Moore would be able to put her elf days behind her and resume her career as a serious journalist.

2

CLAUDIA SHIFTED FROM FOOT to foot, her toes cramping and her thin-soled elf booties offering precious little arch support. She had glanced at her watch at least fifty times over the past hour, but that hadn't made the time go any faster. Instead the day had been measured child by child, reduced to opening and closing the Candy Cane Gate like a traffic cop. She ushered a chubby little kid through the gate, then turned to the next customer in line, a boy with golden-blond hair and huge brown eyes.

"Hey, kid. You're next," she muttered.

He blinked, then hesitantly looked up at her. Claudia groaned inwardly at the nervous expression on his face. She'd been sneezed on, drooled on and cried on already today. She wasn't sure what this kid was up to, but from his expression, it looked like he was about to require CPR—or smelling salts.

Talking to children had never been her strong suit. They weren't interested in discussing current events, they had a rather limited vocabulary and they didn't appreciate her caustic sense of humor. She'd never really had many childhood pals, so it was no wonder she couldn't relate.

"So," she said, hoping to calm his nerves, "what are you going to ask for?"

He frowned, his chin set stubbornly. "I think that's between me and Santa," the kid replied.

Claudia laughed. This was a first. Usually the kids

couldn't wait to recount their Christmas lists to anyone who'd listen, especially one so closely connected with the big guy. "Ah, the old Santa-kid confidentiality agreement."

The frown turned to a scowl. "Huh?"

Claudia sighed. "Never mind." After an entire day of talking to kids, she should have learned that if she wanted a laugh, she'd just have to repeat the Rudolph joke she heard from a runny-nosed six-year-old.

"Do you know him pretty well?"

Claudia shrugged. "As well as any elf," she said. The truth be told, Claudia hadn't gotten past basic introductions with Santa. The top elves stood next to him, chatting as they placed children on his lap, and protecting him like secret service agents. As a junior elf, Claudia was relegated to the area outside the Candy Cane Gate, a distance that precluded any probing questions or innocent eavesdropping.

"Maybe you could give me some tips," the kid said. He pulled a letter from his pocket, sealed in a bright green envelope and covered with Christmas stickers. She saw his name and address scrawled in the upper left corner. "I really need him to read my letter. It's very, very, *very* important." Then he pulled a huge Gobstopper out of his other pocket and held it out to her. "Do you think if I gave him—"

The gesture was incredibly sweet, but Claudia couldn't lie to the boy. "Well, Eric Marrin, I can tell you this. The big guy doesn't accept bribes," she explained.

"But, I—"

"You're up, kid," Claudia said, ushering him through the gate. She watched for a long moment as he hesitantly approached Santa. When he settled on his lap, she turned to the next person in line and tried to appear cheerful, a task made more difficult when she noticed Tom Dalton lurking near the Sesame Street Christmas display.

She'd seen him three times that day, passing by, checking out the action at the North Pole Village, watching her. According to the other elves, he'd never paid much attention to them before. By the end of the afternoon, they'd all managed to get their green tights in a bundle, wondering which of them was about to be fired.

The tension was almost unbearable and Claudia assumed she was the cause. She motioned to Blinkie, the only male elf in Claudia's crew, and asked him to take over at the gate. Then Claudia adjusted her costume, hiked up her tights, and made a beeline for the spot where Tom Dalton stood, her shoes jingling with every step.

He seemed surprised to see her coming and, for a moment, Claudia thought he was about to take off. But he stood his ground, watching her indifferently as she approached, the only clue to his feelings the subtle arch of his eyebrow and the tight set of his shoulders.

"You're making the elves nervous," Claudia said, stopping in front of him, her arms braced on her hips. "Do you think you might loiter up in ladies' lingerie instead? I hear they have a new shipment of lace garter belts to peruse."

"Excuse me?"

"Hanging around like this. The elves are nervous. If you're watching for me to make a mistake so you can fire me, then why don't you just get it over with? Give me the ax, send me my pink slip, give me the old heave-ho."

He paused for a moment before he spoke, measuring his thoughts carefully. "Miss Moore, this is my store. If I choose to stand here all day long, it's my right. If I choose to hang from the top of the Dalton's Christmas tree and sing 'Frosty the Snowman' at the top of my lungs, then I can. And nothing you or the rest of the elves say will make any difference.''

''So, are you going to fire me before or after the *thumpity thump thump* part?'' she asked.

With a soft curse, Tom grabbed her elbow and steered her past the Tonka trucks toward the far end of the sales floor. When they reached the elevator, the doors opened and he gently pushed her forward. ''Get in,'' he muttered.

''Where are we going?'' she asked, looking over her shoulder as she stepped inside.

''You're going to wait in my office,'' he said. ''I'm going to join you there in a few minutes.''

''Your office?''

''You've obviously neglected to read the employee manual, the section on respect for your superiors. We'll review together and then I'll decide on appropriate disciplinary action.''

''Oh, please,'' Claudia said, stepping back out of the elevator. ''Loosen up. I'm an elf. According to the other Inkies, you've been having a hard time hanging on to help at the North Pole. If you fire me, the rest of the elves are going to have to work overtime and that will cost you money. Money you won't have for your little charitable acts.''

Tom glared at her, his arm braced against the elevator door to keep it from closing. ''What are you talking about?''

Claudia smiled coyly, glad to see she'd touched a nerve. ''Don't play dumb. I've heard all the stories. You shouldn't be ashamed for doing good deeds. You should shout it from the rooftops.''

''I've heard the same stories and believe me, Miss

Moore, I'd love to tell you who's behind those Christmas wishes. But it's not me.''

She felt a stab of disappointment mixed with a healthy dose of frustration. There was no deceit in his expression. But if he didn't know, then who did? She'd spent an entire day at Dalton's and wasn't any closer to the truth. Maybe she'd have to take the elves out and ply them with liquor to loosen their tongues. Or follow Santa home at night and see the real man behind the white beard. ''Aren't you even a bit curious?'' she asked. ''I mean, if it's not you giving away all that cash, then you're getting great press for nothing.''

He gently took her shoulders and pushed her back into the elevator. ''Wait in my office. I'll be up in a few minutes.''

With that, the elevator doors closed between them. Claudia leaned back against the mirrored wall of the ancient elevator and frowned. He couldn't possibly mean to fire her, could he? She'd only worked at the store for a day and she hadn't really done anything wrong. No, this time he'd just warn her.

The elevator doors opened a few seconds later and Claudia stepped out into the reception area of the corporate offices. Mrs. Lewis looked up from her desk, her smile fading slightly as she took in the sight of Claudia in her costume. ''Miss Moore? Is there a problem?''

''Tom—I mean, Mr. Dalton sent me up. I'm supposed to wait in his office.''

Mrs. Lewis stepped out from behind her desk, then motioned Claudia to follow her. For the second time in her short career with Dalton's, Claudia found herself staring across the wide mahogany desk. When Mrs. Lewis stepped out of the office and closed the door behind her, Claudia slumped back in her chair. Her mind replayed her last encounter with Tom and she tried to unravel the meaning beneath his words.

He was attracted to her, that much was certain. Claudia knew enough about men to recognize that look in his eyes—the curiosity mixed with appreciation. But her experience with men was sadly lacking. After the initial attraction, six months of dating—including occasional sex—had always been her limit. Right around that time the men she'd known began to expect more. The future would inevitably come up and they'd demand more time and attention, something Claudia was unwilling to give. Her career came first and she had no intention of easing into the role of "wife."

But somehow, she sensed Tom didn't fit the usual profile of men attracted to her. He was different... exciting...unpredictable. The kind of man who expected more from a woman than just companionship and the ability to do large quantities of laundry.

She twisted in her chair and glanced at the door, impatient with waiting. When she turned back around, her gaze idly scanned his desk, wondering at how he bothered to keep it so organized. The guy was a real control freak. His pencils were all perfectly sharpened and his file folders all color-coded with those little tabs that...

Claudia slowly pushed from her chair and leaned over the desk. File folders! If he knew anything about the Dalton's Santa, it would have to be here in his office. She glanced back at the door again then began to rifle through the stack of folders placed neatly in the corner of his desk. "Keep calm," she murmured to herself. "You've got three, maybe four minutes. Just focus and make sure you put everything back the way you found it."

After thirty seconds, she'd managed to sort through everything on the surface of the desk. A minute later, she'd covered all the desk drawers with no results. She glanced up at the clock on the wall, then turned to Tom Dalton's credenza, finding a key for the file drawer in his desk. With shaking hands, Claudia pushed the key into the lock and opened the drawer. Her gaze scanned the colored tabs, then froze at the one marked Santa.

She bent down and reached for the folder. "So you don't know anything about your Santa, do you, Mr. Dalton?" But she'd barely pulled the file from the drawer when she heard Mrs. Lewis's muffled voice through the office door. With a soft curse, Claudia shoved the folder back in its place, slammed the drawer closed and flipped the lock. But as she scrambled to put the key back in his desk, she found herself caught, unable to move. She'd locked the hem of her skirt in the drawer!

"Hold all my calls, Mrs. Lewis," Tom ordered from the other side of the door.

Claudia tugged frantically on her skirt, her heart slamming in her chest. If he caught her like this, breaking and entering, her career as an elf, *and* as a journalist, was history. "Come on," she murmured, yanking at the old moth-eaten wool. The sound of tearing fabric split the silence just as the doorknob rattled. Claudia felt herself grow dizzy with fear, fear that she might just faint on the spot.

Then the door opened and Tom Dalton stepped inside.

THE OFFICE WAS EMPTY when Tom opened the door. He expected to find Claudia waiting, dressed in her little elf costume, the fabric hugging her pretty figure. But his office was empty. He frowned, then turned back to Mrs. Lewis. "I thought you said Miss Moore was in here."

The secretary frowned, rising from her chair. "I put

her in your office. I've been here the entire time. She couldn't have left.''

Tom cursed beneath his breath and raked his fingers through his hair. Now he'd have to hunt her down and drag her back. Good grief, the woman had absolutely no notion of responsibility, no clue as to her place in the employee hierarchy! Had she been any other elf, he would have fired her on the spot. He strode across the office and circled his desk, then stumbled. Catching himself on the back of his chair, Tom glanced down to find Claudia kneeling on the floor. ''Miss Moore?''

She glanced up at him and forced a smile. ''Hi! I was just—I'm sorry, I didn't mean to—'' She cleared her throat. ''I lost my tinkle.''

''Your tinkle?''

She nodded. ''One of my bells. From my shoe. I was sitting in my chair waiting for you and—whoops!—it just flew off and rolled under your desk. Regulation elf uniform requires the requisite number of tinkling bells on each boot and if Mrs. Perkins sees me like this she'll—''

Tom sighed impatiently, then reached down to take her hand, pulling her to her feet. ''I'm sure Mrs. Perkins can find you another bell.''

Squeezed between the desk and the credenza, he was acutely aware of how close they stood. Close enough to feel the warmth from her body, to catch the subtle scent of her hair. For a long moment, neither one of them moved, their gazes locked. Tom fought the impulse to kiss her right then and there, to test that perfect mouth and see if it tasted as sweet as it looked.

But instead, he pushed the thought aside and took a step back. ''Go ahead,'' he said. ''You can look for your bell.''

Claudia blinked, her lips parted slightly. ''My what?''

she asked, her voice breathless. "Oh, yes. My bell." She dropped to her knees and peered under Tom's desk, then a few seconds later, scrambled back to her feet. "Found it." Claudia held out her hand and showed him the jingle bell, the threads from her shoe still clinging to it.

He rubbed his hands together and gave her a curt nod. "Fine, then. We can get down to business. Please, have a seat, Miss Moore."

Claudia quickly did as she was told, perching on the edge of the chair and staring at him from across the desk. It was the first hint of compliance he'd seen from her since they'd met. He stared at her for a long moment, then forced himself to drag his gaze away. She was far too pretty for her own good.

Tom snatched up an employee evaluation form from a file folder and scribbled her name across the top. It would be best to carry on this meeting by the numbers. Maybe then, he'd be able to keep his thoughts in line. "Usually Mr. Robbins handles personnel problems, but since your problem seems to be with me, I thought we should talk directly."

"I'm a problem?" Claudia asked, her eyebrow arching, her humor tweaked.

In more ways than one, Tom mused, ignoring the smile quirking at the corners of her mouth. She was baiting him again, testing his resolve. Was she a problem? Sure. But Tom wasn't nearly as bothered by her behavior on the job as he was by the effect she seemed to have on his body and his brain.

He couldn't deny the current that crackled between them. Though Tom couldn't be bothered to flirt, Claudia was obviously an expert at the art, drawing him into a subtle yet intriguing confrontation every time they met, pricking his ego and taunting him with witty wordplay.

"Your attitude toward superiors could show improvement."

"Are you going to fire me?" she asked, peering up at him through thick, dark lashes.

"Do you think I should fire you?" he countered.

"No," she said stubbornly, leaning back in her chair and crossing her arms over her chest. "I'm a good elf! And you know it!"

"You refuse to call me Mr. Dalton," he said.

"Tom is your name. What's wrong with calling you by your name? It would be different if I were calling you butthead or spaz or dipstick."

"Dipstick?"

She grinned. "Usually reserved for people of limited intellect and sophistication," she muttered. "Which isn't you," Claudia quickly added. She cleared her throat. "I suppose I could try to remember to call you Mr. Dalton when there are others around."

"We're employer and employee, Miss Moore. You should call me Mr. Dalton at *all* times."

Her defiant expression gradually gave way to grudging acceptance. But Tom knew he'd won a hollow victory. Though they could maintain the illusion of a business relationship, they both knew there was more between them, interest simmering just below the surface, the gentle banter that hid their real feelings. Forcing her to call him Mr. Dalton would not change anything.

"I'm sorry," she said softly. "Will that be all, **Mr.** Dalton?"

He nodded. "I won't make note of this in your file, Miss Moore. Consider this a warning."

She slowly rose and his gaze drifted down her body, to her tiny waist cinched in by her wool jacket, to the gentle curve of her hips and her shapely legs hidden by baggy tights. Tom swallowed hard. "You should really get back to work. They're probably wondering where you are."

He got up and circled his desk, then accompanied her to the door. She stopped just as he reached for the knob and turned to him. His breath caught in his throat as he gazed down into her beautiful face, her tantalizing lips and her penetrating gaze. If he thought the challenge was gone, he was wrong, for he found it there, in her eyes.

"I promise I'll try to be a little bit more circumspect, Mr. Dalton," she said, in a deceptively seductive voice. "My behavior will be above reproach, Mr. Dalton. And I want you to know, Mr. Dalton, that I really do appreciate the opportunity to be an elf and I know sometimes, I have a tendency to say what I'm thinking but—"

Tom wasn't sure what made him do it. Maybe it was frustration at her lack of compliance, the silly repetition of his name, or the smug little smile that curled the corners of her mouth. Or maybe it was the thought of tasting her lips just once. But rather than let her continue, he grabbed her by the arms, pulled her against him and covered her mouth with his.

The kiss was startling in its intensity, for she didn't fight him, didn't even attempt to pull away. She sank against his body, pressing her palms to his chest and opening her mouth beneath his assault. Every shred of common sense told him to stop, but he found himself caught in a vortex of sensation. The sweet warmth of her mouth, the tiny moans slipping from her throat, they spurred him on until he lost himself completely.

Tom wasn't sure how long the kiss went on, or who finally ended it. But the instant it ended he didn't regret it. Sure, a boss shouldn't passionately kiss an employee. But then an employee shouldn't call her boss by his first name. And neither one of them should have pushed so far. Besides, technically, Claudia wasn't really *his* employee. Her paycheck came out of the TD One Foundation, run by his grandfather. And though Tom had hired her, only his grandfather had final authority to fire her.

She stared up at him, her eyebrow arched curiously. "Mr. Dalton, I—"

"Oh, hell, call me Tom," he murmured, stroking her cheek with his fingertips.

"Tom." She drew in a ragged breath. "What was that for?"

His attention was firmly fixed on her mouth and, for a moment, he considered kissing her again. But he'd leave that for another time. He sensed it was best to quit while *he* was ahead. Tom reached around her and opened the door. Gently he turned her around and pushed her into the reception area. "I do believe I've finally found a way to render you speechless. If you leave now, you'll be able to make it back from your break without having any of your pay docked."

He closed the door behind her before she had a chance to grab the last word. With a soft chuckle, Tom strolled back to his desk and flopped down in his chair. Now the game was getting interesting. Like a game of chess, the power had shifted again and he'd just put Claudia Moore in check. And after her rather lusty response to his kiss, he didn't think she'd have the sense to counter his move anytime soon.

Tom glanced at the clock. Usually his days dragged on and on, but today the time had gone surprisingly fast. Though he didn't want to credit Claudia Moore, he had to admit she made things much more interesting at Dalton's.

As he scooped up the files piled neatly on his desk, he

idly replayed in his mind the kiss they'd just shared. He pulled open his desk drawer and reached for his credenza key, then stopped short when he realized that it wasn't where he'd left it, in the little compartment on the far left. He always put the key there. Tom frowned, then pushed his intercom button. "Mrs. Lewis, did you use the key to my credenza?"

Her voice came back at him immediately. "No, sir. I've got my own key."

He sat back and shook his head. He always kept the key...Tom reached out and picked through the pens and paper clips in his desk drawer. He found the missing key mixed in with the paper clips. Chiding himself for misplacing it, Tom turned to unlock the credenza. But as he pulled the drawer open, a tiny piece of paper fluttered to the floor.

He reached down and picked it up, only to find that it wasn't paper at all, but a scrap of red wool fabric—fabric he found all too familiar. The same kind of fabric that made up Claudia's elf costume. Had she taken his key and opened his files? If she had, what was she looking for?

With a soft curse, he shoved the files into the drawer and slammed it shut, suspicion nagging at his mind. Suddenly their little game had taken on a whole new facet. What did he really know about Claudia Moore, besides the fact that he enjoyed kissing her? His first instinct had been to question why such a bright and confident woman would choose to be a Santa's elf. But his instant attraction to her had overwhelmed his instincts and he hadn't given it a second thought—until now.

"Just what are you up to?" he murmured, leaning back into his chair. He ran all the possibilities through his mind, then felt a smile tug at one corner of his mouth. "Whatever it is, I'm sure going to have fun finding out."

CLAUDIA HAD ALWAYS LOVED Christmas music, but she drew the line at dogs barking out the melody to 'Jingle Bells.' Unfortunately, the patrons at Hooligan's Bar and Grill, a noisy little spot just around the town square from Dalton's, thought differently. The song seemed to be the only choice on the jukebox that evening, a choice that her three companions chose to support with their own hard-earned quarters.

The atmosphere at the North Pole Village had been a little tense all day long. The Inkie elves had been surprised when she turned up at work that morning, certain that she'd been fired the evening before. But Claudia reassured them that everything was fine between her and Tom Dalton. She wondered if they saw the lie in her eyes, or the faint blush that warmed her cheeks at the thought of the kiss she'd shared with her boss, because the elves hadn't been satisfied with her vague assurances and evasive nature.

Instead they plied her for information about Dalton, his intentions, his mood, his regard for their jobs. Ever the quick thinker, Claudia decided she'd use their curiosity to her advantage and buy herself time to put her own thoughts in order. She invited them out after work for happy hour, promising to fill them in on all her keen insight into the enigmatic Mr. Dalton.

In truth, the smooch they shared had offered her a few startling new revelations. Most importantly, Tom Dalton had a particular talent for kissing, the simple touch of his lips and soft warmth of his tongue causing her pulse to race and her toes to curl, even twenty-four hours later.

Claudia could still recall with such clarity the moment

when his mouth first covered hers that her heart started pounding all over again. She had to admit, unexpected as the kiss had been, she enjoyed every moment. She'd never even considered pulling away and slapping his face. Instead she did what came naturally—she just closed her eyes and enjoyed the sensation of his lips on hers.

She reached out and snatched up her gin and tonic, taking a big gulp, then stifling a cough. How much longer was this memory going to bounce around in her head? She'd never had this experience before, never known a man's kiss to affect her so deeply. Perhaps it was just the shock of such an intimacy with her boss. She'd expected him to throw her out of his office, not reach out and yank her into his arms.

The balance of power between them had definitely shifted. She no longer felt as if she could control the situation and was concerned that her journalistic integrity had been seriously compromised. She'd kept her eye out for Tom all day long, ready to seize power once again and put their relationship back in its proper perspective. But he'd been curiously absent from the sales floor, robbing her of the opportunity.

Claudia had been tempted to visit his office, but when she reexamined her motives, she realized that she didn't want to confront him about the kiss—she wanted to *repeat* the kiss, over and over and over again, until she was breathless with desire. With a silent oath, she finished her drink and looked for the waitress to order another.

Though she'd had only one, her co-workers hadn't shown as much restraint. Elves, when released from the confines of the North Pole, had an odd tendency to cut loose. The Inkie crew had already gone through two rounds and were on a third before the jukebox changed to a version of "White Christmas" sung by barnyard animals. The only saving grace was that she could write the entire tab off on her expense account—that is, if she ever got the story.

"So tell me," Claudia began. "Have you heard the stories about Dalton's Santa?"

"That Santa," Winkie muttered, her words slurred from the boilermakers she'd so recently guzzled. The chubby middle-aged elf was a divorced mother of two grown boys and had a rather jaded opinion of the pecking order at the Pole. She could also outcurse a sailor and smoked like a chimney. "I don't trust him. He's got shifty eyes."

"I think he wears contacts," Dinkie said, taking a healthy sip of her martini. A diminutive grandmotherly figure, Dinkie was proving herself to be the elfin equivalent of a space cadet. "My daughter wears contacts."

"Soft or hard?" Blinkie asked. The youngest of the bunch, Blinkie was a college senior who favored piercing, tattoos, and a vivid black Goth haircut that gave him the look of the North Pole's resident vampire. He chuckled. "I like hard. They hurt more."

"I saw that movie *Contact*," Winkie said. "I hated that movie."

Claudia groaned. She'd expected this to be easy, the elves so enthusiastic and helpful in the store. But once the costumes came off, so did the attitudes. Time and again, she'd tried to steer their cocktail conversation into some semblance of an interview. But trying to maintain control was like trying to herd a bunch of cats!

"What about the secret gifts?" Claudia said.

"Oh, forget about the gifts," Winkie said. "No one's giving me any money, so why should I care?"

"Speaking of gifts," Dinkie said, "I've been looking for a gift for my—"

"Wait!" Claudia cried, slamming her hands down on the table. "Can we please stick to one subject?"

"Hey, man," Blinkie said, holding out his hands. "Chill."

"Aren't you guys even a little curious?" Claudia asked. "It's such an interesting story. And Santa has to be in on it. He collects the letters so he must know who this mysterious benefactor is."

"I suppose he does," Winkie replied, "but what difference does it make? It's not my money he's giving away."

"Someone must know something. If I could only talk to Santa outside the store, he'd—"

"No one has ever seen him outside the store," Blinkie said as he carved his name onto the top of the table with a pick from Dinkie's olives. "It's like he's a…spirit of the dead."

"What are you talking about?" Claudia asked, shaking her head.

"It's true," Dinkie concurred. "No one has ever seen him out of the suit. He appears every morning from the Gingerbread Cottage and disappears every night through the same door. I think he might live in there."

The elves certainly hadn't been hired for their powers of observation. How could they work with a man for two weeks and not know anything about him? There had to be a real man beneath the suit, a man who might be persuaded to tell his secrets, a man with a life outside his job as Santa. "So who knows?" she asked.

"Dalton knows," Winkie said. "Why don't you ask him? You two seem to be *very* friendly."

Claudia sighed softly. So she was back to square one!

What was this, a conspiracy of silence? The elves couldn't possibly be so obtuse. Maybe they were all part of the scheme. But as she looked around the table at her half-drunk co-workers, she ruled that notion out right away. She didn't work with the sharpest knives in the drawer and if Blinkie, Winkie and Dinkie knew anything, she certainly had the skills to make them spill the beans.

"You two should go out," Dinkie said. "He seems like a nice boy and he hasn't had much luck with women. That whole mess with his fiancée and the—"

Claudia's attention quickly turned back to the conversation. "He had a fiancée?"

"A very pretty girl," Dinkie said. "Her family is very prominent here in Schuyler Falls. They were only three weeks away from the wedding when she canceled it all. She was fed up with the amount of time he devoted to work. Said he wasn't paying enough attention to her needs. Since then, the poor boy has only had a few pathetic affairs."

For obtuse elves, they certainly knew a lot about Tom Dalton's social life! But even though Claudia was curious to learn more about the man who'd kissed her, she'd vowed to keep her mind on her story and nothing else.

When the waitress appeared at the table, Claudia didn't bother ordering another drink. Instead she asked for the check, tossed down a generous tip and slipped out of the booth, leaving the rest of the elves deep in a discussion of the benefits of deodorizing inserts in their elf booties.

The air was crisp and cold as she stepped outside Hooligan's Bar. Christmas lights glittered around the picturesque town square and shoppers crisscrossed the tiny park, stopping to gaze up at the huge lighted Christmas tree in the center. She drew in a deep breath, pulled her coat more tightly around her and set off across the street.

Dalton's was still open, the "Itsy" shift of elves manning the North Pole Village. She looked up at the windows on the fifth floor, wondering whether Tom Dalton was sitting in his office at this very moment, thinking about the kiss they had shared. Somehow, she couldn't see him lapsing into daydreams about their little encounter. He was nothing if not pragmatic.

Claudia smiled to herself. But she had to admit that the kiss had been a bit more than he'd expected. She'd seen it in his expression after she drew away, the astonished look that he quickly hid behind a cool facade. He might pretend the kiss meant nothing, but she knew differently. She knew he found her attractive. And if the elf grapevine were to be believed, he'd been a long time without a woman.

But just as she was letting that thought sink in, Claudia glanced up to see Tom Dalton standing near the Christmas tree at the center of the square, talking to two women. She stopped short, then stepped behind a nearby lamppost to observe the scene. He seemed to be deep in conversation with a strikingly beautiful blonde in an elegant overcoat. The other woman, shorter with curly red hair, stood watching them, clearly not involved in the conversation.

Her gaze went back to the blonde. Who was she? Claudia wondered. An acquaintance? A business associate? Or the newest woman in Tom Dalton's life? They certainly made a handsome pair, both of them exuding confidence and sophistication. Next to the woman's designer clothes, her elf costume would look laughably bizarre.

The conversation came to an abrupt end when Tom handed the woman a large envelope. He then turned on his heel and started in the direction of Claudia's lamppost. She looked around for an escape route, but then at the last minute, decided to appease her curiosity. She stepped out from behind the post, right into his path.

He was so absorbed in his thoughts that he almost didn't notice her. But then he glanced up and stopped abruptly. ''Claudia!''

''Mr. Dalton,'' she said. ''Or should I call you Tom? Since we're outside the store, I'm not sure of the protocol.''

He glanced over his shoulder nervously, then shook his head. ''Maybe it would be best if we got past this name problem,'' he said.

Claudia gave him a coy smile. ''I thought we already had.''

''You're referring to our...''

''Kiss?'' Claudia shrugged. Lord, it was fun to make him squirm. To loosen the buttons on that stuffed shirt of his. ''No, I was referring to your request that I call you Tom. That came right before the kiss. Remember?''

They stood there in the center of the square, the light from the Christmas tree bathing them in a golden glow, pedestrians weaving around them. ''What are you doing here?'' he finally asked.

''Me and the Inkies went out for drinks at Hooligan's. What are you doing here?''

''I was just going to get something to eat. Would you like to join me?''

Claudia was sorely tempted. After all, she hadn't had anything to eat since the Snickers bar she'd inhaled during her lunch break at the store. ''Are you asking me on a date?''

He paused for a moment, then offered an apologetic smile. ''You're right. We should keep our relationship strictly business. What happened before was...an unfortunate lapse.''

Why couldn't she have just accepted his invitation? Why did she always feel compelled to poke at his ego? She could have spent a pleasant evening in his company and maybe learned a little more about the mystery behind this man—the mystery behind her attraction to him. "Anyway," she said. "I'm really not dressed properly." Claudia opened her jacket to reveal her elf outfit.

Tom pulled up the collar of his coat around his neck. "Right. Well then, can I offer you a ride home? My car is parked just off the square."

Claudia stiffened at the offer. She wasn't about to let him know she lived in a boardinghouse just a few blocks away. He might ask questions she wasn't prepared to answer—like why didn't she have an apartment and how long had she lived in Schuyler Falls? Still, she almost caught herself accepting. Why was she tempted to risk everything for a few more moments alone with Tom Dalton?

Claudia shook her head. "No, I don't want to keep you from your dinner."

She waited, wondering if he'd say something else, praying that he'd lean forward and brush a kiss across her lips. But when he didn't, she forced a smile. "Good night, Mr. Dalton," she murmured. With that, Claudia turned and started back on her way. She wanted to turn around to see if he was still standing there, watching her, but she fought the impulse.

Though this felt like an ending of sorts, Claudia knew it was just the beginning. There was so much more between them, more to come. "Oh, you'll be seeing me," Claudia said softly as she walked. "I'm not going anywhere until I get exactly what I want."

But what she wanted was becoming harder to determine. For there were moments when she found herself wanting Tom Dalton a lot more than she wanted her story.

3

—————

"Where is Mrs. Lewis? She always helps me get dressed! Estelle! I need you!"

Tom stood in the doorway of his grandfather's office and watched as the old man wrestled himself into the padded pants of his Santa costume, rolling around on the leather sofa like a big red beached whale. Though he was seventy-five years old, Theodore Dalton still had the wiry, athletic body of a twenty-year-old.

"I sent her to distribute a memo for the buyer's meeting," Tom replied.

His grandfather growled, then cursed. "She washed these damn pants! She's always sending my costume out for cleaning and this time the pants shrunk."

Tom chuckled as he closed the office door. "Maybe you should have them take out a little of the stuffing," he said. "You can use some of your own padding in its place."

He held out his hand and his grandfather struggled to his feet, then patted his stomach right above his waist. "I'm fit as a fiddle and you know it." He sat down on the leather wing chair near the door. "Help me with my boots, Tommy. With this big belly I can't even see my toes." He laughed as he rolled forward and tried to grab his boots. "Now I know how your grandmother felt when she was pregnant with your father. No wonder she got so weepy."

Tom tucked a file folder under his arm, then bent down and gently guided his grandfather's foot into the coal-black knee boots. When he'd finished the job, he sat back on his heels and his grandfather flopped back in the wing chair. "I'm getting too old for this," his grandfather said, dabbing at his brow with a handkerchief. He glanced at Tom. "You look a little tense."

Tom rose and brushed off the finely pressed crease in his pants. "It's nothing. I've just got some things on my mind." In truth, he had one thing on his mind—Claudia Moore.

"You didn't follow my advice then?"

"What advice?"

"Sex. You need a woman, Tommy. That'll get you right back on track. A feminine version of Metamucil. Clears up all your problems. Remember we discussed this the other day?"

Tom sighed. "Will you stop? I'm not interested in sex!" he said. "I—I mean, I'm interested, don't get me wrong."

"Good," his grandfather said. "Because it's awfully hard for me to get great-grandchildren if you're not."

"I just mean I'm through with shallow relationships. I want...I want something more meaningful."

His grandfather nodded. "I see. And where are you going to find this meaningful relationship?"

"How the hell should I know?" he growled.

A silence grew between them as Tom stared at the toes of his wingtips. His outburst had surprised even him. But then his grandfather had always had a knack for getting to the heart of the matter. There wasn't a person on the planet who knew Tom better than Theodore Dalton. And his grandfather could sense the change in him, the restless edge, the underlying confusion—a change that had started when Claudia Moore walked into the store.

"So, how did your meeting with Holly Bennett go?" his grandfather asked. "Did she take the job for the Marrin boy?"

Tom watched as Theodore squinted into the mirror on the back of the door and affixed the beard to his face. "She would have been a fool to turn it down. George drove her out to Stony Creek Farm and he said she's going to be staying out there. She seems to be quite prudent. I don't think she'll reveal who's paying her salary at the Marrins', not that she knows for certain anyway."

His grandfather studied him for a long moment. "I don't suppose she's single?"

Tom groaned. "I'm not interested in Holly Bennett! Claudia Moore's the one I've been—" He stopped, the words dying in his throat. Telling his grandfather about his attraction to Claudia was the worst thing he could possibly do.

"Who's Claudia Moore?"

"You know her as Twinkie. The pretty dark-haired elf who works the gate at the North Pole Village." Tom had a hard time thinking of Claudia Moore as Twinkie, or as an elf for that matter. To him, Claudia had become an endlessly intriguing woman, outspoken, audacious, and undeniably sexy.

His grandfather nodded. "Ah, yes. Twinkie. Nice legs, that one, and very easy on the eyes, though a bit impatient with the children. But she's an employee. You remember our discussion about wicks?"

"I'm not sweet on her," Tom lied. He slowly stood, then handed his grandfather the file folder. "I had security do a background check. She's staying over at the boardinghouse on Longwell Street, paying almost as much per night as she makes in a day working as an elf."

"Hmm. Not very smart," his grandfather replied.

"She's also a freelance journalist, a stringer with the *Albany Journal* and the *New York Times*."

His grandfather pulled his reading glasses out of his Santa jacket and peered at the material gathered. "You know how your father feels about reporters. They've managed to kill a few profitable deals for us by printing stories that were none of their business in the first place."

Tom shrugged. He'd considered keeping the security file to himself, but his judgment regarding Claudia had already proved clouded. And family loyalty was strong enough to counter his growing interest in the elf. "Maybe she just needs a few extra bucks. Maybe she's between assignments."

"Or she might be interested in our Birnamwood deal. Or your father's plans to purchase Cell Tech."

"Or she might be interested in finding out who's behind the TD One Foundation," Tom suggested. "And Dalton's secret Santa."

His grandfather raised a bushy white eyebrow. "After a secret Santa story? I don't think so. Not much money or prestige in that one." He closed the file and dropped it on his desk. "If you're really that worried, fire her."

Tom blinked, not sure he heard correctly. "Fire Claudia Moore?"

"She obviously lied on her job application. Freelance writer isn't exactly the same as journalist for a couple of major newspapers. That could be grounds for immediate dismissal."

"No," Tom snapped. "I—I mean, I don't want to let her go. Not yet."

"Then I'll fire her," his grandfather said. "I have the final say-so on the elves."

"Not *this* elf."

Hell, he knew his grandfather had good cause for terminating her employment, but if Claudia left, then he wouldn't get another chance to kiss her or touch her, another chance to listen to the addictive sound of her voice or watch the quirky expressions that crossed her face when she spoke. He wasn't ready to let her walk out of his life. At least not until he figured out this overwhelming attraction he had for her.

His mind wandered back to the kiss they'd shared in his office, the passion that had taken hold of him, making him act in such a capricious manner. But why Claudia? Of all the women he knew, why did she elicit such uncharacteristic behavior from him? She wasn't the type of woman he was usually drawn to. He'd always preferred someone more reserved, more sophisticated, more... boring?

Tom groaned inwardly. Yes, it was true. He did tend to date women who were about as exciting as cold oatmeal. Hell, his fiancée had found drapery fabrics and dish patterns exciting. But talking to Claudia was like playing with fire, dangerous, exciting, her words dancing around him and drawing him near. And when he finally felt he'd gained control, she'd singe him, putting him back in his place with a few well-aimed flames.

"Don't let your personal feelings get in the way," his grandfather reminded him as he tugged the huge black belt around his waist.

"What personal feelings?" Tom muttered. "She's an employee. And I want to find out what she's up to."

"I thought you said she just needed extra money."

"Maybe. But she was alone in my office and I think

she might have rifled through my files. And she was in the park last night when I met with Holly Bennett and her associate. Either she's very nosy or she's looking for something. If I dangle a few clues to Santa's true identity in front of her and she bites, then we'll know for sure. In the meantime, I'll have a little fun with her.''

"You *are* sweet on her!"

"I'm merely curious," he said. Curious to know whether her waist was really tiny enough to span with his hands, whether her hair felt as soft as it looked, whether she might kiss him again anytime soon.

His grandfather glanced at the clock on his desk then tugged his hair-lined hat on his head. "I'm late. They'll be lined up back to the Betsy Wetsy dolls if I don't get down there." He reached out and pushed a panel behind his desk and a door swung open. A wooden stairway led down an old elevator shaft, all the way to a small storage room on the second floor, Santa's secret escape route.

"Be careful on the stairs," Tom called as his grandfather pulled the door closed.

When the office was quiet, Tom sat down at his grandfather's desk and opened the file. He scanned the report, then looked at the recent articles Claudia had written for various papers around the state. Though he didn't know much about journalism, he could tell she was a good writer, clear, concise, passionate about her subject. She made even the dullest subjects interesting.

"So why are you hanging out at Dalton's Department Store?" he murmured, fingering an employee photo of Claudia from the *Albany Journal's* publicity department. "What are you really after?"

Tom leaned back in the chair and wove his fingers together behind his head. If he wanted answers to his questions, then he'd have to spend a little more time around Claudia Moore—not a disagreeable prospect, in his opinion.

He leaned forward and pressed the intercom button on the phone. "Mrs. Lewis? Would you come in here, please?" When she appeared at the door, he smiled. "What do you and my grandfather do with all the letters that we get in Santa's mailbox?"

"We read them all and then we file them, by date and year. We have them all the way back to the beginning. I think some day your grandfather might put them together in a book. Wouldn't that be nice?"

"I want you to take a stack of them down to the advertising department and have them mock up a few letters, make some color copies and some envelopes. I want the copies to look authentic."

"May I ask why?" Mrs. Lewis inquired.

"You may, but I'm not going to tell you." She nodded, then turned to leave. "And I need them before noon," Tom added.

When he was once again alone, he leaned back in his grandfather's leather chair and linked his hands behind his head. A satisfied smile played at the corners of his mouth and he chuckled. This holiday season was turning out to be the most interesting in recent memory. And Tom knew that it was all because of one unruly undercover elf.

"Well, Twinkie, I think you're about to meet your match. Before the week is over, I'm going to know exactly what you're up to. And you're going to be the one who slips up."

"Here, kid. Blow your nose before you sit on Santa's lap." Claudia pulled a tissue from her pocket, wincing with disgust, then held it out to the four-year-old waiting in line.

The little girl looked up at her and smiled, but didn't take the tissue. Claudia groaned inwardly, then covered the kid's nose. "Blow," she ordered. "Again." She shoved the tissue back in her pocket. "Now you're ready for Santa."

The little girl threw her arms around Claudia's legs and hugged her. Claudia couldn't help but smile as she patted her blond head. Maybe she was getting better at the job. The kids seemed to be laughing at her jokes on a regular basis and they didn't look nearly so terrified when she talked to them.

Still, there were a few problems she couldn't handle. For some, the stress of visiting Santa seemed to bring out the worst in them. First, they started leaking—tears, runny noses, even a few upset stomachs and embarrassing accidents that required the store's custodial department. And if they were too old to leak, they peppered her with questions, directly aimed at discovering the true identity of Santa.

Claudia had become quite adept at evasive answers regarding the big guy, but the questions only brought home the realization that after four days as an elf, she was no closer to getting at the truth about Santa than a pack of runny-nosed kids. This entire project had turned into a lesson in frustration.

Tom Dalton had been strangely absent from the second floor that day. She'd caught herself looking for him every few minutes, wondering if he was standing in the shadows of the huge Barbie display or loitering near the shelves stuffed with Rock 'n' Roll Elmos.

Winkie suddenly appeared at her side. "Don't look

now," she murmured, "but Dalton's standing over near the Hot Wheels."

Claudia tried to appear nonchalant, but her heart refused to comply. It skipped a few beats, then began to hammer in her chest. She glanced over at her fellow elf. "Who?"

Winkie rolled her eyes. "Tom Dalton, you idiot. The man you've been looking for all day." She sighed. "What do you suppose he wants now?"

"I don't know," Claudia muttered as she watched him approach. His gaze was fixed squarely on her, his eyes intense, his expression determined. She swallowed hard. He didn't look happy. "I think it probably has something to do with me." Winkie turned to make her escape, but Claudia caught her by the arm and yanked her to a stop.

Claudia quickly rewound her day. She'd been a little curt with a group of teenage girls who'd tried to crash the Candy Cane Gate. And she'd politely pointed out the odor of a well-worn diaper to the mother of a two-year-old. And when a bratty kid had spent nearly fifteen minutes reading a prepared list to Santa, she'd lured him away with the promise of a stocking full of candy, then stiffed him.

When Tom finally stood in front of her, she sent him a haughty look and tipped her chin up defiantly. "Are you going to get the elves all upset again? They've finally recovered from your last visit." Claudia crossed her arms over her chest and stood toe to toe with the boss. But this time he didn't retreat. Instead he crossed his arms as if mocking her.

Winkie stood a step away, her gaze shifting from one to the other, her eyes wide with fear. When Tom turned to her, her face went red and her knees nearly buckled. Claudia grabbed her elbow again.

Tom forced a smile for the overwrought elf. "Well—" he peered at her name tag "—Winkie. How is business at the North Pole today?"

Winkie's voice cracked, any trace of her cocky attitude gone. All she managed was a tremulous, "Fine, sir."

"Fine," Tom said, nodding. "Keep up the good work."

The elf continued to stare at him, like a reindeer caught in the headlights of an oncoming sleigh.

"Carry on," he said.

Winkie hurried to leave and Claudia decided to take her own opportunity to escape. But Tom wasn't about to let her get away so easily. "Miss Moore, I'd like a word with you."

Claudia groaned, then stomped her foot, the little jingle bells tinkling wildly. "What is it now? Are my tights sagging? Was I rude to a customer? Or did I break another rule in the Elf's Code of Conduct."

He arched his eyebrow. "I was hoping you might agree to join me for a cup of coffee," he murmured. "Don't you have a break coming up?"

Stunned by his unexpected invitation, she stammered out an answer. "I—I take my break when business is slow."

Tom glanced over her shoulder. "There're only a few kids in line."

Claudia shrugged. "Then I guess I can take my break." She started toward the elevator, but Tom reached out and grabbed her arm. The moment his fingers closed around her elbow, she stopped breathing. His touch sent a frisson of electricity racing through her limb, setting off tiny explosions all along the way.

"Where are you going?"

"To your office," Claudia replied. "Isn't that usually where you prefer to yell at me?"

"I'm not going to yell at you," Tom said. "I just want to have coffee. In the coffee shop."

Claudia smiled. Then he wasn't angry with her? But why would he want to have coffee? Unless, he wanted to spend some time with her. Maybe the kiss they'd shared had intrigued him as much as it had her. She hadn't stopped thinking about it since the moment his mouth covered hers. And she certainly wouldn't turn him away if he tried again. A tiny sigh of disappointment slipped from her lips. That probably wouldn't happen in the coffee shop, in front of Dalton employees and shoppers.

"Maybe we should go to your office," Claudia suggested. "You never know. After all, you are wound a little tight and you may just spontaneously burst into a reprimand. I'd certainly want to you feel free to vent your spleen."

Tom frowned, then drew her along toward the escalator and the first floor coffee shop. "I'm not going to yell at you," he insisted.

When they reached the coffee shop, he found a spot in a quiet corner booth. After the waitress left them to their steaming mugs of Dalton's special blend, Tom reached into his jacket pocket and pulled out a stack of envelopes. "This is for you," he said, removing the top one and setting the rest on the table.

"Oh, I see," Claudia muttered. "Give me the pink slip, or whatever color you use, right here in public. That way I can't throw a fit." Claudia stared at the envelope, then folded her hands in front of her. "You can't make me open it. And if I don't open it, I can't be fired."

"It's your paycheck," he said. "Hourly employees get paid every Friday."

Claudia snatched up the envelope and tucked it into the pocket of her polka-dot jacket. "Thank you." Her gaze wandered to the small stack of envelopes on the table. These weren't paychecks, but colorful envelopes adorned in childish scrawl. Letters to Santa!

"Aren't you going to look at it?"

Claudia drew her gaze away from the letters and sent him a tight smile. "Look at what?"

"Your paycheck?"

She shook her head. "I thought I'd save that depressing prospect for a moment when I can weep openly."

He leaned forward and braced his arms on the table, covering the stack of letters. "Tell me again. Why are you working at such a low-paying job?" he asked.

"Is it my fault it's low-paying?" she countered. "Nothing says you can't give your elves better pay. Throw in use of the company jet and a key to the executive washroom and all the Inkies and Itsys will be happy. What do you make per week?"

"I don't know," Tom said with a shrug. Though Claudia knew the question wasn't quite proper, he'd already become accustomed to her forthright manner and didn't blink an eye. "If I did, I wouldn't be inclined to tell you."

She rolled her eyes. "Is that store policy? Or just a rich guy thing? Or are you afraid that if I know how much you're worth, I won't like you anymore."

"Oh, you like me? And this is how you talk to a friend?" Tom smiled and reached out, running his finger lazily from her wrist to her thumb. Then he drew back as if the gesture were purely accidental and grabbed the pitcher of cream from her side of the table. "The reason

I can't tell you is that I don't know. My pay goes directly into my checking account. And I don't bother to balance my account.''

Claudia shook her head. Her own income as a free-lance reporter barely covered her monthly expenses. She drove a ten-year-old car and took one vacation a year. And this man didn't even bother to balance his check-book. She ripped the paycheck out of her pocket and opened the envelope. "Let's see how the little people live. Ah, $62.98 for two days work. Quick, I have to call Merrill Lynch. I have enough here to buy a share or two of stock.''

Tom grabbed her paycheck. "Really? That's all? Sixty-two dollars? That's terrible.''

"You're surprised?''

"Yeah, I guess I am. I suppose I could give the elves a small raise.''

Claudia narrowed her eyes, curious at his sudden attack of generosity. "Are you giving us a raise because you think we deserve it or because you have other, more nefarious, reasons?''

"Nefarious?''

"Yeah. Depraved, ruthless, wicked.''

"I know what nefarious means," Tom said. "And no, I don't have any wicked motives.''

Claudia sat back in the booth and studied him intently. "Hmm. I thought you might have decided on the raise because you wanted to kiss me again." She arched her brow mischievously. "Or maybe you thought I'd lose my head and kiss you?''

He returned her smile and leaned over the table. "Kiss away," he dared her.

Claudia felt a warm blush color her cheeks. She glanced around to find almost every eye in the coffee shop trained on the two of them. Oh, she should just accept his challenge. He didn't expect her to kiss him in public and with the challenge, he'd once again managed to wrest control of the conversation away from her.

"I would, but I have a sneaking suspicion that it might get me fired." She fanned herself with her paycheck. "And I certainly am not going to risk losing this job. Especially since I just got a raise."

He glanced at his watch then reached down and picked up the letters, slapping them against his palm. "Well, your break is almost over and I've got an errand to run."

Claudia quickly forgot the tingle that still warmed her skin where he'd touched her. Instead her attention focused on the letters. She tried to appear nonchalant. What was Tom Dalton doing with Santa's mail? And what was he planning to do with the letters? Claudia groaned inwardly. She wasn't going to find out sitting here sipping coffee. "What are those?" she asked in a carefully casual tone.

He looked at the letters, as if noticing them for the first time. "Nothing," Tom murmured. "Just some business I need to take care of."

This was her chance! If he was planning to meet the mysterious benefactor behind Dalton's secret Santa, then she damned well planned to be right behind him. Claudia glanced at her own watch, then took a quick gulp from her mug, the hot brew burning her tongue. "Look at the time. I've already burned seventy-two cents in take-home pay." She pushed her chair back. "Thanks for the coffee, Tom—I mean, Mr. Dalton."

She stood and smoothed her elf outfit, then hurried to the coffee shop doors. She glanced back at him before she walked out. He was carefully flipping through the letters, taking each one out of the envelope and reading it, before putting it back. "Patience," Claudia murmured. "All it took was a little patience and now I've finally got my break."

She found a discreet observation spot behind a display of leather luggage. A few minutes later, Tom signed the bill for their coffee, gathered up the letters and walked out of the coffee shop. He didn't even look her way. Claudia let him take a comfortable lead, then followed after him.

Had she been given a choice, Claudia may have picked a different outfit to wear while tailing a source. The polka-dot jacket and baggy green tights didn't do much to make her inconspicuous. And the jingle bells on her boots made stealth impossible.

She followed him on what began to feel like a tour of the store, through parts of the building she hadn't even known existed, trying to remain as quiet and invisible as possible. He turned around twice, both times when the jingle of her shoes echoed through the aisles of the stores. Finally she ducked behind a display of alligator handbags and ripped the booties off, then shoved them up the front of her jacket. But the delay cost her and she watched in dismay as Tom disappeared behind an unmarked door in the perfume department.

She prayed for the door to stay open until she reached it, then prayed for it to be unlocked. As she turned the knob and stepped into the darkness in front of her, she hesitated. Wasn't this what she wanted? To wrap up her story in a tidy little bow and go back to her life in New York?

Claudia drew a deep breath. "Of course," she muttered into the darkness, waiting for her eyes to adjust to the lack of light. "What could possibly keep me here?"

THE ROOM WAS COMPLETELY dark and Claudia waited a moment for her eyes to adjust. But when she stepped forward, she felt something brush her face. She turned, and by the feeble light from the exit signs she saw a hand swing by her head. A scream nearly burst from her throat and she brushed the hand away, only to get tangled in a mass of disjointed limbs. Like a scene from *Texas Chainsaw Massacre,* Claudia stumbled in the darkness. Only after she'd quelled the urge to faint, did she realize that she was in the mannequin storeroom and the limbs were all plastic, not flesh and blood.

Her head spinning, Claudia crouched down on the floor and pressed her hand to her chest to still her pounding heart and to catch her breath. Her duties as a reporter had never taken much undercover work, but Claudia was determined to get her scoop without revealing herself. She'd already followed Tom around most of the store's departments, through a maze of spooky storerooms, and up and down dusty stairwells that seemed to lead nowhere, except to another dark and cavernous room.

Tom obviously knew every inch of the store, every nook and cranny. And no doubt he'd be meeting the mysterious benefactor in a secluded spot where there was no chance of discovery. Claudia planned to be right there when it all happened, ready to commit every detail to memory.

Their winding route had taken them back out on the brightly lit sales floor twice and, for a moment, Claudia had considered returning to her post. She was already late coming back from her break and if Mrs. Perkins caught her, she wouldn't have to worry about Tom firing her—Eunice would take care of that. But she'd believed her quest was almost at an end—until she'd entered this room, yet another musty storeroom.

Claudia heard a sound at the far end of the mannequin room, then scrambled to her feet. Suddenly the lights came on and a door slammed. She held her hand up to her eyes and cried out. It was almost as if he were leading her on this wild-goose chase on purpose!

She hurried toward the door. Could he know what she was after? She'd taken care with her cover but he had wondered—more than once—why she was working as an elf. If he did suspect, then she'd have to move quickly. This might be her one and only chance to get firsthand facts.

The boiler room in the back of the store was the next stop on the impromptu tour and Claudia paused as she thought she heard laughter and a low voice. Had Tom finally found his man? She plowed through a sticky cobweb then jumped as another door slammed behind her. The laughter and the talk suddenly ceased and she knew, without a doubt, she was alone.

Claudia frantically searched for a way out of the boiler room, bursting through a door and discovering herself on the loading dock. The alleyway was dark, the air damp and frigid and promising more snow. The cold seeped through her tights and sent a shiver up her spine.

In the dim light, she caught a fleeting glimpse of a figure at the far end of the dock and made to follow the shadowy form. But in the darkness, she missed the edge of the dock and felt herself lurching forward. Crying out, Claudia braced herself for a fall and a hard landing on the wet pavement below. But instead she tumbled onto something soft—very smelly and soft.

She struggled to sit up then realized she'd landed in an open Dumpster! "Oh, damn!" Claudia cried, plucking shredded paper and old pasta salad from her hair. Something moved behind her and she scrambled to the edge of the Dumpster and threw herself over the side. She landed hard on the alley, thoroughly bruising her backside, yet safe from Dumpster-dwelling rodents.

"This is not worth it!" she muttered as she stumbled to her feet and wiped the slushy muck from her uniform. "Not for some feel-good holiday drivel! I'm through, finished! I don't need the damned *Times* job. This reporter is going home and I'm never going to wear wool again!"

Seething with frustration, Claudia tugged on her booties, circled the outside of the store and entered through the employee entrance. She caught sight of herself in a mirrored window at the security checkpoint and moaned. There were still bits of pasta hanging from her hair. And the front of her jacket was stained with something that reeked of garlic and sour milk. But Claudia was past caring. All she wanted to do was collect her belongings from her locker, turn in her ridiculous elf costume and take the first train back to the city.

She ignored all the stares and the crinkled noses as she rode the escalator up to the second floor. Dinkie caught sight of her as soon as she stepped off and hurried over. "Where have you been?" She frowned. "Eunice was looking for you. What happened? You have…rotini in your hair."

Claudia reached up and pulled a soggy noodle from a strand near her eyebrow as she continued on to the employee locker room. "It's fusilli, not rotini. And where is Mrs. Perkins now?"

"She had to go to a meeting," Dinkie said, trailing after her. "Is that alfredo sauce on your jacket. Why are you wearing today's lunch special?"

"All right," Claudia countered. "If Eunice isn't here, then you'll have to take my resignation." She held up her hand. "I hereby resign my position as elf." She adjusted her jacket, then turned and continued with her escape.

Dinkie followed, this time hard on her heels. "Wait," she called. "You can't quit. Mr. Dalton, Mr. Dalton. Talk to her!"

Claudia froze, then slowly turned around. Tom Dalton stood beside Dinkie, appearing from nowhere, his arms crossed over his chest, his gaze raking her body and taking in her disheveled appearance. "Where have you been?"

She cursed softly, then turned again and headed to the locker room. He was the last person she wanted to see right now. "Don't follow me!"

But Tom didn't bother listening. He followed her and when she yanked her locker open and began to remove her elf skirt, she felt his gaze on her back. "You've been gone for nearly a half hour," he said. "Your break was supposed to be fifteen minutes. I'm afraid we're going to have to dock your pay."

She turned on him then, whipping the paycheck out of her jacket and waving it under his nose. "You want to dock my pay? Here, Scrooge, take this. I don't care about your measly pay. I'm finished. Find yourself another elf."

She worked at the buttons of the elf jacket, but they were slippery with alfredo sauce. Cursing, she grabbed the hem of the jacket and yanked it over her head, leaving her with only a silk camisole and baggy green tights between her skin and his eyes. "Are you going to stand there and watch me undress?" she asked.

"No," he said, his eyes drifting from her shoulders to her breasts.

His gaze was like a caress, silent yet potent. She saw

desire there, clouding the green depths. Her nipples hardened beneath the thin fabric and goose bumps broke over her arms. But she wasn't really cold, she mused. What was this strange sensation she was feeling? Apprehension? Anticipation? Was he going to touch her or would he walk away? She drew a shaky breath and forced herself to turn her back to him. But the instant she moved, his arm snaked around her waist and he pulled her against his body. She opened her mouth to protest, but she didn't have time, for in the blink of an eye, his lips were on hers.

Though the kiss was swift and intense, it felt like the most natural thing in the world. He tasted better than she remembered and she sank against him and wrapped her arms around his neck. How could she possibly leave this? No man had ever kissed her the way Tom Dalton did— with fire and passion and barely controlled need.

His tongue teased at her lips and, with a soft sigh of pleasure, she opened beneath the onslaught. Claudia's mind whirled and, suddenly, she couldn't remember what she'd been so angry about. His hands smoothed over her hips then toyed with the lacy hem of her camisole.

Claudia moaned softly. Why couldn't she resist him? Why, at the very moment she'd decided to escape Schuyler Falls, did he have to touch her this way? His palms burned a path along her skin as he brushed aside her camisole and spanned her waist.

A soft chuckle rumbled in his throat. "I've been wondering about that," he murmured against her mouth.

"What?" Claudia asked, nipping at his bottom lip.

"Whether we'd...fit." He stepped back and looked down into her eyes, idly running his fingertip over her cheek. "What's this about quitting?"

"I—I—" With a groan, she raked her hands through

the hair at his nape and pulled his mouth down on hers for another mind-numbing kiss. For a guy whom she'd considered terminally uptight, Tom Dalton kissed like a practiced reprobate. He wasn't proper or polite, not when she was in his arms. He was powerful and mesmerizing and irresistible all at once.

"Then you're not going to quit?" he murmured, nuzzling her neck.

"I *should* quit," Claudia said.

"Well, before you do, maybe you could tell me why you smell like garbage?"

"Garbage?" Claudia asked. Was he really interested or did he already know the answer? It was his fault she'd ended up in the Dumpster. She tipped her chin up and gave him a cool look. "I told that lady at the perfume counter I didn't like designer scents. This one was Dalton's signature scent, Eau de Alleyway."

Tom reached out and plucked a piece of pasta from her hair and held it up in front of her. "Maybe you should stay out of alleys...and garbage Dumpsters." He dropped a quick kiss on her nose. "I've got a call coming in from New York in five minutes. Why don't you go clean yourself up. I'll let the rest of the elves know you're staying."

"I'm not staying because you kissed me," she called as he walked to the door.

"And I didn't kiss you to get you to stay," Tom said.

"Then why did you kiss me?" Claudia asked.

He shrugged and grinned. "I've got this thing for elves," he replied. "Never been afflicted with the problem before, but lately I've been obsessed."

"You should see a doctor about that," she said. As the door closed behind him, Claudia let out a long breath. She touched her damp lips and smiled, reveling in the aftermath of their kiss. But as she enjoyed the memories, a slow frown creased her features. How could he know she'd been in the alley behind Dalton's? And how could he know she'd fallen in the Dumpster? She moaned softly. Unless he saw her fall. "He knew I was following him!" she cried. "He tricked me into following him with those Santa letters!"

Claudia snatched up her elf jacket and strode over to the sink. As she scrubbed at the alfredo stain, she muttered a colorful string of words aimed squarely at Tom Dalton's character. "If you think you can toy with me, Mr. Dalton, you've got another thing coming. I'll write this damn story if I have to kiss your lips off to get it!"

THE SMELL OF OLD GARLIC still clung to Claudia's costume the next night as she stood at the Candy Cane Gate. She'd had no time to take the jacket to the cleaners and all her attempts to wash out the smell only resulted in a puckered mess of musty old wool, a state that brought a censorious look from Eunice Perkins as she completed her customary elf inspection.

The stinky costume was only part of what was slowly turning into an exercise in futility. First, she hadn't dug up a single lead on her story. Second, she'd convinced herself her cover was in imminent danger of being blown. And worst of all, when she tried to focus on work, all she could think about was her last encounter with Tom.

While she should have been mulling over strategies and tracking down new leads, Claudia had spent all of last night in a detailed retrospective of their passionate interlude, the feel of his fingers on her bare skin, the strength of his hands as he grabbed her waist. He'd been awfully determined to make her stay, refusing her resignation with an ardent kiss and a fervent caress.

But was that really all there was behind his behavior? Was it simple lust, or did Tom Dalton really have nefarious motives? What if he did suspect she was after more than just the satisfaction of serving as an elf? What if he knew she was after the identity of Dalton's secret Santa?

But one thing didn't fit. If he'd deliberately led her on

that wild-goose chase through the musty recesses of the store to discern her motives, then why hadn't he accepted her resignation gladly? Why had he done everything in his power to entice her to stay instead of booting her out of his store and out of his life?

She swung the gate open for another child, then turned to gauge the length of the line. But as she was scanning the crowd of children, she came across a familiar face. Her mind searched for the name of the little blond-haired boy. He had a green envelope...and candy to bribe Santa.

"Eric...Eric Martin," she murmured. Or was it Marrin? "Hey, kid!" she called, moving toward the middle of the line. "What are you doing back here?"

Claudia noticed the little boy was accompanied by an adult this time, an adult she vaguely recognized. But this woman hadn't been with Eric that night. The kid had been alone. No, she'd seen this woman outside the store...in the square. Claudia blinked in astonishment. With Tom Dalton! This was the sophisticated blonde he'd met in the square.

"Hi, Twinkie!" Eric said, his expression bright as he approached. "Look what I brought. It's my Christmas angel."

Claudia glanced between the boy and the strikingly beautiful woman, her hands braced on her hips. "Your what?"

"My angel. Her name is Holly and Santa sent her to me. She's going to make my Christmas perfect. I came back here to thank him."

Claudia turned to Holly, observing her with as casual a manner as she could muster. "Santa sent you?" she asked. "That's not true, is it?"

The angel named Holly suddenly became uneasy, glancing over her shoulder and forcing a smile. "I—I'm really not at liberty to say," she replied. "Come on, Eric, we'll come back a little later and thank Santa. We've got a lot of shopping to do." She grabbed the little boy's hand and rushed off.

"Wait!" Claudia cried as she stumbled through the crowd of children. "I just have a few questions to ask."

She hurried after them with as much speed as she could gain in her felt booties. This was a connection! This Holly person had met with Tom Dalton that night in the square. *And* she'd become Eric Marrin's Christmas angel. Claudia had her whole story right in front of her as long as she could catch up to the pair and ask a few questions.

But the store was bustling with shoppers, all of them crowding the aisles, arms loaded with boxes and bags. She ran into a young man, scattering his purchases all over the floor. Frustrated, she bent down to help him and when she looked up again, they were gone, swallowed up by the domestics department.

"Oh, damn it!" she cried, stomping her foot and crossing her arms over her chest. "Damn it, damn it, and double damn it!"

"Miss Moore!"

Claudia jumped at the booming sound of his voice, then slowly turned around, ready to face Tom Dalton's wrath once again. Obviously swearing in public was against elfin rules. Good grief, this was getting to be a regular problem with them—running hot and cold, bouncing between overwhelming passion and cool professionalism. Too bad she never knew which was next.

"If I didn't know better I'd say you were stalking me," she snapped. "Still having problems with that little elf fetish?"

"I think I have it under control," Tom said with a lazy

grin. "I understand you left your post seven minutes ago. Mrs. Perkins is looking for you."

"Take the time off my next paycheck," she said with a tight smile. "All thirty-five cents. Now, if there's nothing else, I'm going back to work."

He grabbed her hand and laced his fingers through hers, then drew her behind a rack of Egyptian cotton towels. Claudia didn't bother to resist, deciding to take the brunt of his wrath with some sort of dignity. But when she looked into his handsome face, she saw that he wasn't angry at all.

"Actually there is something else," he said, studying her fingertips as if he'd never seen anything quite so curious before. "I was wondering if you'd like to have dinner tonight."

"I—I'm working," Claudia said, drawing her hand away, then sorry once she did. In such a short time, she'd come to enjoy—almost crave—his touch. She moved to grab his hand again, then resisted the urge.

"The store closes at eight tonight. We could eat after work," he suggested.

"Why?"

He frowned at the question. "Why dinner? Because I'm hungry. And because I'm tired of seeing you in that silly elf costume. Because I want a chance to talk to you without every employee in this store speculating over what we're doing. Once we leave the store, we're not boss and elf anymore. We're just—"

"Boss and conservatively dressed employee?"

"I was going to say man and woman."

Claudia glanced down and smoothed the front of her jacket. "I've learned to like the costume," she teased. "I've lost myself in the character."

Tom reached out and toyed with one of the huge jacket

buttons near her waist. "As fond as I am of seeing you in moth-eaten wool and saggy tights, I'd prefer something more...flattering. There's a restaurant on the west side of the square called Silvio's. They make great pasta. Come up to my office after you're finished with—"

"I'll meet you at the restaurant," Claudia interrupted. "How about eight-fifteen?"

He smiled and gave her hand a squeeze. "I'll look forward to it. It'll be nice not spending the night cooped up in my office." He glanced around, then slowly drew her hand to his lips. But his kiss changed course at the last second and, instead, he pressed his lips to the inside of her wrist.

With that, he turned and walked away, whistling a cheery little tune. Claudia stared after him, her mind spinning with the possibilities. If Tom Dalton was sitting at Silvio's at 8 p.m. waiting for her to arrive, then he couldn't be sitting in his office. And if he wasn't in his office, then...

"Here's my chance," Claudia said, under her breath. "I'll get another look at that Santa file, then I'll go interview the Marrin boy tomorrow morning before the store opens. And by tomorrow night, I'll have my story!"

As she hurried back to her post at the North Pole Village, she began to assemble her plan. She'd need to find a way up to the executive offices without being seen by the security guard. Surely one of the stairways she'd encountered the day before would go up to the top floor. She'd have about a half hour, maybe a little more, before Tom began to wonder where she was and whether she was planning to meet him at all.

As she thought about the task ahead, she had only two regrets—that she would be forced to rely on unscrupulous methods and that she'd have to stand Tom up. The thought of an intimate dinner with him, away from the store, dressed in a sexy dress and wearing alluring perfume, was something she'd dreamed about. The possibilities of what might happen after that dinner sent shivers through her body.

"You've got a story to write," Claudia reminded herself, schooling her thoughts in a more professional direction. "And after you write your story, you'll go home and forget all about Tom Dalton."

But Claudia knew that even after the story had been published, she wouldn't easily put her short stint as an elf behind her. She'd always wonder what she and Tom might have shared—if she hadn't been an elf and he hadn't been her boss.

THE STORE WAS POSITIVELY spooky once the lights were turned off and the employees went home. Claudia slowly made her way through the Juniors department, keeping to the cover of racks of sequined tube tops and hip-hugging bell-bottoms. She'd changed out of her elf outfit into a deep purple cashmere sweater, leather miniskirt and tights she'd purchased a few days ago.

She'd hoped the dark colors would make her more inconspicuous, but after glancing in the dressing room mirror, Claudia decided she looked more like one of Charlie's Angels than a real undercover reporter. Still, if she got caught, she had to look as if she were on her way to meet Tom and simply got trapped in the store after closing time.

She made her way down the escalator, tiptoeing over frozen steps. The door behind the perfume counter led to a stairway and, if her guess was correct, that same stairway passed right behind the Gingerbread Cottage. But did it go all the way up to the fifth floor? "There's only one way to find out,'' Claudia murmured. She grabbed the doorknob and turned it. Nothing but blackness and stale air greeted her.

Claudia reached into her pocket and pulled out the cigarette lighter that she'd borrowed from Winkie. The feeble flicker of the flame gave her just enough light to navigate by. She slowly climbed the rickety stairs and when she reached the second floor landing, she pushed open the door and peered out.

The door led directly inside the Gingerbread Cottage! ''Now I know how Santa comes and goes.''

She quickly closed the door and started back up the steps, to the third floor and then the fourth. But it was there that the stairwell came to an end. Claudia turned full circle, searching for the rest of the route to the fifth floor. To her dismay, the lighter began to sputter and a few moments later, she was stuck in total darkness.

''Oh, God,'' she moaned, reaching out for the wall and cursing her lack of a proper flashlight. Her fingers searched for the railing to lead her back down to safety, but she was afraid to take a step for fear that she'd tumble down the stairs. Suddenly she heard a click and the wall beneath her fingers gave way.

Light filtered into the stairwell and Claudia waited for her eyes to adjust. When she could see again, she couldn't believe what she'd found! The wall she'd touched was a hidden door and behind the door another stairway. ''Up!'' she cried. These stairs were lit by a bare bulb that burned above her head. At the very top, she encountered another door, this one operating with the same hidden latch.

She wasn't prepared for what she found on the other side. She stepped into an elegant office, paneled in rich mahogany and lined with plush Oriental carpets. The room was softly lit by a small lamp that burned on a credenza. And hung on a hook near the door was a red Santa's outfit.

This wasn't Tom Dalton's office, though it was furnished much the same. This was the office of someone more important—the man who played Dalton's Santa. But who was he? Nothing in the office gave her the slightest clue—no name tag on the desk, no business letters lying around.

"I guess I'll just have to find out," she said as she closed the door behind her.

"WOULD YOU LIKE ANOTHER Scotch and soda?" the waiter asked in a thick Italian accent.

Tom glanced at his watch, then tossed his napkin on the table. He'd waited nearly an hour at Silvio's for Claudia to show up and he could no longer deny the obvious. "I've been stood up," he said.

"Ah, Mr. Dalton, this is a shame," Carlo cried, picking up the champagne bucket from beside the table. "And this is your first date in such a long time."

Tom glanced up at Carlo, sending him a withering glare. "Just give me the check," he said. "And I'll take the champagne with me. And the antipasto platter, too. In fact, throw in an order of spaghetti and a salad. Since she won't be joining me, I can go back to the office and get some work done."

"Yes, Mr. Dalton." Carlo handed him the full bottle of champagne, dripping with icy water, then hurried off to the kitchen. Tom usually ate at least one night a week at Silvio's so he was considered a regular. It gave him a break from Dalton's coffee shop and the vending machines that usually kept him alive. And when he did bother to go home, to a huge empty house with an even emptier refrigerator, he ate pretzels and popcorn and anything else that came in a bag or a box.

Tom rubbed his forehead, then furrowed his fingers through his hair. He'd thought everything was great between him and Claudia, that they'd finally gotten past their little dance and admitted their attraction to each other. When they were together, they couldn't take their eyes off of each other. And when he kissed her, she responded in his arms with passion. So why had she chosen to stand him up, to avoid the next step in their newfound relationship?

He took another sip of his watered Scotch, then set the glass on the table in front of him. When Carlo returned with his food and the check, Tom tossed a few bills on the table and said good-night, grabbing his coat from the rack as he walked out the door.

The square was quiet as he crossed back to the store. The night security guard would be on duty at the door, locking down the store after nine and beginning his rounds. Tom could still put in three or four hours work before heading home. "So this is what my life really is," he murmured. "Take-out Italian and a broken date, followed by a night of sales figures."

He crossed the street and headed to the employee entrance, ringing for the guard. The door buzzed and he entered the security lobby, then waved at the camera. The interior door clicked open and Tom walked into the darkened store. As he strolled toward the elevator, he drew in a deep breath.

It still smelled the same as he remembered from his youth, the scent of serious business. He loved walking through the store when it was dark and silent. There was a wonderful feeling of fulfillment, like he'd made all this possible, from the smallest bottle of perfume to the prettiest dress. Yet that feeling had been harder and harder to conjure lately. He was ready for new challenges.

Still, he had transformed the store from a liability to an asset. Competition from the large chains and the shopping malls had made family-owned department stores a relic from the past. But he'd worked hard to buck that trend. And now, with the store's future safe, someday, maybe his own son would run Dalton's.

Tom drew in a sharp breath. His son. Until now, the thought of a family had always been part of the distant future. Even when he was engaged, he'd known it would be a long time before he was ready for the responsibility of children. But now, the notion didn't seem so outlandish. He was ready to settle down and begin his life anew.

Perhaps Claudia had brought this on. Not that he wanted to marry her. It had been such a long time since he'd had a woman in his life, he'd just put the whole idea of marriage out of his mind. Why had he thought of it now? Though he and Claudia had shared a few romantic moments, he'd been foolish to think of what they had as a relationship. A relationship would have required at least a phone call before she broke their date.

So what did they have, except an incredible knack for caustic wordplay? "She's the most fascinating, irritating, mysterious, beautiful woman I've ever met," he muttered as he shoved his passkey into the elevator controls and punched the button for the fifth floor. "What more do I need to know right now?"

Tom leaned back against the wall of the elevator and watched the ornate sunrise dial tick away the floors as they passed. The door slid open and he stepped out and turned toward his office. But something made him stop, an instinct that told him everything was not right. He glanced around, then noticed his office door was ajar. He glanced in the opposite direction and noticed his grand-father's office door was also open. Odd, he mused. His grandfather never stayed past closing.

Tom considered putting in a call to the security desk, but decided to appease his curiosity first. Silently he approached his office and peered through the door. The lamp on his desk was lit and a shadowy figure was bent over his desk, flipping through a file folder.

He sighed. Claudia! So this was where she'd been, hiding out in the store until she could break into his office. What was she after now? He reached out to throw the door open, anxious to find out. But if he exposed her now, then everything between them would be over. He'd be forced to fire her, she'd leave Schuyler Falls. And he'd go back to his old, boring life of merchandising reports and fourth-quarter sales goals.

Tom stepped back from the door, then returned to the elevator. If he played his cards right, he could turn this entire night to his advantage. He could find out what she was doing in his office and he could find out how she really felt about him. He drew a deep breath and started to whistle a cheery Christmas tune. A tiny gasp drifted out of his office and he heard her scrambling to put everything right.

He glanced down at his watch and decided to give her an extra thirty seconds so she'd have time to formulate a decent excuse. He set the bag of Italian food down on Mrs. Lewis's desk and rummaged through it noisily, muttering to himself. When he'd wasted a full minute, Tom grabbed the champagne bottle and bag of food before he strode through his office door.

Claudia had curled up on his leather sofa and was pretending to be asleep. The elf outfit was gone, replaced by a sexy sweater, a short leather skirt, and ankle boots that revealed an enticing view of her long, slender legs. Her hair fell across her face in loose waves and he fought the urge to touch her, to skim his palm along her calf to her hip.

A smile curled the corners of his mouth. If he couldn't touch her, then maybe he could scare her. "Claudia!" he shouted, his voice splitting the silence.

His shout had exactly the effect he'd wanted. Her eyes snapped open and she jolted up to a sitting position, her face pale. Then she remembered she was supposed to be sleeping and rubbed her eyes and yawned for dramatic purposes. "Tom," she murmured.

"What are you doing here?" he asked. "You were supposed to meet me at Silvio's."

She shook her head. "I—I thought I was supposed to meet you here. I came up after closing and waited, but you never showed up. I guess I must have fallen asleep." She threw her legs over the edge of the sofa, then ran her fingers through her hair. "What time is it?"

"Almost nine," he said, amazed at her smooth way with a lie.

"Oh, I'm sorry. I suppose it's too late for dinner now."

He held up the bag of food and the champagne. "I brought dinner back from the restaurant after I realized you stood me up. We might as well eat since we won't be going anywhere for a while."

"We won't?"

"No," Tom said. "We're locked in for the night."

Claudia gasped, her eyes going wide. "What?"

If she could employ her rather paltry acting skills in this little scene, then so could he. And he'd be the one to come out with the Academy Award and the big box-office gross. "Yeah, once the store closes, there's no way out. Everything's alarmed, the security guard has left for the night, and the gates are locked. We're stuck here.''

"Well, turn off the alarm," she said, scrambling to her feet.

She braced her hands on her hips, the sweater pulling tight across her breasts. A stab of desire twisted in his stomach and he tried to maintain his composure. Fantasizing about Claudia's body wasn't going to help. "I don't know how," he lied.

"But you stay in the store late at night all the time," she countered.

He blinked. "How do you know that?"

"Well, everyone talks about you at lunch," she explained, crossing her arms in front of her. "They say you have no social life, you spend all your time working, and that's why your fiancée walked out on you."

"You heard that over lunch?" Tom asked.

"Never mind where I heard it. We have to find a way out of here. Can't you call someone? This isn't a prison, it's a department store!"

"The switchboard closes when the store closes," he said, another lie. "When I came in, I told the guard he could leave. Hey, it won't be so bad. We have food and a warm place to sleep. Everything you could possibly want on four floors of carefully selected merchandise. Think of the fun we could have."

"Fun?"

"I've got spaghetti and antipasto from Silvio's. We'll go down to the coffee shop and get a couple of plates and some dessert. Or we can hit the gourmet department in the basement if spaghetti isn't to your taste. After that, we can visit lingerie and get you something more comfortable to wear. And domestics for some blankets and pillows. And if the sofa isn't to your liking, we can always sleep on a bed in the furniture department.'' He handed her the bottle of champagne and wandered out to Mrs. Lewis's desk to scare up a few coffee mugs.

"I'm not sleeping with you!" Claudia called through the office door.

He strolled back through the door and took the champagne bottle from her hand.

"And I don't want any champagne." She plopped down on the sofa and regarded him with ill-disguised hostility. Claudia even looked beautiful when she was angry. Her eyes were brighter, her color high. She was a passionate woman and, right now, he was tempted to turn that passion toward something more enjoyable than an argument. All it would take was a few short steps and she'd be in his arms. She might resist at first, but he'd come to understand the chemistry between them well enough to know that she'd melt in his embrace once his mouth came down on hers.

"I get the impression you think this is my fault?" he said with a smile.

"Isn't it?"

"You told me you'd meet me at Silvio's. I distinctly remember that. I can't imagine why you would have come to my office instead."

An uneasy look crossed her face. "I don't recall what I said."

"So, we might as well make the best of the situation. After all, this is our first date. It should be memorable."

"This isn't a date," she countered. "And I don't like spaghetti." She stood and looked around the office. "There has to be a way to get out of here. A window or a fire escape. Or we could go out the loading dock." She walked to the door. "I'm going to try. Are you coming?"

For a moment, their gazes locked and Tom felt a current of attraction spark between them. Time seemed to stand still and he saw himself walking over to her to tip up her chin and kiss her. But then, as quickly as the connection was made, it snapped.

"Go ahead," he said with a shrug. "But don't ask for my help when the sirens go off and the police show up." He crossed to his desk and reached into the drawer to pull out his credenza key. For effect, he tossed it up in the air a few times, making sure she saw it. "I suppose I could do some work. I have some files to look through."

"Files?" she asked, her voice cracking. She drew a deep breath and pasted a conciliatory smile on her face. "Maybe we could go find something to eat. I am a little hungry."

Tom tried not to grin as he circled his desk. He held out his arm and when she refused to take it, he grabbed her hand and tucked it in the crook of his elbow. "We've got the entire store to ourselves, Miss Moore. Your every wish is my command, as long as we sell it at Dalton's."

She glanced up at him, a reluctant smile touching her lips. "I actually could use a few diamonds," she said. "Maybe some emeralds. And I love rubies. You do have rubies, don't you?"

Tom chuckled. This night promised to be a challenge, especially if he had any romantic intentions. But he'd learned that Claudia's mood could change in a heartbeat and a prickly attitude now didn't mean a night filled with unfulfilled longing. No, he'd charm her and sooner or later, she'd accept the inevitable.

They were meant to be together. They *would* be together. And no matter what the reasons she'd come to Dalton's Department Store, there was only one reason she'd stay—because she wanted him as much as he wanted her.

5

THEY STROLLED SIDE BY SIDE down the main aisle of the first floor, their footsteps echoing in the eerie silence. Claudia had already examined the jewelry cases and declared in a haughty tone that there was nothing she really fancied. But as they wandered around the perfume counters, she realized that wasn't really true. The one thing she wanted was the one thing she couldn't have—Tom Dalton.

"This is nice," Claudia murmured, picking up a bottle of Chloé and sniffing at it. "Everything's so quiet. No kids waiting in line to see Santa, no noses to wipe nor tears to dry."

Tom braced his arms on the counter and glanced over at her, his gaze disturbingly intimate for such a casual conversation. A shiver skittered down her spine. He'd looked into her eyes before, hundreds of times, but never with such intensity, such...possession. Something had changed and she wasn't sure what it was.

"I used to dream about being locked up in the store overnight when I was a kid," he continued. "I had all sorts of plans of what I'd do. Once, I even hid in one of the storerooms at closing time, hoping that I wouldn't be caught. But my dad found me."

Claudia laughed, but the sound came out forced. Perhaps that was it, she mused. When he looked at her, he was looking directly into her soul. Did he suspect she'd

stayed in the store on purpose? Was his childhood rec-
ollection just a fabrication to make her feel guilty? Her
little lie about meeting him in his office weighed heavily
on her mind. She didn't like deceiving Tom Dalton. And
not because he was her boss, but because she valued his
trust.

She set the perfume bottle down and picked up another. If he suspected she'd stayed in the store deliberately, he wasn't showing it. Her mind wandered to the
stolen file folder tucked in her bag upstairs. How could
she have done something so underhanded? It went completely against her character. But then, she really hadn't
been herself lately. All the pressures of landing a permanent job with the *Times* had taken a toll. And since
she'd met Tom Dalton, she hadn't really been acting like
herself.

Claudia turned and started down the aisle. He fell into
step beside her and grabbed her hand, lacing his fingers
through hers. The contact was like a jolt of electricity
coursing through her body. Good grief, they'd shared the
most passionate of kisses and yet the simple touch of his
hand had the capacity to throw her completely off balance. This little struggle for control was becoming hopelessly one-sided! "And—and what would you have done
if you hadn't gotten caught?" she asked.

"First, I'd have spent a few hours jumping on the beds
in the furniture department. With my shoes on. Then I'd
have gone to the toy department and played with every
toy there. And then, to the coffee shop for ice cream and
pie and a whole jar of marshmallow fluff."

"Is that all?" Claudia asked.

"Well, back then, I would have eaten dirt if I had to
spend my night with a girl." He bumped her shoulder

playfully. "But now, I kind of like the idea. It adds some tantalizing possibilities to the evening."

"Funny, that's not how I imagined you as a kid," Claudia said. "I would have pegged you as an executive right out of the womb. A little toddler-sized suit and tie. Spending your night in the store balancing the books and marking up the merchandise. Maybe dusting the jewelry vault."

Tom laughed out loud. "This is not my dream, believe me. And I'm not such a stuffed shirt, am I?"

She stopped in the middle of the aisle and observed him shrewdly, rubbing her chin with her finger. "You could be reformed, I suppose. Given the right attitude, the right look." She strolled over to a display of men's Hawaiian shirts and pulled a hanger off the rack. "Take this little item. Pineapples, palm trees, orchids. This would look great on you."

Tom regarded the shirt with thinly veiled distaste. "I've never worn anything like that in my life."

"Well, live a little," she teased. "Take a chance. You wanted a memorable first date. No girl would ever forget you in that shirt. Besides, there's no one here to see but me and I certainly won't tell." Claudia sighed dramatically. "Or maybe you really are a stuffed shirt."

Tom shrugged out of his jacket and loosened his tie, accepting her challenge. "I can be spontaneous. Given the right circumstances." He tugged his shirt out of his pants and worked the buttons open. Claudia expected a nice white T-shirt beneath, probably starched and pressed. But when he slipped out of his shirt, he revealed a very naked, very muscular chest, a sight that seemed to render her speechless. She opened her mouth to toss off some lighthearted comment, but all that came out was a little squeak.

Claudia's fingers convulsed as she thought about smoothing her hands over his warm skin. She couldn't tear her eyes away as he grabbed the Hawaiian shirt and took it off the hanger. He seemed to have no idea of the effect his state of undress was having on her state of mind. His chest and belly rippled as he moved and when he turned to toss the hanger aside, Claudia nearly gasped at the sheer masculine beauty of wide shoulders tapering down to a narrow waist.

She opened her mouth again, ready to ask him to forget the shirt. Or at least, pull it on very, very slowly. But he'd already covered his naked torso, and was reaching for the buttons. She held out her hand to stop him. "No!"

"No? You don't like it? What, wrong colors?" He glanced over his shoulder. "I could try another one."

"No," Claudia said, suddenly fascinated by the sharp angle of his collarbone and the tiny indentation at the base of his throat. Her lips would fit perfectly right there, she mused. "You're—you're supposed to leave it unbuttoned. For the attitude."

Tom smiled and held up his hands, then slowly turned in front of her. "So, how do I look?"

Claudia's knees wobbled a bit and she felt a flood of heat kiss her cheeks as her gaze trailed down to his flat belly. He looked like a man she'd love to seduce. And she'd never deliberately seduced a man in her life! She wasn't even sure how to go about it.

"It's better," she said, gulping down the desire that welled up inside of her. "But now those pants don't go." She turned and surveyed the men's resort wear for something, anything, that would compel him to remove the bottom half of his business suit as well. In truth, she was surprised that he'd agreed to go along with her. Tom Dalton didn't seem like the type to just toss aside propriety *and* his clothes all in one night. Maybe this *would* be a date to remember.

She grabbed a pair of baggy surfer shorts in a shade of deep blue and handed them to him. "Here, try these." She pointed to his shoes and socks. "Make sure you take those off first. Nothing wrecks a cool look like ankle socks and wingtips." He took the shorts from her and headed toward a nearby dressing room. "Too modest to change in front of me?" Claudia called. "I already know what kind of underwear you wear. Boxers. Silk. Small patterns, no pastels."

He chuckled. "I'm not changing my underwear as well. Attitude has nothing to do with choice of underwear."

Claudia waited for him to return, her mind plagued with thoughts of Tom, dressed, undressed. She took a few steps toward the dressing room, wondering if he'd bothered to pull the curtain. But then she stopped, unable to summon her courage.

She hadn't expected such an intense physical reaction to him, a rush of desire flooding her body at the mere sight of him. Was it just the realization that there was an incredibly sexy man beneath the suit and tie? Or had all their teasing and testing been a prelude to something much more intimate—something that they'd share tonight?

"What do you think?"

Claudia blinked, her brain yanked back into the present. "Oh. Nice." Very nice, she mused. In addition to having the sexiest chest and shoulders she'd ever seen, he also had gorgeous legs, long and muscular, covered with a light dusting of hair. Even his feet were beautiful!

Tom stepped up to a mirror on the wall and stared at

his reflection. "It's not bad. I look like a slacker, but I guess that's in fashion."

Claudia moved to his side, smoothing her hands over the shoulders of the shirt, enjoying the feel of his hard flesh underneath. When she'd smoothed enough to make her fingers tingle, she drew her hands away. "It's missing something."

"I'm not wearing one of those silly straw hats."

"I'll know what I'm looking for when I find it," Claudia murmured. "Come on." She started toward the aisle, determined to continue their walk through the store, hoping it would take her mind off her thoughts of lust.

But this time, when he joined her, he didn't take her hand again. Instead he draped his arm around her shoulders and pulled her against his body. In return, she casually slipped her arm around his waist, her fingers splayed across warm muscle.

"I think this is much more fun that dinner at Silvio's," he said.

The feel of her body against his sent her mind spinning. Where was all her carefully cultivated control? This man shouldn't have such an effect on her. Claudia ground her teeth and tried to remember why she'd come to Schuyler Falls in the first place. This was all about the story, that's why she was pursuing this relationship with Tom Dalton. Simply for the story!

They strolled past the beauty salon tucked into a corner of the store near the coffee shop. An idea slowly formed in her mind, a way to put her and Tom back on their usual track of witty banter and friendly hostility. "I know what you need," she said, staring at a display at the entrance to the salon.

"A haircut?"

She picked up a tube of Funky Color from the display.

A shade of hot pink, the color that all the Schuyler Falls teenagers preferred. "This would make the outfit. A nice streak of color at either temple."

He looked at her dubiously, then shook his head. "No way. I'm not putting pink in my hair."

"It's not permanent," she said at the very same moment she was reading the word "semipermanent" on the box. Technically, in the world of beauty parlor parlance, she wasn't lying. "It'll wash out. Come on, Mr. Spontaneity." She grabbed him by the hand and dragged him into the darkened salon. She found the light switch and the entire salon came to life, all mirrors and track lighting. When she found the shampoo sink, she pushed him down into the chair. "I guarantee you're going to love this. It'll make you feel like a whole new man."

"A whole new freak," he corrected, grudgingly taking a seat. "I want you to know I'm only doing this for entertainment purposes. This in no way reflects my lifestyle nor my personality."

"This has to go on wet hair." Claudia pressed her palm on his forehead and he leaned back, resting his neck on the contoured edge of the sink. She turned on the water, waited for it to warm up, then sprayed it over his head.

But what she thought would be a silly lark took on an entirely different mood the instant she ran her fingers through his thick, dark hair. His eyes were closed and, for a long moment, she stared at his features, taking in the details of Tom Dalton's profile. Maybe she'd misjudged him. When she'd first met him she'd considered him nothing more than a straitlaced suit, a guy who considered business more important than life.

But time after time, he'd surprised her, with sudden kisses, with unexpected caresses. She idly furrowed her fingers through his wet hair as she considered the man she thought she knew. With crazy clothes and pink hair, he had suddenly become someone different, more than just a roadblock on her way to the biggest story of her life. He was warm and funny and thoughtful, silly and self-deprecating and even a little vulnerable.

He was a man she could probably fall in love with— if she gave herself the chance. Claudia squeezed the excess water from his hair then opened the tube. She hesitated, wondering if she should really go so far. After all, the guy did have an image to cultivate. And what would the store gossips say about a pink streak at his temple?

But Claudia put her doubts aside and squeezed a bit into a lock of hair at his temple. This will be a memorable first date, she mused. He certainly wouldn't be forgetting it, at least not until his hair went back to its regular color. As for her, Claudia wondered if she'd ever be able to forget Tom Dalton. Or if she'd ever want to.

"I THINK ANOTHER GLASS of champagne would be just wonderful."

Tom glanced over at Claudia, taking in her flushed cheeks and her bright eyes. She'd already had at least a half bottle of bubbly and the effects of the champagne were starting to show. Tipsy or sober, she was still the most beguiling woman he'd ever met. But tonight, he wanted her vision clear and her mind lucid.

He grabbed her glass and set it down on the coffee table, then handed her an open can of smoked oysters. They'd raided the gourmet market in the lower level of the store, right after they'd finished up in the beauty salon, coming away with a feast that could keep them alive for a week rather than just overnight.

Claudia had chosen Belgian chocolates, tinned oysters,

English crackers, caviar, canned pâté, and three different kinds of French cheeses. As she loaded the basket, Tom realized that had she asked for fresh-baked baguettes, he would have found a way to fly them in. It was hard to deny Claudia anything and Tom found himself anxious to please her.

She plucked another oyster from the can and popped it into her mouth, observing him as she chewed. "I know exactly what you need," she said, waving her finger in his direction.

He reached out and grabbed her hand, then wove his fingers through hers. He pulled her fingers to his lips and playfully kissed the tips of each one. "You do? And what is that?"

Claudia scrambled to her feet, yanking her hand away, then nearly tripped over herself climbing over him. She giggled, then sent him a sexy smile. "I'll be right back. Don't go anywhere!"

"I can't," he reminded her. "We're locked in."

She hurried out of the office. When he heard the elevator doors close behind her, he let out a tightly held breath. It had taken every ounce of his resolve to keep from tossing her down on his office sofa and having his way with her. If he'd known spending a night alone with Claudia Moore would cause such stress on his libido, he may have opened the front door of Dalton's and let her out himself.

Maybe he should just tell her the truth, that all they had to do was punch a few numbers into the security system and walk out of the store. But he was curious as to where the night would lead. Something had changed between them, the tension had relaxed, and he'd found the chance to look at Claudia through different eyes.

The games they'd played fell into the past and he could

see what they might share in the future. She was the most captivating woman he'd ever known. When he was away from her, he spent his time wondering when they'd see each other again. And when they were together, he found himself disappointed they couldn't be together every minute of every day.

But was he living in a fantasy world? He glanced over at her bag, sitting on the floor near the end of the sofa. He grabbed it, then looked inside. As he suspected earlier, he found one of his files tucked among her belongings, a reminder that though he may have feelings for Claudia, there were still too many secrets between them.

"Santa," he murmured, reading the block letters on the label before flipping through the contents. "I guess this proves my suspicions right." He stood up, fully intending to put the folder back in his credenza. But then he changed his mind and returned the file to her bag. After all, he'd wanted this whole secret Santa business to go away, didn't he? Why not let her expose his grandfather and be done with it?

The whole tradition had become a burden, a burden that had increasingly fallen in his lap. What would happen when Theodore Dalton no longer wanted to play Santa? His father certainly wouldn't take over. And Tom had never been able to refuse his grandfather anything. He'd be stuck in Schuyler Falls for the rest of his life, spending the holiday season in a fuzzy red suit!

"Better for the deception to come to light, than for Claudia and me to end now," he said softly. He leaned his head back and closed his eyes, wondering whether they'd ever be completely honest with each other, or whether Claudia would be out of his life before that happened.

He could finish the charade tonight if he wanted. When

she returned, he could toss the folder in her direction and demand an explanation. But Tom wasn't willing to throw it all away. For now, they could live in this little fantasy world. Morning would come soon enough.

"I have exactly what you need!"

Tom opened his eyes and found Claudia leaning against the doorjamb. She scampered into the office and she handed him a small card with a pair of faux-diamond studs attached.

"Earrings?"

"Earring," she corrected. She reached for her bag and rummaged through it, not noticing that the folder had been disturbed and not bothering to hide it. She must have had more champagne than he realized.

When she found what she was looking for, she held it up. *"Ta da!"*

"A sewing kit?"

"A needle. I'm going to pierce your ear!"

"Oh, no," Tom said, holding out his hand in protest, sliding to the far end of the sofa. "You are not sticking a needle in my ear."

"But you'll look so cool with a stud." She giggled. "A stud for a stud. I'm a poet and I don't even know it."

"And you have had entirely too much champagne," he said. "I'd be taking my life into my hands letting you come anywhere near me with that needle."

"Come on," she said, kneeling on the sofa. "I used to do this all the time when I was in high school and college. Here's a deal. If you let me pierce your ear, I'll let you kiss me."

He reached over and ran his hand along her thigh. "I could kiss you right now if I wanted."

Claudia wagged a finger at him. "But I wouldn't kiss

you back. You know, I find pierced ears very sexy. Almost irresistible. And I've never kissed a man with a pierced ear. There's no telling what might happen.''

Tom had no doubt she'd stick that needle in his ear. Claudia Moore had no fear. And with any other woman, he'd probably turn down the chance for a kiss. But with Claudia, he'd jump into the icy Hudson River if it meant she'd warm him up. He'd dance naked in the square, if she'd be the one to take off his clothes. Getting his ear pierced seemed like a small price to pay for one of Claudia's kisses. "We don't have any anesthetic. Is it going to hurt?" he asked.

She reached into the champagne bucket and withdrew a handful of ice. "Not at all," she said. She slapped the drippy cubes to the side of his head. "Here, hold these on your ear and when you can't feel it anymore, we'll go ahead."

Tom did as he was told. A few minutes later, he could truthfully say his ear was completely numb, though he wasn't quite sure he was ready to trust Claudia with the fate of his left earlobe. She'd sterilized the needle and an earring in a tumbler full of vodka she got from his grandfather's office and now knelt down beside him on the sofa.

"We could do both," she said. "Or two in one ear."

"No, I think one would be just plenty." He winced and waited for her to begin, watching her out of the corner of his eye. But every time he turned to look at her face, screwed up with concentration, she'd sigh and yank on his ear. In her slightly inebriated state, he might just end up with a needle in his eye.

"Just relax. It'll be over in a few seconds."

And it was. Tom heard a tiny pop and then another, followed by a long sigh from Claudia. A few seconds later, she slipped the earring into his ear and sat back on her heels.

"Am I bleeding?"

She shook her head and smiled, then stared at the earring. "You look...different." Her grin turned impish. "Dangerous."

Tom growled then grabbed her around the waist and threw her down on the sofa. "If my ear dries up and falls off, I'm coming straight to you." He smoothed the hair out of her eyes and looked down into the amber depths. "I believe we had a deal, didn't we?"

She reached up and lazily wrapped her arms around his neck. "One kiss," she said.

"Only one?"

Claudia nodded, her gaze dropping to his mouth. "Just one."

"Then, I'd better make it a good one."

This time, Tom took it slow. There was no one around to interrupt and nothing to stop him from kissing her all night long. He bent closer and ran his tongue along the seam of her lips. She sighed softly and opened beneath him.

The taste of her was like nothing he'd ever sampled before and he savored it, like a glass of fine wine. He took her face between his hands and molded her mouth to his, like a man parched with thirst and unable to stop drinking. He wanted more, so much more.

He stretched out above her, taking some of his weight with his arms, but she drew him nearer, wriggling beneath him until there was nothing between their bodies but a few layers of clothes. As he'd always known, they fit perfectly, her breasts against his chest, her hips and his pressed together, legs hopelessly tangled.

She moaned and arched against him and Tom felt himself grow hard with desire. Was this really the place and the time to act on their need? All these little lies standing between them didn't bode well for a good beginning. No, it would be better to wait until both of them knew exactly where the other stood. He slowly drew back, determined to wait.

Claudia's lips were softly parted and her breathing ragged. Through heavy-lidded eyes, she stared up at him. "You can kiss me again," she said. "I don't think just one kiss is really a good trade for a pierced ear."

Tom groaned and lowered his mouth to hers, eager to take just one more taste. But one turned into two and then three, and before he knew it, he'd lost count of how many times he'd kissed her. Kissing a woman had always been a prelude to something more, but he could kiss Claudia all night long and never tire of the sensations that raced through his body and warmed his bloodstream.

But he wasn't ready to make love to her. The lies acted as a roadblock to real intimacy. Her motives, his games, their desire. He rolled over, pulling her against his body and tucking her into the crook of his arm. Her fingers found the open buttons of his shirt and she idly smoothed her hand over his chest.

"Kiss me again," she demanded.

Tom chuckled. "If I kiss you again, I might not be able to stop kissing you. And you've had enough champagne that you might not be able to stop kissing me. So maybe we should just stop while we're both able to stop."

"You're just too honorable for your own good," she teased.

Tom closed his eyes and kissed the top of her head, sliding his fingers through the soft strands of her hair. Maybe he was. But he wasn't willing to risk everything he'd found with Claudia for a quick night of passion. If and when they made love, it was going to mean something.

"If you won't kiss me, then what are we going to do?" she said, running a finger along his bottom lip.

"We could talk," he said. "You could tell me all about yourself. I want to know everything."

She peered up at him, a frown wrinkling her forehead. "What do you want to know?"

"Whatever you want to tell me," he murmured, his gaze locking with hers. For a moment, Tom was certain she was ready to tell him the truth—about why she'd come to the store, about the job she was doing, about his stolen file. And when she hesitated, he nearly filled in the words for her. But in the end, Claudia simply smiled uneasily and told him about the house in Buffalo where she spent her childhood.

By the time she got to kindergarten and a tale about eating crayons, her words had grown slower, her voice softer. And when her story stopped completely, Tom glanced down to find her eyes closed, hints of a smile still touching her lips. A flood of affection washed over his body and he drew her nearer in a protective embrace. Someday soon, she'd tell him. And when she did, he'd know that what they shared between them had become more important to her than any story she could ever write. All he had to do was give her time.

Tom spent the hours until dawn just enjoying the feel of her beside him, the rhythm of her slow breathing and the tiny sounds she made in her sleep. For hours, he stared at her pretty face, cataloging each feature until he knew them all by heart—the perfect little nose, the Cupid's bow mouth, the soft, lush lips that tasted like sweet nectar. Her skin, silken and warm. And the dark lashes that ringed her eyes, now fluttering softly on her cheeks.

Looking at Claudia, Tom saw a woman he could truly love, a woman who stood apart from all the others he'd had in his life. He closed his eyes and tried to work out their future, the next few days, the next year, the rest of their lives. But everything was unfocused, marred by confusion. And when sleep replaced conscious thought, the dreams continued on, disjointed and frustrating until he forced himself to open his eyes.

He was certain he hadn't slept more than a few minutes. The clock told him differently. Claudia still lay curled against him, her hair tumbled around her face, her fingers clutching the front of his Hawaiian shirt.

Outside his office door, the elevator rumbled to a stop and the doors opened with a soft *ding*. No one on the fifth floor worked on Sundays...except his grandfather. Tom cursed, then carefully withdrew his arm from beneath Claudia's head. When he'd settled her without waking her, he rolled off the sofa and made to close his office door.

But his grandfather stepped inside before he had a chance to get halfway across his office.

"What the—" The old man stopped and stared. "Tommy?"

Tom put his finger to his lips and hurried out the door, closing it behind him.

"What the hell did you do to your hair?" He squinted. "Is that an earring you're wearing? Good Lord, what happened to you?"

"I can explain everything, Grandfather. But not right now."

His grandfather stared at him with a suspicious glint in his eye. "You're not having a...what do they call it—

identity crisis, are you? You know, when a man thinks he might be a woman living inside a man's body?''

"No!" Tom said. "It's an earring and a little hair dye. I'm not wearing a dress and ladies' underwear!"

"Well, don't yell at me. After all, you have been a little tense lately. And when I mention sex, you get all irritable. And I've seen this on Jerry Springer. Normal guys just losing their marbles for no reason. Come to think of it, your great-grandfather liked to wear an apron in the kitchen. I always thought that was a little strange.''

"I didn't do this to myself," Tom said. "Claudia did it.''

His grandfather blinked in confusion. "Claudia? My elf Claudia?''

"We spent the night in the store." He touched a hand to his ear. "This was our entertainment.''

"And she's still in there?" his grandfather asked. "She's not wearing Jockey shorts and a fedora, is she?''

Tom shook his head. "No, she's asleep, in her own clothes. And before you ask, nothing happened last night.''

"That's not what I was going to ask. I was going to ask why you spent the night here.''

"Well, probably because I told her we couldn't get out of the store until it opened," Tom replied, grimacing.

"So you lied to her?''

"I neglected to tell her the truth," he added.

"Well, no wonder she did that to you," his grandfather said. "If I were her I would have added a little lipstick and rouge as well.''

"She doesn't know I lied to her and you're not going to tell her," Tom said.

"Well, you're going to have to wake her up and get her out of here. Your father's been trying to reach you,'' his grandfather said. "He needs you in New York. That land deal you set up is going south and he wants you to meet with the sellers and their broker today. He set up a meeting for three. If you can't make it down by train, he'll send the plane up to get you. He says pack for at least three days. He's got other business he needs to go over with you early in the week."

Tom glanced back at his office door, then at his grandfather. "I can't leave. Not now. Not today." He wanted to stay right here, with Claudia, shut safe in his office where the outside world couldn't interfere. But a summons to corporate headquarters couldn't be ignored, and this land deal was the one thing Tom had hoped would get him out of Schuyler Falls for good.

"If I wake her," Tom said, "she won't be in the best of moods considering the amount of champagne she consumed last night. I think I'll just leave her a note and call her later." He glanced over his shoulder again at his office door.

His grandfather nodded. "You do realize you're getting involved with an employee."

"Well, that's the pot calling the kettle black, isn't it? Or had you forgotten that Grandmother worked at the candy counter?"

"I didn't forget that," his grandfather replied. "But I married the girl. Are your intentions so honorable?"

Tom muttered a soft oath, then turned and opened his office door. He quietly crossed the room and squatted down next to the sofa. Without thinking, he brushed a kiss across Claudia's forehead and stroked her cheek. But he couldn't bear to wake her up.

He levered to his feet and went to his desk. A quick explanation scribbled on a piece of Dalton's stationery would have to do for now. He added a promise to call

Claudia at the North Pole Village once he'd reached New York, then left the note beneath the handle of her bag. As he walked out of his office, he wondered if this might be for the best.

He didn't want to risk seeing regret on her face when she woke up. He didn't want to watch her walk out of his office with his file folder and act as if nothing were amiss. There would be time to straighten out everything that stood between them. And he planned to start the minute he returned from the city.

CLAUDIA WOKE UP WITH a headache, a throbbing so painful that at first she wasn't sure where she was. She knew she wasn't in her tiny little apartment in Brooklyn. She also wasn't in her room at the boardinghouse. As her vision gradually cleared, she realized precisely where she was.

"Tom Dalton's office," she murmured, pushing up and brushing the hair out of her eyes.

The office was empty inside and out, with no sign of Tom and no sounds coming from Mrs. Lewis's desk outside. "Sunday," she murmured. No one worked in the offices on Sunday. She rubbed her bleary eyes and looked at the clock, then moaned. It was nearly ten! In fifteen minutes she was due at the Candy Cane Gate and expected to look perky and elfin.

As she swung her feet off the edge of the couch, the events of the previous night slowly came back to her. "Oh, God," Claudia murmured. "I dyed his hair pink! And I pierced his ear." It had all seemed like such a lark under the influence of a little too much champagne. But behavior like that could get her fired! What would he do when he found out the color didn't wash out? Or when his earlobe got infected and fell off?

She snatched up her shoes and pulled them on, then stood. But a wave of dizziness overcame her and she quickly sat back down. As she waited for it to pass, other details of the night came back to her. They'd slept here together—at least, she thought they had—right on his office couch. And he'd kissed her, deeply and deliciously, again and again. Her blood warmed at the thought and, for a moment, her headache disappeared.

Perhaps she should wait for Tom to come back. After all, they had spent the night together. Running out was usually considered bad form. She should thank him for the lovely evening, for the food and the champagne. And the fun. Her mind returned to the pink hair and the earring.

"Maybe it would be best to leave." She found her coat draped over a wing chair and her bag near the end of the couch. A piece of paper fluttered to the floor as she picked it up. With an impatient sigh, she grabbed the paper and dropped it back on the end table where it belonged. When she reached the door, Claudia looked both ways, then made a break for the elevator. After punching the Down button for a full agonizing minute, the doors finally opened and she hurried in.

The bell signaling the opening of the store sounded just as she stepped off the elevator and Claudia groaned. In a few minutes, the line in front of the Candy Cane Gate would be ten children deep and she wasn't even dressed yet. As she hurried toward the employee dressing room, she raked her fingers through her tangled hair and wiped the mascara shadows from under her eyes. But just when she was certain she'd make it to the dressing room unobserved, Mrs. Perkins stepped out from behind a huge bin of rubber balls, stopping her in her tracks.

"Miss Moore, do you realize that you've been late to

work or late coming back from your breaks at least fifty percent of the time you've worked for Dalton's Department Store?"

She swallowed convulsively. Her mind was so fuzzy from the champagne hangover that she couldn't come up with a plausible excuse. "Really?" Claudia asked.

"It's highly unacceptable."

"Yes. Yes, I understand. And I'll try to do better. I promise."

Mrs. Perkins' eyebrow arched. "Aren't you even going to bother with an explanation, Miss Moore?"

Claudia sighed, then rubbed her temple, trying to eliminate the ache that had settled there. "I suppose I could, but you wouldn't believe me, so why bother?"

"I'm sure I'd appreciate at least the effort."

"All right," Claudia said. "I spent the night with Tom Dalton. I drank too much champagne and fell asleep in his arms and I overslept."

Eunice shook her head and sent her a condescending look. "This is not a joking matter and I certainly don't enjoy sarcasm. This is your final warning, Miss Moore. If you don't focus on punctuality, you will not be a part of our North Pole team. Do I make myself clear?"

"Perfectly," Claudia said. "I'll just go get dressed now and I'll be at the gate in just a few minutes."

She turned and hurried toward the employee dressing room. She really ought to quit right now. She'd managed to mess up this assignment so completely she wondered if any story was salvageable.

When she tossed her bag into the bottom of her locker, it fell open. Her heart lurched and she reached out and slowly pulled the file folder from inside. "Oh, no," she murmured. A flood of guilt assailed her. She'd meant to put it back but there hadn't been a chance. Actually there had been plenty of chances this morning had her mind been clear enough to remember she'd taken it in the first place.

Claudia's shoulders slumped. How could she have done this? What had led her to this point? What desperation? She'd never broken the law to get a story, and though she wasn't sure taking the file was illegal, it certainly wasn't ethical. And it was taking advantage of the growing intimacy between her and Tom.

"I have to put it back," she said, groaning softly. "This is no way to get a story." She knew Mrs. Perkins would be watching for her and she ran into her supervisor halfway to the elevator.

"Miss Moore, you're not dressed."

"I—I know, Mrs. Perkins. I've got a little emergency. I promise, I'll be right back. And—and I won't take any breaks today to make up for my tardiness. I'll be back in five minutes. Just five minutes."

She stepped around Eunice and headed straight for the elevator. To her relief, it opened on cue. She waited impatiently for the crowd inside to exit, then stepped inside and punched the button for the fifth floor. But the elevator went up to four then started back down.

Cursing silently, she hit the button again. But after picking up passengers on the first level, she rode up and back down again without reaching her destination.

When she finally reached the first level for the third time, she stepped out of the elevator and approached the security guard standing near the front entrance to the store. "Excuse me," she said. "I—I'm trying to take the elevator to the fifth floor, but it won't go up that far. It always stops on four."

"The corporate offices are on the fifth floor," the guard said. "And they aren't open on Sunday. You need a special key for the elevator to make it go to five. You can get down from there, but you can't get back up.''

"But I have something I need to drop off. For Mr. Dalton. In his office."

"Well, I could drop it off," the guard suggested.

She glanced at his name tag. "Well, LeRoy, that would be nice. But I have to do this myself. It's a personal matter."

The guard shrugged. "Then you'll have to do it between eight and five, Monday through Friday."

"But, I—" Claudia snapped her mouth shut. She was about to say that she'd been on the fifth floor last night after eight. But then she realized how she'd gotten there—through the secret stairway. She clutched the file folder to her chest and nodded curtly. "You've been a great help," she said, her tone dripping with acid.

She turned on her heel and strode toward the escalator, her mind spinning with new strategies. She could use the stairway again, to put the folder back. But she didn't know who might be working in the office on the other side of the secret door. If she waited until after store hours, she'd risk getting caught trying to leave. Maybe she could arrange to meet Tom up in his office for lunch and then ask him to fetch her a cup of coffee or a glass of water. She'd only need a few seconds to unlock the drawer in his credenza and shove the file inside.

Claudia stepped on the escalator. "This is exactly what you deserve. You develop a serious case of lust for the subject of your story and you immediately lose all your objectivity. If you were a real journalist, you'd keep the file and write the damn story."

She sighed softly. Maybe she wasn't cut out to work for the *Times*. But right now, that job didn't mean as much to her as the glimmer of a real relationship she'd found with Tom Dalton. And though he may be wearing an earring and sporting a pink streak in his hair, thanks to her, he was still a businessman at heart. A man who wouldn't look kindly on someone rifling through his private files—even if it was a woman he couldn't stop kissing.

"I'll find a way," Claudia vowed. "I'll make this right."

6

CLAUDIA SAT ON A BENCH in the elves' dressing room and tugged off her new booties. The new costumes had arrived on Tuesday and though they were made of a much more comfortable polyester blend, the design was even more ridiculous than the old costumes. Sparkling sequined trim clashed with gold braid and the faded colors of the old costumes had been replaced with garishly-bright greens and reds.

In truth, they could have been made of the finest silk, hand-beaded by Italian artisans, and she wouldn't have been satisfied. The tiniest things seemed to set her off lately. And though she could have blamed Tom Dalton for her mood, she wasn't about to give him the satisfaction.

After the crazy night they spent together Saturday, she'd assumed things had changed between them. They'd moved from a leery mistrust to a tenuous romance all in one night. But then he'd just disappeared without a trace, leaving her to wonder how much of the evening was real and how much was part of a champagne-induced fantasy.

With a soft sigh, she lay down on the bench and threw her arm over her eyes. Five days with no word. No one in the store seemed to know anything regarding his whereabouts; he'd just vanished. A good reporter could track him down, a good reporter could blithely question his secretary or check his house. But right now, she didn't feel like a good reporter. In truth, she felt like a hack—a very lonely, confused hack.

Standing at the Candy Cane Gate, she'd found herself scanning the sales floor every few seconds, waiting for him to appear. Claudia shuddered to think of how unbearable life had become without the possibility of his stirring touch...his soft kisses...

Claudia sat up, refusing to give in to her fantasies. After all, what did she want with Tom Dalton anyway? Sure, maybe a romance would be fun for a while, but sooner or later, he'd be asking for the same things all the others had. He'd want a wife, someone to tend to his life and do his laundry and make his dinner. A woman to throw parties and take care of the kids and look pretty on his arm.

Well, she wasn't that woman! She was a tough, accomplished journalist whose only goal in life was to write for a major metropolitan newspaper. And no man, not even the irresistibly sexy Tom Dalton, was going to sway her from her goals. She glanced up at the top shelf of her locker, at the file folder she'd stolen from Tom's office.

Over the past five days, she'd reached for it countless times, curious to see what was inside. Each time she told herself she'd simply be doing her job as a good investigative reporter. But her conscience always interfered and she left the file untouched. She stood up and reached for the folder, now determined to see what was inside. After all, what loyalty could she possibly have to a man who just deserted her after spending the—

"What do you think of the new costumes?"

Claudia's hand froze and she spun around to find Tom Dalton standing in the locker room, dressed in a tuxedo and looking more handsome than ever. The pink streak was gone, along with the earring, but he still looked dangerous. Her heart warmed and she couldn't help but smile. But then she remembered how angry she was and replaced the smile with a tight frown.

"Well, well. Look who's here. I was beginning to wonder if I'd ever see you again." She had every right to be angry! Sure, she wasn't his wife or his fiancée, not that she'd ever want to be. She wasn't even his girlfriend. Claudia cursed inwardly. Oh, the hell with it. "It looks like you got a new costume, too. Is that what department store owners are wearing these days? I haven't seen you in such a long time, I guess I might have missed a new fashion trend."

"I'm on my way to a party." He frowned. "Are you angry with me?"

"Oh, no. Why would I be angry?"

"Why would you?"

Claudia laughed harshly. "I don't know. Perhaps because we spend a romantic evening locked in your damned department store and then you desert me without a word. It's Thursday! That's five—count 'em—five days without hearing from you!"

"I left you a note," he said. "And I've been leaving you fax messages two or three times a day. Mrs. Lewis put them in your mailbox."

"My mailbox?"

He pointed to the dressing room door. "It's right next to the lunch tables. The little gray bins. That's how we distribute memos around the store to all the employees."

"I—I didn't know I had a mailbox," she answered defensively, her anger slowly dissolving. He'd left her fax messages? Two or three times a day? That was...well, it was romantic. "But that still doesn't excuse you," Claudia grumbled.

He smiled warmly, then wrapped his hands around her waist. When she refused to meet his gaze, he bent down until he was even with her eyes. "I'll have to make it up to you, then. I came up here to ask you to accompany me to a small Christmas party. Family, business associates, a few community leaders. What do you say?"

She reluctantly met his gaze. "I hope this party is sometime next week and the reason you're wearing a tux is because all your other suits are at the cleaners. It would be really uncouth of you to invite me to a party an hour before it begins."

"Actually, it starts in an hour and a half. Plenty of time for you to get ready. You don't need to bother with the hair and the makeup and—"

"I beg your pardon!"

"I mean, you're beautiful exactly the way you are," he said, sending her a charming grin. "You have a natural beauty. You don't need all that paint and powder."

"Good save," Claudia muttered dryly. "But the answer is still no."

"Why? Because I asked too late? That doesn't seem like a very good reason."

"Where did you take dating lessons?" Claudia demanded. "The World Wrestling Federation School for Social Graces? You should have asked me earlier!"

"I did. I left it in a message on Monday morning. Can I help it if I was called away on business?" He sighed. "But that's all right. I understand if you don't want to go. You're under no obligation to…I mean, just because we spent the night together…and it's not like we're…I suppose I could always ask Janine in accounting. Or Lila in—"

An unbidden rush of jealousy surged through her body.

She wasn't about to let another woman get near him while he was dressed in that tux! "Yes," Claudia said.

"Yes, you're under no obligation? Or yes, you'll come to the party with me?"

"Yes, to both," Claudia said. She paused, her spirits rising and falling in the space of a few seconds. "Wait. I can't go to a party. I don't have anything to wear. I can't wear my elf outfit, attractive as it is. Not when you're dressed in a tux. I need a dress. And I don't have shoes or jewelry."

Tom grinned. "I could scrounge up an elf outfit in my size. Would we match then?"

"Don't be silly," Claudia said, her disappointment acute. Now he'd be forced to take Janine or Lila or some other well-dressed hussy who would hang all over him and stroke his ego. And maybe, at the end of the night, he'd kiss the hussy like he'd kissed her.

"Well, I just happen to have a little store," he said, "with dresses and shoes and jewelry." He glanced at his watch. "The store closes in five minutes. I'll let security know you're going to be shopping after hours. Just take whatever you want. I'll have someone stay late in shoes to fit you with the right size."

"I couldn't accept a gift like—"

"Call it a loan," Tom said. "You can give everything back at the end of the evening."

"People will talk," she warned. "Dishing out evening wear to one of your elves is bound to cause a little gossip."

"I pay my people well to keep their comments to themselves. You have nothing to worry about. No one at the store will know I'm dating one of the elves."

"Is that what this is? A date?"

He considered her question for a moment, then nodded. "Yes. We'll call this our first date."

"I thought our night in the store was our first date."

"Then this is a big step," he teased. "A second date." The bell sounded over the store's public address system. "The store is closing. Why don't you start to look for something to wear. I've got some calls to make up in my office. Come up when you're ready. I'll have the guard leave the elevator unlocked."

Claudia nodded, then pulled her elf booties back on. By the time she left the dressing room, the store's lights had already been dimmed and there were only a few sales associates left on the floor. She climbed up the escalator to the third floor where ladies' evening wear was tucked into a tiny salon. The dresses, some of them with designer labels, were displayed like fine works of art.

She was drawn immediately to a deep blue gown with a silk shantung jeweled bodice and a wide velvet skirt. In the low light it sparkled like stars in a twilight winter sky. Claudia reached for the price tag then dropped it as if it had burned her fingers. "Fifteen hundred dollars," she said.

"That one would look lovely on you, dear."

She glanced over her shoulder to find an elderly sales associate standing at the entrance to the salon. "I—I couldn't. Besides, I'm not sure how formal the party is. Maybe something a little less flashy. A simple black dress? Something...cheaper?"

The sales associate bustled up and snatched the hanger from the hook. "This would be perfect. Go on, try it on. I'll run down to the shoe department and find something for your feet." She glanced down at Claudia's elf booties. "Size seven?"

"Seven and a half," Claudia corrected.

"Fine," she said. "I'll be right back." The sales associate paused. "My name's Millie, by the way. Mr. Dalton told me you'd be coming for a dress."

"Claudia. I'm Claudia." She wandered back to the fitting room and stepped inside, pulling the door closed behind her. With a soft sigh, Claudia sat down on an upholstered stool and stared at herself in the mirror. This might be every girl's fantasy, but she knew that it could turn into a nightmare in the blink of an eye. She was an elf, not some Schuyler Falls socialite.

"Just consider this part of the investigation," she murmured. "It's not a party, it's an opportunity. And he's not your date, he's a way to get to your story."

She stared at herself for a long time, trying to reconcile her feelings. Being a reporter had always been the most important thing in her life. But now, that all seemed mired in confusion, mixed up with thoughts of a future with Tom Dalton.

She slipped out of the elf outfit and examined her underwear. It was a shame to put on such a pretty dress over plain cotton underwear, so she yanked off her camisole and panties then stepped into the gown. She slid the strapless bodice over her hips and up her torso and she held it in place with her hands, staring at her reflection in the mirror.

"Oh, my," she murmured. Claudia had never seen herself as a beautiful woman. At best, she considered herself attractive. Cute, even. But never, ever beautiful. Except all that had changed the moment she stepped into the dress. The deep blue brought out the ivory tones in her skin and set off the rich mahogany color of her hair.

Humming the first bar of 'I Feel Pretty,' Claudia swayed from side to side, her skirt rustling as she moved. She couldn't remember the last time she wore a dress.

She usually preferred a tailored pantsuit when she was forced to dress up. But this dress was made to get a girl noticed. "Maybe there will be dancing," she murmured. She'd love to dance with Tom, wrapped in his arms, hips pressed together, moving sensuously to the—

"I've got your shoes," Millie called from outside the fitting room. She knocked, then pushed the door open and handed Claudia a pair of midnight-blue satin pumps with a jeweled buckle. A pretty handbag followed and a matching velvet wrap with a shantung lining.

Millie helped her zip up the dress and slip into the shoes, then gently convinced her to try a bit more makeup as she drew her back into the salon. As Claudia put on a second coat of mascara and reapplied her lipstick, Millie twisted her shoulder-length hair up into a jeweled clip then pulled out a few tendrils around her face.

"Perfect," Millie said, staring at Claudia's reflection in the three-way mirror. "You're a lovely girl. I'm sure Mr. Dalton will be pleased."

"I am." Tom stood in the entrance to the salon, his eyes fixed on Claudia, an appreciative smile curling the corners of his mouth. "Are you ready?" he asked.

Claudia smoothed her trembling hands over the velvet skirt and nodded. "As long as we don't go near any food or drink, I think I can get the dress back to the store without making a mess of it. But if I spill something, you're going to have to pay for it. This dress costs more than an elf makes in a year."

"I found this downstairs," he said, holding out a diamond and sapphire necklace. "It seems we have a jewelry department in this store and I've got a key to the vault."

Her eyes went wide as he stepped behind her and strung the necklace around her neck, fastening it with gentle fingers. It went perfectly with the dress, the glittering stones simple yet elegant. "Thank you." Claudia giggled and stared at herself in the mirror. "The necklace, the dress, the party," she murmured. "This is all very Richard Gere-Julia Roberts. Except I'm not a prostitute and you're—well, you *are* rich." And much better looking than Richard Gere, Claudia mused.

"Prostitute?"

"Yeah. Julia Roberts. Richard Gere. *Pretty Woman?*" She shook her head at his bewildered expression. "Don't you go to the movies?"

"No," Tom said. "I never seem to have time."

"I'll have to rent *Pretty Woman* and we'll watch it," she suggested. "We can call that our third date."

He smoothed his fingertips along her bare shoulders, his touch as gentle as a balmy breeze. "I'd like that." A tiny shiver skittered down her spine and Claudia fought the urge to turn around and kiss him right there. She felt as if she'd been dropped into the middle of a Cinderella fairy tale, complete with a handsome Prince Charming. Wasn't this every girl's fantasy?

But would Prince Charming be so charming after she exposed all the palace secrets? She'd already decided to put the file back but that was much easier said than done. The clock was ticking and sooner or later he'd notice it was missing. At first, he might brush it off and assume it had been misplaced by Mrs. Lewis. Only after he searched for it would he realize she'd taken it. And that would be the end of it. The Cinderella fantasy gone up in smoke as fast as she could say bibbidy-bobbidy-boo.

"Are you ready?" he asked.

Claudia drew a deep breath. If it did go up in smoke, then at least she'd have this night. One romantic night with a handsome man, dressed in a beautiful dress. Nothing, not his anger nor his mistrust nor his disdain, would ever take that away from her.

CLAUDIA STARED OUT THE CAR window, watching silently as they left downtown and turned into a residential area. She hadn't taken the time to tour Schuyler Falls and the striking beauty and grandeur of the neighborhood surprised her. They passed huge stone mansions, set far from the road, once summer retreats for New York City's wealthy.

Tom swung the Lexus into the next driveway and maneuvered the car on a winding path through thick woods. Suddenly the bare-limbed trees gave way to a wide, snow-covered lawn and a stunning stone mansion. Claudia sighed as she took in the brightly illuminated house. "It's like a castle," she murmured.

If she didn't already feel like Cinderella, she certainly did now. A hypocritical fairy-tale princess with a secret that just might turn her into a pumpkin before midnight and send her prince looking for another princess.

"My great-grandfather built it," Tom explained. "My grandparents lived here until they moved to Arizona. My parents lived here for a while, but they prefer New York City. Now it's mine."

A gasp burst from her lips. "This is *your* house?"

"I know it's a little big for just one person, a little ostentatious. But it's home."

"It's a little big for *ten* people!" Claudia cried.

"But it would be perfect for a family, don't you think?" He turned to look at her, his gaze direct, penetrating. Claudia felt the blood rush to her face and she was glad of the dim car interior. Though she'd tried to avoid it, there were times when she wondered what marrying Tom Dalton might be like. She'd even imagined them with a few kids. But the fantasies were just idle whimsy, something to occupy her time at the Candy Cane Gate.

Claudia Moore wasn't the kind of girl to go all sappy inside over a guy, even a guy as handsome and charming as Tom Dalton. And she certainly wasn't the kind of girl to dream of a big diamond ring and a fancy church wedding. She was a mature, driven career woman who knew better than to let passion interfere with her professional duties. And even if she did indulge in passion every now and then, she could walk away when it came time.

"Why would someone throw a party at your house?" she said, scowling.

"It's my party," he explained. "As general manager of the store, I'm supposed to throw one every holiday season. I invite some of the town's prominent businessmen, our local politicians and bankers, a few friends and relatives."

"Wait!" Claudia cried. "This is your party? And I'm your date? Does that mean I'm expected to—"

"Don't worry." He reached over and took her hand, lacing his fingers through hers. "You're not expected to do anything except be your witty and beautiful self. As soon as you'd like to leave, I'll take you home."

As they pulled beneath the portico, Claudia drew a deep breath. Until this moment, the invitation to the party seemed so benign that she hadn't really thought before accepting. But now she'd be expected to socialize with Tom's circle of friends and acquaintances. People would whisper and wonder about the woman he brought. There would be speculation and questions she wasn't prepared to answer. And something told her this crowd wouldn't be as forgiving as her rowdy bunch of reporter buddies.

He stopped the car and turned to her, draping his arm

over the back of the seat. "Don't worry," Tom said, as if he could read her mind. "You look incredible. Just smile and you'll render them all speechless."

She tried to smile, but failed miserably. "Thank you," Claudia said.

He leaned closer and brushed a kiss across her lips. They should have stopped there, with the parking valet standing outside his car window, but the sensation of his mouth on hers again was too much to resist. His hand found the hair at her nape and he slid his fingers through it, molding her mouth to his, tasting her with his tongue.

"Maybe we should just skip the party," he suggested. "I know a nice place to park. No one would miss me. The caterers have everything under control."

"And maybe we should save the steamy windows and groping hands for the fifth or sixth date," she teased. "Come on, we should go in. It's your party."

"If you promise there will be a fifth and sixth date, then I suppose I could wait."

"Of course there will be more dates," Claudia replied lightly. But her promises were hollow, empty of truth. Though she wanted to believe there would be hundreds of dates, once her work was finished in Schuyler Falls, she'd leave.

Tom hopped out of the car, tossed the keys to the valet, then circled to open her door. He held out his hand, ever gallant, to help her from the car, then rested his palm on the small of her back. The gesture was faintly possessive and endlessly comforting. When they reached the door, it opened in front of them and Claudia stepped into a foyer glittering with Christmas cheer and buzzing with conversation.

Everyone turned to greet Tom and to observe her with curiosity. She pasted a smile on her face, but the introductions went in one ear and out the other. Finally, when they'd finished running the gauntlet of Schuyler Falls society, they retreated to a quiet alcove just off the dining room.

"That wasn't so bad," Tom said, giving her hand a squeeze. "Why don't I go get you a glass of champagne?"

Claudia nodded, the smile still tight on her face. "Just one glass. Just to calm my nerves."

She watched as he disappeared into the crowd of guests, then turned to study a Chinese vase on a nearby pedestal.

"It's beautiful, isn't it? It's from some dynasty, I can never remember which."

She turned, her elbow bumping the vase. It wobbled on its stand and she cried out as it began to topple. But the elderly gentleman reached out and steadied it with easy calm. "I—I'm sorry. I should be more careful," she said, her cheeks flaming with embarrassment.

"You're Claudia, aren't you."

"You know me? I'm afraid I don't remember meeting you." She had a keen memory for names and faces—a reporter's instinct. Her gaze scanned his features and her breath caught. There *was* something oddly familiar about this man, but she couldn't place him.

"I'm Tom's grandfather, Theodore Dalton. I've seen you at the store. You work as an elf."

Claudia held out her hand and met his smiling eyes, intensely green like Tom's. "Mr. Dalton, it's a pleasure meeting you." Perhaps it was the resemblance to Tom that made him seem familiar. It was there in the eyes, in the devilish smile and strong profile. "This is a lovely party."

He nodded and perused the room, then turned back to her. "So, Miss Moore, have you figured it all out yet?"

"Excuse me?" she asked, taken aback by the odd question.

"Have you figured out who the real Dalton's Santa is?"

Her heart leaped to her throat and she blinked back her surprise. "I—I'm not sure I understand," Claudia said. Did Tom's grandfather know who she was and what she was up to? How had he found out?

"You're a reporter, isn't that right?"

Claudia's heart dropped from her throat into her expensive jeweled pumps. "How did you know that?"

He smiled mischievously, a smile that reminded her so much of Tom's. "I have my sources. You know, I've often thought the direct approach was much better than all this subterfuge you journalists seem to enjoy. Why not just ask your questions and have it over with?"

Claudia opened her mouth, then snapped it shut again. That couldn't possibly work, could it? After all this hassle, the answers couldn't possibly be so simple. "All—all right," she began. "I'll ask you. Do you know who's behind the gifts that Dalton's Santa gives out each year?"

"Yes," he said.

"And who is that?"

"It's me, of course. And before me, it was my father. And after me, it will be my son and my grandson. There's a foundation that Thaddeus Dalton began when he opened Dalton's Department Store. Besides our secret Santa contributions, we give away quite a bit of money to charity."

A twinkle glittered in his eye and Claudia gasped in

recognition. "It's you," she murmured. "You're Santa. I've been working just ten feet from you all the time?"

He nodded. "You're a terrible elf," he said. "You just weren't cut out to wear the booties, were you?"

"I wasn't," Claudia moaned. "But I thought it was the quickest way to get to the story."

"And now you have it."

"Yes," Claudia murmured, the full implications hitting her. Now she had her story. And once she had a few more facts, she'd have no reason to stay in Schuyler Falls, no reason to be near Tom Dalton, no chance for a perfect future with a perfect man.

"But, I don't think you'll report your story," Theodore said.

Claudia blinked, surprised by the confidence in his tone. "Why not?"

He chuckled softly. "Because you're in love with my grandson, and to betray my secret would betray our family. And him. I don't think you'll do that."

"But I have to report my story. I can't go back to the *Times* with nothing. This is my chance for a full-time job with them."

He nodded solemnly then smiled. "Well, then you have a difficult choice ahead of you, Claudia. I certainly wouldn't want to be in your place."

"Why did you tell me this?" she asked.

He shrugged. "I love my grandson and I want the best for him."

"Then this is a test?"

"Call it what you want," Theodore said.

"And if I want the rest of the details for my story?"

He paused, then nodded. "I'll have Mrs. Lewis copy all the files. You can pick them up tomorrow morning."

"And are you going to tell Tom who I am and why I came here?"

He smiled. "I think that's up to you." With that, he tipped his champagne glass to her and walked away.

Claudia slowly lowered herself into a wing chair and tried to regain her composure. Would he keep his word or would Tom's grandfather feel compelled to reveal her true motives? And what exactly were her true motives? The more time she spent with Tom, the more she wished her story would just go away.

Who really cared about a small town Santa's generosity? Sure, it would make a nice article, but would it help the economy or promote world peace? It was just a little, insignificant story, meant to make people feel good during the holiday season. A story she could easily forget, along with a job that might come along with it.

"Let it go," Claudia murmured to herself, her decision suddenly becoming clear.

There would be other assignments and other stories. And maybe even other job offers. But she knew in her heart she had only one chance with Tom Dalton and she wanted to make the best of it.

TOM BARELY SAW CLAUDIA during the rest of the party. Though they passed each other a number of times, exchanging a few soft words or a fleeting caress, he'd been unable to tear himself away. He watched her now from a quiet spot near the entrance to the living room. She was chatting with the mayor of Schuyler Falls, involved in an animated conversation in front of the glittering Christmas tree.

At first, he'd worried about her. She'd seemed uneasy and out of place. But once she'd mingled for a while, her naturally witty nature took over, bolstered by the self-assurance she'd seemed to find in the beautiful dress. Every time the sound of laughter erupted, he turned to find her in the middle of it, charming everyone she spoke to.

Tom scanned the room. The crowd had thinned and those who had to work the next day had made their good-byes before eleven. Now, there were only the die-hard party-people who would stay until they stopped serving food or liquor. He watched as Claudia spoke to a well-dressed city councilman whose name he couldn't recall. Bob or Bill. What he could recall was that the guy was a notorious womanizer!

He crossed the room in a few determined strides and caught her hand in his. "I hope you'll excuse us," he said to the councilman. "I haven't had a chance to speak with Claudia all night long and that's no way to treat such a beautiful lady." Tom tugged her along toward the kitchen, pushing open the swinging door and leading her through the butler's pantry.

"Where are we going?"

"Someplace where we can be alone." He perused the food left on the huge worktable in the center of the kitchen, then began to place tidbits from the half-empty trays on a pair of plates. When he finished, he grabbed a bottle of champagne from the refrigerator and two champagne flutes from the counter and handed them to Claudia. "Come on, I'll give you a tour of the house."

They headed up a back staircase that led to the second floor, and when they entered the grand hallway upstairs, Claudia stopped and stared. Tom knew it was a little startling. A second Christmas tree, filled with heirloom ornaments stood at the far end of the hall. Oriental carpets covered parquet flooring and wood furniture glowed with a warm patina. "It's lovely," she breathed.

He wanted her to love it, though he wasn't sure why it mattered so much. "I didn't do any of the decorating," Tom said. "The party planner did all the Christmas stuff and my mother and grandmother are responsible for the rest of the house. Besides a few new drapes and some fresh wallpaper every ten years, the house hasn't changed much since my great-grandfather built it." He slowly turned around. "I've always loved this place. I spent my childhood in this house."

"Show me your room," Claudia said.

He motioned her down the hall, and when they reached the door at the end, he opened it. If she expected remnants of his childhood, a few Little League trophies and model airplanes, she wouldn't find them here. His room was dark and masculine, dominated by a huge four-poster bed on one side and a sofa-flanked fireplace on the other.

Tom glanced over at her and found her gaze flitting over the bed as she shifted uneasily beside him. "This is very nice. Now show me the rest," she said.

Tom chuckled and nudged her inside. "Don't worry, nothing will happen here that you don't want to happen."

"I—I'm not worried. I know you're a perfect gentleman."

A perfect gentleman with imperfect thoughts. How could he be near Claudia and not think of kissing her so deeply she'd feel it in her toes, or of gently undressing her until she stood naked before him? She was a woman who would make a monk question his vows of celibacy. And though it had been a long time since Tom had enjoyed all the pleasures a woman could offer, he'd never subscribed to celibacy.

He sat down on the bed and set the plates of food beside him. "Come on, we'll have a picnic."

"Shouldn't we go back down to your guests?"

Tom shook his head. "They'll go home sooner or later. I want to spend some time with you." He popped a crab puff into his mouth and studied her as he chewed. "You were wonderful," he said.

"Me?"

"Tonight, at the party. You were beautiful and charming and everyone fell in love with you."

She glanced down, clearly embarrassed by his compliment. "It was the dress and the jewelry."

Tom shook his head as he swallowed another crab puff. "I don't think so. You'd be just as wonderful without the gown and the sapphires."

The double meaning of his words hit her at the same time it did him. She quickly stood and smoothed her hands over the jeweled bodice of her dress. "We should really go back."

Tom pushed to his feet and slipped his hands around her tiny waist. "Stay," he said. He bent closer and dropped a kiss on her parted lips. "Just for a little while." Another kiss, this one a bit deeper, found its way to her mouth. And when she sighed in surrender, Tom pulled her against his body and kissed her the way he'd been thinking about all night—long and soft and warm, a soul-deep kiss that would shatter the last bit of her resistance.

He gently pushed her back to the bed, then held on to her as they tumbled onto the soft mattress, pulling her body on top of his. He reached over and grabbed a chocolate-covered strawberry from the plate and drew it along her bottom lip. "Are you hungry?"

Her tongue lined the crease of her mouth and she shook her head, her eyes glazing with need. "You said nothing would happen unless I wanted it to," she murmured, her gaze drifting over his features. "What—what if I wanted something...to happen?"

He hooked a finger under her chin and forced her eyes to meet his. "Are you sure?"

Claudia nodded but Tom wasn't entirely convinced. He pulled her up with him, sitting her in front of him on the bed. Then he drew his hand along her collarbone, teasing and testing, searching for her reaction and waiting for a clue to her true feelings. When she closed her eyes and tilted her head back, he trailed a line of kisses from the base of her neck to her bare shoulder, reveling in the silken feel of her warm skin against his lips.

Suddenly he couldn't hold back. He wanted Claudia to melt in his arms, to cry out his name in the midst of their passion, to look at him with more than desire, with love. Tom smoothed his palms over the bare expanse of her chest, feeling her heart beating beneath his fingertips. Then he slipped his hands around her neck to unfasten her necklace. But he didn't grab it in time and the jewels slid down into the bodice of her dress between her breasts.

Tom bit back a chuckle. "That was smooth," he said, staring down at the spot where the sapphires and diamonds had disappeared. "I—I guess I'm a little out of practice." He paused and looked into her beautiful face. "Or maybe I'm just a little nervous."

"I'll get them," Claudia said, blushing.

He gently pushed her hand away. "No, allow me." He slid his fingers into her cleavage, but as soon as he touched the soft flesh, desire washed over him, stealing the breath from his body and setting his blood on fire. Transfixed by the sight of the jewels slipping out from the cleft of her breasts, he reached around her back and slowly undid the zipper of her dress. The rasping sound was all that could be heard over their quickened breathing.

The bodice loosened and Claudia gasped, pressing her hand to hold it up.

"Don't," he said, lacing her fingers through his and drawing her hand to his lips. The bodice fell away, revealing her body to his eyes for the first time. Tom was stunned by her beauty, by the sheer perfection of her, and with a hesitant hand, he reached out and cupped her breast in his palm. With his thumb, he massaged her nipple until it peaked beneath his touch.

"You're more beautiful than I ever imagined," he murmured.

Again, she blushed and he found it utterly entrancing that she didn't realize the power her beauty held over him. Natural and guileless, Claudia could say more with a simple smile than all the women he'd known in his life. Though she appeared tough on the outside, he'd gradually come to know the real woman inside—sweet, vulnerable, unsure of her own sexual magnetism.

Tom reached up and removed the jeweled clip from her hair. The rich mahogany waves fell around her face into a style that was more bedroom than ballroom. Gently, he pushed her back into the down pillows, stretching out beside her.

And then, as if drawn by an invisible will, he began to kiss her. First, her lips and then her throat. He lingered at the notch in the middle of her collarbone, drawing his tongue over the indentation and tasting her skin. Slowly he drifted lower, spurred on by a need so acute that it suffused his blood and numbed his brain.

When his mouth covered her nipple, she cried out, the protest in her reaction cutting through the haze in his brain. He didn't want to stop but common sense told him something was wrong. Claudia had come to mean so much to him, he wasn't willing to risk what they had found. He pushed up on his elbow and gazed at her flushed face.

After a few moments, she opened her eyes. But he didn't see passion there, only doubt and confusion. "Claudia, we don't have to do this," he murmured.

"No, really, it's all right. I—I want to." Her hands fluttered over his shoulders and she furrowed her fingers through his hair, pulling him nearer.

But Tom knew the moment had vanished and he brushed a chaste kiss across her lips. "Sweetheart, we have plenty of time. I *will* make love to you. You can count on that. But only when you trust me to touch you the way you deserve to be touched."

Claudia bit at her bottom lip as she stared up into his face. That look was enough to test Tom's resolve, those intriguing amber eyes that had skimmed over his body with undisguised appreciation, those tempting lips that made kissing her a religious experience. It took all his will to draw away, but it was the right thing to do. There were too many issues left unresolved between them and he saw them all in her confused expression.

"Why don't I take you home? I'll go down and warm up the car while you…get dressed."

She nodded, a tiny glimmer of relief suffusing her features. Tom rolled off the bed, straightened his tux and started for the door.

"Wait," Claudia cried.

He stopped and slowly turned around, wondering if anything she said could cause him to change his mind. She drew up the bodice of her dress and brushed the hair out of her eyes. "You can just call me a cab. You should really stay here until all your guests leave."

Tom was about to protest, but then realized that proper party etiquette had nothing to do with her request. She'd managed to keep her life outside the store a closely held secret. If he knew that she lived at the boardinghouse, he might be forced to ask the logical questions. Why didn't she have an apartment of her own? Did she plan to stay in Schuyler Falls or was she just visiting? Questions Tom wasn't ready to ask and he knew Claudia wasn't ready to answer.

"My grandfather's driver is still here," he said. "I'll have him take you home."

He turned back to the door, but her voice stopped him again. "I think I might need help with this zipper," she said.

Tom crossed back to the bed and helped her to her feet. When she turned her back to him, he reached for the zipper and slowly began to draw it upward. When the bodice was fastened securely over her naked body, he allowed his hands to drop onto her shoulders.

She turned around and looked up at him and he couldn't resist stealing just one more kiss. "Come on," he murmured. "Let's get you home and to bed."

As he showed her out his bedroom door, he couldn't help but wish he was putting her to bed in his own room. And that he'd find her the next morning, naked, clinging to him in a tangle of arms and legs, soft skin and warm flesh.

Tom drew a steadying breath. There were some things worth waiting for in life and he had no doubt in his mind that Claudia was one of them.

7

"ANOTHER DAY, ANOTHER dollar!"

"More like fifty cents," Claudia muttered to the security guard as she stumbled through the employee entrance to the store. She'd considered calling in sick but since she didn't remember the protocol for elfin emergencies, she wasn't sure who to call—Mrs. Perkins, the personnel department, the Gingerbread Cottage? God forbid, she'd have to call Tom Dalton!

He was the reason she hadn't slept last night and why she couldn't put a coherent thought together this morning. After they'd left his bedroom, he'd put her into the car without another attempt at seduction. His kiss goodnight at the car door was as chaste as a favorite uncle's and when the door slammed behind her, Claudia couldn't help but wonder how she could have let things go so far!

Though she'd had some experience with men, she'd always thought that once a girl decided she didn't want to be seduced then she could simply stop. But she had wanted Tom to make love to her last night and she'd almost gone through with it. And if she had, everything would have changed. He would have expected more, wanted more, and Claudia wasn't sure that she could have given him what all men really wanted—a wife.

He'd told her there would be time; he believed they'd have a future. But Claudia knew better. Last night was probably the end of everything they'd shared. His grandfather already knew what she was up to. How long would it be before he told Tom? How long before he discovered the file she had hidden in her locker? Or realized her true motives?

He was a passionate man, both in business and in pleasure. She longed to experience that passion firsthand. After she was gone from Schuyler Falls, she knew simple fantasies wouldn't be enough. Making love to Tom Dalton would stay with her forever, a memory she could take out again and again, a memory that would ease the ache of loneliness when her career became the only thing in her life again.

Would it all end today, or would she be granted more time to fix things? Last night, as she'd tried to sleep, her mind kept running over the possible scenarios. She imagined what Theodore Dalton would tell his grandson and she pictured Tom's reaction. Then she tried to visualize what their first encounter might be like after that rather surprising revelation.

Would he be angry? Or disgusted? Would he refuse to talk to her and just fire her summarily? Or would she be subjected to a litany of aspersions on her character? Whatever happened, and whenever it happened, she knew she wouldn't be ready. Not that she wasn't anxious to give up her job as an elf. She just wasn't ready to give up her feelings for Tom Dalton.

She climbed the silent escalator up to the second floor, all the while keeping an eye out for Tom. Good grief, if this was what her day was going to be like, waiting for the ax to fall, maybe she should have stayed home! She waved at Mrs. Perkins who was working on one of the registers in the toy department, then pointed at her watch. "Fifteen minutes early," she called.

"Very good," Mrs. Perkins said.

As she walked into the employee dressing room, she saw the elves huddled together over the lunch table. "What's going on?" she asked.

Dinkie held up the morning edition of the *Schuyler Falls Citizen.* "Look. It's Tom Dalton and his new girlfriend. Everyone in the store is talking about it and no one knows who she is. He hasn't dated anyone for years. Rumor has it he brought her to his big Christmas party and before the party was even over, they disappeared...upstairs." The last was added in a scandalized tone.

Claudia grabbed the newspaper and stared at the picture. Though the rest of the elves might not recognize her, she certainly knew the face of the woman standing next to Tom Dalton.

She tried to fight back the flames of heat creeping up her cheeks. "What else are they saying?" she asked, maintaining a cool indifference.

"She's not that beautiful," Winkie muttered owlishly. "But she must be rich if she's wearing all those jewels. They almost look real, don't they?"

"Of course they're real," Claudia murmured.

Blinkie peered over Claudia's shoulder at the newspaper. "She looks familiar," he said before turning back to his Marilyn Manson fanzine. "Either she was in the last Megadeth video or I think I might have seen her around the store."

"She does look familiar," Dinkie agreed.

"Of course, she looks familiar," Claudia said impatiently. "That's me." She shoved the paper into Dinkie's hands.

The three elves looked at her photo, then at her. "You're Tom Dalton's new squeeze?" Blinkie asked.

"No! Of course not." Oh, how she'd love to believe

she possessed that honor. But after he learned of the deceit and the manipulation she'd wreaked on his life, she figured "sworn enemy" and "renegade elf" would be a more apt description of her place in his life. "He invited me to a party, I accepted. That's all. I didn't know the newspaper was there taking pictures."

"Now it's all clear," Winkie said, nodding knowingly. "The raises, the new costumes. He was doing all that because he's got the hots for an elf!"

Winkie might as well have said Tom Dalton had the hots for a sheep, so unfathomable was the concept to her co-worker's brain. "He doesn't have the hots for me," Claudia protested. "We're merely...friends."

"Elves! Elves! Ten minutes to store opening," Mrs. Perkins called from the door. "Miss Moore, you're not dressed."

Claudia stepped over to the locker room door but Mrs. Perkins' voice stopped her. "Miss Moore, I've had a request from Santa. He'd like to see you in the Gingerbread Cottage before the store opens. Hurry up now. We don't want to keep him waiting."

A sick feeling twisted in Claudia's stomach. What did Santa—or Theodore Dalton—want with her now? Was he going to threaten her with exposure? Or would he inform her that he'd already told his grandson everything and she'd no longer be a Dalton's elf? As she opened her locker and took out her costume, she glanced down at her trembling hands.

Everything had been leading toward this moment. From the instant they'd met, Claudia had known deep down inside that she and Tom were meant to share an intimacy more stirring than any she'd ever known. But at the same time, she had a job to do, a job that betrayed any trust that might develop between them. Every instinct had told her to back away, to protect her pride and her heart and her journalistic integrity. But what began with a lie, a faked résumé and a series of evasions, could only end badly. So much deception—and nowhere to go to escape it.

Claudia moaned softly and lowered herself to the bench next to her locker, clutching her hands in front of her. The file folder she'd stolen from his office was still there, tucked on the top shelf beneath her booties. She'd been afraid to take it out of the store, afraid she might not be able to slip it by the security guard. So she'd left it, waiting for the right opportunity to either copy the information or sneak the folder back into Tom's office.

After last night, she had nothing but regret for her actions. If only she could wish the folder back into its proper place, maybe then she wouldn't feel she'd betrayed Tom's trust. Maybe she could go back to the beginning and find some measure of redemption.

She stood and reached for her elf booties, then her costume, hung neatly on the hook. Tossing them both on the bench, she slowly began to unbutton her sweater. Her career had always come first, her desire for recognition as a reporter more important than anything else in her life. She was talented, she knew it in her heart. But no one had bothered to give her a break until now. And how could anyone recognize her talent if her stories never appeared in print?

"The *New York Times*," she murmured as she folded her sweater. She'd already put off her editor for as long as she possibly could. Either she wrote the story soon or it wouldn't be worth writing. The alternative was unthinkable—going back to the *Times* empty-handed. No reporter possessed of sane mind and blazing ambition would turn down the chance she'd been offered.

The door to the locker room opened again and this time Winkie looked inside. "You're not dressed yet?" she cried. "Move your butt, Santa's waiting."

"I'm coming, I'm coming," Claudia said. "Tell him I'm—" She drew a deep breath. "Never mind. I'll be out in a few minutes."

Claudia wondered what she really did want to say to Theodore Dalton. Would any excuse she offered be enough? Maybe if she told him his suspicions were correct, that she was falling in love with his grandson, he'd give her an opportunity to make amends. But even she found that notion hard to believe. Good grief, they'd only known each other for ten days!

She glanced up at the folder. Perhaps she could enlist him in returning the stolen file. He could easily put it back where it belonged. But could she trust him to take her part in this? Or was his loyalty to his grandson unwavering? Her mind whirled, and with a soft moan, she sat down again to collect her thoughts.

"Twinkie!"

Claudia jumped up, pressing her hand to her chest. Mrs. Perkins stood at the door, her expression now filled with impatience. Claudia scrambled to grab her booties and her hat. "I'm coming. I'll be right there. Five seconds, ten at the most."

She slipped out of her jeans, then tugged on her little elf skirt and tights, the new tights twisting as she pulled them up. By the time she had her booties on, she'd already come up with a strategy to convince Theodore Dalton to keep quiet. "I'll appeal to his sense of decency," she said. "I'll remind him of his love for his grandson. And if that doesn't work, I'll cry."

Claudia hurried out of the dressing room and wove her way through the displays in the toy department. When

she reached the Candy Cane Gate, Mrs. Perkins was waiting, the other elves standing beside her. With a reluctant
smile, she opened the gate to let Claudia pass. "He's
waiting in the Gingerbread Cottage. Please don't keep
him long. The store opens in a few minutes and we'll
have children anxious to see him."

Stepping inside the gate should have filled her with
awe like walking into Fort Knox or the Emerald City or
Camelot, at least for an elf of her lowly stature. But Claudia couldn't brush aside the dread she felt. Her hand
shook as she took the doorknob and a faint buzzing in
her head made the entire scene seem unreal. Drawing a
deep breath, she opened the door and stepped inside, then
turned to close it behind her.

An instant later, she felt hands on her waist, spinning
her around. And then, to her horror, Santa, hidden behind
his full white beard, yanked her closer and kissed her!
At first, Claudia couldn't think. Should she give him a
karate chop in the Adam's apple or should she knee him
in the groin? But he was at least seventy years old!
Maybe she should scream or stomp on his instep? All
her self-defense classes suddenly scrambled in her brain
and she couldn't remember whether to kick first and
shout later or chop first and knee later.

She opened her eyes wide and tried to pull away, but
he was insistent. Surprised by the ardor of the old man's
kiss, she had to admit she now knew where Tom got his
talents. What she didn't know was where his grandfather
got the nerve!

When she finally managed to unlock her lips from his,
she gasped. "Stop this!" she hissed. "How dare you!"

His hands skimmed over her hips and snaked around
her waist, while he grumbled in protest.

"Don't do that!" Claudia insisted, trying to push his arms away. "This is highly improper."

He nuzzled his face into the curve of her neck and his beard tickled her skin. She slapped at him, whacking him across his padded chest, but it had no effect. When he just laughed at her efforts, her anger took control. She balled her fingers into a fist and took a swing at him. But her aim was off, and instead of hitting his shoulder, she caught his chin and grazed his nose. He cried out, then cursed in a low voice.

"See what you've done," she accused. "I'm not a violent person, but you drove me to it. You—you're a lecherous old man and you should be ashamed of yourself! I'm an elf and—and you're Santa, damn it! Children adore you. What would they think of you groping one of your little helpers?"

He muttered a curse and rubbed his chin. "They'd probably wonder why I spent a sleepless night thinking about the next time I'd kiss you." His voice now sounded strangely familiar to her ears. When he withdrew a handkerchief from his pocket and dabbed at the bloody nose she'd given him, he was forced to tug down the beard, revealing his face. Claudia's eyes went wide. "You?" she sputtered.

Tom shrugged, then tested his nose with his fingers. "Yeah, me. Am I still bleeding? Does it look like it's broken? Man, that's some right cross you've got. Where'd you learn that?"

"What are you doing here?"

"Our regular Santa wasn't able to work today, so I had to cover for him." He drew her close, but his huge belly still put them at a fair distance. "And I couldn't wait to see you again."

"I—I thought you were him!" she said by way of an apology. "I—I never thought he was you."

"Well, at least I know you're a virtuous elf," Tom said with a lascivious glint in his eye.

Claudia sent him a grudging smile and he laughed out loud, then tossed the handkerchief aside and yanked her back against him. An instant later, he covered her mouth with his, kissing her until every ounce of breath had left her body. She went limp in his embrace, giving herself over to his desire. Why did he have this effect on her? Why did she suddenly go boneless and mindless as soon as his lips touched hers?

"I told you I had a thing for elves," he murmured. His hands skimmed beneath her jacket.

She giggled and patted his stomach, forgetting all the fear she'd had upon entering the cottage. He didn't know. His grandfather hadn't told him. "Is that a watermelon in there or are you just happy to see me?"

Tom kissed her ear, then led her over to a chair. "Come sit down on my lap, little elf, and you'll find out."

Claudia groaned. "Stop it. This is perverse. There are children waiting outside. And Mrs. Perkins is probably pacing the floor wondering what I'm saying to you. If we're not careful, she'll burst in here and shatter the illusions of all those innocent kids."

He pulled her down on his lap, then playfully tugged down the collar of her costume to nibble her neck. "I'll stop, only if you promise I can see you tonight. I'll bring the red suit and you can wear the elf costume."

She wanted to say yes, but Claudia knew she couldn't. There would be no more opportunities for seduction, not until she went back and fixed a few of her mistakes. "I— I can't. I've got some things to do tonight."

"Cancel your plans," he said. "I'll cook you dinner. I'll massage your feet. I'll iron your elf costume. We could rent that video about the prostitute."

"I *really* can't," she insisted. "Maybe tomorrow night?"

Tom sighed. "All right. Tomorrow night will have to do. But only if you promise to pay a few more visits to the Gingerbread Cottage today. Santa has an itch that needs to be scratched. And you're the only elf who can do it."

She reached out and scratched his belly. "This is the only scratching that's going to go on in the Gingerbread Cottage today. I'm not coming in here again."

With a low growl, he grabbed her and gave her a passionate kiss. Then he set her on her feet and adjusted his beard. "There'll only be coal in your stocking, little elf. Santa will see to that!"

Claudia sent him a smile as she slipped out of the cottage. Mrs. Perkins and the elves were still standing where she'd left them, worried expressions suffusing their faces. "Don't worry. He'll be out in a few moments."

She stepped through the Candy Cane Gate and took her place, but her mind wasn't on entertaining the children as they waited. She had only one thought to occupy the next ten hours. She was going to put the file back in Tom Dalton's office and she was going to do it tonight. And, after she did, she planned to call her editor and kill the assignment.

And finally, after that, maybe she'd be free to love Tom Dalton. And, well, he'd simply have no choice but to love her back.

THE NIGHT DRAGGED ON, each sleepless minute measured by the clock beside Tom's bed. He rolled over and punched his pillow twice. He'd tried counting sheep, tried deep breathing, but nothing could relax him. Nothing but…"Claudia," he murmured. The scent of her still hung in the air around his bed. And when he'd pulled the covers back, he'd found the diamond and sapphire necklace he'd removed the night before.

He thought seeing her at the store would quell his need for her. His day as Santa had been filled with chattering children and endless lists. In all honesty, he'd enjoyed himself. For the first time, he'd realized what his grandfather found so satisfying about the job. The children were nervous and goofy and breathless with awe. And they believed he was the one who could make their dreams come true.

But Tom suspected his good mood came not from the children, but from having Claudia so close by. Though she'd maintained her post at the gate, he'd had the chance to look at her whenever he'd wanted—every few minutes when he was busy, constantly when the line of children thinned. And every now and then, she'd sent him a secret smile that only they shared.

He had his own secret he'd wanted to share with her when they were finally alone, a secret that could signal the start of their future together. That morning, before pulling on the Santa suit, he'd delivered an ultimatum to his father and grandfather in the New York office. Either he was transferred to New York by the first of the year, or he planned to find another job in the city—outside the family business.

The threat had worked and in a single instant all his plans had fallen into place. He'd be close to Claudia and maybe they could begin a real relationship. Though they still had a lot to work out between them—her story, for one—he was certain they could overcome anything if they just had time together. Their time together wouldn't end when she left her job as an elf. In fact, they had all the time in the world now.

But when the store closed and Tom looked for her, she was nowhere to be found. Winkie thought she'd gone to get a soda at the coffee shop and Dinkie insisted that she'd left for a doctor's appointment. Blinkie just shrugged and didn't offer any speculation at all. So Tom had slipped up the back stairs to his grandfather's office, struggled out of the Santa costume and headed home.

He couldn't help but wonder what plans had taken her away from the store. His curiosity only pointed out the brutal truth, that he really knew nothing at all about Claudia Moore. She was a reporter, writing a story on Dalton's secret Santa. She lived in Brooklyn and she worked for a lot of different newspapers and was a damn fine writer. But he didn't know about her family or her background, who her friends were or what she liked to do in her spare time.

He'd fallen in love with a virtual stranger. Tom rolled over again and punched his pillow. For all he knew, she could be running off to meet her boyfriend tonight. They'd sit in a noisy, smoke-filled bar and she'd regale him with tales of how she toyed with Tom Dalton's affections, just to get her story.

He cursed softly, then pulled the pillow over his head and moaned. But his lapse into self-pity was rudely interrupted by the ring of the phone on the bedside table. He glanced at the clock again. "Who would be calling me at eleven at night?" His mind went to his grandfather, then his father, and finally stopped at Claudia. He grabbed the phone. "Hello."

"Mr. Dalton?"

"Yes."

"This is LeRoy Varner. I'm the night security guard down at Dalton's?"

"Is everything all right?"

"I think you better come down to the store. We've got a situation here that needs your attention."

"What kind of situation?"

"I've caught a burglar and the perp says she knows you."

"The perp?"

"Perpetrator. She claims she works at the store and knows you. Says her name is Claudia Moore. I'm not sure if that's an alias. I figured the police would be able to tell me."

"Don't call the police," Tom ordered. "I'll be right down."

He jumped out of bed and hurried around the room in search of his clothes, dressed only in his boxer shorts. He pulled on a pair of khakis and a long-sleeved rugby shirt, then headed downstairs.

He found his jacket and his keys and then sat on an ornately carved bench in the foyer and pulled on his socks and shoes. What the hell was Claudia doing in the store after hours again? She'd nearly been caught the last time. This time, he wouldn't be able to keep her little crime quiet. With security involved there would likely be some talk around the store and, for all he knew, LeRoy had already summoned the police.

Was this story so important to her that she was willing to risk her reputation and criminal charges to get it? Hell, he could order her arrested and put on trial for her actions. He could understand her obsession with a story that had more important ramifications—an underworld crime story or a political corruption story—but this was a story about Santa Claus!

He ran out of the house, hopped into his car and raced out of the driveway, ignoring the speed limit through his residential neighborhood. When he reached the square, the streets were relatively quiet, with only a few pedestrians entering and exiting the pubs and restaurants near Dalton's. The Christmas windows sparkled with light, belying the intrigue going on inside the store. He pulled up at the employee entrance and parked the car in a tow-away zone. LeRoy was waiting at the door and let him in.

"Where did you find her?" Tom said.

"Well, sir, I was doing my midnight rounds like I do every night at ten-thirty and I was checkin' out your office when I came upon the perp. That's what we call the criminal element in the security biz. I subdued the perp and upon questioning her, I—"

"Did she say anything?"

"She just said to call you. Then she clammed up and refused to talk."

He winced, then ran his hand through his hair. "I'll take care of this," he said. "Where do you have her?"

"In the security office. I was going to cuff her, but she promised not to flee the scene as long as I called you."

Tom opened the door and stepped into the brightly lit office. One entire wall contained the video monitors that surveyed the sales floor, fitting room entrances and corporate offices from multiple angles. A smaller room contained a table and chairs and he saw Claudia through the window, her head buried in her hands. Tom knocked on the window and she turned and gave him a feeble wave and a smile.

When he entered the room, she quickly stood and

clutched her hands in front of her. "LeRoy called," Tom began. "He said you'd been caught in the store after hours. Would you mind telling me what you were doing?"

"Actually I would mind," she said haltingly. "It's not really important and it would only make you angry, so maybe we could avoid all the trouble? I'd suggest you let me go home and we forget all about this."

He shook his head. "That's not going to happen, Claudia. If we have to stay here all night long, then we will. Or perhaps you'd rather the police question you?"

"You don't scare me," she said, sitting down again and cupping her chin in her hand. "And I don't have to tell you what I was doing. Once I ask for a lawyer, I don't have to talk."

"No, you don't. But right now you're not under arrest."

She sent him a pleading look. "Please, can't we just forget this? I promise I'll never do it again."

A knock sounded at the door and they both turned to see LeRoy standing there. He held out a file folder. "She had this with her," he said. "I dusted it for prints."

"Fingerprints? You can do that?" Tom asked.

"Yeah, I took a class at the community college. Her fingerprints were all over the folder."

Tom took it from LeRoy's hand. He recognized the file as the one she'd stuffed in her bag the night they'd spent in his office. When LeRoy left, Tom turned back to Claudia. "You took this." It wasn't a question, but a statement. He already knew she had.

"I just borrowed it. And I was putting it back when I got caught."

"I suppose you needed this for your story?"

She blinked in surprise. "My—my story?"

"Yeah. Isn't that why you're here?" he asked, slapping the folder on the table in front of her. She jumped in surprise. "To find out about Dalton's secret Santa? You stole the file that night you were supposed to meet me at Silvio's. I saw it in your bag when you went down to get the earrings."

She rubbed her forehead then sighed. "I really was trying to put it back. I decided not to use it." Claudia paused, a frown creasing her expression. "How did you know I was a reporter? Did your grandfather tell you?"

"No, I told him," Tom replied, his voice filled with annoyance. "I did a security check on you a few days after you were hired. I was curious why a woman with your obvious intelligence would choose to work as an elf. Now I know for sure." He stood, circled the table and picked up the folder. "Come with me."

She shook her head, but was forced to follow him when he grabbed her hand. Tom dragged her to the elevator, pulled her inside and used a key to take them to the fifth floor. When the doors opened on the corporate offices, he pulled her toward his. She didn't resist, but he could tell she was frightened by his silence and his anger.

"What are you going to do?" she asked. "Are you going to turn me in? I swear, I was putting the file back when I got caught."

"And then what were you going to do? Just slip away in the night as if nothing had ever happened?"

"I couldn't slip away," Claudia said. "I planned to spend the night in the store."

Tom laughed harshly. "You could have strolled right out! The doors are locked from the inside. Hell, LeRoy probably would have let you out had you flashed your employee ID at him and given him a plausible excuse."

"I wasn't locked in?" She paused, taking in the significance of his words. "We weren't locked in that night?"

"No, of course not," Tom said. "When I caught you in my office, I decided to play a little game. I told you we couldn't get out so you'd have to spend the night with me. I wanted to know what you were up to."

Claudia's color rose and her eyes snapped with anger. "You lied to me. You manipulated me, you—"

"You're angry at *me* because I lied to *you* about the store's security system?" Tom said, his voice laced with disbelief. "What you did was illegal!"

"And what you did was immoral," she shot back. "I spent the night with you because I didn't think I had a choice. That night was tantamount to kidnapping! I should have you arrested."

"Don't be ridiculous!"

"What I did was strictly business. I was after a story and I did what I had to do to get it. What you did was personal. It was emotional blackmail."

"You want your story?" He strode to his credenza, unlocked the door and grabbed a handful of files, setting the file she stole on top. With a soft curse, he tossed them on the desk. "Take them. It's everything you need for your story. All the names, the dollar amounts, the letters from the kids."

"I don't want them," she said.

He gathered them up, strode across the office and shoved them into her arms. "I want you to have them. I want you to write your story. This is what you came to Schuyler Falls for, isn't it?" Tom fought the unbidden urge to brush the folders from her arms and gather her in his embrace. So much anger between them, yet he knew it would dissolve instantly beneath a kiss.

But he wasn't sure he believed her, wasn't sure she'd

been putting the file back. For all he knew, she could have been after more files. The only way to learn her true motives was to give her exactly what she wanted—and see what she did with it.

He slowly walked to the door. "I'm afraid this is the end of your job as an elf. But you have your story now. I'll be looking for your byline."

With that, he walked out, stepped into the waiting elevator and rode it back to the first floor. When he passed by the security office, he told LeRoy to escort Claudia out of the store without questions. It wasn't until he got into his car that he realized what he'd done.

He'd just given Claudia exactly what she wanted. And if she wanted her story more than she wanted him, he'd never see her again. For a moment, he thought about going back into the store and forcing her to admit her feelings for him, forcing her to say what he saw in her eyes that night in his bedroom. But then he drew a deep breath and gathered his resolve.

If she loved him, she'd be back. And whether she published her story or not, it wasn't going to change the way he felt about her. Tom Dalton loved Claudia Moore and it was a love meant to last a lifetime.

8

CLAUDIA STOOD in the hallway outside her room at the boardinghouse, the phone in her hand. She clutched a tiny piece of paper with the number of her editor at the *Times* scribbled on it. Closing her eyes, she gathered her thoughts. Should she or shouldn't she? In all her years as a journalist, she'd never been faced with a decision like this. Even after an hour of wavering, she still wasn't sure what she should do.

Her story was due at the *Times* tomorrow evening. She'd typed out a rough draft on her computer an hour ago, but couldn't go any further. It was a good story, warm and touching, the kind of story that defined the season of giving. Three families who had been affected by Dalton's secret Santa opened their homes to her and each family offered a unique perspective on hope and charity.

It was all there, including the truth about Dalton's Santa, and Claudia knew in her heart it was the best thing she'd ever reported. If this feature didn't get her the job at the *Times,* then she'd never be a good enough writer for them. Marshaling her resolve, she punched in the number for her editor's desk. It took at least ten rings before Anne Costello answered, and until she did, Claudia still wasn't sure what she was going to say.

"There is no story!" she blurted out when Anne picked up. She hadn't bothered with introductions or greetings, her nerves frayed and her mind muddled with indecision.

"Who is this?"

"Anne, it's Claudia Moore. There is no story."

"Claudia? Where are you? I've been calling your apartment. Where's my story? When can we expect the copy? We're saving a nice spot in Wednesday's edition, below the fold on the first page of New York Report. How many column inches can you give them? We'll need photos. I'll arrange for a stringer to get something for us tomorrow. Just give me the info and I'll set it all up."

Claudia drew a deep breath. "There is no story, Anne," she repeated, enunciating each word slowly.

"No story? Of course there's a story. Someone is giving away thousands of dollars every Christmas and isn't asking for public approval. Haven't you heard, Claudia? Altruism is dead. Unless you can sell your brand name along with your charitable good deeds, there's no point in giving! There *is* a story."

"Well, I haven't been able to find it," Claudia countered. "On the surface, it seems like feature material, but after I did a little digging, I—"

"Do you know who this secret Santa is?" Anne asked.

"Well…yes."

"And have you talked to the families he's helped?"

"Yes."

"Then why isn't there a story!" Anne shouted in her best no-nonsense, hard-nosed editor tone.

Claudia pulled the phone away from her ear and waited until Anne had calmed down. "Because maybe this Santa wants to keep his identity a secret. And maybe we should respect that. Once the story is out, he may feel pressured by the public. People will ask for charity when they really don't need it. And though the families were happy to tell their stories, I'm not sure they understand the ramifications of plastering their personal problems all over the *New York Times*."

Though she couldn't see Anne's face, she could almost hear the anger and impatience over the phone line. "I want copy on my desk by tomorrow morning, Claudia. *I'll* decide if this is a story or not. You just give me the facts."

"And what if it isn't?"

An uneasy silence raced over the phone line between Schuyler Falls and New York City. "Then I'm not sure I can recommend you for the job in statewide features," she finally said. "We'll have to look at other candidates."

Anger and despair clutched at Claudia's heart and she fought back tears of frustration. "I'm a good reporter and you know it. I've given you lots of solid stories. Just not this one."

"Tomorrow morning. I'll be looking for the copy." With that, the other end of the line went dead. Claudia slowly lowered the phone back into the cradle. Tears pushed from the corners of her eyes and she brushed them away. She'd already ruined her relationship with Tom over this story. After their argument last night, he'd never trust her again. Any feelings he had for her were gone, tossed back in her face like the files he'd thrown at her.

Why not turn in the story and get on with her life? A new job at the *Times* would go a long way to soothe the ache in her heart. She'd have a regular paycheck, a byline all her own and a job at a paper that was read all over the free world. She could have everything she'd ever wanted.

Except she wouldn't have everything. She wouldn't

have Tom. She wouldn't have passion and excitement and love in her life. She'd only have regret and guilt to remind her of their time together. Claudia crumpled the phone number in her hand and shoved it into her pocket. Then she walked back to her room, closing the door behind her.

Her laptop computer hummed, the screen bright and awaiting the revisions to her rough draft. She crossed the room and sat down at the small desk, and reread the first line. Then, as if her fingers had been disconnected from her mind, she began to polish her story. She didn't really think about what she was doing, just let the words flow from her heart to her hands.

When she finally typed the three "#" marks at the end, she realized she'd been working for nearly two hours. Leaning back in her chair, she stretched her arms over her head and massaged a crick out of her neck. Then she reached down and sent the Print command to the tiny portable printer she'd brought along.

She fed a sheet of paper into it, and then another and another and ten minutes later, her story was finally finished. The words were perfect now, every idea clearly expressed, the quotes following the flow of the story. A smile touched her lips and she felt a small measure of pride in her work. But then she remembered what the story had cost her—the chance at a life with the man she loved—and the smile slowly faded.

Claudia stood, closing her computer. Maybe this wasn't over yet, she mused. Maybe there was still one more thing that she had to do. After all, this really didn't have to be her decision. Someone else could make the decision for her. She grabbed her jacket from her bed, yanked it on and tucked the rolled up story into her jacket pocket.

As she opened the front door of the boardinghouse, she noticed that it had begun to snow again. Her car was parked at the curb and Claudia searched her pocket for her keys. The car sputtered and coughed before it started, but a few seconds later, she put the car into gear and headed away from the downtown area.

She wasn't all that sure she'd find her way. The one and only time she'd been to the house, it had been dark and she hadn't paid much attention to the route. But instinct seemed to be on her side and she found the wide street almost immediately. Claudia leaned over the wheel and peered through the frosty windows of her car, searching for the right house through the heavily wooded lots.

She'd nearly run out of road when she saw it, the huge stone mansion with the fairy-tale turret to the left of the entrance. She turned the car into the driveway. The store closed at five on Sunday evenings and it was nearly six. Claudia wasn't sure he'd be home, but she was determined to wait as long as she had to. Facing Tom would be much easier away from the scene of the crime.

As she pulled up to the house, she noticed his Lexus in the nearby garage. The breath slowly left her lungs and she realized she wouldn't have time to think this all over, to ponder her approach. Though what she was about to say to him could mean the difference between lifelong happiness and bitter regret, Claudia felt at a complete loss for words. Would her heart take over once she saw him again? Could she summon the courage to say what needed to be said?

She loved Tom Dalton and no matter what passed between them, that fact wouldn't change. But how did he feel about her? If he truly loved her, then he should be able to forgive her for her deception. But after their last encounter, she knew his anger could be fierce and his pride unwavering. She'd hurt him and nothing she could do would make up for that. Still, there had to be a way to get beyond this.

Claudia switched the car off and opened the door, her heart pounding in her chest, her breathing quick and shallow. With each step toward the front door, she tried to gather her courage. Her hand trembled as she reached for the doorbell and she said a little prayer that she was doing the right thing.

Before she'd pressed the bell the door suddenly swung open in front of her. Claudia screamed in surprise and jumped back. Her heel slipped off the step and she struggled to maintain her footing, her arms and legs flailing for balance. And then, out of nowhere, a hand snaked around her waist and pulled her upright against a lean, hard torso. She ventured a glance up and met Tom Dalton's stormy gaze. The only thing she could do was force a smile and a soft "hello."

A moment later his protective embrace was gone. He stepped back and regarded her with a hostile eye. "You're the last person I expected to see. What are you doing here?"

Claudia reached in her pocket. "I brought this," she said, holding the story out to him.

He took it from her fingers and glanced at it. "I don't need to ask what this is."

"I—I want you to read it."

"Why? Are you in need of a proofreader? Or do you think I'll change my mind and forgive you?"

"Forgive me?" Claudia shook her head. "No. I don't expect you to forgive me. I don't even expect you to understand."

"Try me," he said.

"This article means the difference between a future of

just scraping by and a byline seen all around the world. Ever since I first stepped into a newspaper office when I was a kid, this has been my dream. And now that it's finally within my reach, I—I can't seem to make it happen.''

He waved the sheaf of papers in the air. ''Hey, if this is what you want, then you should have it. I want you to be happy.'' His words were tinged with an edge of bitterness.

''Oh, please,'' Claudia said. ''Don't lie to me. You want me to be miserable. You want me to write my story and regret every moment. You want me to lose sleep and then, all of a sudden, come to the realization that I'm madly in love with you, so in love that I'd give up all my goals and aspirations.''

''Are you in love with me?'' he asked, his gaze direct, intense, some of the anger gone.

She drew a sharp breath, then looked away. ''I—I don't know. I'm not sure.''

Tom reached out to touch her, then at the last moment pulled his hand back. ''I wouldn't ask you to do that—give up your dreams.''

''And why not?''

This time he did touch her, cupping her cheek in his palm. The contact sent a current racing through her body, making her fingers and toes tingle and her heart skip a beat. Her knees went soft and she reached out and grabbed his wrist.

''Because maybe I'm in love with you, too,'' he murmured.

Tears threatened to spill from her eyes and she gave him a tremulous smile. ''I didn't think you'd ever forgive me,'' she said, shivering from the cold, ''even now that you know I'm not going to submit it.''

"I should take part of the blame," he said. "I pretty much knew what you were after early on. I could have stopped you. I could have fired you or confronted you. But I didn't want to lose you."

"Then we're all right?" Claudia asked.

He handed her the story. "Yeah, we're all right."

She nodded, not sure what to do next. She wanted to kiss him, to reassure herself that his words matched what he felt in his heart. But she couldn't bring herself to make the first move. "I should go then."

"No," he said. He took her hand and pulled her into the house, then kicked the door shut behind her. She expected him to kiss her there, but in one easy motion, he scooped her up in his arms instead. His actions took her by complete surprise and the pages of the story dropped from her fingers and scattered on the floor of the foyer.

"What are you doing?"

"What I should have done that night after the party," he murmured. He carried her up the winding stairs to the second floor. Forget about feeling like Julia Roberts, Claudia mused. Now she felt like Scarlett O'Hara!

When they reached his bedroom, he gently set her back on her feet, then wrapped her in his embrace and kissed her, cradling her head in his hands, his fingers furrowed through her hair. He was a man with a hunger so deep and desperate that his kiss consumed her, a fire raging out of control. Their mouths melded, twisted, searched, until she couldn't imagine they'd ever draw apart. Tom had kissed her before, but this time Claudia knew where his kisses would lead, to an intense intimacy that only they would share. And this time, she wouldn't stop him.

With hesitant hands, she reached for the buttons of his shirt and slowly worked them open. Though she'd longed to touch him, this was the first time she'd actually felt free to explore his body, to feel the powerful muscle and sinew beneath. He was warm and hard and smooth, exactly as she'd imagined, and she skimmed her hands over his chest and brushed his shirt off his broad, angular shoulders.

Claudia had wanted him for so long that, after only a few seconds, the heat of his skin and the smell of his hair already seemed familiar. And though they'd met only two weeks ago, she felt as if she had known Tom her whole life. Since she'd first noticed boys, he was there, just beyond the light, waiting for her to find him. And just when she'd decided she didn't need anything more than a career to make her happy, he'd stepped from the shadows and stolen her heart. Claudia smiled inwardly. Though she'd never expected to be dressed in a silly elf costume when it happened.

"We're not going to stop this time," she murmured, pressing her lips against his chest, the soft dusting of hair brushing against her chin.

He growled and tipped his head back as she kissed his nipple, his hands sliding down to the small of her back. "Sweetheart, I'll promise you one thing. I'm never going to stop wanting you and we're never going to stop doing this."

Clothes dropped away, piece by piece, tossed to the floor with a growing impatience, jackets and shirts, jeans and socks, all discarded along with their restraint. And with each item shed, their passion grew more frantic. She should have been nervous, tentative, but with Tom's tender fingers on her body she felt safe. Before they'd even finished undressing they fell onto the bed, Claudia still wearing her panties and camisole and Tom in his silk boxers.

He lifted the hem of her camisole and nuzzled his face

into her belly. "You're so beautiful," he murmured, trailing kisses from her stomach upward, his lips soft, his tongue tasting.

"For an elf?" Claudia teased.

A smile curled the corners of his mouth as he gazed up at her. "You stopped being just an elf to me a long time ago."

Tom pushed her camisole up further, discovering the soft crease beneath each breast, exposing her skin inch by inch. And when his mouth reached her nipple, Claudia moaned, the sound slipping out of her throat like a sigh of contentment. His tongue teased at the hard nub, drawing her into his mouth with exquisite care and sending waves of sensation through her body.

She shoved her fingers through his hair, pressing him closer, while his hands moved lower, slipping beneath the edge of her panties, still searching for the perfect spot to linger. And when he delved between her legs, Claudia cried out in astonishment at the heat that shot to her core and radiated through her body.

Slowly he stroked her, his mouth still fixed to hers, following the same rhythm, leading her to the edge then allowing her to retreat. Her breathing grew ragged and her mind spun with unspoken pleas. Over and over, she felt herself on the verge of shattering, and at the very last moment, the feeling subsided, always controlled by his sure touch. And when she couldn't stand it any longer, Claudia whispered his name, begging him to stop the torment or give her release.

He drew back and she looked into his eyes, seeing raw emotion swirling in their deep green depths. Claudia reached out and ran her thumb over his bottom lip and he turned into her hand, kissing the center of her palm.

She wanted to make him feel the way she felt, powerless and powerful at the same time. Claudia took his hands, then rolled over, kneeling beside him. He reached for her again, but this time she pinned them above his head. "It's my turn now," she said, her voice low, persuasive.

She grabbed the hem of her camisole and pulled it over her head, then drew it from his face to his belly, teasing him with the soft fabric. She playfully tossed it aside. "Now your boxers," she murmured.

He sent her a wicked grin then hooked his fingers beneath the waistband and slid the silk off. They followed her camisole, flying across the room. Claudia's gaze took in the beauty of Tom's form, her eyes trailing to the hard ridge of his desire, ready and waiting. She skimmed her hands over his body, exploring every angle and plane, his broad chest, his rippled belly, his narrow hips. And when she finally wrapped her fingers around his erection, he lost all sense of control.

After just a few soft strokes, he groaned and gently drew her hand away. "Now you," he challenged, hooking his finger in her panties. The instant she'd slipped out of them, Tom grabbed her and rolled her back on the bed, pinning her beneath his weight. When she'd finally stopped wriggling, he brushed a kiss across her lips then handed her a condom he'd retrieved from the bedside table.

"Do this for me," he said, tearing open the package with his teeth. "And don't take your time."

After she'd smoothed on the condom, she drew him on top of her, reveling in the feel of his weight on her body, his hips pressed to hers. And when he slowly moved inside her, Claudia's entire body came alive with sensation, each muscle and nerve taking on the rhythm of their lovemaking.

They began slowly, enjoying the newness of their joining. But then, passion took over and their lovemaking turned fierce, almost primal. And when her climax overwhelmed her, her body shuddering in its release, Claudia was sure she'd never felt such a powerful connection to a man in her life. And when he joined her, plunging deep and arching against her, her name slipping from his lips, she knew that he'd be the only man in her life. Now and forever.

A long time later, after they'd sated themselves completely, the bedroom fell silent, the strange sounds of the house keeping Claudia awake. She closed her eyes, exhaustion pulling her toward slumber, yet exhilaration pumping adrenaline through her bloodstream. Tom moved beside her, throwing his leg over her thighs and wrapping his arm around her waist. His head was cradled in the curve of her arm. She glanced over at him, touched to witness such a boyish and vulnerable side of him.

"Are you asleep?" she whispered.

"Mmm. Halfway there. I'm spent. Just give me thirty minutes."

She stroked his temple and kissed the top of his head. "Sleep," she said.

Tom nodded and nuzzled closer. She thought he'd drifted off, but a long time later, he spoke. "I want you to go ahead with the story," he murmured, pressing his lips against the curve of her neck. "I want you to have the job at the *Times*. Tell me you'll promise to send it."

Before long, his breathing became slow and even and she knew he finally slept. Claudia stared up at the ceiling, the shock of his words causing her heart to ache with every beat until she didn't want it to beat at all. Had she done something wrong? Why was he sending her away? Her mind ran the evening backward and she tried to recount everything that was said, each caress and longing look.

She must have misunderstood. He'd told her he loved her and she'd admitted the same to him! That was supposed to mean they'd have a future together. But did the words mean something else to Tom Dalton? Were they simply a line he gave a woman before he took her to bed? How could they possibly have a future with him here in Schuyler Falls and her in New York?

She turned her head and looked at him again. And how could she live now, knowing how she felt about him yet not being able to see him every day? Would he think of her at all, or would he simply go on with his life? God, she didn't want to go to New York. She didn't want to go anywhere without him!

"Maybe you really don't forgive me," she whispered.

She took his arm and gently moved it aside, then carefully slipped out of bed and gathered her clothes. Once she thought she could be satisfied with a single night of passion with Tom Dalton. But now that she'd had that night, Claudia found herself wanting so much more. She wanted a life and future!

As she slowly dressed, she watched him sleep, tempted to crawl back into bed with him and accept whatever he was willing to give. But she knew it would never be enough. She wanted all of Tom Dalton. His love, his trust, his passion. She couldn't settle for anything less, not when she loved him with every ounce of her being.

Claudia stood in the room for a long time after she finished dressing. She studied every detail of his body, memorized the way his face looked in the pale moonlight streaming through the window. And when she couldn't stand it anymore, she stayed just a few seconds longer— and then she walked away.

The pages of her story were still scattered where they'd left them. She bent down and picked them up, arranging them carefully. A tear dropped from her eye and marked the first page. With a soft curse, she wiped it away, refusing to give in to her emotions.

She could put this all behind her and stop loving Tom Dalton, she vowed. She'd have to or risk spending the rest of her life wrapped in regret. Claudia pulled the front door open and the cold night air hit her in her face. Only when she closed the door behind her, did she realize the significance of what she was doing. She'd never see Tom Dalton again, never feel the passion that blazed between them.

She left, knowing that the ache that had settled in her heart would stay with her the rest of her life.

TOM EXPECTED CLAUDIA to be there when he woke up. He expected to find her wrapped in his arms, her face nuzzled up against his shoulder. But he woke up to an empty bed—and an empty house. With a soft curse, he rolled over and threw his arm over his eyes, blocking the early-morning light streaming through his bedroom window.

Why had she gone? Though exhaustion still plagued him, he wasn't going to get any more sleep. And he was determined to find her. He sat up and raked his hand through his hair. The scent of her perfume drifted up around him and he reached over and grabbed her pillow, crushing it to his chest.

He thought they'd settled everything last night. She'd turn in the story and take the job at the *Times.* And after a few more weeks, he'd gather up his things and move to New York. He'd planned to explain everything to her in the morning, how they'd get married and find a place in the city, how they'd start their lives together and how, someday, they'd have a big family. He could make it all happen for them, if she was willing.

As for the story, he was certain his grandfather would get over it. After all, it meant that one of the heirs to the Dalton legacy would be getting married to the woman he loved. A little family secret revealed was a small price to pay for Tom's future happiness and the promise of grandchildren and great-grandchildren.

He rolled out of bed and crossed the room, searching for the handiest thing to wear. Now that his future was all planned, he wanted it to begin right now! His jeans from last night were crumpled near the bed and he tugged them on, then found his T-shirt tossed over a nearby chair. Tom didn't even bother combing his hair. There wasn't time. He had to find Claudia.

He finished dressing in a few minutes and raced downstairs to search the house. But she was nowhere to be found, her car gone from the driveway. There were only two possible places she could have gone—her room at the boardinghouse or the store. He'd stop by the store first, explain everything to his grandfather and then go down to the jewelry department and choose the prettiest diamond ring in Dalton's vault. After that, he'd find Claudia and ask her to marry him.

The ride to the store seemed endless as he mulled over what he planned to say. Though he'd proposed once before in his life, the first time, he hadn't, in truth, really cared how she answered. Now, he wanted Claudia to say yes. He wanted her to throw herself into his arms and promise to love him for the rest of his life.

Tom pulled up in the tow-away zone and left the car there, unwilling to waste time walking from his spot in the lot a half block away. When he entered the employee entrance, he waved to LeRoy and the guard stepped out from behind the window checkpoint. "LeRoy, I want you to track down one of our employees," Tom said. "Claudia Moore. Find out where she is and give me a call in my grandfather's office. You should have her home address on your computer—some boardinghouse over on Longwell."

LeRoy nodded. "Is that the same Claudia Moore I caught in the store the other night? The perp who broke in to your office?"

Tom wagged a finger at him and smiled. "Be careful what you say about her. You're talking about my future wife."

An expression of mortification crossed LeRoy's face. "I—I'm sorry, sir. No disrespect intended. I'm sure once she's married to you, she'll leave her criminal past behind."

"Just find her," Tom said as he pushed through the door to the store. It was nearly ten and he hoped he might catch his grandfather upstairs in his office. If he had to drag him out of the North Pole Village, he intended to do exactly that, for what he had to say was much more important than a bunch of kids and their Christmas wishes. He hurried to the elevator and hopped on, tapping his foot as he passed through each floor.

When the doors opened, he strode out and headed directly to his grandfather's office. To Tom's relief, he found him there, struggling into his Santa suit.

"Tommy," he cried. "Am I glad to see you. Mrs. Lewis washed these damn pants again. I swear, they shrink five sizes every time she does that. It takes me days to stretch them out. By that time, they need to be washed again."

"Forget the pants, Grandfather. I've got something important to talk to you about."

"What's more important than my work as Santa?" he said, struggling to his feet and hitching up his suspenders.

"Actually, it's your work as Santa that I want to talk about. Claudia Moore has written a story about Dalton's secret Santa," Tom explained. "It's going to be published in the *New York Times*."

He grandfather scowled. "What? And you didn't try to stop her?"

"No," Tom replied. "I want her to have the story. If she turns it in, there's a good chance they'll give her a full-time job reporting for the paper. And she wants that job more than anything. And I want to make her happy." He paused. "I'm going to marry her, Grandfather. I love her and I want to spend the rest of my life with her. And I hope my future happiness means more to you than keeping your work as Santa a secret."

His grandfather pondered the news for a long moment. "You barely know her."

"I know all I need to know. If I let her walk out of my life, I'll never forgive myself."

"Then, you have my support," Theodore Dalton said. "I hope you'll be as happy as your grandmother and I have been."

Tom smiled, then stepped over and gave his grandfather a hug. "I'll do my best."

His grandfather chuckled. "I guess I was right all along. You didn't really need a woman. You needed a wife." The phone rang and his grandfather drew away to answer it. He listened for a moment, then handed the phone to Tom. "It's for you. Security."

LeRoy was on the other end. "Mr. Dalton, LeRoy here. I've tracked down the perp—I mean, the lady you were looking for. She's in the store right now, down in the employee lunchroom behind the toy department. Would you like me to detain her?''

''No, I'll go find her. Thank you.'' He hung up the phone and turned to his grandfather. ''Well, wish me luck.'' Tom stared at him for a long moment. ''Did you know this was going to happen?''

His grandfather shrugged. ''I knew you were ready for a change in your life,'' he said. ''And I suspected that change would be Claudia the minute you first said her name. I guess that's why your father and I figured you were ready to move up to corporate.''

Tom clapped his grandfather on the shoulder and grinned. ''I am. Just as soon as I buy Claudia the biggest ring we have in the store. And just as soon as she says yes.''

''And if she doesn't?''

''I won't take no for an answer.'' He started for the door, then turned back. ''By the way...thanks,'' Tom said.

His grandfather nodded and smiled. Tom jogged out to the elevator and took it all the way down to the first floor. The store hadn't opened yet, but all the sales associates were at their posts, including the manager of the jewelry department. Tom strode over to the glass cases and skimmed the selections.

''Can I help you, sir?''

''I want the biggest diamond ring we have in the store,'' he said. ''Show it to me.''

''We have a three carat ring in the vault. Perfect color and clarity in a very simple platinum setting.'' The sales manager disappeared to the ancient vault and emerged a few seconds later with a tray of rings. He plucked one out and held it up to the light. "This is a very special ring."

Tom took it from his fingers and held it up to the light. "She's a very special woman." He took the ring and shoved it into his jeans pocket. "Charge my account."

"Yes, sir," the man called as Tom strode away. "And may I offer my best wishes?"

He nodded, then ran to the escalator and rode it up to the toy department. But when he burst in to the employee lunchroom, there were only three elves gathered around the lunch table. When they saw him, they all jumped to their feet.

"Good morning, sir!" the elves chimed, standing at attention like little soldiers.

"I was told Claudia Moore was here," he said.

Dinkie pointed to the door to the locker room. "She's inside, cleaning out her locker. She told us she quit. Are you going to get her to stay, sir?"

"Would you all excuse us?" Tom asked. "I have a private matter to discuss with her."

The elves nodded and Winkie, Dinkie and Blinkie scurried out. Tom crossed to the locker room door and quietly pushed it open. She didn't hear him enter and he watched her for a long moment as she picked through her belongings and tossed them into a Dalton's shopping bag. "I missed you this morning," he murmured.

Tom watched as her shoulders stiffened slightly. She slowly turned to face him, but he didn't find a smile on her face, only a cool, indifferent expression. "I—I was just cleaning out my locker. I'm leaving for the city later today."

He frowned. "Leaving. Why?"

"I'm finished with my story," she said with a shrug.

"And I've got a lot of things to wrap up if I'm going to take that job with the *Times*."

"But we have so much to discuss."

She shook her head. "We've got nothing to talk about, Tom. You made your feelings clear last night." Her voice was distant, angry, trembling with suppressed emotion. From the expression on her face, she looked as if she were about to burst into tears.

"Yes, I did," Tom said. "And I'd think, considering those feelings, you wouldn't be running off to New York the morning after we made love. I'm not ready to let you go yet, Claudia. You can go to the city in a few days."

"Well, you're going to have to let me go!" she snapped, returning to her packing. "I'm not going to stay here just to provide a little fun between the sheets."

He grabbed her arm and spun her around to face him. "That's not why I want you to stay. I want you to stay for us. For our future."

She opened her mouth as if to spit back an angry reply, but the words died in her throat. "I—I don't understand. You told me to turn in the story. I thought that was the end of—"

"The end?" Tom reached out and took her face between his hands. "Claudia, this is just the beginning. I told you to turn in the story, because I want you to be happy. I want you to realize your dreams. But I also want you to marry me."

She gasped, her eyes going wide. "What?"

Tom reached into his pocket and withdrew the diamond. "I wanted this to be more romantic. I didn't intend to ask you in some drab old locker room at the store, but I guess this is the place it has to happen because I can't wait any longer for your answer. And besides, Dalton's is the place where this all started.'' He bent down on one knee and took her hand in his.

"What are you doing?" she cried, trying to tug her fingers away.

Tom held the ring out to her. "Claudia Moore, I love you. I know we haven't known each other for very long, but the minute I met you, I knew we belonged together. Will you marry me?"

"What?" The word slipped from her mouth on a soft sigh of disbelief. He looked into her eyes and saw only confusion there.

"Will you marry me?" he asked, this time speaking very slowly.

She stared at him for a long moment, a dumbfounded expression on her pretty face. Then she shook her head. "You want me to marry you?"

He slowly stood, his gaze never wavering from hers. "I have it all figured out. I've asked for a transfer to the city. That's where our headquarters are located. You can have your job at the *Times* and we can start our life together. It will be perfect. We'll find an apartment or maybe a—"

"No!" she cried.

Tom stopped, the word cutting through his heart like a dagger. "No?"

"No. I can't marry you."

He slowly stood, taken aback by her refusal. "May I ask why?"

She searched for an answer, stammering and stumbling over her words. "You—you don't know me," she finally said. "I came here to write a story and I was willing to do anything to get it. I never wanted to be a wife. All I've ever wanted to be is a journalist. And—and I can't have both. Sooner or later, you'll resent my job and then you'll resent me.''

''You can have both,'' Tom said, ''if we love each other.''

She shook her head. ''Why does love always have to mean marriage? Why can't love just mean love—for as long as it lasts, with no strings attached?''

''Because that's not real love, Claudia. That's just marking time until something better comes along.''

''No, no, this is all too fast. What happened between us isn't real. I realized that last night. It began with a manipulation and we just got swept away in it all.''

''Damn it, Claudia, it is real.''

''So what if it is? We want different things. I mean, I could handle a relationship. I could even handle living together. But we can't get married. You'd expect me to be a wife and I couldn't do that.'' She snatched up her shopping bag and clutched it to her chest. ''I—I just can't. I don't know why. Please,'' she pleaded. ''I'm so sorry.''

With that, she turned and ran out of the locker room. Stunned, Tom stood frozen for a long time, unable to make his feet move. Then he took off after her, shoving the ring back into his pocket. But when he reached the sales floor, a crowd had already gathered in front of the North Pole Village. ''Where did she go?'' he called to the elves.

They pointed to the escalator and he pushed his way past the shoppers to get to the first floor. He turned around, looking in all directions, but Claudia had disappeared into the crowd, slipping out of his life as if she'd never been there in the first place. As he stood in the middle of the store, business buzzing around him, Tom cursed his clumsy proposal.

"This is not over yet, Claudia Moore," he muttered. "You will say yes and we will be married. And if it takes me a year, I'm going to figure out a way to make it happen."

9

TOM DALTON STARED at his reflection in the mirror on the back of his office door. The bright red suit, the cheerily curling mustache, the jolly belly, all belied his grim mood. In truth, Tom had come to recognize the virtue of being Dalton's Santa, but without Twinkie, it had barely been tolerable. It was Christmas Eve and he just had to make it through one more day. After that, he wouldn't have to play substitute Santa for at least another eleven months.

"Just get through the day," he murmured.

Tom glanced over at his desk, at the copy of yesterday's *New York Times*. He'd searched the paper for five straight days, looking for Claudia's story. He'd even had Mrs. Lewis go through it a second and third time, but they'd found nothing. Had her editor refused to publish it? Had Claudia decided to pull the story? And what about the job offer with the *Times?*

So many questions and no answers. He'd been tempted to call her nearly every hour of every day. LeRoy in security had tracked down her home phone number, the number for the *Times,* even the address of her apartment in Brooklyn. But until her story was published, or Christmas had long passed, Tom wasn't sure how she'd feel about hearing from him.

"Just get through the day," he repeated. But the days had passed so slowly, filled with thoughts of what he'd shared with Claudia—and what he'd lost. Tom replayed their last moments together over and over in his head and he still couldn't figure out what he'd done wrong.

Maybe he'd moved too fast. If he'd just given them a little more time to get to know each other…Tom cursed softly. Beating himself up over the mistakes he'd made was not going to bring her back. For now, all he could do was play a waiting game, watch the paper and see just what she'd decided to do about the story—and about him.

A knock sounded at his office door and he stepped away from the mirror and opened it. LeRoy stood on the other side. "I've got your paper, sir." He handed Tom the latest copy of the *Times*.

Tom nodded and grabbed the paper. "Thanks. I appreciate you getting this for me. It's a little hard for me to run down to the paper box in this suit."

"No problem, sir." LeRoy smartly turned on his heel and walked back to the elevator.

Though he was already late getting downstairs, Tom took the paper and spread it out on his desk. He flipped to the New York Report and scanned the first page then paged through the balance of the section. "It's not here," he muttered. He grabbed another section, but after paging through it twice, he didn't find anything there, either.

"Where is it? Come on, Claudia, this is what you wanted. This story was going to buy you your dreams. Why isn't it here?"

Sports, entertainment, lifestyles. It was Christmas Eve, surely the story would have been published by now! He slowly lowered himself into his chair. "Unless they're saving it for tomorrow's paper."

Disappointment shot through him. Of course they'd be saving it for tomorrow. What a perfect feature for Christmas! Secret gifts arriving for families in need. Tom tossed the rest of the paper aside and rubbed his forehead. Why did it make a difference? Whether the story was published or not, she'd still refused his proposal.

But if she had any regrets about what happened between them, if Claudia had any notion of trying to salvage their relationship, then he had to believe she wouldn't go through with the story. And if the story didn't appear, then maybe that meant her mind wasn't really made up about their future.

Tom grabbed his Santa hat and headed downstairs, determined to get his mind off his doubts about Claudia and back on the task at hand. But wherever he turned in the store, he was reminded of her. Their night spent in his office, their adventure in the beauty salon, the kiss they shared in the Gingerbread Cottage. Even that night on the loading dock when she fell into the Dumpster.

He cursed softly as he punched the elevator panel for the second floor. Maybe it was best he was being transferred to Manhattan. If a future with Claudia was out of the question, then it would be easier to put her out of his mind in New York…except that she lived in the city. Her apartment in Brooklyn was only a short subway ride away. And the offices of Dalton Enterprises were just down the street from the offices of the *New York Times!* Hell, he could run in to her on the sidewalk or in a deli or on a city bus. And Tom knew his feelings well enough to realize he'd be looking for her around every corner.

No, things would never be settled between them unless he saw her again. He needed to look into her eyes and be sure that she really meant to refuse him, that it wasn't just an impulse to say no. He slowly began to formulate a plan.

He already planned to leave Schuyler Falls right after the store closed at five, making the drive down to his parents' country house in Connecticut to spend the night and the next day with them. Why not take a quick detour to Brooklyn? He'd be there before midnight, if the weather held and the traffic wasn't horrible. How could she refuse to speak to him on Christmas Eve?

But would she even be there? She might be long gone, visiting family or friends for the holidays, maybe working at the paper, or on vacation in a warm locale. Tom stepped off the elevator and walked toward the Gingerbread Cottage. Though he longed to see Claudia this very second, to touch her face and hold her hand, he knew their next meeting might very well be their last.

The elves were waiting at the North Pole Village, Winkie, Dinkie and Blinkie ready to begin bringing the children through the Candy Cane Gate. There was only a small line today. Most of the children had paid their visit earlier in order to give Santa plenty of time to gather their gifts. But some, like their parents who were busy with last-minute shopping, had used every remaining second to decide what they wanted to put on their list.

Tom sat down on the huge chair, tugging at the belt that cut into his ribs. Winkie took her place at his right side. It was her job to lift the children on and off his lap. Dinkie stood on his left with tiny Christmas stockings filled with candy for each child. And Blinkie stood inside the gate, taking Claudia's place, while still operating the instant camera. They hadn't bothered to hire another elf with only a few days until Christmas.

"Good morning, sir," Winkie said. After his last day as Santa, he'd been recognized beneath the beard. Though Mrs. Perkins was the only one who knew his grandfather played the regular Santa, Tom didn't find it necessary to protect his own identity. After the rumors of his relationship with Claudia and her subsequent "resignation" had raced through the Dalton grapevine, playing Santa wasn't going to hurt his reputation. It could only help.

"Good morning, Winkie," he said. "How are you today?"

"Fine, sir. Are you ready for the first child?"

Tom nodded and watched as Blinkie showed a very reluctant three-year-old through the gate. With each step, the little girl looked more frightened. When Winkie plopped her on Tom's lap, she burst into a wail and a torrent of tears quickly followed. Blinkie snapped the picture and Winkie returned her to her mother before full-blown hysteria took over.

The five other children in line went quickly through their lists and after only a half hour, Tom and the elves found themselves with no line at all. "Is it usually this slow on Christmas Eve?"

Dinkie nodded. "The morning can be busy, but we'll have a slow afternoon."

A long silence spun out at the North Pole Village as they watched the shoppers hurry past. Tom wasn't sure what to say to the elves and they were obviously afraid to talk to him. "I'm sorry we couldn't hire a fourth elf after Miss Moore left," he finally said. "I know all of you have been very busy and I really appreciate the effort involved in covering her duties as well as your own."

"I saw Claudia just yesterday," Dinkie said.

Tom gasped and looked up at her. "What?"

Her face turned red and she glanced away. "I—I'm sorry, sir. I know you probably don't want to talk about her. I mean, after the way it ended between—" She stopped. "Not that I know what happened between—" A mortified look crossed her face. "Oh, God. Why can't I just keep my mouth shut?"

"No," Tom said. "I want to know. Where did you see her?"

"In the square," she said. "I didn't actually talk to her. She was walking on the other side, but I knew it was her."

"Then she's still in town?"

"I don't know."

Tom sat back in his chair and smiled. Could this be true? Could Claudia still be in Schuyler Falls? If so, then maybe things between them weren't as bad as he thought. Maybe she'd come to regret her answer to his proposal as much as he had. He glanced out over the crowd of shoppers, automatically looking for some sign of her presence. His mouth curved into a smile and he couldn't help but feel a renewed sense of hope.

"You know, Dinkie, I think this might just be the best Christmas ever."

"Do you think so, sir? Have sales been good?"

Tom laughed. "There's more to Christmas than sales figures. There's hope. And love. And the possibility that, for one day, miracles can actually happen."

THE STORE BUSTLED with last-minute shoppers, all of them scurrying to find the perfect last-minute gift. Claudia stood at a display of designer belts and fingered the leather, trying to work up the courage to find Tom Dalton.

She knew he'd be here in the store. Since she'd walked out on him, his car had been parked in the nearby lot nearly twenty-four hours a day. Though it wasn't technically stalking, she didn't feel good about spying on him. But, since she'd thrown away the job with the *Times,* she really hadn't had much to do with herself.

Every morning, she woke up in her room at the boardinghouse and vowed that today would be the day she'd leave Tom Dalton and Schuyler Falls behind her and get on with her life. She would even pack her bags and tidy up her room in preparation to go. But when the time came to take her bag to the car, she just couldn't bring herself to call an end to everything.

As long as she stayed in town, there was still a chance she might be able to fix things with Tom. Though she hadn't made a move yet, she'd been seriously thinking about her options. At first, she'd considered running into him on the street. She'd make it look like a coincidence. They'd talk, he'd ask her to dinner and they'd end up engaged by the end of the night.

She'd also come up with a more cowardly option—a letter expressing her regrets about her answer to his proposal. She'd pour out her feelings, he'd call her and ask her to dinner and they'd end up engaged by the end of the night.

But after mulling it over for the past five days, Claudia had decided the direct approach would be best. She'd simply confront him at the store and tell him she'd been temporarily insane when she'd refused his offer of marriage. Of course, he'd ask her to dinner and they'd end up… Well, each plan always ended the same.

In truth, she finally felt as if she were ready to face him. This morning, she hadn't even bothered packing her bags. And last night, she'd dreamed of his proposal. Only this time, she'd said yes. This time she'd pulled him to his feet and thrown herself into his arms, shouting her acceptance to the world. She'd put aside her silly fears, all the doubts and insecurities that had been with her since her childhood. She wasn't her mother and Tom wasn't her father. They loved each other and they could have a wonderful life together.

Had she been thinking clearly that day, she might have said "yes" the first time. But with everything that had happened between them, all the accusations and recriminations, she wasn't sure where she stood. The proposal had come like a bolt from the blue. In truth, she'd expected him to toss her right out of his life, not ask her to marry him. Though the thought of spending the rest of her days with Tom Dalton had crossed her mind a few times since she'd met him, she'd never seriously considered the notion of happily ever after. And when he had asked, he'd expected an answer immediately. The word no just popped out of her mouth.

But how could she get him to ask again? Finding Tom and professing her true feelings was a daunting enough task as is. But the possibility that he might not repeat his proposal would be the greatest humiliation of her life, a million times worse than wearing that goofy elf outfit.

Claudia sighed. If only she had someone to talk to, someone who could give her wise advice and careful counsel. Someone who knew both Tom and—

"Santa," she murmured. "I could talk to Santa. He'd tell me what to do!"

Why hadn't she thought of that before? After all, Theodore Dalton had suspected her feelings for Tom long before she'd even acknowledged them. And Tom must have discussed his proposal with his grandfather. The general manager of Dalton's Department Store didn't just up and marry an elf without breaking the news to his family first.

Set on her course, Claudia dropped the belt she'd been fondling for the past few minutes and started toward the escalator. This was a good first step. She'd feel out Theodore Dalton, ask him about Tom's mood, and if things looked good, she'd march right up to Tom's office and plead her case.

There was no line at the Candy Cane Gate when she arrived and all the elves were standing around chatting. She glanced past the gate and found Santa's chair empty. When she stepped up to the group, they all turned to look at her. Shock colored their expressions and they all stammered out uneasy greetings.

"What are you doing here?" Winkie asked.

Claudia forced a smile. "I've come to see Santa. I know you usually don't let grown-ups beyond the Candy Cane Gate, but I really need to talk to him. Is he still here?"

Dinkie nodded. "He's in the cottage taking a break."

"I'll just wait then."

"No!" Winkie cried, an uncharacteristic smile curving her lips. "I'll go get him."

Claudia opened her mouth to protest, but Winkie had already hopped over the fence. She ran up to the cottage and knocked frantically on the door. Then she poked her head inside and spoke to Santa for a few seconds before returning to the group. "He'll be right out," she said breathlessly.

A few seconds later, Theodore Dalton emerged and took a seat on his huge chair. He nodded in Winkie's direction and the elf opened the Candy Cane Gate with a flourish. "Santa will see you now."

Haltingly, Claudia stepped through the gate and approached Santa. Like all the children before her, she felt her heart slamming in her chest and her breath constricting in her throat. Unlike the children, she had more to ask for than toys. She wanted a full-grown, incredibly sexy, devastatingly handsome man for Christmas. And that diamond ring he'd offered her.

When she reached Santa's chair, she stood in front of him, her eyes downcast, her fingers clutched together.

Claudia cleared her throat, then began. "Mr. Dalton, I know you probably don't want to talk to me right now," she murmured, "especially considering what happened between me and Tom. But I was hoping you'd be able to help me, elf to Santa."

He patted his knee. Claudia glanced around uneasily. "You want me to sit on your lap?"

He patted his knee again and she sat down. The elves watched her, wide-eyed and curious. A little boy now stood on the other side of the gate and regarded her suspiciously. "She's too big for Santa!" he cried. "She probably doesn't even believe."

"I do believe!" Claudia said, startling the little boy into silence. She shifted on the old man's bony knee then drew a long breath. "Did Tom tell you about his proposal?"

The old man nodded. "Mmm," he growled.

"You have to understand. Everything just took me by surprise. I didn't know what to say and I was scared. But I haven't been able to leave town. I've been hanging around the square hoping I might run into him, but I haven't seen him. And I just want to tell him…" She swallowed hard, fighting back a flood of emotion. "I want to tell him that I…" Claudia drew a shaky breath. "I love him. I've probably always loved him. And I made a mistake running away. I should have stayed and worked things out." She looked down into his eyes. "So, do you think I still have a chance? Or has Tom put our relationship in the past?"

Theodore pondered her question for a long moment. Then, without warning, he wrapped his arms around her shoulders and bent her back in a passionate embrace! Claudia screamed, but the instant his mouth covered hers she realized that she wasn't sitting on Theodore Dalton's lap at all.

She was kissing Tom Dalton! With a soft moan, she opened beneath his lips, joy welling up inside of her, making her head spin and her heart race. She'd confessed her feelings to him and he still wanted her, still loved her. The kiss spun out, weaving a spell around them until reality subsided into the background and all she sensed was their love surrounding them like a cozy cocoon.

After a minute or two, the sound of applause filtered through their world, and when he finally drew away, Claudia saw a rather large crowd gathered outside the Candy Cane Gate. Parents were chuckling and the few children in the crowd looked confused and somewhat horrified. Dinkie was crying and Winkie was actually laughing. And Blinkie stared at them both and said, "Bogus."

Claudia tipped her head back and laughed. "I've been kissed by Santa Claus," she cried, giggling.

The crowd broke into another round of applause. "No, darling," Tom murmured, his beard tickling her neck, his breath soft near her ear. "You've been kissed by your future husband."

He slipped one arm beneath her knees then stood up. "We'll be right back," he called to the elves. He kicked open the door to the Gingerbread Cottage and carried her over the threshold. Then he closed the door behind him, giving them their first bit of privacy.

She reached out and tugged his beard down, revealing the handsome face of the man she loved. "I never should have walked away," she murmured, as he set her on her feet. "I'm sorry, but I let a bunch of silly fears affect my feelings for you."

"I never should have let you walk away. I should have gone after you and made you tell me what was wrong."

"I'm sorry about all the lies."

"What about your story? I've been looking for it in the *Times.*"

"Forget the *Times,*" Claudia said. "All your family secrets are safe with me. Besides, I don't need the *Times.* I'd rather pick and choose my assignments. And when I don't want to work at all, we can spend the day in bed." She wrapped her arms around his neck and pulled him close. "So, are you going to ask me again? Or do I have to ask you?"

Tom looked deeply into her eyes, his feelings for her there in the depths of his soul. "Claudia Moore, would you please be my wife?"

She smiled, her eyes glazing with tears. "Yes!" she cried. "Yes, I will be your wife."

He pulled her close and kissed her again. Nothing had prepared her for the intensity of her feelings for him. Gone were the doubts and insecurities, replaced by an abiding faith that they truly did belong together. Perhaps it was the magic of the Christmas season, or maybe it was fate. But Claudia had found what she hadn't even known she'd been looking for—a life, a future, and a man who loved her without question.

Tom pulled back, his gaze skimming her face. "You know what this means, don't you?"

"That I'll love you forever? That we'll build a life together and have lots of kids? That we'll grow old in each other's arms?"

He chuckled, then smoothed a strand of hair from her temple. "Well, yeah, that, too. But this also means that when I come in from New York to do Santa duty next year you're going to have to play Mrs. Claus. If you think

I'm getting dressed up in this suit without you standing beside me, then you've got another thing coming."

Claudia wrapped her arms around his neck and gave him a fierce hug. "I've been promoted? Wow, from elf to mistress of the Gingerbread Cottage, all in one season."

"Mistress...what an interesting choice of words," he said, nuzzling her with his bearded face.

"Shouldn't you get back to the kids?" she asked, teasingly trailing a line of kisses along his jaw.

"Not just yet. You see, you told me all your wishes," he said, stepping back to tear off his Santa hat and pulling off his beard. "Now it's my turn to tell you what I want for Christmas."

When he'd discarded the padded jacket, he yanked her into his arms again. Claudia shouted with joy, laughter bubbling from her throat. Then he picked her up and twirled her around in the tiny cramped cottage. And as she stared down into his sparkling green eyes, she knew she'd spend her life making *all* of Tom's wishes come true.

For every day she spent loving him would be just like Christmas.

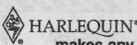

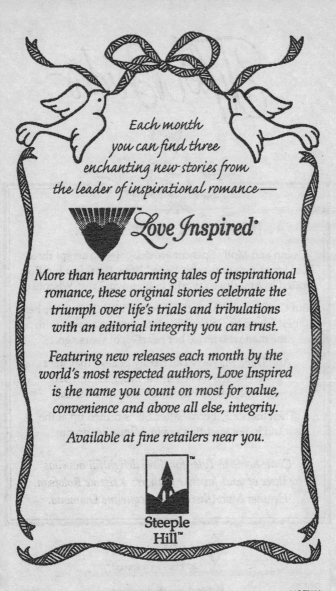

Tyler Brides

It happened one weekend...

Quinn and Molly Spencer are delighted to accept three bookings for their newly opened B&B, Breakfast Inn Bed, located in America's favorite hometown, Tyler, Wisconsin.

But Gina Santori is anything but thrilled to discover her best friend has tricked her into sharing a room with the man who broke her heart eight years ago....

And Delia Mayhew can hardly believe that she's gotten herself locked in the Breakfast Inn Bed basement with the sexiest man in America.

Then there's Rebecca Salter. She's turned up at the Inn in her wedding gown. Minus her groom.

Come home to Tyler for three delightful novellas by three of your favorite authors: Kristine Rolofson, Heather MacAllister and Jacqueline Diamond.

HARLEQUIN®
Makes any time special™

Visit us at www.eHarlequin.com

PHTB